Praise For

INTO THE GORGE

"*Into the Gorge* is both an inventive novel and an unforgettable World War II tour de force of theatrical intensity. Combining meticulous research and a prose style of muscular beauty, master storyteller Rick Burton has given us a timeless epic of love, war, loss—and redemption."

Rus Bradburd, author, *All the Dreams We've Dreamed*

"Rick Burton's words carry adventure and soul in equal measure. This historical World War II fiction pays glorious homage to the Australian spirit through adversity, our beautiful Outback land, and the universal power of love. A beautiful story of action and romance."

Lachlan Wills, Imparja TV and La Trobe (Australia) professor

"Rick Burton skillfully steers us through an obscure World War II adventure that keeps us breathlessly on the move. From Austria to Australia to the Indian Ocean, *Into the Gorge* is a tale of corruption, deception, survival, and finding our way home. Five stars, all day, every day."

Steve Physioc, author, award-winning *The Walls of Lucca* and *Walks with the Wind* series

"*Into the Gorge* is a rich tale of loss and love with enough suspense thrown in to keep any reader up at night. This is a love-poem historical thriller."

Stephen Kuusisto, author of *Have Dog, Will Travel: A Poet's Journal*

www.amplifypublishinggroup.com

INTO THE GORGE

For more information, please contact:
Subplot Publishing, an imprint of Amplify Publishing Group
620 Herndon Parkway, Suite 320
Herndon, VA 20170
info@amplifypublishing.com

Author photo by Andrew Burton

Library of Congress Control Number: 2023900420

CPSIA Code: PRV0123A
ISBN-13: 978-1-63755-686-3

Printed in the United States

For David Castle, who inspired much of this work.
For Gay Hembach and all the others who have faced
loneliness with courage.
And, of course, for Barb.

───────

The author also wishes to gratefully acknowledge the
generous patronage of Syracuse University professors
Pat Ryan and Sean Branagan.

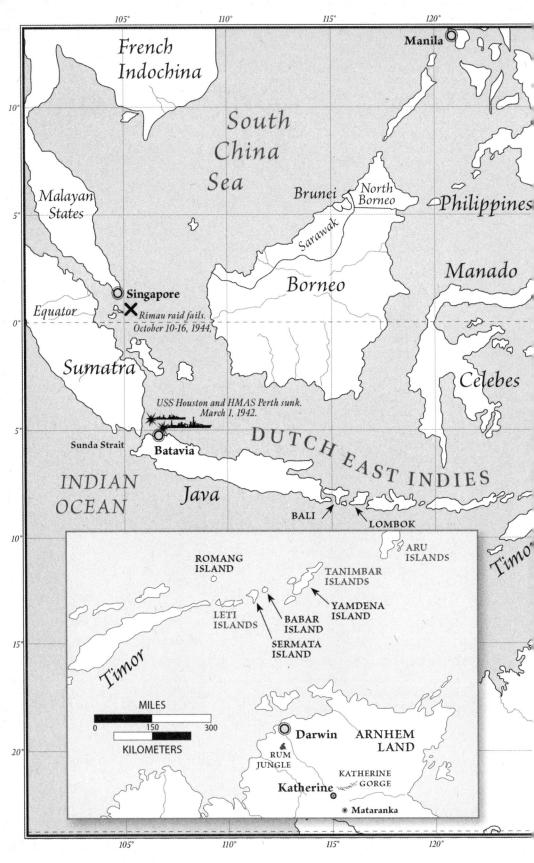

When they gazed down into that hideous chasm, she thought that the earth had just opened, bent upon swallowing them. She couldn't see any bottom, just cliffs plunging to darkness.

G. M. Glaskin, *Flight to Landfall*

I remember. I remember everything.

Paul Kelly, *Leaps and Bounds*

Love never ends.

Saul of Tarsus (1 Corinthians 13:8)

INTO
THE
GORGE

RICK BURTON

SUBPLOT
an imprint of Amplify Publishing Group

PROLOGUE

3 April 1938—Graz, Austria

Ilsa Stulmacher, barely thirteen yet physically and mentally mature far beyond those very short years, knew immediately she and her father had fallen into a deep Alpen crevasse. Germany's chancellor and Führer had caught them filming from Zell's inside garden terrace without official permission.

It was unimaginable. They had barely arrived at her uncle's sprawling mansion, but their mistake, a crime where innocence or ignorance would not matter, had fallen just one day short of the Nazi leader's historic speech in Graz. Repercussions would surely follow.

The original plan called for Ilsa's father, with his new Bavarian 35mm Arriflex, to film Adolf Hitler's stomping, salute-filled oration inside the gargantuan Weizer Waggonfabrik plant. But in visiting Onkel Fritz to get official permission from the German high command, Johann and Ilsa accidentally witnessed something much more troubling.

At the time, the Anschluss Österreichs, the looming creation of a "Greater Germany," was barely a month old. That hadn't stopped Hitler from sending the Wehrmacht into Vienna at dawn on the twelfth. By the Ides of March, just three days later, in front of a packed Heldenplatz, the conquering hero's rapturous coronation tour of Austria was already in full swing.

With formal confirmation issued by Reich minister Joseph Goebbels, Austrian news services began reporting, with growing excitement, how Hitler would visit Graz in early April, presiding over a large unification event at Weizer's factory.

In advance of that moment, the fates conspired to send father and daughter into the tempest, a virulent storm where they would meet the Austrian corporal who had successfully crowned himself supreme leader for all of Deutschland.

Too young to fully grasp the situation, Ilsa tried guessing at solutions capable of aiding her father. There were few, and most would never work.

Worse, she had no way of knowing the random cinematic images filmed that sunny afternoon would rain down on her family like a searing acid, creating a rippling effect of rough scars and reoccurring nightmares for decades to come.

For now, though, the dark clouds of danger were building, gathering their forces, all around her.

CHAPTER 1

January 2005—Katherine, Northern Territory, Australia

"Austrian Ilsa" marched off into the unforgiving Katherine Gorge one blazing afternoon and, with little fanfare, engineered her own death. She was eighty. Old by some standards. Unlucky, I suppose, not to reach eighty-five or ninety.

The local coroner, a tubby man covered in fine red dust coating his Coke-bottle spectacles, indicated her death was a suicide. His slender report was accurate, as far as the facts were concerned, but I knew there was no chance he would've understood why the Stulmacher woman, probably smiling as if she'd won the lottery, had entered one of the Katherine River's deep side canyons, the slender Leight Creek cut, with no intention of exiting.

Ilsa's death wasn't brought on by sadness or loneliness. No, it was a strange new sensation she hadn't felt in sixty years: love. Her discovery of this well-known affection, meant when she left her overgrown homestead, heading out into a sunburnt slash of Australian desolation, she was undoubtedly humming an Austrian folk song about the mountains. One my mother would've sung to me as a child.

I was saddened by the news of her death, of course, but I was an outlier.

That's largely because Ilsa's passing didn't create any grieving in Katherine, the rural town where she'd lived alone for six decades. There were no calling hours at the town's one decrepit funeral home. No relatives sitting shiva. As the *New York Times* sometimes tells its readers, "No immediate family members survive."

Ashes to ashes. Gray fumes and thin flakes of bone surging out of a crematorium's slender smokestack. Another ancient spirit joining forces with the undulating antipodean winds headed eastward, sailing on dusty waves surging out of Australia's Great Sandy Desert.

In honesty, if I hadn't made a promise to my mother as she approached her own deathbed in 2004, I would never have met this World War II refugee. Not come anywhere near her. But Mom, in one of her final afternoons of clarity, stressed I needed to find her old friend Ilsa and tell her something about two movies they'd watched. At the time, it didn't make any sense…even though Mom had talked about Ilsa before.

"Hitler coming into Austria in 1938," she said, her voice raspy from a lifetime fighting asthma. "The first is where his motorcade comes to Graz, and then, ach, there's the dangerous one. At Zell's house. When Ilsa was there with Johann. They saw Hitler up close. In person."

"What do you mean?" I asked, thinking Mom was perhaps confused and she'd seen a newsreel short with Ilsa and her boyfriend in Graz.

"Just that. Tell Ilsa…she lives in Australia…I've told you that before… in a town named after a woman. I think it's Katherine. Or maybe Alice. Tell her they're safe. The two reels. I separated the tins before we left for Minnesota. Left one where it was hidden but moved the other. I buried it in the park where we used to meet."

Mom's German accent was still thick, but this was the first time I'd ever heard anything about an Austrian childhood friend producing a movie. For a teenager to have created a motion picture showing Hitler, especially in the thirties before World War II, was beyond preposterous. It would rank right up there with finding E.T. in your closet.

Worse was Mom refusing to say exactly where the movies were hidden. All she gave me was Graz and an unnamed park, saying Ilsa would know where.

CHAPTER 2

Mom's ability to focus on any one topic wasn't so great at the time, and she didn't linger on this crazed concept of an Australian visit long. Instead, she started up again on why her single son, a man in his forties, hadn't settled down and started a family. I tried brushing off the familiar discussion only to have Mom reverse course and start in on the importance of finding the mysterious friend who lived seven thousand miles away.

As if anyone could jet off to the Land Down Under on a whim. *God help us*. I'm sure that's what I said. Or, *for the love of God*. In either case, I was exasperated.

Everything might have ended there, with me casually disregarding the whims of my elderly mother, but it didn't, because of an old Hebrew expression that sometimes plays out rather quickly. It's the one about man planning and God laughing.

I'm convinced we sometimes get that parable wrong. God outlines the plan, and we shrug our shoulders, thinking we've got things under control and can trust in the schemes of our own making. We imagine we're the ones calling the shots.

As it turned out, the Almighty's recipe—call it a set of serendipitous coincidences—fell into place a few days after I left Mom's nursing home. I just didn't recognize God's firm hand scraping the ingredients into the smoldering pot.

It was the point where a string of interrelated incidents started to get interesting.

Because of Mom's cryptic comments, the next day I pitched a human-interest research project to my editor at *World War II Magazine.* Over beers, I told J. B. how Mom and her friend, a woman named Ilsa, who lived in Australia, had possibly seen Hitler visit Graz in April 1938. I thought a story about two high school girls witnessing a historical event was unique and might drive female readership. Might nudge our circulation numbers.

J. B. sneered, noting Hitler's imperial tours had been done to death. Worse, the publisher would have his head. A "chick" story would scare off our shallow male readers. But then he produced an alternate concept, one that involved ordering me to visit Oz to dig around on why Darwin was unprepared for a massive Japanese air attack just two months after Pearl Harbor.

"Okay. So, you're heartbroken about that hot number you were telling me about the other night. Get over it. I've got the perfect solution. Tied to a story I've been sitting on for months. Right after Christmas I want you to go investigate why the USS *Peary,* alone and completely unprotected, got popped in that supposedly nice, safe, Australian harbor," he said. "Same as the *Arizona.* Sunk in minutes, and nobody knows about it because no one thinks the Aussies ever got attacked. They got whacked good in early forty-two."

At this point, he pulled a photo out of his desk drawer. It was a creased and wrinkled clipping from the *Katherine Times* showing the *Peary* lying on the bottom of the Timor Sea. Proof that two months after Pearl Harbor, the American military still hadn't fully figured out what Japan's Imperial Navy was doing.

"You were in the Air Force. Fighters, right?"

"Yeah, F-15s," I said. "Tactical stuff. No combat."

"Well, I'll give it to you straight. I think the *Peary* was cursed. Get me that story and answers on how a bunch of Aussie and American desk jockeys missed seeing the Rising Sun sneak up on them. Especially after Japan had already clobbered Singapore and was pounding the snot out of Manila."

I smirked. Who was I to argue with a snarling editor? I told J. B. I'd bring him back five thousand words on the single worst attack ever to hit Australia. Anything to get out of Dodge.

I had good reasons for wanting to disappear. They started and ended with Fiona, the beautiful brunette who'd recently left a note suggesting my Peter Pan traits, my lingering immaturity, were nothing more than testosterone in a sport coat. She'd had enough.

That breakup bruised my ego, in large part because I'd convinced myself Fiona was "the one." When I woke up to the hard truth of her departure, not to mention some less-than-festive holiday parties involving Cuervo Gold, my free fall accelerated like some fool stepping off the Grand Canyon's Rim Trail.

"While you're down there," J. B. offered, "you can look up this Ilsa you're so keen on finding. Maybe she'll have you over for a barbecue, tell you about Hitler's visit, and introduce you to Elle Macpherson. Get you back on the dating horse and stop your moping."

Remembering old *Sports Illustrated* swimsuit calendars, I doubted Macpherson's doppelgänger existed. I also questioned whether I wanted to go to the trouble of finding some old crone who remembered my mother from the 1930s. But free airfare is reliable catnip for me, and if Ilsa lived in Alice Springs or Katherine, a lightning-fast visit could be arranged.

And here's where God entered the picture again.

Ilsa, when I finally got to know her, had called Katherine home for sixty-five years. Never married, no kids. Her claim to fame was serving as the town's longest-settled loner. The eccentric geriatric who outlasted the history she'd observed. The one who knew where the figurative bodies were buried.

My mother had said in her more lucid times Ilsa operated a family-sized ranch since 1945, growing enough local produce to stay afloat. Her specialty was mangoes with a sweet, distinctive taste, and a box of them always showed up at Mom's place during the holidays. The address on the most recent shipment, in fact, arrived in timely fashion, saving me from having to investigate Alice Springs or any other feminine town name in the Outback: Emungalen Road, Katherine, NT, did the trick. In many ways, Ilsa was the human version of that fruit. Fleshy and colorful on the outside but, as I learned the hard way, one hard pit of a heart on the inside.

On the night we met—this was in January 2005—I drove down to Katherine from Darwin after grabbing details on the Japanese bombing from a local historian. Katherine was about three hours south, and as part of my agenda, I'd arranged an official visit to Tindal, the RAAF base located just outside of town.

That day's research portion had run smoothly, and after I promised to quote the base commander, a group of his 75th Squadron pilots decided they would show off their machinery and fly me over the famous gorge. In return, they would let me "shout" them a round of drinks.

Grabbing four F/A-18s, one a two-seat trainer, the flyboys took me up for an afternoon sweep over the sandstone cliffs of Nitmiluk National Park. Tindal is minutes away, and popping their turbofan engines, they had their sonic beasts up over Mach 1 quickly. From there, the Hornets zoomed down along the Katherine River's tectonic ridges, showing how the watery snake was always nibbling away at the region's geology, carving out waterfalls, lagoons, and secluded beaches rivaling any of Hollywood's most exotic movie sets.

In multiple places, the river flowed over a series of chiseled ledges before dropping into stretches of sunbaked solitude. It was stunning, especially from the air.

Landing back at Tindal, the fliers dispersed to pick up their partners with a plan I would meet them at their favorite hotel, the one where the Air Combat Group was still flying its 2003 Iraq Operation Falconer flag on the back wall.

Arriving early, I immediately felt at home. There were some Bundaberg Rum and XXXX Beer neons blinking their yellow messages and, off to one side, a miniature tin water tank, constructed by one of the locals. Hanging from the ceiling were two inflatable crocodiles, one wearing jungle fatigues and the other dressed as a fighter pilot with old night-vision goggles.

The combined craftsmanship and artistry must've passed for remarkable, and I'm certain if Mark Twain were still writing, he'd have called Katherine a drinking town with a military problem. He would've also admired the pub's journalistic décor. That's because the owner had posted a series of framed newspaper stories throughout the place. One from the 1960s showed a massive 27-foot saltwater crocodile attacking a small boat. It was supposedly the largest reptile ever on record.

Another clipping featured a drunk who found a big snake and stuffed it in a bag on his truck's bench seat. He intended to bring it back to his favorite watering hole for their glass terrarium. A classic bad idea because once the king brown got loose, it latched onto the driver. The journalist failed to reveal if this knucklehead survived the ensuing crash but did note that while the king brown isn't Australia's deadliest snake, when it gets angry, it doesn't bite. It chews. All while injecting a toxic venom.

Katherine was that kind of place. The locals were the equivalent of big browns. Locked in on their patch of dirt and, often enough, loaded. They laughed at their outback isolation (and misplaced tourists) while holding on to traditions brought on by untamed weather and regional custom.

To understand how empty this part of Australia is, Katherine is best described as a coffee-and-bathroom-break kind of town. It sits no more than a par-five dogleg off the four-lane Stuart Highway, which stretches from Adelaide in the south to Darwin in the extreme north. In between, for about 1,900 miles, there's only one significant town, Alice Springs.

That means gunning down the Stuart equates to driving from Boston to Denver and not seeing anything but an occasional roadhouse or triple-trailer road-train hauling cattle. On all fronts, drivers are surrounded by near-endless desert scrub with Alice's restaurants serving as no more than a few bleary distractions.

The "Top End" is also famous for its extreme heat and dryness. Except when it pours. When the "Wet" hits, flash torrents rage, roads wash out, and the water floods the north in near biblical fashion. The two distinct seasons help explain why so many no-stoplight towns in the NT bear liquid names such as Daly Waters, Tennant Creek, and Emerald Springs.

My unplanned, unexpected meeting with Ilsa came shortly after our pilot group, with look-the-part swagger, entered the restaurant. They could've been sunburnt extras from a *Top Gun* remake, especially when they removed their aviator Ray-Bans, in a choreographed way, to better view the bar's dark corners.

Alongside this group of buzz-cuts, the pilots' wives and dates did little to abuse the stereotypical mirage of women in action movies. With their big hair and long legs, they played their clichéd parts with no apparent guilt. This was Australia in the early 2000s, and despite the inherent sexism, nobody in the smoke-filled room stirred. This was *their* local.

As we settled in at a long eucalyptus table, a cacophony of bar noises bouncing loudly off the rough-hewn walls, I noticed a thin, white-haired woman with horn-rimmed glasses sitting at an empty booth about fifteen feet away. Her striated arms, sprouting from a sleeveless gingham smock, were wrapped like skinny pythons around a tin container. She looked maybe five foot eight, with a straight back, not at all stooped. She was older, but sturdy, almost stocky.

My first impression was someone's wayward grandmother had somehow escaped her nursing home and stumbled into the wrong bar. With her rugged facial creases, set in an almost painful grimace, and unkempt locks, she looked that much out of place. Yet, here she was, standing out in this rowdy setting, a rocking metronome, mouthing the words to an unknown song, blissfully ignoring everyone else's reality.

In her youth, I imagined a tall blonde with prominent shoulders. Perhaps sixty years ago she'd been a looker. Now, she was no more than a regional oddity, someone the regulars wished they could ignore. She was a fender bender, a crash site they tried driving around with no more than a glance at the unlucky driver.

For an instant, our eyes connected, and I felt a monstrous tractor beam of visual acuity transporting me back to my F-15 days. During training missions, pilots worked on spotting and identifying "bogeys" or "red air bandits." It was when someone locked in on a target.

The last thing I wanted was a local zeroing me out, so I quickly adjusted my sightline, studying her battered box that once contained cookies. I wondered about its importance before looking back at the laughing pilots. If this lunatic woman had mental health challenges, I remembered enough from my Barroom 101 "classes" at Virginia Tech to give her plenty of space.

Things might've stayed disengaged if she hadn't waited for my curious return glance and nailed me a second time. This time she fired fast, beckoning me, with one very long index finger, to join her. That sunburned digit wiggled in the air, an upside-down oil derrick bending and straightening. And behind that finger, glittering blue eyes sparkled as if she were flirting.

At six foot two and with a lengthy military career, I've long known how to give and take orders. I suppose it explained why I excused myself from our raucous table and started reliving Coleridge's *Rime of the Ancient Mariner*. I was the "one of three" stopped. The put-upon wedding guest drawn into some kind of mysterious sideshow.

When I sat down next to her, Ilsa wasted no time ladling out her name before launching into two implausible but elaborate tales. The first involved an ill-timed 1938 meeting with Hitler's sinister propaganda minister, followed by a daring escape from Nazi pursuers. The second involved two World War II men fighting to save her. Two heroes she wanted memorialized.

Three months later, after many hours spent researching missing parts of her story in various libraries and military museums, I found myself in Jakarta typing this improbable tale about an Austrian beauty, an Australian commando, and a Black American sailor.

My three A's.

The two men fought for their countries during a brutal war that stopped in 1945. The misunderstood woman's battle ran another sixty complicated years. She stayed tough through all of it and never buckled under the weight of their serendipitous collision.

CHAPTER 3

I sat down with Ilsa that first night, the two of us enveloped by loud Australian accents, INXS blaring on a jukebox, and a blue fog of cigarette smoke. The combination swirled, with great mischief, like a bothersome genie intent on infiltrating our private gathering. All while the old woman suggested I ignore how everyone was watching.

"Don't worry about them," she purred. "I'm just the mysterious spinster from the run-down property outside of town. The secretive old Nazi witch who's hidden here in Australia with Hitler's gold since 1938. The spy who worked for Rommel. They have no idea. We'll get to all that silliness, but not quite yet. By the way, my name is Ilsa Stulmacher."

At that moment, my eyes instantly widened at the shocking coincidence, my face breaking into one of those epic conspiratorial grins associated with finding needles in haystacks.

"Hey, I've been sent to find you," I said with notable disbelief. "I'm Greta's son. She wanted me to let you know…"

"Not yet," she interrupted. "I knew you were coming. But don't tell me her message until I'm finished. You have a role to play in all of this."

Glancing at the oblivious fighter pilots, I shrugged my shoulders in resignation. They were laughing, undoubtedly fabricating a story to explain my behavior. Perhaps they were taking pity, thinking the exiled Austrian fruit lady reminded me of my mother.

It was impossible making out their conversations, so I returned my accommodating attention to Ilsa's mysterious overture. That was the moment she started a veritable recital about something from a few days earlier. On that Tuesday morning, she'd looked in the bathroom mirror and knew the blood in her stool and urine meant something ominous had started. She was dying, she said, and didn't have much time.

"Why me?" or "why now?" didn't matter. Making a long-considered plan work did. And the timing of my presumed arrival was now critical to its success.

Ilsa's headful of once-blonde curls, bleached white by the sun and cut short to minimize the irritations brought on by farm work, made clear she wasted little time on daily upkeep. Hair care, beyond a stroke or two, was low on her daily priorities list. It was the same with makeup, although I did observe some blush on her cheeks, which kept her from looking ghastly.

Speaking as if I was already a co-conspirator, Ilsa explained she'd been born into a middle-class family in Graz, a major Austrian city, and during her time at school, befriended my mother. She'd spent much of her youth climbing in the Alps with her father.

As recently as three years earlier, at age seventy-six, she'd run the unpaved, rutted Gibb River Road from Darwin to Broome in a rented Land Rover. By herself. That alone sounded like she didn't lack for toughness.

Ilsa asked what I had learned about the Northern Territory. I said something about it being one of the world's least traveled areas and that I wanted to visit Kakadu National Park and Devil's Marbles. Maybe even Mataranka Hot Springs.

She begrudgingly acknowledged their natural beauty but fancied Australia's far north for a different reason: people left her alone. I presumed it meant she could shop peacefully in Katherine's shops during her irregular visits, because her spikey, abrupt mannerisms caused harried retailers to greet her with caution or indifference. It was that or she scared the crap out of them.

Her exclusion undoubtedly owed a great deal to a traditional Austrian childhood and a strong German accent. Or decades of vicious rumors generated by gossipers who never met her.

She was a witch. A Nazi. One of Hitler's consorts. Or conquests. The prevailing rumor, she noted, had her playing the part of Australia's Lizzie Borden, supposedly murdering her parents after an intense argument. Those allegations and others were passed down for close to sixty years by the stockmen in Katherine's pubs, the unwelcoming members of the Ladies' Auxiliary, or teenage boys known to steal fruit when they could reach it without triggering a shotgun blast from her back porch.

To her, the rumors were like Australia's ever-present flies. Bothersome, best ignored, and waved away without a second thought.

What she needed was an unsuspecting accomplice who would come to the surface and swallow her bait. That night I was the walleye swimming into the Crazy Ilsa Fishing Derby.

"Have you visited a doctor?" I asked with a level of professional distance.

She dismissed that question with a wave of her hand, saying she merely felt hungover. As if she were fuzzy and off balance. In the tropical heat, despite the aromas coming from blooming frangipani and fragrant bougainvillea, her agricultural priorities, much like her physical condition, were meaningless.

She had decided to stop worrying about inconsequential acts. Feeding chickens and a few Merino sheep or sweeping sand from her rotting verandah. Chores no longer mattered. They could all drift away like swallowtail butterflies, flitting among overripened stone fruit.

Watching those very delicate wonders, she said she'd recited a specific line from either Ecclesiastes or Ecclesiasticus. "It's the one about the sun rising and setting yet everything remaining utterly meaningless."

I smiled. I occasionally recognize Bible verses but not in noisy Australian pubs with a drink in my hand. She said it didn't matter. She could recite the verse in her sleep. "There are some who have no memorial, who have perished as though they had not lived; they have become as though they had not been born."

"And the doctors…" I persisted, missing her real intention.

"I have no time for quacks."

By this point, I regretted having joined her and was rapidly calculating how to extricate myself and return to my hosts. If that emotion showed, she paid it, as my mother often said, "no never mind."

Without waiting, she initiated a verbal journey to an outbuilding that had long stood at the eastern edge of her family's original holding. A crumbling woolshed hand built by her father in the late 1930s standing about seventy flat yards from the house. After years of neglect, it offered a partially collapsed roof, musty smells, and a single false floorboard near the rear wall.

I visualized her grabbing a flimsy handrail and, with creaking joints, maneuvering her way down cracked porch steps. She even joked about looking into the fenced-in chicken yard and eyeing her lone rooster clucking, pleased with himself, judging by the proceedings.

"Stop that," she'd said to the bird. "I want silence. We have started the mission."

Ilsa proceeded to paint a powerful word picture, her fierce nature on full display. I gathered, as the rooster would have, the old bat was on the warpath and the comment about the mission was intended for me.

She walked out, perhaps striding like someone entering a holy maze that, in this case, ran in a straight line. Not like the looping labyrinth she later said she'd traced at Chartres Cathedral in France. On this day, Ilsa wanted a streamlined discussion.

"I talked to Him that day," she offered. "I said, 'God, what if that priest hadn't fed us near Innsbruck? What if we hadn't finally found the convent that night? We were freezing to death, out of food, the Nazis all around us. For that blessing, I thank you.'"

I don't know what my face showed. The noisy room was getting more crowded by the minute, and the regulars were starting to slosh their beers. My pursed lips must've revealed some passive irritation.

Ilsa didn't seem to care and kept trudging through her memory, remembering the noisy ruckus of screeching cockatoos in flight, watching minuscule detonations of sienna-colored dust settling around her feet, amber particles catching sunlight before falling back into place.

Evidently, two thousand years earlier, Aboriginal women had trod similar dirt, worshipping a rainbow serpent named Bolung. A creator god living in the Katherine Gorge.

"Bless his long-ago daughters. Their dust then. Mine soon enough."

By now, the strange monologue had delivered her to the ancient toolshed.

Undoing the hut's single weather-beaten latch, she cracked open the sagging oak door and stepped into the gloom. Without thinking, she pulled on the frayed twine cord hanging inside the jamb. Responding to a quick double jerk, the bug-encrusted bulb blinked on, doing its sickly yellow best to brighten the claustrophobic darkness.

"It goes without saying it was an oven. Book of Daniel hot. A furnace. Not at all like springtime in Graz."

Ilsa lurched to the far end of the rectangular room, extending her wrinkled hand, noting the presence of slight tremors. Then, with practiced force, she extracted a wooden stool wedged under a thick pine shelf. Twenty inches below, covered in white latex paint chips and weeks of dust, lay a small waterproof crypt.

"One of my better hiding places."

Leaning forward, Ilsa confided she'd never pitied herself or the series of events she'd defiantly endured. She said she'd carried on, loyal and lonely, like a solitary Japanese soldier foraging on a Filipino or Indonesian island long after the war ended.

"It was hard focusing my thoughts," she said about the shack. "Above me there were silvery orb-webs hanging from eaves we had long ago stained with creosote. But there were also killers. Redbacks. Funnel-webs. Waiting for an ungloved hand."

"Did you speak to them like you spoke to the rooster?" I hoped my light-hearted cynicism wasn't too obvious.

"Yes, in fact, I did. I told them, 'Not today, you lot.'"

But here, her timbre dropped. As if she was making an eerie confession. She detailed how she reached into her calico apron's deep pocket and withdrew a claw hammer determined to pull two protruding nail heads, both rusting, out of a special floorboard. The spikes screeched but still ended up on a splintery ledge. Then, Ilsa removed the fitted meter-long board guarding the crevice she'd opened. With a sudden quickness, the rotting wood produced an earthy musk that rose with the cloying heat.

Steadying herself, she reached into the shallow opening, grabbing out a leather satchel. She said the feel of the Driza-Bone oilskin was warm and explained how she used her fingers to untie the pack and remove a rusting Arnott's biscuit tin. It was the same one she had brought to the rollicking bar.

Recalling her efforts in the toolshed, Ilsa painted an image of an ancient milking stool and, sitting on it hunched over, an old woman mumbling a monastic four-word phrase in German.

"My prayer. A chant I'd hung onto from Graz."

In my mind, Ilsa removed the covering before prying off the sticky lid with a bit of twisting. Inside were two resealable freezer bags. The first held odd items. Newspaper clippings and old photos. The other contained a bit of torn and frayed fabric.

As she zipped back the first receptacle, Ilsa's gaze fell on an empty matchbox from an Austrian hotel. She said Papa used the last match lighting his pipe on March 31, 1938. That was when it all started.

Behind it lay a single cracked black-and-white photo of her mother and father dancing. The nicked edges were yellowed with age. Written on the back in bold German script was a location and date. Zell's, 1936. Graz. The couple on the front stared stiffly at the camera.

"Mutti was dressed up that night. Not at all like an Austrian housewife. She looked elegant. She must've felt so proud of Papa. Of his connection to Zell."

A Darwin newspaper clipping came next. It described the Japanese aerial attack in late February 1942. Then, a shell casing from a spent bullet. Fired from an American .45-caliber Colt. It was followed by a modern reprint about Australian boxers in 1936. Men preparing for the Berlin Summer Olympics. And here was her burgundy hair ribbon, made of crushed velvet.

Finally, Ilsa said she'd run her fingers over perforated frames of brittle 35mm film. About ten seconds' worth. There was more, but she decided discussing the other antiquities would wait. It was the second bag she wanted to explain. This one held a faded blue shirt sleeve that had been ripped away at the shoulder, its thin cotton weave saturated with dried blood.

In my mind's eye, she lifted the soft fabric to her cheek, touching it in the way of Belgian Christians at the Basilica. She'd visited Bruges in the eighties, and if those holy droplets, supposedly taken from the base of Christ's Cross, were precious, then so too was this sleeve.

"Brad Tucker had worn it once. Father's work shirt. He looked so handsome in it."

I didn't know who this good-looking guy was but guessed he might've been a husband lost in the war. Maybe a long-ago boyfriend. She then launched into a tale about murderous, unrecorded Nazis moving through the near-empty Northern Territory in 1944, culminating in a horrific battle in the Katherine Gorge.

And then, as if she were back in that broiling hot shed, Ilsa returned to her metronomic rocking. In the cacophony of that gregarious bar, she started humming a melody from an old Austrian love song. One played on the state radio channel sixty-seven years earlier.

It was haunting…this self-imposed *Liedlein* of her youth serving as an Aboriginal songline from her adopted country. The soothing musical bars brought on a trancelike state centered around the memory of her life's unexpected and extraordinary tipping point.

"I still see the gorge," Ilsa uttered softly when she finished humming. "I go in there all the time."

CHAPTER 4

31 March 1938—Graz, Austria

"Can you believe this, Ilsa?"

"What is it, Papa?"

"This Anschluss with the Germans. It has happened here in 1938, of all years, and in less than one month. We had rioting on the first, an invasion on the twelfth, Jews marched through Vienna's streets with toothbrushes, and now our Austrian army is part of the Wehrmacht."

Ilsa was sprawled on the floor, her long legs close to the fire. Dressed in a crisp, white-collared blouse and knee-length blue school skirt, she was close to finishing her homework, absentmindedly twirling lengthening blonde curls.

Nearby, in his great stuffed chair, her father continued scanning his evening paper, humming the symphonic music playing on the Austrian state radio. His tightly cropped hair was modeled on the race car drivers and mountaineers he idolized. He kept tapping a reddish walnut pipe on his thigh.

"Is it bad?" Ilsa asked.

"I don't know. It's unsettling. I am surprised how many Austrians have embraced rejoining Germany. The troops poured into Vienna the day after the canceled referendum, the plebiscite. Just three weeks ago. But now they are in Linz and Salzburg. In reunification, the German army runs all over us. And instead of talking football or Matthias Sindelar and the Wunderteam, we are talking about wiping out a religion."

Ilsa braced herself for a lecture sensing her father's anxious tone. Confiding in his eldest daughter was always a delicate process, especially in a country where the ugliest news was rarely discussed. But tonight, *die Presse* must've been extra troubling.

"Have you overheard me talking with Mutter about Baron von Rothschild?"

"He is the banker, yes?" asked Ilsa.

"Correct. He's been arrested. Apparently because he is Jewish. The paper says they've placed him in protective custody."

"Is being Jewish wrong, Papa?"

"Most certainly not. But my Jewish friends at work are all very nervous. They say the unthinkable is unfolding. It is beyond their comprehension. Already, there is a concentration camp at Woellersdorf, overflowing with prisoners. Many of them Jews. When that one fills up, the excess will go to Prussia or a camp they are expanding in Bavaria at Dachau."

"Aren't the Nazis rebuilding Germany? That's what we are learning at school."

"It depends on who the teacher is, young miss. And whether their facts are accurate. Leaders bend the truth these days. I think they lie when it suits them or push for laws that suit their agenda. By the way, how is your English class progressing? Your teacher taught German at Stoke-on-Trent in England, yes?"

"She did, Papa. And I am making progress. But many of the English words sound identical. There is *two, to*, and *too*. Or *there, their*, and *they're*."

"It's better than learning French. That country is usually drunk or delirious. They have an American woman funding their Grand Prix racing team. The one with the Delahaye 145s. Ach, they drink too much wine for their own good."

At this comment, he fiddled with a match, making it flare brightly before inserting it into his wheat-colored meerschaum pipe.

"But maybe we are a bit wayward ourselves," he continued. "Our Teutonic version comes with rioting and persecution. By the way, this matchbox is now empty. Can you use it for your dollhouse?"

Ilsa nodded. She had moved beyond dolls more than two years ago but accepted the gift without comment, watching her father rise from his chair. He walked over to a nineteenth-century walnut side table and picked up the March 28 issue of *Time*. He scanned the cover photo of Bette Davis before flipping through the magazine to find a specific page.

"Listen to what they have written about our Anschluss: 'Typical of the thoroughness with which Nazi adherents had prepared for "the day" was the fact twenty-four hours after Nazification, the Nazi guard at the remotest frontier post was armed with a fully tabulated, thumb-indexed book of many thousand names on the Nazi blacklist.'"

"That list sounds horrid."

"Indeed, Ilsa. But to be honest, I don't know what to think. All this saluting and Sieg Heils. By everyone. All the time. What is happening to us? Ach, this is enough news for tonight. Let us help Mutti with Hans and the cleaning up. You are singing for Herr Hitler on Monday? After his factory visit?"

"Of course, Papa. Everyone knows how important a day it is."

Johann smiled as if someone was watching him. As if he needed to be careful. He coughed into his right fist and rubbed it up and down on his muscular stomach as if that would clean his hand.

"Remember five years ago when Herr Hitler first came into power? One of his directives—this would have been 1933—was telling the directors at Mercedes and Auto Union that Nazi drivers, in German-built cars, must start winning Grand Prix races."

Ilsa enjoyed her father's motorsport stories. He would recite racers' names, the types of cars they drove, and where they finished in key races. All with great fluency.

"So, my child, you know these names I am always mentioning. In 1937, this past year, the Germans Hasse, Caracciola, and Manfred von Brauchitsch won the five big Grand Prix races. But at Nürburgring in July, Ferrari's Nuvolari, a good driver, I will admit, but not German. An Italian. Nuvolari kept Hasse off the podium by finishing fourth."

"A great shame, yes?" said Ilsa as if her words had been scripted.

"Correct again. Germans failed to take the top four places. Herr Hitler reportedly erupted and demanded a complete sweep this July. I would love to see such a historic event. Do you think I could convince your mother to let me motor up to Nürburgring?"

"She will ask if you can't do something closer to home. With your expensive new movie camera. And your children."

"Hmmm…you are unusually wise. I must ask again, how old are you?"

Ilsa giggled. "Papa, you know."

He shrugged in a conspicuous way. "I have my doubts about your birth certificate. Sometimes you are more seventy than thirteen. Each day you remind me more and more of your Oma in Vienna. Perhaps you were really born in the last century."

"Papa! How can you?"

They laughed together, but it was here, at this very moment, the seed of something clever began sprouting.

"I have an idea, Papa. Could you use your new camera to show Herr Hitler coming to Graz? It will be ever so special. Everyone will be there. Might I even miss class and instead help you film his historic visit?"

Johann considered the young girl's bold suggestion.

"This is interesting, Ilsa. But not easy. We need a wide platform for the camera's tripod. An unobstructed view. And no one banging about and making faces in front of me."

"As young Hans does in our garden, Papa?"

"Exactly."

Ilsa studied her father's strong face, offset by his bushy mustache that called for a good trimming. She could tell he was calculating how to film Germany's supreme leader on extremely short notice. And how his daughter might help. He stroked his dimpled chin in concentration.

"Does such a setting exist? This I ask you."

He pondered his question while Ilsa closed her schoolbook, glancing over at a new Hitler coloring book Hans had left in the room.

"Ahhh, but wait, I have it. Karl Schmidt's crow's nest. The foreman's perch. The little place where he watches over the workers. It could be perfect. We will go tomorrow and investigate…which means I must inform your headmaster. I will do this because right here in Graz, in our very own village, we might be training the next Leni. The next great storyteller."

CHAPTER 5

1 April 1938—Graz, Austria

Like everyone else in Graz, Ilsa knew when the sun rose on Monday, April 4, Adolf Hitler's entourage of sleek black cars would roar into town for the Führer's speech at the Waggonfabrik factory. Along the parade route, schoolboys would try to keep up with the snaking motorcade, charging past cheering villagers throwing their voices and right arms at the German leader and his troops.

On the boulevards, corseted housewives would not allow themselves to be upstaged by dirndl-wearing Gasthaus maids. All of them would cheer from their flower-box windows and granite front steps. Hanging over the streets from every building on the parade route, Nazi bunting and flags would flap lustily in the early spring breeze, guiding more than thirty thousand Austrians toward the scrubbed Weizer factory where the German Führer would speak.

The combination of history and spectacle was what finally persuaded her father he must film the event. Unfortunately, as father and daughter had discussed, the SS would cordon off a raised platform toward the back of the red brick building for news photographers. An accountant would never warrant a media credential. Something more imaginative was needed.

Johann would need to leverage his role as one of Weizer's senior accountants. Few outside the executive circle had ever visited the foreman's overlook, but it would offer an unimpeded view of the Führer's podium.

Arriving at the factory, Ilsa was shocked when she estimated the distance from the foreman's rough platform to the elevated stage. From the floor, the observation room appeared to be an afterthought, but what it lacked in amenities was more than compensated by its proximity.

Climbing a series of ladders and traversing two iron catwalks, Johann and Ilsa looked down on the immaculate factory floor to see workers in boiler-suits busily hanging blood-red Nazi Party banners in front of Waggonfabrik windows and stringing rectangular streamers from steel I-beams behind the stage. All of them were stark black and bold red, lightly fluttering in the spring breeze. Everywhere she looked, Ilsa saw swastikas.

Schmidt's platform was perfectly placed, but that was the problem. It made the setting even more desirable. Weizer's top executives might warrant the front row or placement along the main aisle, but schemers would seek out this room. There were even rumors floating that Hitler would discuss Germany's intentions to annex the Sudetenland in Czechoslovakia.

What Johann needed was permission, formal notice he was the sole cameraman allowed to use the foreman's nest. Making that happen required something official indicating the small room was off-limits. As her father explained it, that would require a lot of Glück. In other words, more Macht than anything a Weizer official could grant. For such a historic speech, permission must come from a high-ranking Nazi. Someone beyond challenge.

"How to do this?" he asked Ilsa, appearing to forget she was a year-eight girl.

"Could Onkel Fritz help? Didn't you say Herr Hitler is staying at his estate the night before his speech? If anyone can provide permissions, it is der Onkel."

Ilsa's father was far junior in social stature to Fritz Zell, but through family misfortune and a bit of good luck, the two men had spent summer holidays together near Klagenfurt. Left fatherless after the Great War, Johann had been unofficially adopted by the wealthy Zells to give their son a playmate during annual camping retreats along Austria's most popular lake, the darkly forested Wörthersee.

The gap between their respective social classes was wide, but over the years, the two men had stayed in touch. Fritz Zell had even guided Johann into finance. "Uncle" would surely know if connections with Hitler's advance team was possible.

"Wunderbar. It is inspired thinking, mein Schatzi. We will call him the very moment we get home."

That evening Johann placed the call. Following a confirmation from the switchboard operator, a connection was made, and an imposed-upon voice answered. When that individual departed, Johann held the black handset away from his ear and whispered that a butler had answered and dispatched someone to find Herr Zell. To this, Johann playfully pantomimed the role of an officious servant marching off in the grand mansion, tilting his head from side to side.

"Zell here."

"Fritz. It's Turnip. Your good-looking younger brother."

"Johann, I'm surprised you call me with the Führer coming this Sunday. Everyone is scurrying to be ready."

"Exactly so, mein Herr. I'm calling for that very reason. A simple request. You are aware I have recently purchased the same camera as the great Leni Riefenstahl?"

"Yes, yes, of course. Everyone wants to know how a man with three children can afford an Arriflex 35 from München. Have you stopped feeding Ilsa and young Hans?"

"Nein. They are eating me out of my home. And the newest one, Frederick, is worse. Up all night, always nursing. There is no rest for my poor Heidi. Somehow, I saved for this wonder and used the last of my inheritance. I told young Ilsa the other night the triple-lens concept is magnificent. It gives me framing comparable to what Leni used in *Triumph of the Will*."

"So…go on, make your request. But don't ask to meet the Führer. He is fastidious in how he prepares for public appearances. I am not to bring guests near him while he rehearses his speech. He becomes a man in a trance, often in a special chamber."

Like many of her friends, Ilsa had seen Hitler shouting with unscripted fury during news shorts at the moving pictures. Now, if the plan worked, she might witness him firsthand.

"He speaks in tongues, Fritzi," said Johann. "Very passionate. With a slight Bavarian accent…which is not unusual for an Austrian."

"Turnip, you are taking up precious time. Be quick here."

"Ahh, so. I am wondering. Herr Goebbels will be with him this weekend. Could you ask the minister for permission for Ilsa and me to film Herr Hitler's speech from a special room in the Weizer factory? It is one of our accounts. There is a closet, a foreman's observation room. It looks onto the factory floor. Perfect for recording history."

"Is that all? No handshakes? Nothing more?"

"I swear, my brother. Just permission to place a sign on the door saying, 'Do Not Disturb.' If it is signed by the Reichminister, no one will dare think about throwing us out. Of that I am certain."

"Come to the house Sunday exactly at four before our dinner and meet me on the back stairs. Enter through the servants' sector, not the front door. I will arrange for your credential. You can thank me later. Do not hope for an unexpected invitation to dine with us. Our grounds are shut from noon today, and the guest list is final. You will be met at the gate by the German security detail."

"Of course, of course. I will bring Ilsa with me. You have always been good to us, Fritz. Always helping with my tent and pack. But this is the most ever. I will bring the Arriflex and show you how these three lenses work."

"I will not have time. If we screw this up, the Führer may never visit Graz again."

The two men hung up, her father smiling. Ilsa pictured Onkel Zell overseeing final preparations with maids and butlers scurrying up and down the stairs. If permission was granted, she would soon see the Nazi leader making clear how foreign treatment of Germany angered him. How European leaders restricting the Reich made his blood boil.

At school, her best friend, Greta, said if a guest were to sit near Mozart or Beethoven while they played, they would not move so much as a finger out of fear they would distract the maestro. Germany's new leader was evidently just as intense.

Ilsa countered that she'd heard Hitler didn't use notes. His words came from some deeper source. It was cold water from a village well. But instead of a sloshing liquid, he pulled up buckets of words, the well's rope making him strong. A Bavarian giant. But so short. With a rectangular mustache.

The two girls giggled, agreeing Hitler's gyrations came across as manic, almost frantic. He chopped at the air as if he were possessed. His vicious forearm jabs and enraged facial expressions transmitted such anger. And everyone was always yelling "Sieg Heil" in unison.

Now, Ilsa might get to see him. Right after the Anschluss with Austria had been signed. She would learn what all the adults were talking about. That would make Greta, with her long yellow braids, so very jealous. Greta would murder her for getting such a lucky break.

CHAPTER 6

3 April 1938—Graz, Austria

Just prior to the drive to Zell's chateau that Sunday afternoon, Ilsa's father fiddled with their black-and-yellow Volksempfänger radio, darting between celebratory reports of the Nazi dictator's imminent arrival to baroque interludes and orchestral leitmotifs. Already, state newscasters were proudly reporting how local police and military would restrict access on all major boulevards in advance of Hitler's extended motorcade.

For a moment, father and daughter found themselves listening to static-laden snatches of Wagner's *Tristan und Isolde*. It was followed by a famous Austrian love song about the Alps and then classical works from Mozart, Liszt, and Strauss. Each piece fit the mood of coronation and historical occasion.

The appointed departure time having arrived, the duo departed to the garage where Johann stored his car. Rumbling out of the city, Ilsa stared out the Opel's windows, noting how the late March snow continued to linger under conspiring Austrian pines. Above her, towering firs and larches crowned the winding country road leading to Zell's historic bastion in Eisbach. It was a special day, bright blue with golden promise. If all went to script, her father would secure permission to film on Monday.

At Zell's gate, two muscular SS men shouted at Johann to park on the far side of the estate's service lane. It was all quite efficient, and as the pair exited the car and approached the mansion, Ilsa could see Zell's hedges and flowering trees were manicured to perfection. Above them, twin spires rose from the corners of the mansion's gothic entrance.

The residence was not a true castle. Not as grand as the palace owned by the Herbersteins in Eggenberg. But what it lacked in baronial grandeur, it made up for with forested grounds landscaped for hunting. In addition, Eisbach's nearby lakes had undoubtedly provided countless summer holiday activities.

"I was here for a large bank party in 1936 following the Berlin Olympics," said Johann. "That year little Austria won four gold medals and, some said rather begrudgingly, a controversial silver in football. It was a magical night for your mother and me."

"Did you dance under the stars?"

"Yes, of course. Mutti looked beautiful. We posed for a photo. But don't get me started on the past. I get lost there too easily. We must focus on the present and successfully influencing the future. Just so. We move to our assigned meeting place."

With purposeful strides, the pair walked past numerous stone-faced guards before opening a thick wooden door and descending the back steps to the home's indoor private garden. Inexplicably, Johann halted at the top of the mansion's rear stair landing and requested Ilsa descend to the carpeted middle landing.

"I will load the film here," he said, undoing the first circular lid and starting to engage the film roll onto the axle before threading the loose end into the camera's one-way sprocket. "This always takes a moment or two to get the magazine set up, so wait patiently, young miss."

Ilsa guessed Johann was simultaneously calculating how things would look with sunlight pouring through the chateau's skylights. For the moment, his daughter would serve as a stand-in while he constructed the shot. The bulky Arriflex was far from quiet, its film whirring away inside the magazine housing. At that moment, she wondered whether the Führer had a lighter side. Would he stop to play with the Zell's family dachshunds?

Unexpectedly, there was a rough jostling noise emerging from a room at the base of the stairs. The door was shut, but two loud male voices were either encouraging or chastising each other. A scraping, dragging noise suggested someone was possibly moving furniture during a heated exchange.

"*Schießdreck!*" one of the men cursed.

It was similar to the many times Papa had carelessly smashed his thumb with a hammer. Turning around to look back up the stairs, Ilsa realized her father was pointing his camera toward the disturbance. It was worse than bad luck. If anyone came out of the noisy room, they would see an intruding filmmaker.

"Keep looking up here, Ilsa," Johann was saying to her.

"Papa, we have come at the wrong time."

Just then, with the sound of a muted explosion, the door below flew open, and a wild-eyed man with very fine blond features stumbled out, his pupils enlarged with anger. He was naked from the waist down. His long dress shirt barely covered his private parts. And then from out of the room, for a fraction of a second, the Führer emerged. He was infuriated.

Ilsa hoped the two men had not seen her and her father—or the new Arriflex, with its three great eyes, filming.

From above, Ilsa's father was hissing. They needed to leave. Quickly. From below, Germany's all-powerful leader was instructing the second man to return to the room. His direct order conveyed how important it was to prepare his remarks. Didn't Karl recall other speeches they'd worked on in Munich and Nuremberg?

Johann urgently motioned for Ilsa to move up the stairs away from the lower landing.

"Gott im Himmel," he frantically whispered through his cupped fingers. "We must return to the car at once."

They slashed their way toward a side door to the outside garden, the wooden tripod banging clumsily against their legs. Ilsa hoped no one else had seen them.

But then, out of nowhere, materializing like an evil goblin or gargoyle come to life, Hitler's propaganda minister, Joseph Goebbels, was upon them, his angular frame blocking their path of retreat.

"What have we here?" said Goebbels, his scowl moving from overt suspicion to mild intrigue. "You are Zell's friend, Stulmacher, yes? But who is this beautiful young Fräulein?"

"I am Johann Stulmacher, Herr Reich Minister. And this is my daughter, Ilsa. We were departing. On our way out."

Winded, it was clear Johann was doing his absolute best to appear calm. Goebbels, on the other hand, his dark, menacing eyes appearing to burn brightly, had begun a different assessment. One involving Ilsa.

"I understand you have come for my blessing," Goebbels offered. "For paperwork to film tomorrow at the factory. You wish to see our great history unfold. To witness it firsthand."

Given the intensity of the minister's fearful countenance, Ilsa's father began stammering. She deduced his mind was frozen or lost, a climber in one of the Alpen whiteouts when flying snow weakened even the strongest ascending toward a dangerous peak.

Johann blinked repeatedly as the minister's stare drilled into him, a slow-grinding auger digging into her father's soul. Goebbels was probing, searching for deceit. For a reason to deny the request. Ilsa's mind raced.

What would happen if the film showed Herr Hitler? For certain, Zell and her papa would be ruined. It must not happen. She must answer for him.

"It would be our honor to film such an important day, Herr Reich Minister," she said with the confidence of a bold teenager. "Austria will make der Führer proud."

"Indeed," Johann stammered in hurried agreement. "If we are so fortunate, Herr Reich Minister. I am inspired by the great Leni. She is showing the way for those of us with moving-picture cameras in Austria. I am hoping young

Ilsa will find herself similarly inspired."

"I see. You are using the new Arriflex 35. This is good. Very professional. Far better than the piggish American version. It is lighter, yes?"

"Assuredly so, Mein Herr. The Bavarians make it easy to see what you are filming. It is so much more powerful with three focal lengths on the bayonet."

"Ahh, yes, a Bavarian Bayonet." Goebbels paused. "A good term. Most appropriate for what is to come. We must remember to use it in an upcoming speech. And I assure you, there will be many. Our moment is rapidly approaching."

"I do not understand, Herr Reich Minister."

"Nor should you, Stulmacher. But there is a chance your film will assist the Fatherland. As you pass the SS guards near the cars, you will find my assistant, Günter. He is set up at a field desk. I have arranged for him to provide your notice for the factory. He will handle this matter in Herr Zell's unfortunate absence. Zell's chef has not yet attained the level of our German culinary standards. He wishes you a pleasant evening. As do I. Perhaps we will show your footage to the world, and your daughter will be inspired. She is quite lovely, Stulmacher."

"Danke, Herr Reich Minister."

Johann attempted clicking his heels, as the German military did, but failed to generate a sound worthy of respect. Given his awkward bowing, Ilsa hoped he'd avoid making further small talk.

But now, as they were striding away, Goebbels called to them.

"Fräulein Ilsa…how old are you?"

She stopped, dead in her stride, and turned around.

"Thirteen, Herr Reich Minister."

Goebbels nodded. "A fruitful age, Fräulein. Do not forget your duty to the Fatherland. You are quite right for the Reich."

The words somehow felt wrong, but Ilsa pushed her discomfort aside. She and her father faced a much more pressing issue. The clock was ticking and by now Germany's all-powerful leader was dressed. Would he alert his men to detain the Stulmachers before they reached the gate? Would her mother ever learn what happened the day they went to get the signed permission at Zell's?

"Danke vielmals, Mein Herr, und auf Wiedersehen." She spoke the words, hoping they might buy father and daughter enough time to get home.

But then, seemingly against all odds, the miracle was birthed. Goebbels waved them off. There was silence.

Günter, with great officiousness, handed over the signed order and, as they returned to the Stulmacher car, no one yelled for them to stop. No one came with guns raised. They were welcome to leave the grounds.

Ilsa's father primed the Opel's underpowered engine, engaged the balky clutch, and left Zell's mansion with great caution. Sitting on the far side of the car's bench seat, Ilsa wondered if he understood the gravity of their problem. In the safety of the automobile, she pressed the matter.

"Papa, der Führer saw us, right?"

"I don't know, Ilsa. I think so. But maybe not."

"You had the camera rolling, Papa." Her voice sounded tense. "It showed Herr Hitler and a man with no pants."

"You must not worry, my child. I will have that roll of film destroyed. For now, history is happening on our doorstep, and we have permission from the Reich minister. We will proceed with our plan and record the Führer's speech tomorrow at the factory. It will be all right."

That night, the family worked its way through a meal of lentil soup, leftover venison, and apfel strudel, but Ilsa's father was clearly distracted. It was only too obvious to Ilsa because Mother did most of the talking, announcing where she and the two younger children would watch the historic motorcade.

After the ritual of evening baths, Johann announced to his family, he would retire early for the evening. "Tomorrow is a long day, and tonight I am feeling too much excitement. I am thinking Ilsa and I will leave early but come home for the evening meal. And then we can discuss the day's events."

Ilsa listened for her parents' voices that night, but nothing was sounding from their twin beds. Undoubtedly, they were pulling Mutti's eiderdown quilts, her prize-winning Federbettens, up to their respective chins. Mama still did not know.

As the silent house settled down, Ilsa prayed to Jesus but found she could not concentrate on her words. She imagined uniformed men massing nearby. In that devilish dusk, the crunching sound of German Wehrmacht boots was approaching.

She finally fell into a deep slumber but tossed and turned. In a dream, Minister Goebbels chased her on skis. Racing through Olympic slalom gates high above the Bavarian village of Garmisch-Partenkirchen, he tore down the hill toward her.

It made no sense, but what she remembered on waking, with a sense of impending doom, of vulnerability, frightened her. Goebbels had caught her. And she was alone. Everyone else was gone.

CHAPTER 7

4 April 1938

True to her father's plan, Ilsa and Johann were gone by 6:30 the next morning. She hoped the Führer hadn't seen anything and hadn't asked Goebbels to investigate Zell's accountant friend. If he had, they could get stopped almost anywhere, but most certainly would be detained at the factory.

After her father parked the black Opel, he sternly repeated careful instructions for carrying his burlap satchel filled with film canisters. They entered the Weizer factory alongside shift workers, both expecting Johann's specially secured papers to receive intense scrutiny from grim black-shirted men. At each checkpoint, Ilsa gripped the bag of silver tins more tightly.

It was obvious the signed documentation from Herr Goebbels had paved the way.

"I think only Herr Himmler could overrule a Goebbels order," Johann said with confidence to Ilsa. "Minister Goebbels has served Herr Hitler since the 1920s. Now, watch closely while I set up our camera so you can see how it works."

At 1:00 p.m. there was a dull roar from outside the open steel doors. Then, amid much fanfare, German's supreme leader strode into the building, saluting to various throngs all shouting, "Heil Hitler." At different points, almost as if scripted, he veered toward select members of the crowd to accept flowers.

His camera rolling, Johann turned to Ilsa and said, "Are you seeing this, my child?"

"I do, Papa. He is so popular."

The crowd roared in unison as Hitler announced Germany and Austria were once again a single entity. That Austrians, the people of the Alps, were the newest members of the Reich. Others were certain to follow, but the country of his birth was clearly special to him.

To Ilsa, Hitler's performance was that of a festival hypnotist, someone able to place everyone in a spell. His shouting and savage gaze, his stomping and frequent saluting, produced the equivalent of a verbal mist covering the factory floor. When he called out, they responded with throated fury.

Below her father's camera, row after row of uniformed men and hoarse civilians thrust stiff arms into the air, while Hitler berated Neville Chamberlain and his recent address to the English House of Commons. After that, Hitler targeted the people of France. None were as pure as the Germans or Austrians. Purity was a mandate for the Fatherland.

At one point during his tirade, Germany's leader paused, staring at the cameraman in the crow's nest. At that moment, Ilsa felt the man with the unusual mustache perceived the Stulmachers as two birds on a perch...with no cage protecting them.

When the ceremony's final ovations ended, Ilsa said, "Papa, did you notice when Herr Hitler stared at us? Do you think he recognized us?"

"I think so, Ilsa, but I am not sure what we make of that moment. The German chancellor is skilled at speaking to cameras and into microphones. I'm sure he does that all the time."

On the way back to their car, the bell tower on Schlossberg Hill began casting its late-afternoon shadow like an angry finger of doom. Around them, Austrians openly proclaimed their expectancy of prosperity, smiling at the father-daughter pair, and, on seeing the bulky camera gear, asking if they had filmed der Führer. Yes? They had? You are lucky, they would roar.

Echoing words Ilsa had already heard from Herr Goebbels, many also commented on her looks and importance to the Reich. In their festiveness, they suggested she would produce fine sons for the Fatherland. It was unsettling. Total strangers thinking of her as a breeding cow.

"You must not put stock in these comments, Ilsa. You are soon a woman. But these words are ignorant."

They were almost home, coming up one of Graz's slight inclines, enjoying warm rays of spring sunshine, when from out a side alleyway, a frail hand beckoned for them to step into the cloaking darkness.

"Pssst…"

"Ach, was ist los, Herr Stein?"

Ilsa was abruptly nervous, afraid of the unbidden intrusion, but her father was smiling at the man in the shadows.

"What a pleasant surprise."

"You may not act so pleased when I reveal my purpose."

Under a side street awning, Ilsa learned Stein was a bookkeeper assigned to profitable Jewish jewelry accounts managed by her father's firm. Ilsa thought the little man with the extra folds of skin and wild dark eyes was afraid, almost agitated. Had he been waiting for them, hoping they would follow this route home? Or had he followed them and run ahead? The latter didn't make any sense given his age.

"I understand the Gestapo and their coming agenda, Johann," the bookkeeper said in a hoarse whisper that swirled aggressively amid the smells of the dank alley. "I'm sorry to tell you this in front of your daughter, but I've known for hours. I couldn't find you. Listen to me. You do not have much time. A friend of mine recognized your name as orders were given. Whatever it is, you are under suspicion."

"You risk yourself, my friend. Yet you take the time to warn me?"

"My people know of betrayal. Persecution. Be aware. You are numbered with us now."

"But—

"It doesn't matter," Stein said. "You have a car. Disappear or lose everything. In fact, my own time approaches. Another pogrom, the most cruel yet, is coming."

"I am grate—"

"Don't waste your time with gratitude. Leave now, you fool."

Nervously, the gnomish accountant turned on scuffed black heels and walked deeper along the side street, his footfalls ominous in the narrowing space. The echoing was still hanging in the cold air when he interrupted her father's final question.

"When will—"

"During the evening. In force. Do what I cannot. What my foolish, ignorant family refuses to believe."

Waving his hands in exasperation, the wild-looking man departed, sliding through the door to a Jewish jewelry store further down the alley.

"We must hurry, Ilsa. We cannot doubt that Herr Hitler saw us. So, tonight, when I give commands, you must obey them."

Reaching their neighborhood, Ilsa witnessed Austrians pulsing up and down the elm-lined Straßen. They no longer mattered in the slightest. They were marked. And what had Hitler asked of his private staff? He'd undoubtedly demanded to see the film.

Ilsa wondered if Hitler had grilled Goebbels. *Who were the people in the foreman's loft? The man with the camera. The modern one. With a young blonde girl assisting.*

"Where is this film?" Hitler might've asked in a rage. "Find it. Mach schnell."

"Jawohl, Mein Führer," she conjured Goebbels saying. "Immediately."

He'd seen father and daughter on Zell's stairs and stopped during his speech to make that very point crystal clear. The Stulmacher film could destroy his new Reich.

Ilsa tried imagining what would have been uttered next.

"Joseph…be sure to tell him I have decided to view this footage from Graz before anyone else. Bring it to me undeveloped."

Goebbels's two heels would've clicked together perfectly while his right arm shot forward like a large-winged bird taking flight. Behind them, an orderly would have been scratching out a reminder note, watching for Herr Hitler's perfunctory half wave.

"The wrong people must not penetrate our inner circle, Joseph, even accidentally. Deal with this. You may have the girl."

"It shall be done, Mein Führer. With pleasure."

Ilsa hoped her runaway imagination was flawed. That her family was not at risk. But deep down, she predicted Goebbels and his men were coming. They must destroy their film.

"So. Herr Himmler has given orders," her father said, interrupting Ilsa's daydream. "That is more than unfortunate. We must leave tonight."

"But Papa, to go where?"

"I don't know. I don't know. There may be just enough time to reach Innsbruck and the mountains. After that, we must find someplace where no one knows us."

"In my book, Papa, with the woman from Australia, there are no people around them."

"Is that the Never-Never book you are always carrying around?"

"Yes. The one about Mrs. Gunn and Elsey Station. It sounds so empty. There is no one for hundreds of kilometers."

"Funny that your book about Australia is so popular in Austria," said Johann. "Both beginning with A-u-s-t, no? Is it a solution? I don't know. Herr Stein was very certain about getting out. Right now, we face bigger problems. We need Italian money and a plan."

"How will we destroy the film if we are running away?"

Ilsa recalled her father talking about the blacklist in the international edition of *Time* magazine he brought home from the Graz library to stay up on world affairs. All over Austria, according to the article, people were killing themselves for having supported the wrong political party. In Vienna, Austria's former vice chancellor Fey had killed his wife, nineteen-year-old son, and then himself. Fey tried suppressing Nazi sympathizers while commanding Austria's nationalist paramilitary group, the Heimwehr.

In the mountains, Tyrolean magnate Friedrich Reitlinger instructed his daughter to shoot him before turning the gun on herself. Gustave Bayer, a Home Guard supporter, administered fatal doses of morphine to his family before turning up the gas in their oven.

Every day, Austrian Christians and Jews were leaping to their deaths or shooting themselves. That was how much they feared the fast-moving Nazi Party. If Herr Stein was right, Ilsa's family had less than an hour. It meant she might have no chance to tell Greta goodbye.

"Papa…you know how I had the idea to film der Führer's speech at the factory?"

Johann nodded his head, distracted, not unlike a chess player considering his next move. Ilsa guessed the safe, comfortable world he had built in Graz was inexplicably falling in on him. Where could he take his family?

"I'm partly responsible for what has happened," she blurted out.

"No, my darling. This is my doing. I wanted to film something important, and instead we have filmed the unimaginable."

"Yes, that is so, but it doesn't matter. I have a solution."

"You do? How is that possible?"

"Because Greta and I share secrets, we hide little things. Forgive me, Papa, but we write notes we don't want our parents to see. If you give me the film, both canisters, I will give them to her, and she will hide them. In a place where no one will ever find them. Then, if we leave, we have nothing with us. If this matter blows over, we can get them back, and you can do what you must."

Johann looked down at the street's round stones, gripping both temples with his left thumb and index finger.

"When we arrive home, I will give you an order. I will put the cans in a satchel by the fireplace. I was going to burn them. If you are certain Greta can hide them and not tell anyone, then, on my order, you will give them to her. When it is safe, we will come back. Perhaps this film can be used to put an end to this madness. But as I've been saying all day, I just don't know. If they come after us and I say I destroyed the film, I doubt they will believe me. At least if it exists, and we are caught, I can bargain with it. Safe passage for the family in return for handing the reels over."

"Safe passage, Papa?"

CHAPTER 8

Arriving at their house, Johann raced into the kitchen, imploring his wife to turn off the stove and start packing the children for an abrupt journey, one filled with shelterless nights in the Alps. They would need boots and thick socks. Heavy jumpers. Food that wouldn't spoil.

Heidi turned. "What are you saying, Johann? What is this wild ruckus about?"

"Do not ask."

"And why not?"

"Trust me. Quickly now. Or we are doomed. Ten minutes. The loden jackets for the children. Ilsa, you must help your brothers. Grab three wool blankets. Winter boots and scarves. Put them in my biggest climbing knapsack. Leave it for me by the door. Do it now."

Ilsa's mother was dumbfounded. She had been baking Tyrolean pastries for this special night, her creased apron still warm from pressing up against the oven. Now, her husband and daughter were home safely from the rally.

"Where is this coming from?" she cried. "What is this? Are you mad?"

Would Ilsa's father scream? No, he wouldn't. The nearby neighbors always listened for raised voices or private news.

"I have learned something horrible, Mutti. News I cannot tell you here," he hissed. "You remember the Röhm-Putsch in 1934? The Night of the Long Knives? When Hitler killed his own men. Not even four years ago."

"Of course, but—"

"Hundreds of good German soldiers. Murdered in Munich. Berlin, all over. They came for Dollfuss that July. We are next. Because of what Ilsa and I saw at Zell's."

"But my dinner…"

"Let it burn. The men coming for us are not the SA. Not the storm troopers. It's Hitler's secret force, the Gestapo. They will take us to their cellars. If we get that far. Trust me, my darling, we must leave at once. If you don't pack the children immediately, they will die. We are marked, Heidi. Doomed. Ilsa, get new boxes of matches. From the fireplace. Schnell."

Ilsa knew she mustn't look around or scare her mother. Or spend even an extra minute hunting for belongings. Her father was already grabbing a leather backpack and stuffing summer sausages into the outer pockets. A wedge of hard cheese followed. Whirling around, he took a pitcher and filled a container with water. Five minutes had passed since they had arrived home. As he reached for his woolen winter coat, the one with the big collar, it caught on the brass hook.

The beating in Ilsa's heart surged as her father struggled. Was she imagining the sound of screeching tires?

In her head, Greta mocked her. *The Alps are killers in April, Ilsa. You know that. Avalanches and whiteouts. Cold winds knifing through your wet clothing.*

Heading into Austria's Salzburger Land, the infamous East Tyrol that rose majestically toward the Italian border, was madness. Were the Alps their only hope?

You'll fall into one of the deep ice crevices. You'll be entombed in ice for centuries.

"Listen to me." It was Papa speaking. "We must do what they least expect. We'll split up until I get the car. If all five of us leave the house together, someone will notice. Instead, we go in opposite directions. A family adventure."

"Papa, what is my assignment?"

"You are the oldest, Ilsa, so you go first. Pack for climbing. Our ropes and burner. When that is done, you will walk down the Tummelplatz, then along the Bürgergasse, past the Mausoleum of Emperor Ferdinand II. If anyone approaches you, including your school friends, tell them you are running an errand for Mutti. That will explain your bag. At the emperor's monument, sit on the steps with your Australian book until you see us all again."

He nodded his head at her, and after grabbing her heavy coat, she left the room to get their gear and the rucksack filled with film. In the kitchen, her father continued his instructions.

"My darling, Heidi, I'm sorry about this. I will explain in the car…but for now you must take the boys and go a different route. First, through the alleys to the Dom and then into the big courtyard next to the mausoleum. Carry Frederick, but Hans must walk on his own. I will bring the car around and collect everyone. No one is to run."

Ilsa was moving toward the door when her father swept her into his arms.

"You will be fine, Ilsa. Don't worry too much. Think of this as a more exciting version of your famous hide-and-seek. When you are tricking your brothers."

Ilsa felt his firm arm steering her toward the door. He opened it and squeezed her two arms, indenting her biceps with his thumbs, before kissing her forehead. With that, she was skipping out the door, her tentative first steps revealing just how much she feared the Gestapo's arrival and the arrest of her family. Where would she go if Papa didn't meet them? She had seen Austria's fanaticism during the speech. She would be brought to Goebbels.

I must be brave. For Mutti und Papa. I mustn't let my thoughts run wild. They will all arrive at the monument.

To calm her nerves, Ilsa began humming one of the songs that had played on the radio during the drive to Zell's. At first, she tried whistling the melody, but it was hard hitting all the notes. So she clamped her teeth and lips together and made the lyrics fill her head.

Reaching the first corner, she looked up toward the Schlossbergbahn funicular, keeping her mind fixed on Papa's instructions. After running to Greta's, she must turn at the Bürgergasse and make for the emperor's mausoleum. On reaching the crypt, she would sit down and pretend to read her Never-Never book.

In the distance, Ilsa saw Frederik III's ornate memorial. Greta's house was around the corner from it, two blocks over. Increasing her pace, she began rehearsing how to convince her friend to risk everything. Hopefully, the two girls could talk in private.

But now some Glück. Racing over the round cobblestones, she saw her friend playing hopscotch, oblivious to the coming conspiracy.

"Quick. A new secret. Can we talk in your room? Someplace alone?"

"Of course, Ilsa," said Greta, instantly understanding an adventure was afoot. "I'll tell mother we must discuss our schoolwork."

"Good. I won't be long. Our family is going away to do some climbing this week, but don't say anything at school. It's kind of an unexpected holiday."

"Lucky Mädchen."

"We shall see."

Sequestered in Greta's tight bedroom on the third floor of their townhouse, Ilsa began unpacking her father's rucksack. As she set the silver canisters on the floor, she saw the gleam of envy in Greta's eyes.

"You filmed today at the rally, yes? How was it? Amazing?"

"You cannot believe the passion, Greta. Everyone. The crowd. Der Führer. And we were so close to the stage. But there is an issue," she said, starting the fabrication she'd barely found time to construct. "We may have filmed at the factory in the wrong place. In a setting where we shouldn't have set up the camera. My father could be in trouble. He thinks the Germans want his film and might come to our house and search for it. I told him you and I had a secret hiding place, and because this footage is so special to him, we could hold it until this silly matter blows over."

"You think so? You think the Nazis will want it? It was just a noisy rally to get Austrians excited about the Anschluss."

"We don't know. But I told Papa, 'Better safe than sorry.' Regardless, can you put these tins in our special place and make sure no one sees you going there? One is of the rally, and the other is just some silly footage out at Onkel Fritz's."

"Yes, yes. Of course. And when you return next week, I'll give them back."

"Perfect. That's all I ask. But if something happens while I am climbing, you must never look at them or show them to anyone else. It's our secret. When I return, I'll tell you about the speech. Herr Hitler looked right at me while he was speaking."

"No."

"He did. As if he knew who I was. He was so intense. Staring with his black eyes."

Ilsa's last sentence was truthful, but its darker meaning, the omission threatening everything, was obscured. It didn't matter. Greta would hide the films, never revealing where she took them. It was their newest, best-ever secret.

Giving her friend a hug and kisses on both cheeks, Ilsa bounded down the stairs, yelling a cheery but staged "auf Wiedersehen" to Greta's mother. Once on the street, her gait composed, she kept close to the towering city walls leading toward the mausoleum.

What happened to the dead? Did their skeletons eventually turn to dust? What would happen to her bones when she died?

You mustn't think of such things.

Sitting on the freezing steps, Ilsa left her pack on for warmth but also in case she needed to run. If soldiers turned up, she wouldn't want any fumbling.

If I had to escape, I would go back to Greta. She would loan me money for the train, and then I would go to Switzerland. I could always come back for the film canisters and use them as blackmail. The Nazis would have to bargain with me.

The thought of entering another country presented Ilsa with a different problem. Did Mutti and Papa know anyone in Geneva or Zürich? She was working her way through the Stulmacher family tree when, out of the corner of her eye, her mother appeared with the two boys. They were winded, even flustered, but safe.

"Is Papa coming with the car?"

"We must hope so, Ilsa. But I am at a loss on what is happening. I don't understand. Yet you do. What did you see that makes us leave everything? Hans, stop that. Sit down next to your sister and behave."

"Mutti, I cannot speak of those things here. Papa will tell you tonight. When the boys are asleep. It is serious."

As she sought to end her explanation, Ilsa's father roared up in the car and with beckoning arms implored everyone to join him. He was mouthing the word "schnell." Ilsa guessed he dared not get out of the vehicle. Were the Gestapo that close at hand?

Moments later, her father merged into Graz's evening traffic, telling Heidi he intended to visit an Oesterreichischen Bundesheer brigade lieutenant named Heinz Jäger. The two men had worked together on winter field maneuvers, with airfield groups at Graz, Innsbruck, and Salzburg. Jäger would know the best routes for entering Italy.

"Tell me nothing," Jäger said curtly as he produced a military map of the Brenner Pass. His strong face was tight with tension. "You are apparently leaving us. If that is the case, I have not seen you, my friend. But there is a Catholic priest near Innsbruck. Father Lambert. I will get word to him. He can help you. Enter his church two nights from now and appear to pray."

"Danke, Herr Jäger," Stulmacher said. "We will say nothing more than auf Wiedersehen."

The visit lasted no more than three minutes before the family was again hurtling down the road. At the entrance to the Inn River valley, Johann Stulmacher turned southwest toward Kufstein and Innsbruck. Rolling through the night, keeping the icy Inn almost always within sight, the family's escape into the mountains would soon rest less on tires or petrol and more on legs and lungs.

CHAPTER 9

5 April 1938

The family spent their first cold night in the cramped Opel, huddled in the looming shadows of Kufstein Castle, the imposing Festung used as a place of torture and grisly executions during the previous seven hundred years. Above them, the fort's sheer north wall soared upward into the cloud-filled sky.

To the south, the Alps rose out of the rocky river valley, monstrous tidal waves of stone and granite. High above the Inn River, round-walled towers revealed slits where crossbow archers once fired their arrows on invading Maximillian I and his Bavarians.

At the fortress's base lay the Auracher Löchl, a tavern, brewery, and dark wooden hotel leaning up against the immense thirteenth-century wall. Löchl literally meant "hole." A hole in the mountain. Through an open door, Ilsa saw the interior of the brewery incorporated a tunneled alcove. Rough-hewn roof-beams and fortified extensions were fitted where the surging river and soaring mountain allowed.

In Graz, Ilsa's father was a respected member of the community. He was prosperous to the point of even buying an expensive movie camera. They socialized with the Zells. But here in Kufstein, it was all different. Around them, drunken merrymakers staggered away from the tavern, debating Hitler's visit to Graz and the Anschluss.

Worse for Ilsa was sleeping in a sitting position. It was cold and cramped. Mother had handed out blankets and wool jumpers but whispered harshly at her husband. She was not pleased at learning the reason for their daring departure.

When Ilsa awoke the next morning, robins and blackbirds were hard at work making their predawn calls. It was the moment she made out a shadowy figure, her father, scavenging for pork spätzle and Tiroler Knödel in the tavern's slop bins. It was unimaginable for a family of their stature to eat these scraps.

Returning to the Opel and deeming it safe to move, Johann started the car, passing quietly under the alley's arched passageways. Just above them, a sixteenth-century cannonball, still black and round, revealed itself embedded in the castle's wall. Ilsa couldn't help wondering if the artillery remnant was an omen of some kind, foreshadowing more shots to come.

Three hours passed before the family reached Innsbruck and the mountainous mouth of the Brenner Pass. In the hamlet of Hungerburg, they abandoned their vehicle and waited in a nearby pine forest until it was dark enough to meet the priest.

Father Lambert welcomed them into the rectory with a hearty "Grüss Gott," listened to Johann's story, fed them, and extended his guidance on which routes to favor. Everyone was ravenous, but Frederick was more restless than normal, and Hans needed constant soothing. The governess role was one Ilsa took on for the good of the family.

As soon as they'd eaten, Lambert ushered the family out his back door, advising them to attack the eastern side of the ridgeline that formed the vaunted Brenner Pass. They must not rush, but if a search warrant had been issued for their arrest, they also mustn't linger. The Gestapo were growing ruthless. Too many German and Austrian Jews were taking to the hills.

Two mornings later, having climbed into the Brenner's near vertical forests, Johann spotted German mountain units off in the distance. He suggested they were the German Gebirgstruppen, patrolling an alpine service road with Alsatians and Dobermans.

Closing in, the Germans, evidently with Austrian help, had set up a roadblock in a deep valley near a spot where the river's flume attacked the bedrock. There were two gray Nazi staff cars, parked nose to nose, with twisting wisps of exhaust smoke spiraling upward over the road's flimsy wooden guardrails. Next to the vehicles, men were gesturing upward toward the stark white flanks of the pass.

Ilsa lay completely still, positioned behind a pine tree covered in a sugar-powder dusting of fine snow. Mucus from her nose was pooling and freezing on her upper lip. Licking at it only made things worse. In the distance stood two utility barns built into the steep hillside for housing summer tools. Around them farm carts and wagons sat abandoned for the winter.

We would be much warmer in one of those huts, but that's the first place they would look, isn't it? We're safer up here.

Ilsa shivered, a violent convulsion, before looking to her mother for reassurance. But with evening falling, she received little more than a hollow stare. Soon enough, the family was moving again, climbing past strands of glistening birch trees into deer runs and minor avalanche chutes illuminated by the moon. Above her, the torn clouds wrestled with black peaks trying to block the advancing Tyrolean fog.

Below them, sprawling valleys nestled under fierce granite faces. In the distance, Ilsa thought she saw a Gothic church steeple, its spire pointing skyward in the night.

Expelling a frozen breath, she whispered, "Papa, wouldn't we be safe at the church? As we were in Innsbruck?"

"Nein. Not tonight. We are not safe in Austria. We must reach Italy. Another full day's hike. Maybe less if the terrain helps us."

The Nazis were one thing to fear, but in a multitude of places, one false step would send them falling to their deaths. Freezing air, meanly vented down steep, icy ravines, was an additional and constant worry because it brought on hypothermia. The best way to stay warm was to keep climbing, stomping with frozen feet through the deep snow.

Twice during that first week in the Brenner, Ilsa saw how her family's fatigue and growing despair might threaten their very survival. It fell to her father, sometimes with Ilsa helping, to break the trail on the mountain switchbacks and carry supplies across the exposed, windblown ridges. Twice he nearly lost his balance, once with Hans under his weary arm.

Mutti often asked if there wasn't an easier path to pick. Ilsa guessed there wasn't, particularly since the peaks towering above the tree line created soaring ridgelines resembling ebony sabers. And when the ice wasn't creating eyestrain, its cerulean blue affirmed the frigidness ahead.

On the other side of the border lay the Italian Alps. Here, they would descend steep slopes, with dark chicanes and ice-crusted crevices majestically falling away under an endless parade of peaks. In some places, that route ahead would almost certainly exceed the skills of a man leading a one-rope party with his wife, teenage daughter, and two young boys.

Ilsa constantly worried her father's strength would give out, but despite the family's exhausted situation, he held firm. He even resorted to telling visually embellished stories about Max Reisch, a great Austrian motoring legend and heroic adventurer. Or the late Austrian climber Paul Preuss.

One night as the family lay huddled in a freezing snow cave, their fire quickly digesting the spindly branches Ilsa had collected, Johann told how Reisch had driven a battered Indian-Puch motorcycle across broad, burning stretches of the Sahara in the early thirties.

They were all fully spent, and Ilsa wasn't sure what benefit her father's story might provide. Worse, Mutti was showing signs of weakening. The boys were also sluggish, their eyes ragged and dull. Around them, the callous evening shadows raced through the sparse trees and barren rock lee of the mountain.

The spiraling red tendrils provided little heat, but all afternoon, Johann had promised the last of their cocoa and a magnificent story. Ilsa guessed Papa intended to create something warm and encouraging because the wind had picked up, its ululation akin to a lone wolf calling for its pack, an eerie sound forcing even the hardiest animals to stick to their dens.

"You see, my little ones," Johann started out, holding Hans tightly, "remember how Max became one of our most famous Austrians for driving across Africa and Asia in 1935 and '36? I saw that famous car in Graz before you, Frederick, were born. But, tonight, I'll tell you something that happened in 1932, six years ago, when mighty Max achieved the impossible. That year he drove a two-stroke motorcycle, not much more than a bicycle, with a sidecar, across the deadly Sahara."

Hans was always cold, but after Johann rebuked his eldest for sniffling too much, he rubbed each of their shoulders, ensuring no one cried. Ilsa could not see beyond the glow of their fire and barely made out the shape of her mother settling the baby in a rough bed of blankets and fir boughs. Ilsa wished to sleep, but fatigue was a slippery ledge even the strongest climbers feared. Inattention could send them into the abyss of overexposure and death.

"It was a bed of hot sands," Johann told Ilsa and Hans with enthusiasm. "So hot that if you touched the metal of the motorcycle, you would be burned. Here, Hans, touch my coat and imagine when you touch it, this sleeve will scorch your fingers."

The child held out his hand with caution but, emboldened by the story, brought his index finger to rest on his father's parka.

"Sssssssss!" Johann roared at the touch, and little Hans immediately yanked his hand away convinced it had been burned.

"Ahhhh."

"You see what it is like in the desert. The place where humpy camels can go on for days without drinking. It is boiling hot. Too hot for the motorcycle. But if Max stays too long in one place, he and his companion will overheat. They must get water. So now, Ilsa, tell me what you must find to survive in this sweltering desert. Where are you safe?"

"Oh, Papa. You must find an oasis, a place with a palm tree and a lovely little watering place. They must go there. I see it off in the distance."

"Yes, but is it a mirage? Will it disappear in the heat as we get closer? Tell me, child, are there animals there? Are they hot and thirsty?"

"I can see it. It is a wonderful place, Papa, with a tent and a fat sultan sitting on a carpet. The camels are drinking. They have long necks, so I am thinking it is not going away."

"Good girl, Ilsa, and just as the camels do, we must drink as well. Because, you see, whether we are in the desert with Herr Reisch or here in the mountains, water is what keeps us going. It is our fuel. Our petrol."

"But mustn't we eat also, Papa?" asked Hans.

"When we can, my young mountaineer. But always we are drinking hot cocoa to keep our bodies lubricated. Max told me once the secret was taking care of his equipment. Your little body, Hans, is like Max's machine."

For three more nights, icy ravines merged with a vortex of cruel snowfall. Winds knifed through frozen layers of cloth, forcing Johann to tell new tales about Preuss, the Austrian climbing legend who had established daring first routes.

"We must be superior to this mountain," Papa said to Hans after explaining how the Alpinist disdained artificial aids, often attacking routes unroped. Twice, Preuss had tackled the daunting Totenkirchl near Kufstein. "We face difficulty. All climbers do, but we have the confidence, from our preparation, to overcome fear."

There were many occasions, on steep snow-covered switchbacks, with numb feet and empty stomachs, Ilsa's father told of Reisch crossing crocodile-infested rivers on lashed-bamboo rafts. If they could cross one more couloir, or traverse the next pass, there would be safety. Always, like a man hurtling down an icy river, he pushed them toward Italy.

Days later, moving under the cover of a night that crept from blue to indigo, purple, and black, the family descended a gently sloping hillside, Johann and Heidi carrying two of the three children in their arms. As they crept silently past a darkened monastery, Italian words on a sign made clear they had reached Bressanone. They had survived the Brenner on foot.

A week later, the family came to Verona, Venice, and finally, after a cramped and vexing train trip, Rome. It was on reaching the frantic capital Ilsa again wondered how the Gestapo had failed to grab them during the Graz rally at the factory. Had they slipped up? Was it possible someone's arrogance or inept disbelief had facilitated their escape?

Ilsa scratched at one ear, pushing a persistent blonde curl aside. Maybe the Germans were not perfectly efficient. Or perhaps they were just uncertain how to navigate in a newly annexed country. Either way, they clearly had not anticipated an Austrian mountaineer, with a roll of Italian lira, taking his family and fleeing into the night.

CHAPTER 10

January 2005—Katherine, NT, Australia

"Looking back," Ilsa said to me afterward, while entering the same pub where we'd first met, "it was nothing short of miraculous we survived the Brenner. I remember one time reaching that Italian convent my father knew about. He was an amateur Alpinist who'd trained in the Austrian Federal Army. He was at home in the mountains. Also, he spoke some Italian."

By now, I had canceled my flight back to Maryland and extended my Australian visit by a week. J.B. would not care so long as my story exploded off the page. I nodded politely to the head waitress as she sized us up: an older woman carrying a laptop and a businessman, a stranger, with a tape recorder and notebook.

She guided us to a booth where dull cutlery, wrapped in ancient ivory napkins, leaned lazily in a repurposed dark-blue coffee can.

"You were saying…" I prodded gently.

"Father later told me that going toward the Hungarian or Yugoslavian borders near Graz or even west toward Klagenfurt would've been madness. He said even Hitler wouldn't think of attempting the Brenner in April."

Once our Great Northern beers arrived, Ilsa looked at hers like it had come from another galaxy. She had brought me through the accidental filming at Zell's and rally in Graz. Then heroically through the Alps. I'd been fascinated by all of it.

The wrinkles in Ilsa's face were many, and her short white locks broke in multiple directions like waves thrashing rocks in a shallow cove. Her mottled age spots, prominent on her serene face, suggested many years getting burned by the sun.

"I was barely thirteen at the time. So it was all very exotic. But I realized how much danger we were in. The real hero was my mother. She was strict, but throughout our escape, she was our rock. But mad as a cut snake at father. More than once, she demanded to know if he'd destroyed the film. She nagged him, but all he would say was that it was gone, stashed in Graz. We had nothing to worry about, he assured us."

Out the bar's window, the NT sky was splashing purple, pink, and orange clouds across the sky. It was a vast impressionist painting the Australians often used in tourism ads.

"Papa's side of the story was simple. He finished packing everyone's provisions and then cut through a series of back alleys to the garage where he stored our car. I think it was a 1936 Opel Olympia. I remember that because the Olympics happened in Berlin in '36. It wasn't very fast, and Papa cursed how a weak engine made handling more difficult. I didn't much care. It was just a car."

"You must have been quite scared."

"Of course. But we were Austrian children of the 1930s, not twenty-first-century ankle-biters who carry on like stuck pigs. Papa made up a story for Hans that we were going on an important holiday. By then, he'd adopted my Australia suggestion. It was truly far-fetched enough."

"I wouldn't have thought Austrians knew about this country."

"I did. *We of the Never-Never* was all about Australia. And I had gotten an English version somewhere around 1937 and was reading it with your mother. You wouldn't believe it, but that book was surprisingly big in Austria."

"Your memory is amazing," I said, encouraging Ilsa.

Ilsa ignored the compliment.

"You know, people have been fleeing dictators for decades. Running from the Germans, the Russians, the Hungarians. I remember reading back in 1980, twenty or so Romanians stole a crop-dusting plane, flew over communist Hungary, and landed in a cornfield near Graz. When you feel you have no choice but to leave a place, you take life-or-death risks. We certainly did."

Ilsa looked out the hotel pub's darkened window, acting as if she were lost in a wintery whiteout. After a few seconds of silence, though, she restarted her travelogue by indicating her father didn't know exactly who was pursuing them, but the armed Germans they'd seen in the last Austrian valley suggested a concentrated effort.

"It was a miserable, painful journey," Ilsa said. "My oldest brother tried not to cry, but Mama and I needed to comfort both of them. Often. It was so cold, and we carried so little in our packs."

"I can't imagine," I said. "But then, you had generated some pretty damning footage. Homosexuality in Germany was illegal. Punishable by death. If Hitler was caught on camera, that evidence would've obliterated the Nazi Party."

"It was easier moving through Italy," Ilsa said, as if my history lesson was unneeded. "The Italians had accepted Mussolini's fascist dictatorship, so their spending money was gone. Still, the peasants in the Alps were good to us. Sometimes extravagantly. Gave us far more than we could've hoped for. I've always thought they'd guessed we were on the run. Passing us down the Italian side of the Brenner the way they did."

"The Italians are good people," I said.

She smiled gently, seeing the moment with the shimmering eyes of a young girl.

"We looked so ragged. Our clothes were dirty and torn. I was embarrassed because I didn't know Italian, and some of the boys were pointing. I kept hugging myself as if I might get hit with something. The Italian mothers sensed my discomfort. One woman, twice my size, jumped into the street and wrapped her arms around me. She was like a smelly blanket, all garlic and onions, but I didn't care."

"Gotta love mothers," I offered, remembering my own.

"They fed us so much and put us in their beds. I never felt so warm or content as I did that night. Stuffed and swaddled. When I woke the next morning, I thought, more like secretly hoped, our journey was over. Except it wasn't. It hadn't even started."

"Were you worried about Nazis in Northern Italy?" I asked. "I read about a German commander there who was so feared even his own men referred to him as the Evil Genius. He was sadistic. Tortured Italian partisans. Extracted confessions. I'm guessing if anyone helped you, the Germans would have picked up your trail."

"Maybe," Ilsa said. "But I don't think so. Remember, this was 1938. The war hadn't started. The German generals weren't in Italy. They were planning Poland."

"Good point."

Rubbing the round coffee can like a fortune teller holding a cloudy crystal ball, Ilsa continued conjuring up unforgotten images of her weary family reaching Rome and boarding a converted ocean liner headed for the Suez Canal, Red Sea, Indian Ocean, Bay of Bengal, Malacca Strait, Singapore, and then Batavia, capital of the Dutch East Indies.

"We'd been at sea almost a month, working our way past Singapore. Coming down the north Java coast. Making stops in Batavia, Surabaya, Bali, and finally Portuguese Timor."

Ilsa spoke the names with ease.

"Near Bali—it must've been the middle of June—Papa thought about switching ships. Perth was marginally more civilized than Darwin, but when he looked at maps, Papa thought Nazi sympathizers in Africa, if they ever came, might go straight across the Indian Ocean headed for Fremantle. He'd determined just south of Darwin there were all these deep gorges. Impenetrable canyons. If the German lunatics wanted him, the Northern Territory was the last place they'd go."

"Didn't people sense World War II was coming on?" I asked.

"Papa said when he was a young boy, around 1914, a Bosnian nationalist, part of the Black Hand terrorist group, murdered the Archduke and his wife, Sophie. In Sarajevo. My father was convinced the Nazis would get far larger than the Black Hand. And no one would see it coming."

The elderly woman swished her latte around the edge of the cream-colored ceramic mug, trying to drag a little extra flavor out of the foam. Swirling her spoon, she formed a slender whirlpool, the spoon clinking against the inside of the cup. Behind her, a chintz curtain billowed lightly in the hard-to-feel breeze.

"I remember asking him, 'Is war coming soon?' This was when we were still far out to sea. I'd been with him that day in the factory and seen Hitler firsthand. I saw the Austrians falling in line."

I lowered my eyes to check the tape recorder, to make sure the red light was still on.

"The first Great War cost my papa his father and two of his brothers," Ilsa continued. "They died in the trenches. Victims of a war that killed two generations of men and financially ruined Germany and Austria for the next twenty years. A second war was always inevitable."

"He guessed what was coming, didn't he?"

"His prediction was spot on, like so many others," Ilsa said. Her voice sounded like a whisper at a funeral. "It started September 1, 1939, in Poland. Not much more than a year after we arrived in Australia. By then, we'd moved inland to Katherine. Father thought we'd be safer there. Quatsch. Utter Unsinn. It was the Japanese in 1942, not the Germans, who invaded. And not just once or twice. Sixty-odd times. Their bombers pounded Australia like the devil."

Ilsa's agitation surprised me because she soon started in on the war planners of the late 1930s. How they should have known Darwin's port was a valuable target.

"The British were always so full of themselves," she said. "They couldn't imagine an Asian power taking Singapore or Manila. I remember seeing in *The Australian* how one British commander said he'd hoped England wasn't getting too fortified in Malaya because then the Japanese might never attempt a landing."

I moved the tape recorder slightly closer to her. Glancing at the spiraling sprockets with feigned curiosity, Ilsa recalled that just out of Kupang, on Timor's southwest coast, their boat, the *Viroma*, finally finished trudging across the Indian Ocean.

Sleep on board was rare, the odors from below-deck compartments disgusting. Searing heat pushed atmospheric rivers of urine and vomit into every opening. Below decks, oil-stained engines spat out thick black fumes like lung-ravaged asthmatics coughing up blood.

At a point when Ilsa was certain the family had reached its absolute breaking point, the *Viroma's* captain sighted Australia's mainland and Melville Island.

"It was July eighth, and Papa wasn't keen on lingering in a foreign port where they wouldn't take kindly to Germans or Austrians. There'd be too many curious eyes. Too many locals talking about non-Australian newcomers. Today, they'd say he was paranoid."

Reaching Australia brought little relief. At customs, Ilsa's father spoke German and Italian, trying to convince officials his family truly wanted to immigrate and could support themselves. In the end, it was Ilsa's heavily accented English that saved them.

"For the customs officer, I made up a story about a simple Austrian family, country folk, seeking to invest in Australian agriculture. Not a mob of German-speaking immigrants on the run from Hitler. I told them about the Fizzer and Quiet Stockman, Katherine, Mataranka Springs, and Elsey Station from my book. It made them smile in a paternalistic way. I imagine it distracted them."

"Interesting."

"Years later, when I saw *The Sound of Music* with Julie Andrews, I saw myself as Liesl. Young but switched on. I was very much bothered, I might add, by how easy they made the von Trapp escape appear. As if there were no checkpoints by then. Or singing their way through the meadows versus sleeping in the snow."

"That's what Hollywood does to a good story."

"Maybe. What apparently mattered most to the Darwin immigration officials was that we weren't Jewish. By 1938, there had been a flood of Jewish settlers coming into Melbourne. But we weren't, not on my father's side, and we had come into Darwin. So it worked out. What happened next is unusual," Ilsa continued, "but make sure to check my facts."

"Of course, of course," I agreed.

"That was a time when you could still see the harbor from the Hotel Darwin's front verandah." Traces of tenderness played at her eyes while I scratched out notes. "Darwin wasn't an international port. In fact, a cyclone tore up Darwin the year before we arrived. Destroyed it. It wasn't at all like Broome with its pearls. There was one military base and certainly no oil money pouring in."

I adjusted my chair, stretching my legs. "Long before anyone thought about developing the harbor area, eh?"

From somewhere outside, a strong scent of bougainvillea floated on the breeze. In the distance, road trains were making their runs for Alice, Kununurra, and Darwin.

"The NT was a strange place back then. It's where failed Australians hid out. Hunting for gold or tin. My father wanted none of that. We were just trying to survive."

Ilsa adjusted her glasses, then toyed with her napkin, folding it over and over. Despite her best efforts, I detected a slight tremble.

"Darwin was the absolute end of the road. Except it had pubs. And during the Wet, there was always water gushing about. Remember, we came here from the Alps. The land of snow and mountain streams. I hated Darwin and Katherine."

I must've looked surprised.

"Was there anything cold? No. Ice? Nonexistent. Air conditioning? A ceiling fan moving heat around. Shifting flies toward a different face. We really wore those hats with the corks hanging off them. The ones they sell in the tourist shops. It was so hot. Made you tired. Desperate. And that was before the Wet started washing roads out."

Ilsa didn't wait for a response. She charged on, talking about the hard men of the NT.

"What was interesting was their gumption. I'll give them that. It was quite remarkable. Written off, yes, but they wouldn't roll over and die. My father certainly saw it that way. And then the war started."

I had studied Australian military history before flying over for the USS *Peary* story and knew how close Japan had come to conquering Australia. Seventy days after Pearl Harbor, the emperor's forces took Kuala Lumpur, Singapore, the Philippines, and Corregidor.

"We didn't know anything about the English or American military back then," Ilsa continued, "but escaping in the middle of the night and surviving those other wretched places made us think we were safe. We were so wrong. The Japanese attacked the Katherine aerodrome in forty-two. Just four years after we'd arrived."

I remember my head arching back, pondering whether German agents had ever come for the film?

That was crazy. But like one of those crocodile cruises, with all the paying customers craning their necks toward the bow of the boat, waiting for the payoff, I sensed the dead chicken on a rope was going overboard, jerking its way toward the water. It didn't take much bait splash to bring the snapping beast over to the keel, just below the surface.

CHAPTER 11

"Hitler would logically have lost his mind," Ilsa continued with increasing confidence, "learning this Austrian filmmaker was missing. When railway officials couldn't produce evidence of a family departing Graz, they'd have blocked the roads into Italy and Switzerland."

"Most Americans don't know much about European history," I offered, "but groups like the Gestapo and SS paid or tortured for details. They must've uncovered something. Maybe someone had seen you with Father Lambert."

The old woman was quiet for a moment.

"Here's what I think. The Gestapo dug around and found ship manifests. They worked out we'd sailed from Rome."

"That's a logical jumping-off point," I offered. "But Hitler had much bigger issues by late 1938. Like dealing with Chamberlain in Munich. Did he believe your father's film showed anything? In fact, if what you said was accurate, it didn't. I seriously doubt Hitler would've sent men from Germany to investigate. He wouldn't have wasted resources trying to get film your father might have destroyed. And he had to've believed the crisis had passed."

"I don't know. My father had read up on the Röhm Purge. He knew footage suggesting homosexual activity would destroy Hitler. Would a mad dictator take that kind of a chance? Had Papa gotten it to the right people, it would've altered the course of history. Instead, he gave it to me, only to spend the next six years worrying about it."

"Hmm…" I was trying to resolve how any high-ranking politician reacts when they know a damning sound bite, photo, or film clip exists.

"It was always in our minds," Ilsa said while poking at her rocket salad. "But I knew where Greta had hidden it. It sat there while bombs fell on Graz and we managed the Katherine property near the gorge. When we first came to it, all we saw was an abandoned homestead overrun by sago palms, mulga, creepers, grasses, and mounds of red sand. It was all crook until we wrestled it back under control."

I was impressed by her recall, the emotions she still held for that era. "To get out of Europe and even think of trying to survive Down Under," I said. "That's pretty incredible."

"It wasn't easy. Even though we were Austrians running from the Nazis, the Australians were suspicious. Not very friendly. Mama used to confide in me that adapting here was hard. They would sell us things at the mercantile but never offer us help. That's why we got our land. It was a tangled pile that no one wanted. During the Wet, the river was quite deadly and could cut us off. The gorge became a complete barrier. Our station was just above the flooding."

"What did you think the first time you saw it?"

"That Papa was insane. Mad. Did you see the railroad bridge here in town? The one with sixteen-, seventeen-, and eighteen-meter water marks painted up the side of the iron trestle. That's how much water the Katherine pushes through the canyons. Staggering amounts. Papa brought us from beautiful Graz to a lean-to with a tin roof. The barn was caving in on itself. I was barely a teen. All I saw was an untamable land. I don't know how my mother managed it. Back home, Papa had been successful. We had shops, a car, could go to the pictures."

"So, what happened next?" I asked. Over Ilsa's shoulders the sun's last rays of early evening were blossoming onto the shoulders of the local ranges. "Did you ever see the whole film? From start to finish?"

"No. Only a shortened version. Just the factory speech, which I dug out of the ruins in Graz in the 1950s. I went back and found the site of our original hiding place. Did you know Graz was one of the most heavily bombed Austrian cities? It was a fuel distribution point, right on the main Allied flight routes after hitting Vienna. They marshaled the trains in Graz."

"You went back? And actually found the film? It was still there?"

"I did. But only one of the tins was still there. The other was gone. I took it to mean your mother separated the two canisters before your grandparents moved her to Minnesota. Sometime during the summer of thirty-nine."

"Yeah, that's when they emigrated. We were one-quarter Jewish. By then the Germans and Austrians were checking bloodlines. We were Lutherans, and our surname didn't immediately give us away…but my grandfather could read the tea leaves. As I recall, it was difficult for them getting out of Austria, but it changed their lives. All of our successive lives."

"We weren't so lucky. On one hand, filming Hitler made us leave long before the bombs fell. But it also led to very real heartache in Australia. Worse, I had no way of knowing how to find Greta, your mother. By the time I got back to Graz and had the one reel developed, I realized more fully our risk. Sometime around the 1990s, I converted the film so it would work as a computer file. Want to see it?"

As Ilsa started booting up an old Dell laptop, my head nodding like a dachshund on a dashboard, she watched my face. I'd come to Australia to write about the sinking of the *Peary*. Instead, I was now watching home movies of Hitler in Austria.

"The Nazi Party first came to power in Bavaria," Ilsa patiently explained as if she were teaching for Elderhostel. "But Hitler was an Austrian by birth. So he had very personal reasons for wanting Austria back. Still, Germany didn't annex Austria, what was called the Anschluss Österreichs, until March 1938."

"Your German still sounds pretty good," I noted.

"I've returned to Graz multiple times trying to make sense of it all. Even visited two of the concentration camps in my sixties. I have trouble with educated twentieth-century German citizens making excuses, denying any responsibility for what happened in 1932 and 1933. I struggle with the rest of the world ignoring Kristallnacht in 1938 or the Night and Fog decree in 1941. Or twenty thousand Jews murdered each morning for months at Treblinka."

"By the way, has anyone, a journalist or historian, ever seen this footage?"

"Certainly not. And I apologize for lecturing."

"No worries," I said. "It's a huge part of your story."

"My story." She frowned as she repeated the words. "Tragedy is more like it. But maybe that's a bit much. Let's simply leave it this way: my life changed because of what I show you next."

Ilsa manipulated a small keyboard mouse, causing a tiny white arrow to hover over an icon marked *Graz 1938*.

Sitting back in the booth, she let the silent film speak for itself. Her father's effort started with an establishing shot, panning left to right, showing a large German banner with the emboldened words "Ein Volk. ein Reich. ein Führer."

"One people, one empire, one dictator."

That first scene was followed by a jumpy segment of three men, two sporting long leather military coats and the third in a short gray tunic, their respective swastika armbands fully displayed. From there it cut to a young boy, in leather shorts, joyously waving a miniature Nazi flag on a crowded street. The pug-faced child, pleased with his act of newfound patriotism, was happy enough to ignore the camera. He had undoubtedly been told the day was solemn and special. He should not pose or preen.

Next came a series of images showing people awaiting Hitler's arrival. The conqueror entering a large village. In the background, I could see men still hurriedly placing finishing touches on building decorations. Workers in Alpine hats hanging twenty-foot Nazi banners from the sides of stone buildings.

The young women's heads were festooned with lusty brims puffed out like filled sails. These weren't quite the vestal virgins of that movie era, but their fashionable faces were starry with radiant anticipation. Hitler's presence in

Graz warranted complete fealty.

They were fools, Ilsa said. If these women had been allowed to kneel, they would've bowed their heads for this unholy First Communion. Instead, the film showed them acting just as vigorously as the men, shooting their arms out at forty-five-degree angles and roaring their approval.

Next on the screen, helmeted men, the protectors of Germany's new values, marched forward in lockstep unison. They moved collectively like panthers, each step precise, eyeing the terrain, waiting for the gazelle. These were not puffy Cheshire cats but stylized gray leopards in a pack. Confident predators fearing nothing.

The Grazians clearly sensed Hitler's authority and pushed forward, collectively raising their hands in the familiar Nazi salute, their eyes filled with awe. Austria's conquering hero returned to lowly Graz.

Look at these Austrians, I thought to myself. These guys aren't the helpless victims of a siege. That's what Austrian historians tried presenting later. These folks bought in hook, line, and sinker.

Despite numerous suicides by the vanquished Austrian Heimwehr, the people of Graz wanted Hitler in power. They believed he'd fill their financial coffers and spare them from future onslaughts. They'd be victims no more.

He won't be there when they die on the Russian front. More than a million will get conscripted and not return. They won't see him in burnt and bombed-out Berlin in April 1945. Or when Soviet tanks bash their way toward the bunker. Not when the Americans bomb them from twenty-five thousand feet starting in 1943. Not when 20 percent of Vienna is destroyed. But at this moment, the Austrians can't sense their impending doom.

Following three seconds of filmic black, the next scene showed an industrial wooden window. Ilsa's father's framing was using muted lighting to go with clashing contrasts of deep blacks, harsh whites, and drenched grays. Even I had to admit it was an impressive cinematic "capture" for a hobbyist.

Johann was using his camera in such a way that the viewer came to the window and stared over the assembly gathered on the industrial factory floor.

Viewers would come out of a darkened room and see the crowd. Anyone watching would witness the audience lifting their eyes in awe. The "supreme judge of the German and Austrian people" had arrived.

Climbing a slender set of steps, Hitler took the stage, unaware his loyal flock was marked for death. That they would become sacrificial lambs slaughtered in a war of unimaginable magnitude. He waited, enjoying the complete control he held. He could intimidate them and would speak when he was ready. For as long as he wanted. He would speak until they were willing to die for Germany.

"I can't believe your father's vantage point," I said, interrupting Ilsa's own viewing. "His proximity makes it seem like a front-row seat."

"You might already know this, but Hitler came to Graz only twice as Führer," said Ilsa. "This time and once again in 1941. At this point, the Anschluss is less than a month old. It's Hitler making nice with one of his first conquests. Just before he moves on to the Sudetenland."

I gathered the Austrian people had welcomed this short man with his infamous mustache and his very sly *Directive No. 1*. That document, a political maneuver, called for the "peaceful" occupation of Austria and armed defense of the Austrian-Czech border.

I leaned forward in the pub's booth as the searing images rolled past. There was no sound, but the camera's intimacy was riveting. I was certain this footage was historic and, even with reams of Hitler's speeches clogging up the History Channel, this one had to be exceptionally rare.

On the screen, Hitler's eyes burned with hypnotic rage. By 1938, he was already projecting great victories over various enemies. The blitzkrieg into Poland and France was already planned.

At one point, Ilsa explained her father had switched lenses and zoomed in. In seeming response, Hitler assessed Johann's proximity. He paused, wiped sweat from his thick brow, and then, before Ilsa's eyes, glared directly into Stulmacher's camera.

Even for a casual viewer like me, it was unnerving. Like that moment when someone knows they are marked for ambush far from the schoolyard. They are certain an attack is coming but don't know when.

As Hitler resumed ranting, I guessed he was revealing his new truth. Not the cliché of "truth to power." No, this one would prove far worse. He was bringing fanatical evil to the distracted. He was a carnival barker convincing the locals to enter the tent. To buy into the promise of something rare.

It was then, in the next few seconds, that Germany's leader made a personal, nonverbal, body-language statement to Ilsa's father—the intense look Ilsa had previously mentioned. The moment when Hitler broke down the distance between his raised platform on the factory floor and a single cameraman operating a bulky Bavarian camera.

Hitler's black eyes convey a simple message: "I know who you are, what you do, where you live. Think carefully about what you do next."

It must've been more than unnerving for a sunny thirteen-year-old to watch Hitler make this threat. Yes, the film was just a few minutes of old 35mm black-and-white film. But in April 1938, for a young girl who had witnessed the unthinkable, this must've been terrifying.

The movie over, Ilsa waited for my reaction. She was swirling her coffee again, acting distracted. Bluffing. She knew I was nothing more than a thrashing barramundi on thick fishing cord. I'd fully swallowed the hook.

CHAPTER 12

B y now, I was certain Ilsa, like any good clairvoyant, could read my thoughts.

She would've envisioned I saw a spinster from an obscure setting with historic film footage. A remote psychic—maybe *psycho* was a better word—holding tarot cards. Like all paying customers, I'd want to know what happened next. What the cards meant. Whether there was an attempt to recover the film.

"So how did you end up alone in Katherine?" I asked as gently as possible.

"You want the short version?"

Ilsa shot me an angry look, like I'd approached a place of buried treasure and swung a metal detector near a secret cache buried in the ochre-colored dirt. As if I'd hovered over her heartache.

"I'm sorry. I know this must be hard."

"You have no reason to be sorry. We chose Australia. But after six years of back-breaking labor, pounded by the Wet, parented by an increasingly illogical father, worrying nightly about the war and a foolish film…now I meet the man of my dreams. An Australian sublieutenant named Brad Tucker. From Sydney. He was in the AIF and very handsome. Had been on a secret mission. Flambeau or something like that. I thought he'd come to save me. I was so lonely. The war had been going on for six years. I'd have gone anywhere with him. Anywhere."

"You sound like you'd had enough by then."

"I had. And the Germans weren't far behind him. Just after Brad and Tom Northgraves arrived in Katherine, so did the Nazis. That night changed me forever."

"Wait a minute," I said, my head snapping up from my notebook. "Nazis officially came into Australia? Up here in the Northern Territory? You mentioned that once before. The first night we met.

And where did Tucker and Northgraves come from? What happened to them?"

I know now Ilsa understood my question came from complete innocence. She expected it. I imagine it was what she wanted. It allowed my aging recluse, the one softening as the night went on, as the cool evening air worked its wonders, to emerge as an enraged shrew.

"I won't say another word," she announced loudly, pushing back from the table, bumping a nearby empty chair, and deliberately rising to make a scene. "I think we're done here. Done with this foolishness, young man. Take me home. Right this instant. I don't know why I agreed to tell this story. I've made Brad and Tom disappear a million times, and now, like an idiot, I've brought them back to life."

"What? What's this all about?" I thought for a moment that somehow these characters had entered the restaurant behind us.

"Get the rest from Brad. If he's still alive. Have him tell you about December 1944."

"I guess that's it, then," I said with embarrassment. I didn't need to be humiliated in an Australian pub with inflated crocodiles hanging from the ceiling. "We can be going. We've both had enough for one night."

"*Going* isn't the word," she barked at me again. "They're all gone. Sixty years of secrecy. All forgotten. Including those Nazi bastards. All of them. Gone to hell."

I didn't try to respond, and the subsequent ride to Ilsa's place progressed in sharp silence. It was a short trip filled with unspoken words about each of our larger agendas.

I was in no mood to placate or even see the old battle-axe to her door. It was time to fly back to the States. Especially after that oral pummeling. Thankfully, she didn't ask for help. But through the open car window, she mumbled a guttural phrase she'd offered me the first night we met.

"Danke und bis bald."

It meant she planned to see me again.

It took me an hour to recover from Ilsa's blindside and a seat in a different pub wondering whether there was a bigger story than the *Peary* wrapped up in a tale about two men named Tucker and Northgraves. Was there something there?

The whiskey told me I'd swallowed the hook. So I ran with it.

After a week in Canberra and Sydney, I tracked down the man she'd mentioned: one Bradford David Tucker. With help from some Aussie military connections, an armchair historian at Tindal, and the best researchers at the Australian War Memorial in the nation's capital, I deciphered one of her key clues.

It was Ilsa's word, *Flambeau*. It should have been *Rimau*. As in Operation Rimau.

This once highly secret Australian sabotage mission had taken place in 1944. But in no account of Rimau, including numerous books written about this specific Australian mission, did Tucker's name ever appear.

It meant he wasn't officially rostered on the mission. But if Ilsa had held onto the name of the operation and one AIF commando, was it possible an Aussie also fought against Nazis in the NT in 1944? It made no sense.

One other looming question was whether this Special Forces fighter was still alive. The historians in Canberra hadn't quite laughed at my questions because one man with that name had served in the Australian 2/3rd Independent and spent time in Australia's Z Special Unit from 1942 through '45. What was strange was their inability to find more than his birthplace, initial unit, rank, serial number, and medical discharge details. Other than that, my assigned historian couldn't give me anything more to go on.

This much was evident: Tucker had been released in Darwin in December 1945, roughly three months after the war in the Pacific ended in Tokyo Bay. There was no record of his death and no photos or mementos supplied by family to the War Memorial. He felt like a phantom.

But, if there's one thing the military teaches its intelligence officers—and I suppose this is true with journalists—it's that you mustn't let go of a lead. My father used to use the movie *The Bridge on the River Kwai* as just such an example. In that book and film, the British commandos needed to stop a troop train filled with military supplies from crossing the Kwai.

"If you can't blow up the bridge," Dad would say, "blow up the train. If you can't get the locomotive, get the tracks. If you can't get the rails, you get the driver. But bottom line, the train doesn't go over that bridge."

I brought some of the same turn-over-every-stone tenacity to finding Brad Tucker and finally, with some additional sleuthing, got a lead that Tucker was still alive, housed in a veterans' facility. The Australians call them RSL War Vets villages. His tidy little room was in Narrabeen on Sydney's Northern Beaches.

Getting through on the phone, but without mentioning Ilsa, I told him I wrote for a monthly American history magazine called *World War II Magazine* and needed to see him.

When I reached the settlement, the old vet met me at the door to his one-bedroom unit. It was clear he was in failing health. He looked frail with his bent body and leathery skin. But his vibrant mind more than impressed. He wanted to know how I'd found him, because he said he'd never once talked to the media about his war experiences or his spectacular escapes.

Taking my seat, I noticed an old washed-out print of some boys playing cricket hanging crookedly over a single photo on the bedside table. It was next to a pair of broken reading glasses and an empty water glass. The 1940s-era black-and-white picture showed a woman in full swim costume. Catching me admiring the photo, Tucker said it was taken at a place called the Manly Harbour Pool.

The old man's hands shook a fair amount, the blood in his blue veins running crookedly away from his cracked knuckles and very nearly popping out of their channels. Bruises on his arms offset a pallid face offering up what seemed like resignation eyes. If Death wasn't getting a coffee nearby, the guy with the scythe was already in the building.

The old man's pupils were the most disturbing thing. They were approaching their last days, their final chance to reveal the deathbed secrets they'd witnessed. To talk about what happened. I took notes and listened as Tucker occasionally nodded off the way some older people do. But when his eyes closed, even sitting up, it was clear he was uncomfortable, as if something invisible was pressing in on him.

In moments of clarity, I eventually uncovered a journey rivaling Ulysses in the *Odyssey*. It started with Tucker hiding in a banyan surrounded by a Japanese search party.

"It was all smooth bark and thick branches," Tucker said. "Big as a Moreton Bay fig. Built like a fortress with flat buttress roots at the base. On an island near what everyone used to call Portuguese Timor."

I listened, imagining tubular branches curving upward toward the sky. All around this giant lay the moss-covered carcasses of other fallen gums. When Tucker finally finished, he dozed off again. That was the moment I knew, without a shred of doubt, I'd stumbled onto the story of a lifetime.

CHAPTER 13

December 1944—Sermata Islands, Dutch East Indies

Tucker cocked his head the moment the noise reached his ears.

It sounded like a wild kookaburra, and the distinctive laughter had somehow shaken him awake. Somewhere in his restless subconscious, the echoing noise, coming through the towering trees and strangler vines, was penetrating his dozing, warning him.

It meant only one thing. The plan he had explained via pantomime, barely a day before, was working. A sturdy man with copper skin and red-stained teeth, standing on the island's uneven shoreline, was blowing a native whistle, alerting the weakened Australian that Japanese soldiers were charging up the worn path, racing for the dirt clearing where Tucker was sheltering in the open-air kampung.

Their faint, pounding footsteps told Tucker he had maybe thirty seconds to drag his hairless, malnourished body away from the uneven bamboo plat-form and attempt climbing into a giant gum tree he'd just barely finished hollowing out twenty-four hours earlier. It was a hiding place fashioned for this very real possibility.

Quick now, lad, or your head sits on a six-foot stake. These bludgers won't bother with interrogations. They'll kill at first sight.

Tucker's twin demons, Dehydration and Panic, hollered in his ears about him needing water or coconut milk. Plus, quinine. Ignoring the two tormentors, he hefted himself over the wooden floor. He'd predicted an enemy patrol would get around to searching this island.

Give us water, or we'll see to it you lie down for good. Just like Page and Sargent.

The inner voices brayed like dingoes, only to have the Australian quiet them.

Get stuffed.

At the edge of the thatched platform, he threw himself forward, lunging toward the darkness of the verdant leaves. The fall wouldn't kill him, but if he wasn't running when he landed, he'd soon be dead.

In that moment of falling, Tucker saw a straw-stuffed training field mannequin tumbling over the uneven wooden edge of the hut. A 130-pound scarecrow, all protruding ribs and scabbed elbows, about to die.

He hit the ground hard but rose to his fragile knees, still squeezing his knife. It no longer mattered how listless he was from not eating or sleeping properly. Or how festering sores, bleeding gums, and bites from ants and bloodthirsty mosquitoes had all but finished him. There was no time for wondering about malaria, rancid wounds, trench foot, or tapeworm.

One more "cut" would surely kill him. A clumsy trip, and he'd reach a thousand. A simple stumble. A foot placed the wrong way. He'd never get back up. Never finish the mission.

To survive yet again, he'd have to soundlessly scramble through twenty-five yards of thick underbrush, listening to the exact words of a not-so-distant Japanese commander.

Tucker had grown up rough and tumble on the Collaroy Plateau, a place where granite ledges stretched high over Sydney's Northern Beaches like a citadel. He'd been the pride of state boxing matches and even fought one of the regulars in Jimmy Sharman's Boxing Troupe at Sydney's Royal Easter Show.

That was in the past. The commando crashing to the ground on an unremarkable island in the Dutch East Indies was half the man who'd started the war.

But here was his moment of luck. Eight years earlier, during a handful of pre-Olympic amateur welterweight bouts in Tokyo, Tucker got the firsthand chance to study Japanese fighting tactics. Watching multiple bouts, he mentally catalogued the distinctive commands yelled from his opponent's corner. In those halcyon days of 1936, the Japanese cornermen always wanted their fighters to "circle around" the Aussies and push them into short corners where they couldn't escape.

Eight years would pass, and then, on a remote island in the Dutch East Indies, Tucker found himself recognizing the same command: "Encirclement. Don't let him out."

The searching soldiers would wheel through the giant ferns and pandani in evenly spaced ranks. But their fast-closing maneuver would require a few extra seconds before they reached him. And those precious moments would provide Tucker the opening he needed.

Careful to avoid low-to-the-ground thrashing, the Australian scrambled through the brush on bony elbows and knees, lunging forward onto the damp peat behind a fallen log. Behind him, hookbill parrots generated a cacophony of screeching, drowning out his movements. He still needed to cover another ten yards to reach the tree.

Seconds later, having crawled forward through the dirt and dead leaves, the Australian reached the gum-colored roots of the gnarled banyan. Without hesitating, he stood up and reached for an inconspicuous scuffed notch, a handhold six feet off the ground that he'd gouged out with his American-made knife.

Was it only yesterday he'd used mud to cover any evidence of his cuttings? He'd dulled all around the tree's smooth buttress, attempting to hide his handiwork. After that, he'd shoved the headman's blazing torch inside the empty trunk to smoke out spiders, snakes, or foot-long rats comfortable nesting in the tree's dead spot.

He'd also constructed a false door, an entrance covering, by taking a large chunk of ground bark and carving it so the opening was undetectable to anyone searching the vine-wrapped tree.

With the last of his ebbing strength, Tucker pulled himself up onto a knotted burl before wriggling into the oblong hole. Slithering like an eel, he slid into the rubbery trunk's soot-black embrace and wedged tight the camouflaged trap door behind him.

Seconds later, the Japanese soldiers were firing their guns into the wall-less hut, hoping they'd trapped the last Rimau man. Voices rang out as rifles recoiled. Tucker shuddered involuntarily. But for the old man's birdcall, they would have caught him.

Reaching down, Tucker touched his spongy, heaving frame. The skin on his dirt-covered skeleton was nothing more than grimy wallpaper plastered over a grotesque ribcage.

Get yourself together, mate. Slow your breathing. Use your nose.

Flaring his nostrils, Tucker wondered if they climbed onto the tree, would he detect human sweat or oil from a gun? Cheap whiskey? It was densely dark in the tree, with just a slight crack of light showing from one poorly cut corner of his improvised door.

This far into their pursuit of Rimau's men, if the Japanese had taken any Aussies alive, they'd have been tortured. The Japanese would have learned there were Australians still unaccounted for. That three men were dodging their search boats.

What the Japanese navy didn't know was that within the last month, two saboteurs had stopped running. Tucker had left captain Bob Page only days before on Leti. The second man, Blondie Sargent, reached Romang, likely dying not long after Tucker and Page had paddled away heartbroken.

Tucker was the only one left. To get home, he'd face longer odds than the miracle escapees who made it back from Ambon in the Dutch East Indies. That was early 1942, not late '44. And instead of Ambon, Tucker was on a far more insignificant island, possibly Sermata or Babar. He wasn't sure, but then again, it didn't matter.

As of this moment, everything came down to one dull knife and whether his crawling along the jungle floor had gouged out the equivalent of a giant directional marker, telltale tracks in the dirt, pointing to this single tree.

CHAPTER 14

The gargantuan gum Tucker had chosen was so large that anyone searching for a man on the run would've spotted the tree's unusual girth and climbed up onto its smooth branches to scan the surrounding area.

Standing on one of those thick limbs, that same man would've looked for evidence of footprints, trampled grass, or bent branches. Any of those telltale clues, left by a frantic man scrambling for his life, would point the way.

If an Aboriginal tracker were on this case, I wouldn't carry a prayer. He'd be on to me faster than…

He needed to not think but fixate on the knife there in his gripped hand, at the end of his skinny right arm. If they found him now, he'd go down fighting. Just as he'd been trained.

In the stillness, he tried concentrating but his mind kept wandering. The blade was American, about twelve inches long, and he'd traded an Aussie rucksack for it with a US marine in Perth. The moment he first held it, that night in the pub, he'd liked the heft and the way the handle was wrapped in black leather bands.

There were seven sections, each with four tight dark rings. He'd used those bands to represent days, symbolic of an imperfect week and tenuous month.

Tiny straps for tracking his tough times. And for counting the islands he'd touched.

Stay focused, mate. Be ready to come at them. Extend the blade toward the opening.

The silver shaft protruded from the fist-guard and ran with a gleaming edge into a point. It was more than enough to kill a man or small shark, but the Americans had cleverly designed the knife to serve other purposes. The handle featured a flat butt end perfect for hammering and a blood gutter if there was gore or moisture. That slight trough provided half a curved straw for the slightest amount of water or a row of berries.

Tucker knew how to kill with different blades, but gutting fish and small animals didn't count for much. A full-grown man would be different.

The knife's last feature was its unfamiliar inscription. *Camillus, NY,* had been stamped on the shaft's base on one side and *USMC* on the other. He had no idea where Camillus was located but knew MC stood for the Marine Corps. Short of a silk bomber map knotted around his neck, the knife was his most important possession.

The pants he'd worn had largely rotted away, too often ripped by pricking nettles and saw grass that sliced skin and cloth alike with the slightest contact. His boots were torn, the leather soles separating from the uppers. They provided no real support other than covering the pulpy soles of his feet. His singlet was useless, pocked by growing holes.

Straining to hear every sound, Tucker began to hear a dull moaning, and when the noise persisted, he knew someone, whimpering, was getting pushed forward. It could only be the island elder, the one who'd signaled with the bird whistle and helped him during the last two days. The man who fed him fruits and wild pork, communicating with sign language dating back thousands of years.

Tucker knew what came next. His protector was about to lose his head. The Japanese commander would make the man beg for mercy in the hopes he'd reveal something, or, through the man's screams, draw a conflicted but stupidly heroic Australian out into the open.

Tucker squeezed his eyes shut but couldn't block his imagination from seeing the native pushed to his knees. The Japanese commander, quivering with indignation, would circle his prey before bringing his sword down on the islander's exposed neck.

Tucker twitched involuntarily until the screaming stopped. There was grunting, scuffling. Then silence. Tucker guessed the Japanese officer was hoarsely commanding his patrol to fetch a bamboo stake and mount the dripping skull as a warning to others.

It was quiet for a few moments before Tucker recognized an order getting barked out. *Be fast. Finish it.* That command was followed by the pounding of a stake into dark earth. And then the Jap captain, his voice raw, yelled, "Find the Australian. For the emperor."

In the gum's bole, Tucker held himself tightly, one hand grabbing the opposite elbow, the other clutching the knife. He rocked slowly on the sore balls of his feet. He'd gone more than six hours without food or water. The putrefying smell of urine, the warm fluid he'd let run down his leg, was adding to his torment.

He was a long way from home, stuck inside a tree as big as a Collaroy surf bungalow. A gum with an above-ground root system so large entire rooms would've fitted into its foundation.

No holiday shacks today, mate. Just Tojo's boys. Watching. Listening. It's December 1944, a full three years on, and, my word, they're still out here killing us.

Thick sweat was building on his eyebrows. If his tree ruse worked, the enemy soldiers would start in on the villagers, trying to learn whether a non-Asian had swum ashore during the last forty-eight hours. He hoped the islanders were good liars.

Ignoring his heaving chest, Tucker prayed to keep silent for the next hour or two. The Japanese captain would certainly leave a sentry in the area.

Ignore them. Go walkabout in your mind. Walk around this island.

Initially, Tucker had trapped shore crabs and fish off prehistoric fishing hooks made of rat bone. He'd long stopped trying to catch wild pigs or cuscus and instead resorted to eating shipworms, Capricorn beetles, and their larvae. From plants, he'd been taking a Sago palm's pith and pounding it into white starch.

None of it was easy, especially when he came upon sulfur-crested cockatoos, fat iguanas, or blue-necked hornbills. They were so close and contributed to his exasperation. In survival classes, they'd been drilled on a coconut's three eyes and safe-to-eat sweet roots. How to get water from tubular plants. That there were ways to fight off mosquitoes with balms and doctor wounds with plant oils and root-mashed salves.

Yes, keeping hope alive was hard. Especially in the jungle. That left him thinking about Laurel, the girl he hoped against hope was waiting for him back home. Had he been stronger, fit as he'd been four months earlier, he might have leaped from the tree and taken his chances. For Page, Blondie, and even the innocent native headman.

His mind wandering, Tucker suddenly sensed movement. It was almost soundless in its stealth, a slight juddering. Emerging from just below him. It was almost certainly a Japanese soldier climbing into the fig, angling for an optimal vantage point.

Moving like a panther, the man was taking his time, probing carefully for the slightest movement in the surrounding vegetation. Sniffing. Poised for the kill.

Tucker held his breath, recognizing his newest problem. He'd encased himself in a near-airless box with one outlet vent, at the top of the tree, far above him. Unable to draw air through his mouth, his knees drawn to his chest, he must avoid hyperventilating. The hunter was next to him. If Tucker sneezed or coughed, he was finished.

Focus on the knife. They think you're in the bush. About to make your last mistake.

In training, they'd taught Tucker's Z unit to go on mental journeys, trips back in time to review something closely. But where to go? What place could distract him long enough while an enemy soldier camped right above him?

What about that time we left the plateau and scrambled right into the German sailors' camp on Deep Creek? Up above Narrabeen. The day in thirty-eight when Don Bradman's wattle branch saved us. The day we beat back the Nazis.

CHAPTER 15

It had been one of Tucker's greatest adventures.

They'd been up on the Collaroy Plateau. This was back in 1938, when he and the boys set off to find a secret location where German merchant marines hid out, supposedly to keep from getting knifed in King's Cross after they docked.

The German community in Sydney was small, but a friendly sympathizer had found a favorable setting further up the coast, past the fibro holiday homes on Sydney's Northern Beaches. That led to wild rumors: Germans were coming into American Bay near the Hawkesbury River.

Then came the real shocker. Their secret hideout was closer than that. Germans were bivouacking just in from Narrabeen Lake, near the lagoon's wide sweeping curve. Right under one of the rocky ridge lines.

A few old fishermen suggested the sailors were part of a militaristic, political group called Nazis. They were up there somewhere, working on military maneuvers, carving strange symbols into the rocks, and singing war songs around huge bonfires.

Like most of his classmates, Tucker believed foreigners shouldn't be allowed to muck about on Australian soil. But if mysterious Germans were holing up where Aboriginal bushmen once painted their images on the rocks, then it demanded a troop of Sea Scouts go exploring. That idea led to a wild adventure.

Armed with swags loosely strapped to their backs, Brad and three of his best friends set off one warm March day, hoping to emulate a *Famous Five* adventure. With any luck, they would return in two days' time with fantastic stories to tell.

For fortification, they raided family pantries and made off with cucumber sandwiches, SAO biscuits, apples, and tin canteens.

Their truest hope was to find an empty camp and maybe rustle up a few foreign souvenirs. Instead, the boys got far more than they bargained for. It was the day Tucker realized he was good at keeping his cool. Particularly when there was no way out.

The four teens hiked proudly off the plateau at Collaroy, working their way up past Oxford Falls and the wallaby-filled foothills tumbling down from the Heights to the Narrabeen Lagoon.

The going wasn't hard and the views out toward the ocean beaches were inviting, but as the day heated up, it was clear the boys had undertaken a strenuous trek. Martin, the youngest at sixteen, was complaining almost from the outset, a behavior prompting numerous threats that one and all would kick his skinny behind if he didn't stop.

Tommo and Denny, though, were as good as Tucker at keeping their pace strong and morale high. As they forded streams or climbed around slate waterfalls, they watched for hard-to-spot platypus and giant orb-web spider nests strung between the barky trees.

Oxford Falls provided a great first-day swim with plenty of cooling down at the height of the day's heat. They'd eaten their lunches, legs hanging over the edge of the sixty-foot falls, and regaled each other with the mock courage of what they'd do if they spotted any Germans.

"Reckon we just should leave well enough alone if we find 'em," said Denny. Tucker knew his friend would end up as a doctor or diplomat. His mood never veered toward the violent. It always sought observation, prognosis, and procedure.

"Ahh, stuff that," said Tom. "If we find the dirty mongrels, we'll wait until they're passed out on the grog and then race in and nick their gear. My Dad says they're up to no good. Looking to bollocks up the world again."

"Not me, mate," said Martin. "If I see 'em, I'm keeping' my distance. They'll have lookouts posted. With tommy guns. Like the ones in those Jimmy Cagney movies."

For his part, Tucker was indifferent about whether they found Germans or not. It would be something to see the sailors in their lair, but then what? Spy on them?

Moving under the noise-reducing racket of the cicadas and screeching birds, the boys came into Deep Creek from the backside, tracking along a slender waterway taking them past various cabbage tree palms, stubby black-boy grass, and speckled Angophora trees. Along the way, they watched for lazy carpet pythons, red-bellied black snakes, and bored bandicoots.

In one area, they came upon giant boulders, fifty-ton billiard balls covered in moss and lichen that were once headed for a slanted thirty-foot slab of rock that looked, at certain angles, like a tilted banquet table.

One by one, they slid down it to the bottom of a small cascading water-fall. At the bottom, they found clear evidence of an abandoned Aboriginal settlement complete with fire-scorched rocks. Given the arching overhang and trickling fresh water, they weren't surprised by the fresh animal tracks in the yellowish dirt. Ancient men would have tucked up into this glen for centuries, waiting for lunch to come down the far hillside.

Pondering Australia's prehistory, the four reared back at the sound of shrieking cockatoos. Without hesitating, they shot across the shallow tributary and headed up a bushy incline to investigate. At the top of the curving ridge, they found a thick strand of red bloodwoods and then a virtual alley-way, each striated wedge at least eight feet high. The impassive blocks forced them toward an open area hemmed in by huge sedimentary rocks. There were no Germans, but the screeching had come from nearby.

Unexpectedly, the boys stumbled onto a series of unusual messages. One said *Stassfurt 8-2-38.* The next showed a strange insignia showing two tangled Zs with the inscription *6-3-38.* An even bigger rock displayed a complex German eagle pattern, the word *Dortmund*, and the numbers *26-X-37.*

"Holy shit," said Denny. "They've been here before."

"No foolin'," responded Tucker. "And they might be nearby, so let's be plenty careful and quiet. We came out here to prove they're stuffing about. Not to stumble onto them and get our hind ends kicked."

"Let's get outta here," said Martin, feeling they'd completed the mission. "No sense pushing our luck."

"For cryin' out loud, Marty, will you give it a rest, mate? Stop acting the goat. Things are just getting interesting."

It was Denny taking control. He was motioning them toward a ledge hanging over the creek. When he got to it, he ran his hand up and down a pockmarked Angophora that had hosted various moth larvae. The squiggled lines caught all their eyes.

"I'm guessing they're just down toward that jumble over there," Denny continued. "You can see some hidey-holes where the rocks bung up against one another. That's where I'd set up. Right near the water. Good spot for fishing. Cool and protected. Keeps 'em in the shade. Out of the heat."

What the boys heard next was the muffle of human voices. Their widened eyes left no doubt they were all thinking the same thing. They'd found them.

The Nazis had somehow worked their way inland from Narrabeen Lagoon by boat, following the lake's shoreline until it intersected Deep Creek. From there, they paddled upstream toward the massive fractures in the Hawkesbury sandstone.

Peering over the top of one final boulder, what the boys saw was three Germans standing around a fire—two near a ragged rubber raft and a third lashed to a pale gum. Judging by the whip dangling from one sailor's waist belt, it seemed clear a punishment or initiation had just been inflicted.

"Have a look at that," hissed Tom. "They're floggin' one of their own."

"You can see the blood coming right outta 'im," said Martin.

"S'ers five of 'em…if you don't count the bludger who's tied up. Only four of us. We're outnumbered," said Denny, his nervousness clear. "Look at the size of the one mongrel with his jumper off. The one with the stock whip. He must go eighteen stone."

"I heard they torture the ones from the boats that ain't Nazi enough," said Tom, watching for Tucker's reaction. "They bring 'em up 'ere where they think no one can hear 'em holler. Reckon they got that itchy bastard good."

"Let's sit tight for a moment, lads," said Tucker. "See what happens."

"I don't like the looks of this one little bit," said Martin, and it was at that precise moment, in edging backward from the ledge, he loosened a hefty rock from the lip of their concealed vantage point.

The bowling-ball-sized marble fell forward, bashing its way over various ledges below, bouncing in slow motion, alerting the Nazi sailors they had unwanted visitors. At once, the half-naked man-beast was snapping his whip, hollering in German, and drawing the full attention of the others. Whatever his words, there was no question he wanted the spies found, caught, and killed.

For the four Australians, their advantage at first was the height of their location. The Germans could not come straight at them without first hunting around for an ascending path. But the boys' weakness was their fear and, considering the density of the vine-strangled setting, there was a good chance they'd stumble as they ran.

The sailors, old hands at nautical maneuvers, began flanking the boys and funneling them toward level ground. There, in the flat, the teens would lose their slight advantage.

What saved them was Tucker's stout commands and bravery.

"Over here, Tommo…through those trees" and "Oi, Marty, keep your head on, mate. C'mon with me."

Immediately, the boys leaped from their perch, shouting to make for higher ground and follow the rock-lined chute that would bring them back up the path they'd just come down. As they fled, Tucker's strong, clear voice guided them. Even with the Germans gaining ground on them, he pointed the way out.

"This way, Denny. Squeeze through here and jump for that strangler fig. When you get down, turn around and help Marty."

Around them branches tore at their shirts and faces while thorns or nettles scratched their legs. Still, the boys ducked and scrambled, scampering over the rocks the grown men would need to maneuver around.

Primal fear overrode rough scratches and turned ankles. A full-frontal fall, however, would wind a boy, which was exactly what Tucker saw happen to Denny on a long, rocky slope leading toward the indigenous campsite under the waterfall.

At first, Denny stumbled but then miraculously caught his step. Unfortunately, Denny's back foot didn't recover in time to take the full weight of his careening body. Tucker watched the teen smash his stomach down on a good-size stump.

It hurt, even seeing it from a distance, but there was no time for sympathy. The nearest German sailor was less than twenty yards away, homing in on the fallen boy, charging through the brush like a big red roo on the hop. He was so intent on catching one of the intruders, he failed to pick up on Tucker quickly circling back through the scrub.

The German was just standing over Denny when Tucker caught him flush in the side of the head with a chunk of rotted wattle. It was unlikely it ever entered the big man's mind that a teenager, not yet nineteen, would have the presence of mind to counterattack.

"That'll go for six," said Tucker as the German crashed to the ground. "And not out, neither. That's how Bradman would've protected the crease."

With that, he hoisted the gutted Denny to his feet and, wrapping the boy's arm over his own shoulder, began pulling him thorough the snagging undergrowth. It was rough terrain, but picking up their pace, they heard the other Germans gathering around their fallen comrade.

"C'mon Denny. Get yer legs going, mate. They might still decide to come after us."

Ahead and moving toward the clearing were Tommo and Martin. They looked gassed but happy to have cleared the scratching brush. Martin was even whooping, readying for how he'd detail every step of running for his life. He'd be chattering about it for hours to come.

The Germans wouldn't want to bring a lynch mob back after them. They'd know better. But did they have pistols? That was worth considering, so Tucker made the lads stay low to the ground, all while moving them back toward the big garden near the lake. From there, they hightailed it out toward the trolley stop on Pittwater Road.

Looking over his shoulder, Tucker wondered if he'd see any of the Nazis coming through the casuarinas. But the bush revealed nothing, not even a slight swaying or bending of branches. Apparently, they'd retreated while the four teens pounded each other silly, reliving their escape.

It was Tucker alone, later on, who predicted if the German sailors had mounted one last attack, they would've caught the boys. Just as the Japanese would carry the day on a remote island in December 1944 if Tucker sneezed or fainted. The tree was his tomb.

Unless he kept his cool.

CHAPTER 16

December 1944—Katherine, NT, Australia

Whenever Ilsa had talked to me in our early meetings about life during World War II, the first thing she always emphasized was the heat pouring down onto the Katherine Gorge. How it lay over everything like a smothering winter quilt.

That December, while still nineteen, she'd convinced herself the Dry, the very opposite of the Wet, missed nothing. The weather's unseen broiler coils hovered over the land, baking it before finally letting up and pouring invasive water all over the inhabitants with the same fluency. When the Wet came, water rained down on every living creature with oppressive efficiency, staggering man, woman, and farm animal alike.

But not the flies. Dry or Wet, they swarmed. For every eye, lip, or cut. It explained why girls in Australia learned to spit early. The flies targeted mouths. And if there was no respite from weather, flying pests, or her father's endless chores, there was also no escaping Ilsa's mounting sense of desperation. Looking back, the last six years had relentlessly delivered all four.

Worse, there were no new faces. No one ever came around. The war had seen to that. For Ilsa and her brothers, their isolation on the outskirts of Katherine was as complete as any prisoner-of-war camp.

"Papa won't even let the local ringers visit," Ilsa said aloud to Dandy, her horse, "and other than Glenno and his missus, there's no one to even tell me what's going on. We haven't seen a swagman in more than a year. Are the Japanese and Germans still winning?"

Looking around the homestead and out beyond the ridgeline that carried straight into the expansive gorge, Ilsa wondered again how Aboriginals knew so much about the land, storms, and strange animals she'd come to identify and understand. The roo and goanna. Different birds, like kites and magpies. Even the freshwater crocs and snakes.

"They don't go to school," she mused about Glen Logan's indigenous family. "And they certainly don't read books like Austrians do. And yet they look at the sky or that old river and tell us next week's weather. How do they know so much?"

Sitting alone two hundred miles south of Darwin, there was no one to answer her question. Like so many other things, Ilsa realized she'd have to work it out alone. She'd gathered a little local knowledge since the family's escape, but her recent education had come from the family's untidy stock hand.

Glenno, with his circular white beard and mustache, explained the Katherine Gorge was the primeval home to a sacred Dreamtime story stretching back to the dawn of time. The Jawoyn people believed a rainbow serpent named Bolung lived in the second pool of Nit-ma-lick. But he could reveal no more. The elders required certain things remain secret.

"We bin here long time, Miss Ilsa," he said, rubbing his rough hands together. "Bolung not for whitefellahs."

"I know, Glenno, but how am I going to learn to like it here?"

"Have to watch and listen," he said. "Land always talking. Telling plenty good stories."

Ilsa wasn't sure about stones or plants communicating with humans, so the stock hand told her about songlines. When Aboriginal men went for their long walks, they sang their way across the land. Some songs told of hardship and joy, but many lyrics simply provided directional signposts for finding food or water.

"Different songs for leaving. Going someplace else. Others for coming back, Miss Ilsa. Some songs for where animals living. Then some for good-eating plants."

For more than an hour, Ilsa wondered how singing her way out of the gorge would work. She played around in her head with creating new words for Austria's national anthem, *Sei gesegnet ohne Ende*. It was an easy song, and where the lyrics spoke of "freundlich schmücken dein Gelände," she could replace the first stanza's green firs and golden spikes with stationary red rocks and large termite mounds.

It was certainly better than *Deutschland über Alles*, the stern ode Germans made the Austrian schoolchildren sing back in 1938. That horrific tune would never do.

To occupy her mind, Ilsa began creating a small verbal map. She started humming a few bars of the Austrian anthem with words about riding out to the great broken rock at the edge of their property and then turning west toward the massive boab. That verse delighted and led to the path cresting the big hill before it dropped down into the gorge.

"What a wonder that would be," she said to the horse. "To ride away from this dreadful place. To follow the river to a city where things happen and people meet each other. A place where they hold dances and girls meet boys. But for that to happen, Dandy, I'd certainly have to learn new songs. Long ones."

The horse kept trotting, barely nickering in response.

"Yes, I agree. It would have to be done when the Katherine River wasn't coming down. We'd go after the Wet. Toward Mataranka and the hot springs. On a day Papa wasn't looking."

Despite her longing, Ilsa knew she couldn't leave her family. Planning an escape, so pleasant as a distraction, was dangerous. It would fill her thoughts, but she mustn't want more. When the war ended and she turned twenty-one, then she might attempt to make personal demands about leaving the station.

Ilsa felt certain her plan could work but faced some notable roadblocks.

Where did one learn new songs in the Australian bush? She certainly couldn't use *Waltzing Matilda*. Or could she? If there were no other sources for songs, she'd have to make new ones up.

"Dandy, what if I used Beethoven's Fifth? You know, dah-dah-de-dah. Dah-dah-de-dah. I could make it into 'Go to the tree, go to the tree, then to the rock…and…turn at the tree.'"

Staring out from under her worn felt hat, she tried imagining keeping all the landmarks and soaring cliffs in their designated places. How hard must it have been for Aboriginals to survive this place, for thousands of years, without horses or canned food or anything.

In her daydreaming, Ilsa imagined the river was part of the answer. If one followed the Katherine long enough, it must go someplace more interesting than the family's property. Darwin was days away. But what about going south? The North Australia Railway went through Mataranka. And that was where Elsey Station was located. The place where Mrs. Gunn wrote her *Never-Never* book.

That was the sole book she'd managed to bring from Graz the day they'd raced out of the house and escaped into the Alps. By now, she knew every line by heart.

She'd even started thinking about writing a story of her own. It would be about an outback doctor and his delightful youngest daughter, who combined her knowledge of horses to help all kinds of remote victims. She'd even started putting down thoughts in a private journal. The story started like this:

THE DOCTOR'S DAUGHTER

The doctor was a lucky man. He had a beautiful wife, a handsome son, two pretty daughters, and a large medical practice, and he lived in a large country house with extensive gardens and grounds. But fourteen years after the birth of his youngest daughter, a big surprise came.

Lo and behold, his wife became pregnant, giving birth to a third daughter. The doctor grew very fond of his youngest because she had inherited his jet-black hair and her mother's emerald-green eyes.

That was as far as she'd gotten, but she knew she must soon make the doctor start to take the youngest on trips in the car to visit his patients. Along the way, she would learn about medicine and how to treat wounds and upset stomachs. Maybe even to assist with baby deliveries.

But for now, she needed to stop her frivolous thoughts about becoming a writer. There were chores to finish before father, the boys, and Glenno came back needing tea. They would be tired and hungry.

"Oh Dandy, I'm just so tired of this place. Of war. And old Mr. Hitler. And that evil Dr. Goebbels. He gave me that look. The same one Angus Wilson, the drover, used five years ago. Do all men think the same things?"

She rode for a while in silence, admiring the red rocks in the distance.

"Remember how angry Papa got that day? It was like he was suggesting I was at fault for Gus liking me. Angus may have been immature, the way he was mooning about, but I'm tired of not having anyone to talk to. It's horrible here. I wish we could fly away."

When the horse said nothing, Ilsa continued, "Maybe I am old enough for Papa to let me get a job in Katherine. What do you think? I believe I shall ask him tonight. As my Christmas gift. I will tell him I don't want anything. Just permission. That will be gift enough."

CHAPTER 17

December 1944—Sermata Islands, Dutch East Indies

S tuck in the steaming gum tree, Tucker fought to keep his cool.
The flaw in his previous thinking was now fully evident. He hadn't determined how long, with limited oxygen, he could squat in this secret "hole"
without hallucinating or passing out.

Well, in for a penny, in for a pound, thought Tucker, using distracting "p"
words. They were all that came to mind. That and *Dark as Death's dunny.*

Burning out the gum's trunk had come off without a hitch, but thoughts
about breathing were something he hadn't had time to consider. His sixth sense
hadn't considered details.

Quiet, mate. Listen.

Above him on an outside silvery branch, the sentry was grunting his way
onto one of the giant gray limbs, a smooth-as-glass shelf, wriggling about,
trying to find the best vantage point. This sniper was waiting for the Australian to make his move. To catch sight of an agitated hand brushing away a
mosquito. Of a man stretching his cramped leg and disturbing the emerald
glade's quiet harmony.

He'll be patient. Pick another place in the past. Start with this mission.

Start with Ivan Lyon, the lieutenant-colonel who'd been scheming, since his escape from Singapore in early 1942, to bring elite Allied soldiers and sailors together to counterpunch in a long and dirty war. Lyon had supposedly lost his wife and child to Japanese bombers after he'd put them on a boat leaving Singapore. He'd decided to channel his pain by planning new and violent ways to disrupt the Japanese and their Greater East Asia Co-Prosperity Sphere.

Under normal conditions, Tucker would never have learned about Lyon because he'd been too busy rising through the ranks of the Australian 2/3rd Independent Company in New Guinea. But life during wartime tipped on the thinnest of decisions made or coincidences.

As Tucker was sweeping back into Sydney on furlough, his captain ran him to ground and redirected him to Melbourne. In August 1943, he'd been interviewed and invited into the Z Special Unit. His appointment came just late enough to miss out on joining Lyon and a hand-picked group of thirteen commandos for Operation Jaywick, a top-secret mission targeting Japanese ships in Singapore Harbor.

Jaywick sank or damaged multiple Japanese boats, and the men from the mission, acknowledged for their heroism, went back to their units until someone in military intelligence brought five back to Lyon. Against all logic, he told his handpicked veterans he wanted to go back to Singapore.

No one doubted returning was suicidal, but none wavered. They supported Lyon's brash will, and this time the military brass agreed to provide Lyon a submarine and guerilla-style insertion near the target.

Stuck in a tree on an insignificant island, Tucker recalled that just after noon on September 11, 1944, Operation Rimau left WA's Garden Island on the HMS *Porpoise*, a tired Grampus-class mine-laying sub. Under the watchful eyes of Lyon and his 2-I-C Lieutenant-Commander Don Davidson (RNVR), the British sub moved up into the Lombok Strait. This time, Tucker had been selected, at the last minute, as an alternate whose job was helping with preattack equipment maintenance and mission insertion.

Spirits high, the twenty-two raiders, two conducting officers, and Tucker squeezed into the *Porpoise's* confined spaces as the sub sliced northward toward Merapas Island in the Riau Archipelago. That tiny speck of land was their drop-off zone and postmission recovery point if anything went wrong.

Lyon's plan involved launching a mix of electrically powered one-man submersible kayaks (known as Sleeping Beauties) and Australian-made folboats, low-in-the-water canoes, to carry more than fifteen tons of guns, mines, and supplies. Each craft would carry two men, gear, and explosives.

The original Rimau plan hadn't called for Tucker to fully deploy with the Rimau team, but working below deck one dawn as auxiliary support for the conducting officer, Carey, things had radically changed. Abruptly, there was verbal hissing, the air blue with swearing. Tucker was ordered to make haste in off-loading ammo and gear.

Somewhere around September 28, the *Porpoise* had located a forty-ton Malayan junk Lyon decided to "steal." It was named the *Mustika*, and the sub was just off the area known as Datu, due east of central Sumatra, west of Borneo.

"They've found one," Tucker overheard someone say. "Skipper says she'll do nicely."

At once, the sub's commander, Marsham, was yelling what sounded like nervous instructions, sending the *Porpoise* to the surface. Immediately, seven armed sailors poured out of the conning tower, swinging into action like Errol Flynn in *Captain Blood*, overwhelming the unprepared Malayan pilot and his crew.

It was just before dawn two days later when Tucker was ordered to start moving folboats, minus their midship frames, through a torpedo hatch and up onto the slippery deck. He'd been topside when an unidentified craft, possibly a Japanese antisub patrol boat, came roaring out from behind one of the islands. Caught with both feet on the sub's outer hull, Tucker heard commands and realized the *Porpoise's* captain was sealing his hatches and preparing to dive.

Tucker pushed the last of the canvas-covered kayaks off into the foaming water just as the submarine jerked and initiated a rapid dive maneuver. The intense drop caused him to tumble awkwardly off the glistening starboard prow into the gurgling, monstrous suction of the descending whale.

The drowning sensation was immediate. Tons of water pushed down on him, but as the tension on his ears increased, Tucker followed his training and determined the direction of the ballast bubble. That allowed him to streamline his way toward the surface and the bow of the captured junk.

Stroking over, one thought loomed in Tucker's mind: Lieutenant-Colonel Lyon wasn't going to like finding his alternate, a man not even listed on official records, climbing up into his pirated ship and accidentally joining his raid.

Lyon, however, was preoccupied with off-loading the captured Malayan fishermen and ensuring his raiders gave enemy patrols no reason to investigate. Finally noticing the dripping wet Tucker, Lyon established contact with the sub's commander, indicating he had an extra man. Here, Marsham argued against another risky surface procedure, suggesting Tucker could help on the *Mustika* and stand guard over supplies at the rendezvous point.

At 10:00 p.m. on September 30, the British sub turned south for Fremantle. There was no longer any chance of Lyon turning back. From that moment on, the Rimau commandos were on their own until *Porpoise* returned to Merapas Island on the seventh of November, a gap of thirty-eight days.

Unfortunately, the fight that led to the *Mustika's* sinking came just over a week later.

On the afternoon of October 10, near Kepala Jernith and Batam Island, the junk encountered a Malay patrol boat that gave no doubt it intended to investigate the *Mustika*. Tucker's memory suggested they might've avoided trouble, but one of the Rimau men opened fire. The bursting muzzle flash instantly gave them away.

For the next four days, hunted, Lyon motored the junk toward his target, dividing his men into attack groups and making the decision to scuttle the *Mustika* near Bulan Island. On his orders, most of the men went over the side into the folboats and canoes.

"Into the water," Lyon commanded them. "Scatter. I'll head to Kepala

Jernih and sink her there. The rendezvous is at Merapas on the night of the seventh and eighth. Godspeed, gentlemen."

All of the Rimau men were strong swimmers and strong kayakers. With luck, they might've reached their "safe" island. But as the firefight's adrenaline wore off, Tucker understood the enormity of their challenge. They were swimming for their lives in the very middle of the enemy's ocean.

"Go for your life," said Bob Page, Rimau's third in command and the mission's sole captain. "You there, Tucker—move into the stern seat. Lieutenant Sargent, take the bow. Start paddling. I'll take the first stretch in the water."

At the time, there had been a large group of them. Maybe an even dozen, paddling and kicking through the night, knowing their lives depended on covering more than sixty nautical miles in heavy seas if they were to reach Merapas. If they stayed undetected there, the sub was due back soon. But it also meant an incredible amount of ocean paddling with at least one man in the water the entire time.

At one point, a predatory Japanese cruiser came out of the fog to their distant left, its yellowy-white search beam prowling the blackness, sliding across the water like a ravenous snake. It slithered, leaping at the three bobbing heads in ripples, but each time the trio ducked under, pulling the canoe's frame down to avoid the freeboard showing. Twice the serpent's silvery tongue passed over their frantic heads but both times missed catching them.

Making the decision to not wait for the British submarine at Merapas, Page maneuvered the trio through two thousand miles of ocean, sliding down Sumatra's east coast before successfully jumping to Java's northern coast. On Tucker's silk map, it had looked impossible.

From Surabaya, they'd moved down the line islands from Bali to Romang in the Wetar Strait. Their plan was to catch the trade winds and easterly currents leading toward the Leti Islands, Sermata and Babar. If they reached Kobror in the Arafura Sea, then they might acquire the jagged line of islands stretching up toward the southwest corner of Dutch New Guinea.

That was so long ago, and now Tucker was alone. Stuck in a gum, shaking with heat tremors. If the sentry heard him, no one would ever learn how he died.

The same will hold for Page and Sargent. If I don't get back, then who records what happened? So, hold on, lad. Stay in the past.

He'd review how he and Page lost Blondie at Romang.

By then, their great giant of a companion was gaunt, his eye sockets like craters. The lieutenant was completely hairless. Covered in hideous red scabs. They had no quinine for malaria and were forced to keep him in the canoe to shield him from sharks. When they made land, they'd dragged him ashore, but his fever was worsening.

There hadn't been much ceremony when Captain Page decided to leave the unconscious man. The Japanese navy was closing in, and with impossibly long odds facing them, Page hoped cooling shade could buy Sargent extra time. Another day on the water would kill him. But staying together might kill all three.

Tucker and Page continued paddling east, but when they stumbled ashore in the Leti Islands, just before dawn, both men were fighting severe dehydration and exhaustion. Tucker hauled Page, with his sunken eyes and salt-encrusted mustache, across the wet-black beach into the brush, collapsing almost immediately to catch a few minutes of sleep. Awakening, as rays of light arrived in irritating waves, it was clear the canoe would reveal their position.

Tucker couldn't hide the boat alone. The tree line was too far away, and the tide was too rough for hoping it would float away. His only choice was to puncture the flotation bags and fill the boat with rocks.

It took an enormous amount of time, all of it on an exposed beach, but the moment Tucker returned from the ocean's blue-white edge, he understood Page was finished. He cradled his brave commanding officer for a few moments, found some tepid groundwater, and forced it past Page's cracked lips, but it was futile. Page's shark-colored skin was literally sloughing off him.

His fading eyes weren't focusing. It was a combination of sunstroke, dehydration, and starvation.

A godsend arrived not long after when a local villager checking for early-morning tidal treasures came upon them. Shortly after she'd run off down the stony, root-strewn path to report her unexpected finding, a "friendly", round, brown man, appropriately cautious, came down the dirt track bearing lifesaving papaya, breadfruits, and drink.

Tucker was able to eat and swallow the precious fluid. Page couldn't.

With haste, the chief's men retrieved the dugout, two men taking it away for salvage, with the others constructing a bamboo litter for Page's stretchered journey back to their village. During that first hour, Tucker held onto a naïve belief Page might make it. He had revived a little following an application of herbs applied by the native women. If a man could do such a thing, Page was trying to convince his shattered body to fight on.

Thinking back, Tucker knew Page likely wouldn't have made it, even if he'd been stretchered into Royal North Shore Hospital in Sydney. There was nothing to him but skin and bones.

A day later, the outcome was obvious. Page could no longer travel—he'd lapsed into a near coma—and Tucker was told, in pidgin English and diagrams in the dirt, the enemy was coming. Their short instruction was simple. Tucker must leave, and they would hide Page. That was the best they could offer.

Sitting up that last night in the bush, staring at the stars, Tucker prayed an interceding hand would save Page.

"Sir, rather hard to tell you this," Tucker started. "I've got to leave you here. Got no choice. We'll hide you out back. In one of their secret huts where they won't see you."

The captain, pallid in his near-death state, nodded. Encouraged, Tucker continued.

"See, the thing is, they'll find us if we're both here. I've talked it over with the headman. If I shove off tonight, I have a chance to make Sermata, maybe Babar. I'll find one of the coast watchers and get him to send for help. In the meantime, you rest up and try to regain your strength. Reckon the sisters here are pretty good at mixing the salve."

This time, Page didn't respond. Tucker gripped Page's hand and squeezed. The captain was finding his own inner peace.

After that, Tucker followed the younger village men down a worn trail, skirting the moonlit shore. In an hour, they came upon another group, and after a series of grunts and curious hand signals, the huskier ones put Tucker in a fifteen-foot wooden dugout and, with two teenagers in a separate thatched-roof craft, shoved him off the eastern edge of the island. Behind them, on the horizon, the glowing moon had started its evening journey across the sky.

The hollowed-out palm bolt, Tucker's new craft, contained four unopened coconuts and some leaf-wrapped dried pork bits tied tightly to a thwart. As they forced their way out through the reef's broken-tooth gap, the roar of ugly, crashing breakers closing in on them, Tucker waved the support boat away.

Triangulating a rough heading based on his reading of the Southern Cross, he pointed himself east toward the next group of islands. If he was right, the Sermata-Babar-Yamdena Island chain lay reasonably close. Absent a North Star, men in the Southern Hemisphere needed a bit more calculation. But as he paddled away, he kept checking and rechecking the stars. It was like playing two-up. One bad flip would finish him.

When he sighted the next island, chanced upon after more than thirty hours of painful open-water drifting, he was spent. His immediate routine remained unchanged: stash the dugout, find drinkable fluids, and sleep.

Where are the sodding coast watchers? he asked himself the next morning. *Woulda thought one of those geezers would've turned up by now.*

It was not that Tucker lacked respect for them. They were nothing less than brilliant, surviving off the land, calling in radio reports about enemy ships, all while Japanese units hunted them across every inch of captured territory.

Snapping out of his reverie, Tucker tried guessing where he'd come ashore and his luck at coming through the coral reef safely. There was no evidence of a Japanese beach patrol, but a Jap cutter could be anchored in the next bay over.

Tucker shook his head like a soaked dog. He needed fresh water. There would be droplets on nearby leaves. But as the sun rose above the latticed canopy, the waxy leaves would curl up, and the lifesaving water would evaporate. Tucker cursed.

The rest of that morning was foggy in his memory. He'd been exhausted. And then, once again, God answered one of his prayers. He was discovered. Again. By another friendly islander who fed him. Helped bathe his wounds. Watched him build his hiding place in the giant gum.

Bloody oath, I'm a long way from home. Who's ever heard of three men on the trot, traversing this many islands, over two thousand miles, living on nothing for nigh on three months?

The sudden vibration, slithering along the tree's great vertical axis, suggested something was happening. The Japanese sniper had slid down the tree and was stamping around like he wanted to get his circulation going again.

Whatever it was, Tucker would wait him out. He'd push through the suffocating heat and sweaty odor of dank and vaporous decay. He had no choice.

Sweat pouring down from his forehead, Tucker licked at parched lips with a sticky, desiccated tongue, suffering in the claustrophobic sauna of his own making. Around him, the gum's sooty walls pressed in on him. It'd take a miracle to not accidentally nudge open his concealment door.

It was like boxing in the later rounds. When an opponent's punch connected, good fighters pushed through the pain. Counterpunched. Tucker needed that fighter's trance mentality now. Needed to bundle up commando training, bouts with his brothers, fending off the old man on the drink, and mix it all together.

Steady on, lad. Stay alive. Get back to Darwin. Report in and tell them what happened.

It was then he heard the footsteps, kicking through the dead leaves. Departing.

CHAPTER 18

December 1944—Katherine, NT, Australia

To Ilsa, it felt like weeks had gone by, when, in fact, it was mere days. The barbarous, punishing heat in the gorge area had not abated. Nor the imminent arrival of the annual Wet. That seasonal disturbance always changed everything. But not Ilsa's desire to escape. Especially since Papa had said no to working in Katherine.

Despite Ilsa's wish for wage-earning labor as her Christmas gift, Johann hadn't given her much more than a stern rebuke. He gave no reason. Some part of it was the war. Another was the family's need for her to work at home and help with her brothers. The truth of it was their dark secret.

It was so hard, she thought, living with parents who never allowed anyone other than poor old Glen Logan to come near their station. It was utterly miserable.

Ilsa would have killed for a new book to read or something that resembled schooling, but not since September 1939, when the Germans roared into Poland and England pulled Australia into the war, had she been given much of a chance to learn with others. When the Japanese attacked Darwin in February 1942, the incendiary bombs finished any discussions about leaving Katherine for a bigger town or city.

There wasn't much to do during one's free time except hope the war would end and for Papa to reconsider. Talk of a Japanese invasion persisted, especially after the Adelaide River was bombed in November 1943. But that was more than a year ago. As far as Ilsa could tell from listening to the sputtering wireless, the panic in the Northern Territory was only just possibly settling down.

Long ago, father and daughter had sat in their Austrian parlor, talking about the Anschluss and how Austrian bankers were afraid.

"Was it really more than six years ago Papa moved us from Graz?" she asked the horse, riding out to one of the family's remote paddocks. "If that was April 1938 and now it's December 1944, that's six and a half years. You wouldn't know about this, Dandy, but Papa made us hike through those snowy Alps to avoid the Nazis. Next was that horrible ship with its disgusting diesel fumes and unbearable heat. Gave us all manner of rashes. It was dreadful."

Ilsa surveyed the humble work clothing she was wearing at that moment and noticed her physical shape. She understood her body had changed. She had a distinct bosom, much like Oma Maria. Where had her teenage years gone?

Somehow, she'd survived 1938, 1941, and 1944. But things certainly got harder the older one got. There was only Dandy and Glenno, and neither said much. The stockman often used his hands to talk or uttered strange phrases she'd never heard in English or German sentences.

Dandy, named by Ilsa for the outgoing character in Mrs. Gunn's book, spoke with scraping hooves and snorts. Then there were her brothers, who didn't count. As she was their older sister, they worked at excluding her.

Not that there was much time for playful frivolity. One thing was certain: it was hard coming of age in Australia's Northern Territory. Thankless during the Wet and near impossible during a war, when the Japanese might bomb them all at any moment. Such was her lot. Perhaps she should ride over to where Papa stored his special things. She would check and make sure everything was safe for the first big downpour.

If there was one certainty, it was this: November was always dry, and December would bring three things: Christmas roast, daily storms, and prodigious humidity. Plus river flooding, invasions of mice or flies, and unending chores.

The deep alcove, always cooler in the rock's covered crevice, might be a little nicer. A place to take off one's hat and wipe the sweat away. Why not now? Tugging on the reins, she steered the horse toward a back trail leading under the cliffs.

Managing the Wet meant learning not to complain. That was Rule Number One to Australians. No whining. What they called whinging. It was something of a tradition in the region. If something broke, it got resolved on the station, or its repair waited until others could assist.

Regardless of status, everyone in the NT suffered since there was no escaping the annual torrents. The billowing clouds would appear, but unlike seasonal snowstorms in Austria, here the rains, sometimes with thunder and heat lightning, came every day.

The other piece of the Wet puzzle was understanding how hard it was to travel any distance since most passable routes were destroyed or cut off by water. And crossing a watercourse was never safe since various potential tragedies lay just below the surface. Horses had been known to get swept off their feet, and saltwater crocs traveled inland on rushing rivers. Poor swimmers drowned in rip-like currents.

Unfamiliar with horses when she left Graz, Ilsa had quietly revealed a gift for working with the large animals her father purchased. And in the absence of girlfriends, she told her brown mare everything.

"When we get there, Dandy," Ilsa said, "I shall leave you to graze. But I must inform you, I will ask Papa to let me travel to another station when the Wet ends. I will be almost twenty, and in many places that makes me of marrying age."

The horse snorted at the remark and pulled his head back.

"In Graz, there would have been dances and Gasthäuser where I might've worked or been invited for a meal. I would've met a nice soldier or the son of a nearby farmer. Oma Maria would have known all the right families, and

Papa would've conspired with men from his accounting firm. Things would have been arranged."

Under the awning of the overhanging rock walls, all was still. Far above her, kites and magpies drifted on invisible carpets of air, their flight creating corkscrew helixes. To the north, cloud banks built, collecting the water droplets slated to fill Bolung's mighty gorge.

"I know what you are thinking. That these things will not happen for me here in Katherine. But Papa must let me travel, when it is safe, to meet my future husband. And what shall he be like? What will kissing be like? Do you think I shall like it? I have no experience in these matters, and Mutter has not yet shared with me her knowledge."

At this comment, the horse looked away, seemingly embarrassed.

"I do hope I like being married. That is, if ever I meet the right man. I will know how to bake damper and work a cattle station. I will be good with children. First, I must meet him. But, Dandy, it would be helpful if he came here first. To meet Mama and Papa. That will be my Christmas wish," she said with naïve confidence. "If I can't work elsewhere, I shall wish for a visitor. Or a new book."

CHAPTER 19

23 December 1944—Sermata Islands, Dutch East Indies

Stuck in his tree-bound trance, Brad Tucker conjured up his favorite vision of the girl he believed was "the one." In this iteration, his head was there in her lap. They were stretched out on a wind-blown grassy knoll high above the Warriewood Drop. Just in from the cave where the explosive tide washed over an immovable flat shelf and its impressive blowhole, far below Mona Vale's sheer cliffs.

Laurel. Wearing her engagement ring. Floating so close he could touch her. Near a setting that could've been described in pirate books. In fact, if Stevenson's fictional buccaneers, or any real ones, had ever come near Australia, they would have buried gold at Warriewood, where the snug cove was that inspiring. Surrounded by spikey banksia plants and bottlebrushes, with casuarina trees standing guard, Tucker saw a wild dollop of brownish, spindly reeds growing among the wind-warped Norfolk pines. And far below the headland, coppery stripes shone brightly on the cove's spectacular rock face.

The fantasy's itinerary called for the two of them to picnic before making the steep climb down the crumbling shale into the foaming whitecaps and sapphire blue of the ocean. They'd worn their bathing costumes under light jumpers and spent the day riding bicycles, a little Raleigh and his rusty Malvern

Star. They'd come down off the plateau, just the two of them, working their way to his favorite swimming spot.

Dee Why and Turimetta Head were regular beaches. The "drop", by comparison, was more of a box canyon. For teenagers, the setting was perfect because, after a few lateral traverses, anyone could leap from the head's various rock ledges. It was an isolated place, far removed from the umber ridges running off to the north.

Today, there was only a touch of offshore breeze and minimal cloud cover. They'd gotten perfect conditions for entering the drop's famous ocean-eroded tube and stroking through the exploding exit spout where they'd shoot up out of the surf like seals or otters onto the smooth shelf at the base of the cliff.

In his mind, Tucker helped Laurel down a treacherous path before they climbed down a knotted rope to the final rock outcropping. It was just above the point where the cave's channeled water smashed into a sheer rock wall.

To the right of the spitting fissure was one of the dark entrances to the tubular hole in the cliff, and it was the rare teenager who didn't think twice about entering the massive pipe from the other side. Getting caught in the murky tunnel when a swell raged was bad news. The offshore tide could push swimmers up against the unevenly eroded ceiling, and on the wrong day, a weak swimmer could drown, trapped against the rock roof.

The only other thing to consider was guessing what else was swimming in the black water roaring into the headland. Some of the locals said reef sharks came by and rested on subterranean shelves. But Tucker always believed they were merely black wobbegongs, nasty-looking (but harmless) carpet sharks, lazily curled up on the sandy bottom just below the cliff's open face.

On the other end of the horizontal pipe, the Warriewood beach side, there was a brilliant set of jumps into twenty or more feet of glittering aquamarine water. There, great turquoise waves mingled with swirling patches of dark blue.

Sliding into the water, the two of them worked their way around the seaside labyrinth. Bobbing at the grotto's entrance, smashing together as the tidal breakers boomed against the rocks, they waited to launch themselves into the gurgling funnel.

"Whaddya reckon? You right to swim through the next time the surge goes down?" Tucker asked, spitting out a mouthful of saltwater.

"Of course. Are you?" she said.

"No fear."

He knew more than a few of his mates, Marty for one, would've been pumping the brakes, offering a wild litany of nervous excuses. It took a steady swimmer, stroking with the wave's mounting curl, to stay on top of the foaming wave.

Laurel would have giggled, as if she didn't have a care in the world, and then, timing her forward thrust as the water level initially dropped, she would've shot into the cavern's ominous entrance. Riding a large breaker, he imagined her surging out of sight.

"Right as rain," Tucker whispered. "Right as bloody rain."

Under the water's lifting and falling surface, Tucker glimpsed the vague outline of Laurel's fluttering feet. Below, in the trough, dark fish were making for the pocked side walls. Poking his head up for air, Tucker stroked toward the opening, watching Laurel's blonde head cutting a powerful swath through the cobalt waves.

As they went further along, it darkened, but both swimmers could see light at the far end of the tube. He gauged they had a good five feet of gap between the surface and ebony ceiling. If a rogue wave came in from offshore, it would squirt them out the far end.

"C'mon, keep up," she said with encouragement.

She turned again, her voice still bouncing across the dripping walls, stroking swiftly toward the hole's explosive spout. Projected by the wave, she flew upward with a thunderous splash, almost five feet in distance. Tucker thought it was like watching a porcelain doll pumped out of a whale's snout. She gracefully landed on the slick ledge jutting out of the water. Around her, thousands of gallons of ocean washed over the uneven shelf, pouring back into the ocean through eroded channels.

Now it was Tucker's turn. He didn't hesitate, and timing the next wave, he replicated her feat. With an extra-hard kick during the surge, the squirting wave lifted him, and he landed in a standing position. Around him small waterfalls drained into the sea.

"Shall we go again?" she asked.

"Reckon not," Tucker said. "Might be pushing our luck. But climb with me, and I'll show you some jumps."

She nodded her agreement, and within minutes they were leaping from various heights into the inviting waters away from the throaty flume. After three such jumps, they climbed back out, dried off, and lay in the grassy meadow above.

Tucker stared up at her face. Just below her smile, hidden behind her costume, two full-sized breasts nestled in their cups. In his mind's eye, he could think of nothing more than her leaning over him further, laughing at one of his jokes.

Emerging from his fantasy, Tucker vowed that when he got back to Sydney, he would take Laurel to Warriewood and propose. There was something about her beauty but also something else. It was her unavailability. She could choose anyone. Why not him?

But stuck in a tree, trapped in a fantasy of his own making, he stiffened. His hands would not move. He reconjured her covered breasts when she looked away. His adrenaline was mounting, but where were his arms?

In the darkness, he finally saw rough outlines. Two hands. One held a knife. The other, showing a slight tremor, was balled into a fist, the thumb curled under the scarred knuckles. Fighter's hands. Hardened bones that had once been taped and shoved into Everlast boxing gloves. For bouts in the Tokyo fighting dens against Katsutoshi Naito's famous stable of boxers.

The old man had somehow arranged for him, an undersized welterweight, to accompany the Australian team during its pre-1936 Olympics tour of Japan. The one with Olympians like Leonard Cook and Henry Cooper. But to medal in Berlin, the managers wanted to fight proven competitors on foreign soil.

"You were seventeen in 1936. Full of spunk. Got ahold of those Japanese language books. Started learning their language, didn't you?"

Tucker recalled that to his way of thinking, the Japanese were the most mysterious of the Asians. The Chinese were food merchants. The Japanese were a different story. The trip to Tokyo and Osaka had revealed firsthand a storied culture wired in codes of honor and rigid discipline. Their fighters were constantly bowing to their sensai and came across as uncomfortable fraternizing with the Australians. They weren't like the Poms or Kiwis. Those lads would chat a bit after the fights.

Still, Tucker had found one Japanese fighter who sneaked similar curious glances at the tanned Australians who'd journeyed so long just to fight. When there was a bit of downtime, he attempted an awkward friendship built around trying out each other's language.

⁓

Tucker squirmed again in the gum, trying to reposition his aching knees and thighs. In the dark dreamscape of the Jap fighting den, he clenched and unclenched his fists. He was circling, looking for his opening, his chance to strike first. The arena was smoky, thick with sweaty humidity. He did not want this mirage. He forced his mind black.

He squeezed his eyelids, searching his imagination. Where was she? And then, she was there. A beauty, sparkling in a backless swimsuit, the denounced fashion of that year. Motioning for him to swim into the drop's infamous tunnel.

In the giant gum, he relaxed his shoulders, not wanting to miss even a single moment. They were lying alone on the Warriewood hillside, listening to the surf. Tucker looked at her, wanting to kiss her, hold her, roll her on her back. She was looking at him. But what was it in her resisting eyes? Did she somehow already know what was coming?

She stared at him, her eyes a piercing blue. She was floating over him, gentle hands twirling his thick hair. Her face was the whole of perfection. Couldn't she tell he was tired and afraid?

Pull her down to you. Kiss her. Talk to her. Tell her what you are thinking, mate.

But his fighter's hands were still, constrained. As if they were tied. Would she not allow him to hold her?

Come home to me, Brad Tucker. It's safe. Start now. Come to me.

CHAPTER 20

Tucker blinked. Had he heard Laurel clearly? Or was it just the asphyxiating tree pushing down on him? It felt like the hollowed-out banyan was intent on squeezing the life out of him. Was Laurel instructing him to start moving? That today was not his day to die? Not on this speck of an island in the Arafura Sea. Or was it the South Banda Sea?

Shaking from fatigue, dehydration, malaria, or maybe all of them, Tucker wondered what he would've given for a single day at Warriewood. For one hour in her arms. At that moment, his mind's eye showcased her clearly.

She'd been fearless, swimming into Warriewood's sloshing vagueness without a second thought. She'd laughed. Made it through. Popped out the other side. She must be sending him a message now, telling him to make his move.

No fear. That's what I said to her that day at the Drop.

Tucker drew a deep breath through his nose, hoping it was early evening. Dusk. It would work to his advantage if he took his time.

Reaching down, his outstretched fingers twitching from exhaustion, he felt for the rough surface of the trap door before pushing it open. Immediately, a cool breeze curled into the tree's lower cavity, moving the stagnant air skyward. Silently, Tucker drank from the sensory overload, knowing he must wait a bit longer, until the night animals came out, using their noisy foraging to cover his escape.

He needed one more mental journey, and while praying didn't come naturally, divine intervention had popped up as they'd fled the *Mustika*. It arrived as a wad of paper, torn pages from a Bible that someone had shimmed into the underside of the submersible canoe's gunwale. Initially, Tucker thought it might work as toilet paper, but after a day of drifting, he'd dug out the folded-up paper. It was three pages of Paul's letter to the Romans, with Paul providing instructions to the Christians in Rome.

"Orders," he'd grumbled. "Even in the Bible."

Tucker remembered that day's sunbaked agony and how he'd spoken aloud about his discovery. It took too much effort to talk during the frying-pan days, but at sunset, when the heat started to break, the escapees, a virtual three-man chain gang, revived enough to search for rain clouds and ponder their fates.

Page, almost always positive and invincible, was wearing thin and asked how another world war possibly fit into any deity-designed plan. He was weak with rashes and blisters, and Tucker recalled just how painful it had been watching him paddle.

"How do you think this all fits together?" he asked the other two. "Part of a big plan?"

Neither answered.

"Does say something in here about salvation. Says we'll be saved. Reckon that would be good news."

The other two stayed silent. There were no Allied ships coming. The three of them were becalmed off Sumatra in the Java Sea, drifting through the Bangka Strait, cursing the canoe's creaking. They had reached the point of hating everything.

Baking sun and madness-inducing thirst had stretched them to their physical limits. They were skeletons mumbling various obscenities like prisoners chained to a castle's dungeon wall. Soon enough they would give up talking altogether.

As Tucker stared down at Paul's Roman epistle, it seemed as if a laser beam of sunlight was drilling into his head. Tilting back in pain, he squinted up at the searing yellow ball. Instantly, his vision went black, interrupted by an image of himself in short pants.

He was up on the plateau, looking out to sea. Out beyond the breakers that were tearing ashore at Narrabeen. Out beyond the makeshift boxing ring his father had constructed.

Below him, Long Reef's solitary ridge rose from the Dee Why lagoon. He and his brothers had been all over those beaches, a teen boy's paradise.

On this morning, though, the old man was teaching. How to clinch. How to get into a slight crouch allowing elbows and forearms to shield his stomach and ribs. When to duck and weave. Or counter.

Each of his brothers had been through the same training and knew it was the only way to win Mick Tucker's difficult accommodation. Fight your way to the old man's love. Brad complained once to his eldest brother, but it did no good.

"This is us, mate. We fight. Whether we want to or not. You'll learn quick, or you'll get smashed. It's how the old man is. He learned it from his pa, who got the same from some dirty relation of ours. Rough end of the stick for all of us, hey?"

Brad knew it was true. Some fathers took sons fishing or, on the odd weekend, into Manly, where the pier and diving boards served as a gathering point. The men would amble into one of the many seaside hotels, usually the Steyne, while the nippers thrashed the water.

Not Mick Tucker's kids. On Sundays, the Tucker boys fought short matches up on the scrubby plateau. They fought so often, they didn't need to engage in the normal scrapes that develop when brothers share bunks or work rough chores. They fought, nearly from birth, with each successive elder holding a height, weight, and experience advantage over the next one. Each of the Tucker Five (except Peter) could "punch above his weight" and knew how to avoid a throttling by the old man for whichever boxing sin was committed.

"Oi, Brad. You dropped yer guard there. Serves you right when Ben steps into ya. He should knock you rotten." At this, the old man would generally try walloping Brad or Ben. Brad for being slow and undersized or Ben for using his advantage. "Use yer speed...like a king brown...move yer arse if yer too fagged to throw a punch. Circle 'round him."

Then he'd teach a feinting move or how to reverse out of a clinch. "Drop this shoulder and see if you can get him to throw a cross there. Get the bludger off balance, Brad."

Brad hated fighting his brother but knew no one dared challenge the Tucker boys at school. Their reputation for fighting was legendary. And where the five grew to see each other as rivals and their mean-spirited father as a tyrant, no outsider took them on. It was widely believed that even their mum, with her tea-stained molars and curlers, would put up her dukes.

That momentary vision of home gave him strength. From down on the beach road, the imposing cliff made certain Collaroy homes look like castles, all flashing windows and garrets hanging over the edge. It was a wondrous sanctuary. The heaven he needed.

The Americans liked throwing around the phrase "In God we trust," and the Commonwealth countries always shouted, "God save the king," but the Almighty must've been too busy or distracted. To make it home, he'd need a bit more of Mick Tucker's tough love, special-unit training, and the possibility of marrying Laurel.

C'mon, darlin'. Tell me again that it's safe.

And then, in a mad moment of hallucination, Tucker sensed Laurel nodding her assent. She was giving him the "all clear." Tucker could climb down from the gum's embrace and make his run for Babar, Dutch New Guinea, and finally, Darwin.

CHAPTER 21

23 December 1944—Katherine, NT, Australia

Ilsa's favorite holiday period, three special days that unfolded in magnificent succession, were imminent. Christmas Eve, Christmas Day, and Boxing Day, celebrated by all Australians, would arrive tomorrow. In Austria, the day after Christmas was known as *der zweite Weihnachtstag,* which seemed far prettier than something about boxes.

Ilsa knew they would start singing *Stille Nacht* at the station soon and hand out meager gifts to one another. As in years past, she had encouraged Mutti and Papa to provide extra food to Glenno and his family for their tireless work. The same had been done in Mrs. Gunn's *We of the Never-Never* less than forty years earlier.

Ilsa had long ago built her seasonal calendar around Christmas. It was a time of giving for others, but in the far north, Christmas only meant the Wet was on or overdue. It could mean chicken on the table or possibly lamb. But it never meant snow or glittering icicles. There was one other thing: the finishing of a calendar year.

Glen and his wife, Annie, had consistently been good to Ilsa in ways her parents could not. They explained things as big as Australia and as small as the very dirt she walked on. They couldn't speak on her behalf, since offering opinions to the boss, the Maluka, was verboten, but they sensed her frustration. It was most evident when she rolled her eyes behind Papa's back. Both remained impassive, never letting on or making her mutinous situation worse.

Ilsa tried talking to Glenno about the Alps and mountains covered in snow. Of Franz Gruber sitting on a hillside at Christmastime, writing about a silent night when the white landscape was not filled with gunfire or bombs. How the very same full moon that hung over Australia was there in Austria.

To explain, she tried using lamb's wool and said that after some snowstorms, the land would be covered as far as the eye could see with white fleece. He asked if it was like a red dust storm. Those fiery storms came into Katherine every so often, the sky filled with fine amber-colored sand blotting out the sun. Within minutes, the sifting particles would find their way into everything.

Was snow like a sandstorm? he asked. Ilsa said it was. Except white, of course. And cold. People could ball it up into a snowball and throw it at one another. The stock hand scrunched up his massive nose and snorted about white rain a man could hold or throw. He shook his head of wild, white curls, offering an aside, something she couldn't translate.

Harder still for Ilsa was explaining a world war. How it was that far north of Darwin, men were invading islands and trying desperately to kill soldiers from a country called Japan. The stock hand's worldview did not include bombers, destroyers, or invasions. His country had already been invaded. Instead, he spoke of spirit beings. This prompted Ilsa to attempt to explain her desire to learn his language.

"You see, Glenno," she began, "in my special book, there's a part where the missus—that's Mrs. Gunn—she goes down to the creek to learn the language of the stockman. And she struggles, like I do, with pronunciation. Your words are so hard."

"Have to keep trying, Missa Ilsa. We learnin' your language all the time, and then sometimes when we go too far away, we have to learn other man's tongue. Up Kakadu way."

By this time, Ilsa had learned Glen was a member of the Jawoyn people, with stories centered on the cicada dreaming. Johann, though, was uneasy about Aboriginal folklore and any kind of foreign kindness. This was becoming more and more apparent the longer the family lived outside of Katherine.

Looking back, Ilsa saw that ever since April 1938, Johann suspected everyone. Glenno and his wife were still the only people allowed any kind of ongoing contact with the family. Everyone else, the ringers and stock hands, were hired on a need-by-need basis and efficiently sent off the moment the work project was completed. Ilsa, now in her late teens, was always sequestered away from them.

The most she ever heard from the outside after September 1939 came via the four-valve Argosy radio that ran on a two-volt battery. The brown-paneled machine itself had been brought north from Melbourne and sold cheaply to her father for £7/10 because the aerial and earth wire insulators had gotten damaged in the Wet.

Trained by the Austrian army, Johann had fiddled with the valves and condensers and somehow found and rigged up enough wiring to pick up occasional news flashes. The first big story came in December 1941, when Australian prime minister John Curtin gave his New Year's message and told the country he was no longer counting on England to save Australia but turning his hopes to the United States. Curtin's voice had rasped out of the big permagnetic speaker, and Johann muttered that if the Japanese took Singapore, the Philippines, and Dutch East Indies, Australia would surely follow.

Two months later, the Japanese attacked Darwin, and the Australians started curtailing information about the war. To Ilsa, little of interest came out of the big box during the next two-plus years other than suggestions the Japanese were getting routed and an indication in November 1944 the prime minister had suffered a heart attack.

One of the commentators said Curtin's war minister, Frank Forde, who occasionally stood in as acting PM, needed to be ready for action. Did it matter? War or no war, Ilsa and her brothers worked, world without end, in the paddocks, gardens, and livestock pens.

The maddening isolation gave Ilsa little chance to find out from anyone her age how to think about becoming a woman. Too much remained mysterious. The combination of never-ending labor and absence of girlfriends, those logical open-minded sounding boards, was making Ilsa very steely. Something just short of strident. Severe and on some days, when her brothers misbehaved, cruel.

Turning her thoughts back to the Christmas dinner, Ilsa's mother would need help with the special puddings, breads, and preserved foods pulled from the ice chest that didn't use ice. They would also start emptying the smooth Fowlers jars in the shed where Mutti performed her open kettle canning. They wouldn't get a proper Austrian meal with a glazed ham, but for the NT, it would suffice.

The day would undoubtedly stay hot and humid with the imminent specter of buckets, no mere sprinkling, hanging over them. When the Wet came, the Stulmacher family would once again find themselves isolated, cut off from reaching town without a dangerous river crossing. That usually brought out the card games: whist, bridge, and euchre.

Still, tomorrow was Christmas Eve, and somewhere, someone, a soldier or a sailor was still stuck in a war zone. Ilsa imagined those poor men had it much worse. She, at least, would eat a full meal and sleep soundly in her family's home. Not in some miserable jungle or bombed-out building.

She didn't have other people trying to kill her. There would be no shots fired in the gorge anytime soon. Of that she was certain.

CHAPTER 22

24 December 1944—Sermata Islands, Dutch East Indies

Tucker couldn't believe it. He'd outlasted them all. They were gone.

His legs still shaking, he slid down the tree's wide, gray barrel, hugging it, before reaching the moist ground. Then, bent over, hands on his knees, Tucker drew in three deep breaths before slumping next to the gum.

All over his body, various joints hurt. Worse, his thirst and hunger made him realize he would black out if he didn't close his eyes. It was risky, but his head was spinning. For the longest time, he sat thinking about his situation. If the village elder had been killed, the village wouldn't want Brad in the area. His best chance was getting off the island that night.

Do you have it in you?

He wasn't sure, but as he had done previously, he knew he must keep moving. Otherwise, his struggling spirit might cave in on itself. He could live with his emotional anguish a while longer, but the avalanche of insect bites, swirling flies, leeches, bats, parasites, creeping rats, coiled snakes, and hundred-leg crawlers was burying him alive.

On reflection, Tucker guessed he'd caught everything Mother Nature could throw at him. Malaria, beriberi, dysentery, dengue fever. They all worked on his body with fiendish glee, bacterial armies seeking his mouth, anus, and bowels. Especially when he dozed off. He imagined if he ever reached home, he'd never sleep normally again.

Between clutching vines, stinging nettles, putrid mangroves, knee-deep swamps, and quagmires of quick mud, the torment never stopped. But in every agonizing step, his eyes sought patterns or clues in the unforgiving geography. All of it determined whether anyone ever learned what happened to the Rimau men.

He fought those images, hesitating over every step, scanning for unusual shapes or colors. Vigilant for any oddity that made him freeze or sink silently behind a solid tree.

"Careless or careful," they'd said in training. "One kills, one kindles."

After an hour, Tucker realized the hunters had vanished, ordered somewhere else on their interisland cutter. They had vanished, but they weren't gone. The Japanese were good at "relentless," especially when saving face was involved.

That first night away from the gum, making sure he couldn't be seen from the water, he'd found an old dugout canoe, not far from where he'd been hiding. It had belonged to his executed "friend" and contained one paddle, a fresh coconut, and a small gourd for carrying water.

Poor bugger. Got himself killed on my account. And then I steal his boat.

After loading the narrow boat with as much fruit and ripening coconuts as he could manage, Tucker paddled toward a speck in the ocean the American bomber map called Babar. The island existed about eight degrees south of the equator and was maybe twenty miles at its widest.

To get there, he would need to cross fifty miles of open water, under intermittent clouds. With easterly breezes blowing coolly on his back, the following sea kept moving him along. Then, just as dawn was breaking, an inquisitive white pelican dropped from the sky onto Tucker's sloping wooden bow.

Initially, he'd been tempted to catch the mighty bird and eat it but remembered that Coleridge's ancient mariner had killed an albatross and was forever haunted by his decision. Instead, Tucker chucked the bird a few bits of fruit.

For a while the bird eyed Tucker's wretched state with distrust.

"Oi, whaddya think, Molly?"

The pelican arched and fluffed a wing in response, never once breaking eye contact.

"Back home, your lot has got black feathers round the tail. Not all white like you're showing here. We see your cousins down at Long Reef. Stacks of yas. They're a bit bigger. Hold more fish in their gobs."

Tucker kept paddling, glad for what he treated as female company but ever aware the increasing sunlight meant a Japanese patrol could, at any moment, come roaring over the horizon and the rim of the dugout's smooth prow.

"You know I can't be out here too much longer," he continued. "The island I saw on the map better come up on that horizon in the next thirty minutes, or I'm stuffed. Still, if you've flown out from somewhere looking for an early feed, we can't be too far away. That right?"

At the gentle question, the bird opened its large wings, rearranging itself before returning to its coiled position.

"How about I send you out like that dove in Noah's Ark. That's the reason for your visit, right? I bet Laurel sent you."

Tucker wondered if he was out of his mind talking to the bird like it was a human sitting in the pub. He'd been stroking for more than six hours, every so often switching sides to keep a straight nautical line. Slapping waves and sparkling troughs of varying depths made his effort tiring, but Tucker believed he'd held a solid northeast line amid the South Banda's circular current.

His next thought was about his meager possessions. They included a brown gourd, the ever-present knife, his map, and a paddle. Add a torn singlet, two rotted-out boots, and a few coconuts. He had no fish.

Not much to go on. And me out here talking to a pelican. I've gone mad.

Lifting his paddle from the water, Tucker broadly swung it in the direction of the bird, finishing with a slap of the ocean's ultramarine surface. If he was lucky, the pelican would take wing, giving him a navigational heading.

Following the startled bird's flight, Tucker saw a rising black line of low-lying coast he'd failed to detect in the early-morning mist. The bird's timely flight pattern had come just in time and kept him from veering out into the emptiness of the Banda Sea.

After an hour more of paddling, Tucker navigated his entry over the splashing outer reef, and with a solid series of strokes, rode a long shore break onto a deserted rocky beach. Jumping out, he pulled the dugout up beyond the high tide's last marking.

Scattered across the beach was a series of smooth gray-black rocks giving off the appearance of beached whales or seals. Their distinct waterlines made clear a big set of foaming rollers could take the boat back out to sea. Still, moving it any further up around the island's uneven coastline created too much risk of exposure. If the boat stayed put, he could reuse it. If it didn't, bad luck.

At his feet, he noticed a large orange starfish with round black studs running from each tip up into the humped center. It was magnificent in its construction, with five elongated arms gripping the sand. The creature's core was topped with sharp protective points. Yet on this shore, waiting for the next big wave, it lay dying.

What chance outcome had ripped this iridescent sea star out of its natural environment? Could it survive until the tide came back in? Had it been carried onshore by the same chain of waves that carried one weary Australian to safety? The thought, just trying to understand life and death, perplexed him.

Dizzy, he rested for an hour in a palm-shaded recess, dozing in fits before climbing to his feet and limping up a seaweed-covered scree guiding him toward the island's unknown guts. As a matter of safety, Tucker knew to avoid moving any further inland until his strength returned and he found fresh water.

Wakened early the next day by pestering flies, Tucker began exploring the island's prominent elevation and happened upon a gurgling brook whose origins lay somewhere deep in the island's interior. The rippling black line of water had long ago eaten its way down the hillside, but its presence delivered an idea. He would go up the mountain, keeping the slashing creek and its steep bank to his left.

Within minutes, he'd moved fifty or so yards into a copse of trees, but the stream edge he'd been navigating now started to drop away. One misstep, a flapping heel slipping over the lip of the river's slick chasm, would send him tumbling to his death. He'd snap his neck on the rocks or drown after bouncing down the slope.

Laurel would never know why he had failed to court her. Down at the RSL, they would post on the active service board he was missing in action. Presumed dead. A corpse unlikely to be found. She'd have no choice but to move on…if she hadn't already.

Obscured by trees, Tucker looked back to see a patrol boat approaching the coastline he'd just left. The Japanese were not letting up. There was no choice now but disappearing further into the darkness. Inland, there might be ravines or caves, hidden places for staying dry.

Ahead, he saw nothing but an upwardly sloping terrain. An untamed tangle of massive ferns, vine-draped palms, bamboo, yoli myrtle, pandanus, and araucaria pines. Every step forward would leave a marker.

Frantically, Tucker pushed aside the tall saw grass and dead limbs of the surrounding flora. Insects swarmed his every step, but brushing them away meant one less arm brought to bear on obstacles and obstructions. For a while, he clawed like a deranged man. The vines and ferns, equal to the battle, scratched back.

Pushing through dense undergrowth, Tucker scared off a massive goanna that might've been a giant Komodo or dragon lizard. It hissed with territorial displeasure before scuttling further down the hillside, disappearing among the twisted strangler figs and taro roots.

At his breaking point, Tucker heard splashing water, a sound almost certainly suggesting the presence of a waterfall. He slid down a leaf-slick runoff and, moving among a set of half-submerged cube-shaped boulders, sprang forward into the surging stream. It was bracing, but he lowered himself until only his forehead broke the surface.

As far as he could tell, no one was pursuing him, but his torn trail was easily followed. If he cut across the watery channel, a swirling eddy, and worked his way through a fast-moving section, one where the riverbank was too steep to climb, he could wait and watch.

Here, the canyon's walls narrowed and the current increased, slamming him back a bit, but the alternative option was free-climbing a series of ladder-like cuts, primordial gashes in the land where tumbling stones had smoothed the black igneous rock. It was too risky.

The process of moving upstream required taxing physical effort, and each time Tucker launched himself forward, he grabbed desperately at slippery handholds. In some places, the bubbling stream pushed him backward, filling his mouth. Pausing half in the water and half out, Tucker estimated the uphill gorge led to a volcanic cone.

Limit your exposure. Slow down. Listen.

Fashioning a type of rope from the "wait-a-while" vine he found dangling from one tree, Tucker drew his knife and nicked off the barbs to create a poor man's lasso. With quick practice, he'd figured out how to loop the cord's opening around a prominent crag, enabling him to wiggle his way forward. With each successful toss, he moved forward like a drunken barge operator swinging behind an inattentive tugboat.

Ahead, a massive multitiered waterfall with an inviting viridescent pool appeared. To the right, partially overgrown, lay a stair-like formation in the rocks leading up a trickling overflow. It smelled like a trap because anyone further down the valley, looking ahead, hearing the thundering roar, would likely see him climbing through the cascading spray.

To the left, fanned palms extended like bowing ballerinas over the onyx rock. But it was their intricate root system that provided Tucker his solution. Hand over hand, the tired commando pulled himself along the rough brown tubes, cautiously pulling himself up into the brush.

The abundance of water made him think of food, and Tucker knew if he didn't get something soon, he'd lack the strength to hide for long. Somewhere, nearby, there were pawpaws, kumaras, bananas, and mangoes. If he pushed through another hundred yards, he might reach an area where fruits grew.

Below him, the oxygenated stream tumbled over the rocks. There was a power and beauty to the water, and under different circumstances the numerous water holes would have led him to one of those boyish adventures on the Northern Beaches.

Push on, lad.

Just then, he saw a distinct cleft in the rock wall. It was more of a vertical couloir, a rectangular crack the width of two men, slightly above the water but with an overhang ensuring no one could easily see into it. To find him, a searcher would have to enter the water.

The beauty lay in the angle of the steep bank as it veered out over the river. Encouraged, Tucker hoped he could show the same courage as Page and Sargent.

By God, those Rimau men were rare spirits.

And what was the meaning of Romans 8 about the Holy Spirit? The thing about the Spirit helping a man in his weakness. If men didn't know how to pray, the Holy Spirit would intercede. It said something like "The Spirit will intercede with groanings which can't be uttered."

Tucker was wondering about the groaning when he saw the very thing he feared. A tan-uniformed Japanese soldier moving toward him, doggedly picking his way along the riverbank, and peering forward with great intention. For a moment, it appeared their eyes had met.

Tucker immediately feared the worst. He'd been seen.

CHAPTER 23

"Ahh, shite. They've found me," Tucker whispered.

Silently easing his body out of the water, the Australian slithered toward the nearest covering. If a man was approaching with a gun, staying in the water was suicide.

The Japanese scout, a smallish man in a tattered olive-green uniform, was working his way along the uneven river, watching the placement of his feet and free hand, carefully navigating around the giant roots and drinking from the stream.

As he advanced along the ravine, Tucker saw sweat running down the man's neck. His tunic, soaked with dark stains, was as flimsy as his pants.

Had the tan man been ordered to investigate someone's hunch? That one of the Australians was on this island? But was it also possible this man didn't want this fight? Was just as weary of war as his prey? It didn't matter. One of them must initiate the coming fight.

Tucker hoped the Japanese private was short on nerve and started drawing that conclusion as he watched the man fidgeting with his wet uniform, continually taking one hand off his weapon. Here was the opportunity to surprise. To strike first and kill.

When the gap between the two men was down to twenty yards away, the man placed his right hand around the stock of his gun in order to free his damp shirt again. His anxious eyes kept darting to the darkening skies, as if a torrential downpour might provide an excuse to abandon the mission.

In less than thirty seconds, the two men would meet, and gripping his knife, Tucker drew his thumb along the back of the flat edge. It was time. His commando drill sergeants had rehearsed the men for these exact moments.

Assume a crouch. Give the legs coiled strength. In one motion, bring the tip over the victim's throat. Run the insertion from ear to ear. Drive the blade forcefully through the jugular and windpipe. Rip fiercely through the cords of the neck.

The problem with that plan was evident. Tucker was no longer the warrior the Z Special Unit instructors had trained. He could map out the moves but surely lacked the strength to kill in man-to-man combat.

Is there another way?

Was he strong enough to stick the blade in? To yank it through muscle or organ?

God, guide me.

Watching through the thick foliage, Tucker saw his pursuer continuing along the edge of the stream. When the man was less than fifteen yards away, the Japanese soldier darted a quick glance across the tumbling water. For a moment, he paused, resting his gun on a hummock before wiping his wire-rimmed glasses. Then, lifting his rifle's trigger to his cheek, he panned the barrel at the surrounding trees before freezing.

Did he hear something?

In another ten yards, he'd find Tucker. Did a possible solution, maybe his only option, lie not in a cricket bat, like hitting the German at Deep Creek, but in bowling him out? Could Tucker somehow hit him? A quick glance down revealed a variety of stones. A round one, the rough shape of a cricket ball, launched on target, might stun the man.

Can I throw it hard enough? Take the wicket?

Slouching down, cautious to not create any movement, Tucker blindly felt frantic fingers running over rounded rocks at his feet.

Too flat. Too small. Too hard to dig out. Too...hang on, this one.

The stone was slick with moisture, but its heft felt solid. If he connected, it could kill.

I'll only get one chance.

The Japanese scout was moving again, now with great intensity, his eyes squinting from the light bouncing off the watery pools. He was still fumbling with his glasses.

Coming. Still coming.

Tucker cocked his arm in the standard bowler's pose and tensed. If he missed, he'd have to charge out and tackle him.

Stay strong now. ATTACK.

Calling on his limited Japanese vocabulary, Tucker leaped from his hiding spot, bellowing the single word Japanese boxers feared most: the call to surrender.

"Kosan!"

Tucker yelled it with as much anger as he could muster, before firing his stone.

Caught off guard, the small man was bringing his arms up to cover his face when the rock smashed into his nose. Stunned, he sagged into the stream, dark-red blood pouring over his quivering upper lip.

Tucker was sure he'd missed killing him, leaving no choice but to finish the job with his knife. Lunging through the undergrowth, grabbing at coarse vines and roots, he stopped, amazed to see his armed enemy hastily backing away in defeat. The Japanese soldier had moved off about fifteen yards, his free hand clamped to his face. But then, tossing his gun aside, he knelt as if he were on a summer picnic, and began laying out a thin blanket and dented food tin from his pack. Rising, he bowed toward Tucker as if he were engaged in a sacred ritual, one requiring he make a sacrificial offering.

Let him go, mate. Hold up and leave it to God. Vengeance is his. Not yours.

Not today. The Japanese bloke doesn't want this fight. And neither do you.

The word "kosan" had come to Tucker at the last second. And it had apparently worked, stopping any further pursuit, but when the man returned to his patrol boat, if he ever did, he'd undoubtedly suffer a beating for failing to kill.

Drawing on his Tokyo boxing tour experience, Tucker bowed in return before scooping up the ratty sheet, silver container, wet gun, and a three-inch piece of colorful paper that had fallen from his pursuer's chest pocket.

This enemy had essentially surrendered.

Sizing up the gun, Tucker knew it was an Arisaka, given its long black barrel and bolt-action breech. Strangely, the bayonet was missing. There was one bullet chambered, but the river water would've removed any chance of the gun working. At least until it was properly dried out.

The piece of paper was Japanese currency, a fifty-sen note in faded bluish ink. On one side it showed Mount Fuji, the mountain shrouded in clouds.

"That was sure a close one," Tucker said in a conspiratorial whisper watching the small man fade into the jungle's bamboo quilt of greens and blacks. "Bit of a very lucky toss, if you ask me."

"He'll report the attack, which will bring out more hunters. So why didn't you kill him?"

"Because. I didn't need to."

In allowing the man to retreat, an inner verbal battle started to emerge. Tucker imagined there were two of him fighting for his sanity.

"Coward."

"In the kayak. The Romans stuff when I was with Page and Sargent, paddling away from Merapas. It said showing kindness was like pouring burning coals on their heads."

"Maybe you really wanted a completely different outcome?" the first voice said. *"Like maybe if he'd shot you dead, you'd be free from this crap?"*

"Piss off."

"Maybe you thought you'd go all chums and roast up a leg o' lamb."

The adrenaline rush of combat was subsiding, but not the voices.

"So, now what happens? Want to chase him down? Why didn't you kill him?"

"Get stuffed."

If he reports you're here…on this island…you're dead."

And maybe he runs off and hides himself. And never comes out.

Tucker shook his head to clear it. He was wasting time.

The river's steep ravine required scaling, and reaching higher, dryer ground was his priority. After that, he could try finding food and plot the rest of his latest escape. The Japanese patrol knew he was on the island. After he rested, they could try again. Or he might just crawl back down the roaring creek bed and go back out into the swirling Banda Sea.

He would paddle to Yamdena and then the Kai group, the last isolated batch in the Dutch East Indies chain. After that, he'd find Kobror. It was hard thinking about another open-water journey, but staying on Babar was undoubtedly a death wish.

Keep moving, mate. Forage for food, get a kip, keep moving.

Tucker found food while plodding upward toward the island's volcanic roof. He'd stumbled onto plantains and coconuts. Nothing would cure him, but nourishment would keep him going. Especially coconut milk.

Not sensing pursuers, he rested in an unremarkable shaded area near the summit. Cooled by ocean breezes, he scraped out a shallow pit in a leafy furrow he'd discovered. Covered with branches and palm fronds, his trench would let him observe most of the hillside he'd just climbed. If his pursuers came anytime soon, he'd pull the ground cover over him. It might not work, but it was all he could muster until he was rested up.

Over the next two days, Tucker crawled out at dusk and dawn to drink from a spring feeding into the stream he'd climbed. He wasn't getting any stronger in this setting, but the sunlight and food helped fight the deterioration consistently plaguing him.

From his elevated position, Tucker identified the logical track to take and its approximate distance. The island was maybe ten to fifteen miles wide, and if he worked his way east-northeast, he could traverse the island's saddle and acquire a steepish concourse heading down the island's lush flank. It would follow another mountain stream flowing eastward.

A day later, having regained some strength, he'd just started out when he once again heard the unmistakable sound of splashing water. After nearly stumbling over a sharp ten-foot cliff, he came upon a thin cascading waterfall pouring over a rocky escarpment. It was collecting in a smooth, perfectly rounded bowl and was shallow enough for him to see the bottom through the crystalline water. Around its edges, flat sandstone-like rocks had been smoothed by centuries of overflow grinding down the curvaceous surfaces. A flat ledge offered a drying platform.

At the pool's far end, a plunging chute of water gushed noisily out across a stairstep of flat brown rocks and threw up a slight spray of ghosting mist. This flow of water kept the bowl filled, and Tucker never hesitated. He eased his filthy body into the solar-heated basin.

The warm sensation was extreme, and for a few moments, Tucker hung on the edge, savoring the tingling sensation before hefting himself up onto the beveled rock. After months in saltwater, mangrove swamps, and stifling heat, he felt revived. Maybe it was even something more. Refreshed.

Twisting around to check on the Japanese rifle and American knife, Tucker sensed a metallic reflection, a glistening near a low rock ledge about four hundred yards away. It looked like a place with a possible cave. When the same pinprick of light flashed again, he stiffened, slid to the ground, and commando-crawled away from the pool's rim.

What was that? A helmet? A handheld mirror?

There was no question about the light's frequency, he thought. It was deliberate.

Was it a signal? The Jap soldier trying to alert his crew? A distant plane?

There was nothing in the sky and no boats evident at sea. Along the ridge line, Tucker saw no further movement. Had those two strobed moments fired up his imagination? He'd been on high alert for months, but the flash spooked him.

Assume you've been seen. How long do you have?

The silent dialogue drilled into him by commando trainers erupted in Tucker's mind. Fight or flee? But running away created new problems. He either built a boat, stole one, or, illogically, started swimming.

Tucker focused on the light's point of origin. Until now there had been no movement, but as he scanned the brush, he made out the unmistakable shape of a brown, shaggy man ambling over rock. There was no uniform. Based on height, it wasn't a traditional native, but he was certainly dressed like one.

Is he coming for me? Yes. He surely is. Get the knife.

CHAPTER 24

24 December 1944—Katherine, NT, Australia

Ilsa had long ago stopped wondering if Father Christmas would visit their station on Christmas Day. He had come to see them at the grand house in Graz, where the snow would fall on the lamplights and eaves. In town, it piled up around the festive markets that sprang up around the ancient walls. But that was years ago.

For a moment, she wondered whether St. Nicholas needed snow to make things official. That might explain why Australians never made much of a fuss about the holiday. It was too hot, and the people of the NT simply "got on with it." The old saint would not have found any of the powdery white stuff near the gorge. Nor the entire Northern Territory.

Long ago, back in 1934, Ilsa saw herself wearing a taffeta dress and a shiny tiara. She'd been pushed forward by Mutti to make the sign of the cross on her forehead. For this she would receive an apple from St. Nicholas. The traditional procession by the white-bearded saint started with him knocking on their wooden door. They had all been there, watching for him through the frosted window. He'd come that Christmas morning in his long white robe with three dancing devils leaping about in hideous masks. The year before, Greta said her

St. Nicholas brought six demons.

In the outback, young men didn't waste time wearing masks trying to scare children. There were enough hellish spirits among them, including windy dervishes swirling up the dirt, throwing it everywhere, and making sure "chores" were never neglected.

They had sung the songs on Christmas Eve, but other than her little brothers believing in miracles like kindness and an extra helping, that day in Katherine passed like most others. There were the usual chores: feeding animals, tending to crops, oiling equipment.

Ilsa imagined most Australians had never lived anywhere else, so they couldn't hold the perspective of two different worlds. If someone lived on a farm in Katherine, they had never seen snow. And Darwin was "the big smoke." That was ironic because compared with Vienna or Salzburg, even Innsbruck, little Darwin was nothing. A port town with sagging timbers or tarped-off shanties.

Losing herself in a mental fog, Ilsa wondered what had become of Greta. There was no way to stay in touch. Father had forbidden writing, believing any correspondence back to Austria might be traced. What had happened to her friend? Had Graz been bombed? Had Greta met a soldier and married him? Maybe she was already a widow at nineteen. Poor Greta.

Or had Greta's family also gotten out ahead of Hitler's war machine? There was no way of knowing. And what of the hiding place for the film? Had it remained safe all these years? Would her friend have been tempted to do anything with the moving images?

Worse, what if someone knew Greta met with Ilsa that day? Would the Gestapo have come for her? Tortured her until she told where the camera canisters were hidden?

They were not pleasant thoughts for Christmas Eve. Not the kind featuring the Christ child in a manger with wise men coming to visit, escaping from a wicked king intent on killing newborn Jewish males.

CHAPTER 25

24 December 1944—Sermata Islands, Dutch East Indies

The bearded man heading for Brad Tucker moved fluidly through the rough brush, grabbing each tree's low-hanging limbs, propelling himself fluidly. He was moving with extreme confidence, dipping in and out of sight as he hugged the mountain's contours.

Without hesitating, Tucker dropped to the ground, wondering if it was a coast watcher and whether a miraculous rescue could be arranged by radio. But what if...

For months, Tucker's life had depended on trusting his instincts and little else. As he'd seen on Romang, there were times when an escaping man simply took a chance. Right now, he could cover up or prepare to fight.

Slithering along the edge of the rock pool, Tucker reached a point where he held the widest possible vantage point. He'd see the dark man's approach, and from this modest point, he could gauge how to stage the fight to come. There was no time to run because with each stride forward, Tucker's visitor was approaching with a brazen casualness.

It didn't ring true because even though calendar year 1945 was just days away, forty-eight hours earlier, the Australian had scared off a Japanese soldier who probably believed west of New Guinea, the Japanese navy was still in charge.

He's a strange one, this bloke. Looks Aboriginal. Like he's ready to go walkabout.

After a short disappearance, the brown visitor swung up a tree-lined ravine along the edge of Tucker's spring-fed water hole. The bearded man's scant loincloth had not been issued with the dirty military shirt. He was whistling a tune, much like the ones the lads whistled coming out of pubs back home.

And then from out of his mouth came the unmistakable twang of an American.

"Hey there, mister…I can tell you're sittin' up here somewhere in these weeds. Know that 'cause I've been watching you for the last day. Seen you laying around the shack like you was all day lazy. Was starting to think you should pay me rent for squatting on this side of town."

The comment was so foreign, the thick southern accent so improbable, that even as the big stranger kept jabbering away, Tucker stayed silent, covered.

"Hey…cat got your tongue? It's okay, you know. Seaman First Class Thomas Northgraves, US Navy, present, accounted for, and at your service. That's right—the US Navy is here, and it's safe to come out. I'll serve the first round of drinks."

The Black American was now just feet away from Tucker's simple covering, and the Australian marveled at how the sailor moved up the ridgeline like a tomcat. He was healthy if nothing else.

"Yer jokin'" was all Tucker could think to say as he slowly came to his feet, cautiously nudging branches away from his head. It took a moment for him to set his stance, but as his demanding father had taught him, his ever-alert eyes never left the sailor's face.

"Ahh, there you are."

Alive with caution, Tucker simultaneously used his Japanese gun barrel and pig-sticker to brush away the mint-colored palm leaves he'd just finished drawing around himself. His hands remained protectively curled around both.

The American didn't seem to notice the gun or else didn't care. Dropping the rifle, Tucker stuck out his scratched right hand.

"Sublieutenant Brad Tucker. AIF."

"Well, what do you know about that?" said Northgraves with a firm shake. His warm greeting made no sense. "Ha. I knew you couldn't be too far yonder when I sent you that signal. Used a bit of quartz and conch shell to get 'er done."

Tucker stared at the man in disbelief, his brain struggling with the improbability of a Black Allied soldier on this island. It made no sense.

"My bleedin' word. What's a Yank sailor doing out here in the bush?"

"I was gonna ask you the same thing. Yer an Aussie, right? That's what that *A* is in AIF, right?"

"Too right it is. And am I ever glad to see you. You beauty. But hang on… where are we, and what are you doing here?"

"Ho, ho. I get that all the time. Well, truth be told, I haven't gotten that in two years or so. I guess it's been about that long since the *Houston* went down."

"Oi, slow down," said Tucker. "You were on the *Houston*? That means you were with the *Perth*. Both boats sank in the Sunda Strait in 1942. Got slaughtered there."

"Sure did. Both of 'em sent to the bottom in a matter of minutes. Don't know if too many men from either ship survived. So, you're an Aussie, eh?"

"Yair. Been on the run about three months. By the by, any of them rotten Japanese bastards around up here? Should we be keeping low to the ground?"

"Nahh, they don't come inland these days. Too dangerous for the little pissants. They fear the Wild Man of Borneo…even though we're nowhere near Borneo."

"Said your name is Tom, right? I had a mate back home in Collaroy with that name."

"That's great. Pretty common name, I guess. There was even a book once called *Uncle Tom's Cabin*. That didn't help me none. My folks sure didn't do me no favors naming me Tom. And how about you? Where y'all from? I can't say I heard that part clearly."

"Collaroy. It's near Sydney."

"Aha. Me, I'm from Mason Neck, Virginia. That's near Washington, DC.

By God, it's purty good loggin' and farmin' country when we get enough rain and the tornados aren't killing us. I expect yer hungry. Am I right?"

"You are. I'm starvin'. What I wouldn't give for a proper feed."

"Great," said Northgraves. He dug into a flapped pouch woven together from strips of palm before producing what looked like a reddish shaft of raw vegetable root. "Gnaw on this for a while. There's good juices in it for you. Already had mine for the day."

"Thanks. Back home we'd say, 'I'm starvin' like Marvin,' so you can't know how much your kindness is coming at just the right time. Speaking of home, you got a guess what island we're on? Is it Babar? I mean, if you were on the *Houston*, you're a long way from Sumatra. And that was more than two years ago."

"Had been working my way east toward Dutch New Guinea and Hollandia. Wasn't bothered with hurrying. Just trying to avoid them Japanese sum' bitches. They ain't been around as much lately."

"Good. So, where are we?"

"Dunno. Northeast of Timor is the best I can figure. Haven't seen a map in quite a while…but then I haven't needed one. Been living off the land. Stole a few native boats when I needed 'em. Came ashore here. Built a place where no one bothered me. Set a few homemade traps, poached a few eggs from nests. Birds, turtles, lizards. You name it. If it lays an egg, I've been first into the nest. Mostly, though, I've been waiting for someone to find me."

"Right, see the problem is, I don't have much to offer. An old Jap gun with one soggy bullet. A dull Marine Corps knife and a faded silk chart of islands mostly west of here."

"More 'n me. All I had was a jackknife clipped to my belt when I started. Got a bit more as I borrowed from the natives." Northgraves tilted his head at the word "borrowed" to make sure Tucker knew he was bending the truth.

"Hmmmph."

"So, what's your story? How'd y'all get here? And where'd you get that useless rifle?"

"Pinched it off a Japanese private couple of days ago. Other side of the island. Further down the west side track. He'd been sent out to find me, but I knocked him back. He got away."

The two men continued sizing each other up. It was hard coming to grips with the concept of an Australian escapee finding an American castaway deep in Japanese-controlled waters. But for Tucker, here was a partner who could help.

"You should've killed him. Now, we may have to split this joint," said Northgraves, apparently bothered by the Japanese soldier's likely survival. "I know I'd have killed him."

"Yeah, should have. But it just didn't seem right. And here's the strange thing. This bloke kind of surrendered. Left me his blanket and a small tin with rice balls in it. I think he'd had enough of this war, so I figured I'd leave things up to God."

"Lord almighty. Have mercy! Well, yer a better man than me. So, what's your story?"

"I'm from an Aussie commando mission that set out in September forty-four. We were going after the shipping in Singapore. Come out of Fremantle. Got jumped by a Malayan patrol boat. We went into the water around October tenth. We paddled a submersible canoe for seven weeks, but my two mates didn't make it. They're gone now, and so's the canoe."

"Lookin' like we stuck here."

"Not much choice, is there? Funny thing is, I wasn't even supposed to be on the mission. I was an alternate. They had me topside off-loading kayaks when the sub cleared out. She dropped out from underneath me."

"How many men in your unit?"

"We were officially twenty-three. I made twenty-four. I'm probably the last one going. They likely killed the rest. Gives me the shits."

"As it should. But look at the bright side. You've got your little swimming hole. Fresh source of good water. Could use a few ol' gals to liven the place up, but I guess we can't have everything during a war."

"Too right, mate," said Tucker. "It's sweet and all, but tell me how you survived the sinking and lasted so long. We heard they were rounding up Yanks and Aussies all over Java the first month you geezers went into the drink."

"Lucky, I guess. I had just finished bringing coffees up to the bridge when the final fight broke out. The *Perth* had already gone down. Captain Rooks, well, he went right after them peckerheads. Straight at 'em. We fired at their cruisers, but then a round hit us, and boom, everything around me is flyin' splinters, smoke, and flames."

"Were you scared?"

"Yeah, it was pretty hot on that deck," said Northgraves, his drawl ever broad. "But then we started listin'...tiltin' hard to starboard...and not long after, I heard our bugler blowin' 'abandon ship' on the ship's PA. Then the ol' *Houston*, well, she just kind of rolled over. I don't 'member the details too good. The old girl, I reckon she went down fast at the bow."

Tucker tried envisioning a big boat sinking fast. The water would have been filled with thrashing sailors.

"What happened next?"

"I seen some of these crates floatin' nearby, and I made for them. Growin' up near water and all, I could swim. But some of our sailors couldn't. And the rip through the Sunda Strait that night was strong. Taking all us straight out toward the Indian Ocean."

"What'd you do?"

"First off, I climbed on a few boxes, but then I had to keep ducking. Jap sailors were shooting us. And I mean poppin' men surrendering. Just blastin' 'em in the water like fish in a barrel. It was a slaughter. Hate every one of 'em sum bitches did that to us."

"Seen any Aussies from the *Perth* at that point?"

"Nahh. Not originally. But later I did. The *Perth* went down near us, but like I said, they got hit first. After we went down, there were boys everywhere, on rafts, rescue rings, boxes, all of us thrashin' in the water. For the next day or so, half-dead sailors were turning up everywhere. But the more men in a group or raft, the easier it was for them to get shot. Japan's navy was already in Java, unloading troops. All of 'em, pouring like mad ants into Batavia."

"So, you stayed in the water?"

"As long as I could…but I had to come to shore at some point and make a run for it. Was hopin' I'd meet up with the Dutch or someone friendly but kept to myself. I could hear riflemen on land firing at men as they come up out of the water. Strange as it sounds, I figured I was safer stayin' in the water. Or near it. Gettin' out of Dodge was my goal, if you know what I mean."

"Don't know much about Dodge, but good onya, mate. Somehow you made it."

"Yeah. Pure luck. I grew up outdoors, so I'm comfortable sleeping rough. I'd come ashore at night. Sleep a bit. Finally, I took to the hills. Didn't trust anybody. Hid out, found a flint and machete, stole food. Mostly papaws and coconuts. Then, I headed southeast. Went through a lot of empty plantations. Kept hopin' I could steal a boat. Wasn't to be."

Northgraves's voice was a welcome salve, but in the back of Tucker's mind, tickling his subconscious, he continued worrying about the Japanese soldier who had seen him.

"Looks like we've both beat the odds, but we're still a fair cow from home. These two other lads and I paddled down the entire Sumatran coast from further north, the Rhio Archipelago. You know, Bintang, Batam, that lot…but then they couldn't go on. I have to finish the job. Hard to believe I've made it this far. And as good as meeting up with you feels, I'm not out of it."

"Not hardly. But tell you what. Let me bring you back to my place and get some food into you. You're looking like you haven't had a decent meal in a good long spell. Maybe put a poultice or two on those infections of yours."

The American jutted his chin down the hill, leading Tucker along the palm-strewn trail he'd previously climbed. Behind them, the fiery sun was sinking lower in the pink-orange western sky.

Barely able to keep up and using the Japanese rifle more as a crutch, Tucker hobbled after Northgraves, hoping the American had more than pulpy roots back at his camp. He also began calculating what it would take, physically and mentally, to get back on the water again.

If there was plentiful island food and no enemy troops, it meant there was a low risk of getting captured. Maybe they could wait out the war, luck into a battleship, and get home. Maybe. But it wasn't going to be like 1943 and Operation Jaywick.

Food sounded like a luxury. Particularly since Tucker was nothing but wire and whipcord. Back home in Australia, they would've said he was as skinny as a nine-penny rabbit. It would not take much to bloat his stomach.

"You've gone quiet. What are you thinking, Mister Brad?" asked Northgraves as they worked their way around a thick strand of bamboo and headed in a looping way toward a leveled promontory of ferns and tall grasses.

"Wish I knew how far to the next island. We weren't even remotely studying this area before the Singapore raid. When we started paddling, Captain Page knew about Romang, Leti, Sermata, and then Babar. Which is where I think we are. But if we miss the next island, Yamdena, we're done for. Plus, the Wet is due, and that means whitecaps and tiger sharks."

"Depends on what you're sailing in."

"Say again?"

"Depends on the boat. Back home, one of our expressions is that if you have trouble, you're up the river without a paddle. Course, we don't have many rivers or canoes where I come from, but that's beside the point. We won't be in a canoe. We'll have to go in something local, with fresh water in tins, good fruit, a guide who knows his way around, and a motor. That would be a different story, wouldn't it?"

"Wait a minute. Are you saying there's a boat like that on this island?"

"For certain. Up on the northern tip. I've seen it before. I imagine the local headman uses it to serve up native supplies."

"Stone the bleedin' crows."

"Huh?"

"That's unbelievable. We get some sleep and grab the boat."

"How do you like that? You land on my island and all of a sudden like you start giving out orders. How about if we slow down and feed you. Nurse you back to something more than a walking beanpole. Figure out what the enemy is thinkin' 'bout doing. You clobbered one the other day, right?"

"Yeah, but…"

"Think 'bout it. Look at the crappy rifle in your hands. I'm telling you, if those bastards are around, I ain't going down to the beaches carrying some an old gun that don't work, a jarhead shiv, and a jackknife between us."

"Yeah, sorry 'bout that. But listen, I was just trying to say I've got a lot more appetite for the next leg of this escape if there's something seaworthy to consider. A Malayan junk or Timor prau. How long a walk is it to have a look at this beauty?"

"Less than half a day. But now I'm the one needs time to think. I've been here almost a year. Everybody's left me alone. If I'm pulling out o' here, I'd like some assurance what I'm getting into. Not saying I won't go…just saying I'd like to think about it over dinner. You still hungry like Martin or whatever his name is?"

"Marvin. Hungry as."

"Okay, that's more like it. Let's settle in at Fort Northgraves for the night. I'll show you that boat in the morning. Might get my tired ol' self motivated to make a run for it."

CHAPTER 26

Northgraves's bivouac looked like something out of *Robinson Crusoe*. Rugged and entirely spartan. Which didn't matter because Tucker felt safe making small talk about food with another Allied soldier.

The heavily bearded Northgraves said he'd become a hermit on Babar. He'd adapted to the near isolation while watching Japanese activity around the island. Like a hidden coast watcher without a wireless. He guessed brown-skinned natives in the region knew he was there but had decided to leave him alone.

For the last year, the Japanese patrols had landed on the island less frequently, but then, during the last two months, he'd noted a flurry of naval activity. Northgraves said he mocked their infrequent visits from a distance, watching the empire's wind-shredded flag, with its red ball, receding in the distance. Something had stirred them up.

"They chasing you, ain't they?" he said, approaching his smoldering fire pit, tending to a few embers. The gravel in his voice sounded like a man who didn't get to talk much.

"Reckon they are. It's why I've kept moving. To avoid getting run to ground."

"Wonder why I'm not getting the same treatment," Northgraves said while coaxing a small flame into existence. Next, he took a hanging burlap bag from a branch and poured a measure of rice into a burnt coconut husk.

"If I had to guess," said Tucker, "it's coz we attacked them. Right outside Singapore. Caused 'em to lose face. Last I heard, the top officers have to kill themselves for stuff like that. Think it's called Harry Carey."

"Hmmm…"

"But mate, in your case, you were having a go at them. You got sunk but did the honorable thing by escaping. Those buggers don't tolerate surrender. It's bad form. In training, we were told to fight to the death if we got surrounded coz the Japanese never give up. We heard from some of the boys that made it out of the Philippines that they'll just shoot a man or bayonet him if he surrenders. Even chop off his head. Right on the spot. Healthy or not."

Tucker spit away from the fire in disgust. The American broke some lengthy branches down and moved the kindling closer to the fire.

"Wonder if Uncle Tojo knows the game's up? I mean, we're winning out there, right?"

"Hmmm. You haven't heard anything since February 1942, right?"

"Yeah, been a while, hasn't it?" Northgraves dabbed a bit of his cooked concoction on his dirty finger and tasted it. "Needs another minute, okay?"

"Sure, no worries. For the last two years, we've given it to 'em everywhere, with your side doing most of the heavy lifting. Back home, our PM was mad as hell at the Poms. Says he's done with England. Turned us to counting on America. That's why he's given them the MCG."

"What's that?"

"Big cricket ground in Melbourne. It's a military base now."

"You mean, like a big baseball stadium?"

"Yeah. Anyways, the American navy's been working their way up the islands that lead to Japan. Reached the Admiralty Islands in May. But who can tell who's winning for sure?"

"Whaddya mean? The marines must be making quick work of them."

"Not so fast. This past March, Japan was supposedly invading Western Australia. Every man and his dog got shifted around. Turned out, it was faulty intel."

"So, what you're saying is nobody knows nuthin'."

"Yeah, that'd be about right. The Japanese were having a go at India about the same time, which means they still have some fight left in them. Last I heard, the Yanks were in the Marshall Islands, starting on Palau. But that'd be old news now. I haven't a clue what's on. I know the Kaiser is taking it on the chin in Europe."

"Crazy, isn't it? Two of us sitting here around a campfire on some island like we're on a fishing trip. Course, back home I doubt we'd be fishing together. Me being a Negro and all. We'd never do this together."

"I guess that's right," said Tucker. "Wish it weren't the case coz it's all rubbish in the end. But I dunno. Given what we've both been through, it'd give me the shits if someone said we couldn't be mates."

Tucker wasn't sure about his answer, whether he'd said the right thing, but didn't bother to ask for a response. It was a difficult topic, one never discussed back home, and at the moment, he felt his thinking was jumbled. He was barely functioning. Without medical supplies, his condition would worsen. Food and rest would help a little, but any chance he had of surviving depended on the American.

Fighting his fatigue, the Australian noticed Northgraves had whittled a few utensils from his surroundings and designed his fire pit to shield the flames from any distant visibility. He'd also built his bed frame off the ground using bamboo timbers and then softened it with various pandanus leaves. It wasn't extravagant, but the dirt trails through his camp made clear Northgraves was grounded. This was his nest.

"Mate, my guts must be shot up from the grubs and rotten tucker I've eaten the last two months. So, tell me what's on the menu tonight. I haven't had Shanghai Surprise since the last night on the sub."

"It won't be much. See, a while back I snuck down the hillside and grabbed some rice from their storage shed. Must've been about two weeks ago. They came in late one afternoon on their motor launch. Got smashed on sake. While they slept it off, I crept in and dragged away a couple of bags. Been miserly with it, but tonight, we celebrate. We'll mix in my version of collard greens and a bit of mango."

"Can't wait."

"Lookin' at your overall appearance, I think we need to make sure you don't come down with scurvy. Gots to add some vitamin C into your diet. You look like a bag of old bones."

"The proverbial sack. That's me, mate. Fact is I don't know how I've kept going. Just stubborn, I guess."

"Dumb luck," said Northgraves, smiling.

The rest of their meandering conversation covered the length of the war, Allied victories, Japanese atrocities, their escape routes, missed food, and the possibility of rescue.

For a hermit like Northgraves, three years of news was like watching a movie-length newsreel. His brown eyes were bright with amazement, and each new battle or political upheaval brought on a new set of questions. Finally, Tucker claimed exhaustion and asked where he should lie down.

The American offered his bamboo bed and pushed aside a few things, creating space near the fire. Both men agreed they'd start figuring out an approach for the local boat in the morning.

"One other thing before you hit the sack, Mister Brad."

"Yeah, what's that, mate?"

"Do you know who won the forty-two baseball World Series? I know y'all wouldn't be following American baseball…but I've been wondering about it the last year or so. Like whether the New York Yankees won again."

"Couldn't tell you. Not many of us were thinking about sports. They canceled the Olympics in 1940, and then, like I said before, your mob took over the G in Melbourne. They even shut down the Shield, the interstate cricket. Guess saving the world's been a bit more important."

"Good idea. See, I was just curious. Sport takes your mind off things.

Listen, get a good night's sleep. We've got a big *game* tomorrow if you're up to it."

"No fear. As we say back home, I'll be right as rain."

Tucker closed his tired eyes, trying to hold on to his dim goal of moving east toward New Guinea. Falling into a deep sleep, he was still wondering how the two men would reach the next island.

CHAPTER 27

It wasn't long after dawn when the two men awoke.

Tucker recalled dreaming about finding himself surrounded by angry German sailors, but then waking up to see the fire's glowing embers and was comforted by how that reassured him. He was drifting back to sleep when the Virginian started asking questions about the war and forcing hospitality on his new arrival.

Lying on Northgraves's improvised bamboo bed, Tucker's immediate goal was crossing the island's serrated face and reaching the island's leeward harbor. Staggering to his feet, he saw doubt in Northgraves's eyes.

"You're wondering if I can make it, aren't you?" asked Tucker.

"Sure am. Y'all look like death warmed over. Crippled and broke up. Shot to pieces."

"Last night was the first time in forever that I slept where I wasn't worried about something chewing on me. Or ambushing me."

"That's a good start. You and Marvin hungry again?"

"You know I am."

"Good. We'll see how you do with some rice and banana."

After breakfast, the two men descended a forested slope, moving from the cooler ridge line back into the humidity of the lower jungle. Walking downhill, Tucker leaning into and bracing himself against each trunk, they agreed on the weaknesses in their plan. First and foremost was detection by the Japanese. At any moment, from any obscured area, they could find themselves attacked.

A second one was understanding that by engaging a local tribesman, they'd learn too late if he'd been bought off by the enemy. Thinking their luck could last even a day longer ignored what every gambler knew: the tables eventually turn. Tucker couldn't dwell on the negative if he wanted Northgraves to pack up and leave, especially since the natives had apparently come to accept sharing a small portion of their island with a Black American.

The big decision was determining whether to steal the boat or convince an islander to provide an interisland transfer. If they stole the boat, they'd lose navigational knowledge. On the other hand, if they asked for help, they rolled the dice.

"Think the kanaka running this skiff would take the gun in exchange for ferrying us?" Tucker asked as they approached the bay where the boat was tied up.

"Can't hardly say," said Northgraves. "If he gets caught with one of their rifles, it might get him strung up by the next patrol that comes in. But these islanders don't have much firepower. So the chief might like showing it off."

"If that piece of junk impresses him, and he'll guide us, I'd trade it straightaway. I don't fancy stealing his boat. We don't know the tides, the reef breaks, or where Yamdena is."

"I agree. For what it's worth, though, we mightn't have much choice. Once we come down out of the hills and the headman sees us, he's either gonna help us or sound the alarm. What I'm saying is, if it doesn't go to plan, we take the boat by force."

"Agreed. I don't like the thought of waiting near shore where he can see us or trying to race back up that hill with them chasing."

"They come here twice a day. Early in the morning and late in the afternoon," offered the American. "And the headman takes his siesta in the heat of the early afternoon."

"You think we could creep up on him while he's knackered?"

"Maybe. I think if we get close, we either walk up on him friendly or surprise him."

"Wonder whether he speaks any English," said Tucker absentmindedly, scratching at an insect bite. The red welt around the open wound was inflamed.

As they reached a heavy section of hanging vines, Northgraves motioned for the two men to stop. There was no sense pushing into an open space when they could rest in the shade. In the near distance, they heard waves rolling onto the beach. Finally, after almost two hours, Northgraves signaled it was time.

"Let's stroll in on him like we make local check-ups all the time."

"A fine sight we'll make," replied Tucker. "My oath."

Emerging from the hillside's jumbled shadows, the two shipwrecks saw the local tribesman tending a fire in a grove of coconut trees. Twenty yards away, his battered launch was tied up in a finger-like channel fed by one of the island's many streams. The crystal-clear creek sheltered the narrow-beamed craft nicely.

As a seagoing vessel, it wasn't much. The battered gunnels looked like nothing more than lashed-bamboo poles. The hull looked strong, likely made from an island gum with generous amounts of sealing resin. Tucker guessed the salt-and-oil-stained four-cycle outboard motor was a fifty-horsepower unit from the mid-thirties. Likely slow but reliably steady.

The squatting native, a brown man of about forty, did not react at finding two bearded men approaching from the island's scrubby clutches. In fact, he kept stirring his coals, his eyes never leaving them. When the two were nearly upon him, he let out a strange guttural noise that made no sense to his visitors. If it was a greeting, it sounded pained.

Rising to his feet, his black hair hanging thickly behind his head, the elder nodded as if he were greeting two field hands. Tucker thought him about five foot seven, maybe 140 pounds with a squarish face, darting black eyes, massive pug nose, and a piece of bone through his nasal septum.

He wore a deeply stained shirt, and next to him sat a woven bag covered with feathers. His leathery arms were muscular, far more so than either of his White guests, and his powerful legs extended from his trunk like ham hocks. He wasn't tall, but his low center of gravity ensured he'd stand his ground. If things got physical, he would win easily.

With Northgraves making no move to speak, Tucker took the lead, his shaking hand firm on the Arisakas.

"G'day, mate. How ya goin'?"

"'Mercan?" asked the native, squatting back down while moving a leaf-wrapped object out of the fire.

"Nahh, mate. 'Stralian. But this bloke's a Yank."

"Jap man not like."

"Reckon they wouldn't. You speak English, hey?"

"Little. What you want?"

At this opening, Northgraves carefully extended his arm as if to shake hands. He was ready to talk.

"I've been on this island a while—you know, up in the hills—and my friend here, Mister Brad, he came by to visit. Been showing him around, but he wants to visit a bigger island. Told him you might be able to help us. It's Yam-a-dena, isn it?"

"Yamdena." The native considered Northgraves but didn't take his out-stretched hand.

"Okay, thought it rhymed with Pasadena. That's where they play our big Rose Bowl football game every January."

"How you pay?"

"You can see we don't have much," said Tucker. "Reckon we could trade you this rifle."

"Jap man gun. No good. They not like you have. Or me have. Plenty trouble. Shinohara kill hundreds at Emplawas village."

"I dunno anything about that. One of their men gave it to me the other day, other side of the island. Looked like he didn't want to fight anymore."

"Fighting all bad," said the islander, spitting a stream of red betel juice on the ground away from his two visitors. "Islands different now. Bad Dutch then. Bad Jap man now. Bad, bad, bad. Want all go away."

"Righteo," said Tucker, sizing up the native's displeasure. "We're just as keen, but we need help. How far to Yamdena on your boat?"

"Go at night. Come in on morning tide, near side of island. Away from Jap man boats."

"If you'll take us, we'll leave," said Tucker. "We don't want to be here any longer. We're trying to get to New Guinea."

"Much danger," noted the brown man. He spat again in the same spot, but this time it appeared he was hesitating, as if he were hatching a scheme on the spot. "Very far."

"But we…"

"You pay in fifty coconuts, fifty bunches of 'nanas. Go get. We leave tomorrow night. When sun is all the way down. Go 'way until then. Not good you here with me. Everyone see."

Tucker and Northgraves looked around to see who might be watching, but there was no one. Done talking, the brown man turned back to his fire, unafraid, and began unwrapping the taut vines he'd used to hold two blackened fish in a broad leaf. Each one was roughly six inches long. Tucker guessed they were stream-caught in an eddy from one of the mountain streams. They'd been cooked in the ancient way, the shallow pit serving as a convection oven.

"Coconuts and bananas, you say? How about forty of each?"

"Fifty and fifty. Now go 'way."

The smell of the cooked fish tempted both men greatly, but more exciting was sensing they'd booked their one-way voyage. If the situation didn't turn into an ambush, it had gone easier than expected. There was a fare, but they could keep moving toward New Guinea.

"No worries, mate. See you tomorrow night. We'll bring the goods with us."

The native grunted and continued poking his coals. He showed no inclination to invite the two starving men to join him.

Shrugging their shoulders, Tucker and Northgraves moved back into the jungle, conversing on what had transpired and how to handle their ferry fee. Northgraves didn't seem worried the islander would betray them.

"Cheeky bugger," said Tucker.

"They can get coconuts and fruits whenever they want," said the American. "For my nickel, he's just lazy. Wants us to do his work. I bet that's his chore when he comes here. Collect fruit and coconuts. Bring them back to the chief. He's just an errand boy."

"Maybe. At least he's willing to give us a go. Confident little bludger. There was two of us. With a gun no less. If he wasn't careful, we coulda nicked his boat and left him sitting there with his baked fish."

"I'd be careful about that plan," said Northgraves. "We might get to Yamdena on his boat, but his people would find us and bring a posse out to settle the score. Listen, as we said before, he knows the ocean currents. We don't."

For Tucker, the choice was clear. Work for the native or stay hidden at Fort Northgraves. The latter option still held notable risk because the native knew there were two White men on the island. And the Japanese soldier Tucker had beaned with the rock might return with a full patrol.

"Right you are. Listen, I'm good with trusting blackfellahs. Truth be told, one of 'em—and he paid for it—saved my life two islands ago. Let's find his produce and deliver them."

"You better be good with this," smiled Northgraves, "because, right now, you got no choice. Remember, I'm awake while you sleepin'."

After returning to camp, the two men discussed the best locations for coconut collection and storage points for payment the next night. For the rest of the afternoon, there were trees to climb and a host of other decisions to make.

"Think he turns us in?" Tucker asked during their evening meal.

"Nope, and I'll tell you why," said Northgraves. "If he was going to sell us out, I think he would have acted friendly and kept us around with food. He would've assumed we didn't know their schedule and might've thought the coast was clear. Instead, he sent us away. Proof's in the pudding. Otherwise, someone would already be up here scalping us."

"We know he didn't follow us back into the bush…at least not that we know of. So, he doesn't exactly know where we are. Then again, this island is pretty small."

"That's true," said the American. "But tomorrow night, we can scout all around his boat before bringing in the goods. Make sure we check for a trap."

As the moon began its nightly climb over Northgraves's camp, both men slumped down in the leaf-covered dirt. They'd used the last of their waning energy, with Tucker stumbling frequently, but collected the required number of coconuts for the morning. They would pick low-hanging bananas early the next day.

"What do you say we wander back to my swimming hole and wash off?" asked Tucker. "Reckon it would give us a lift."

The Black man looked exhausted from the day's exertion but happily pushed his large hands down onto the dark soil before climbing to his feet. It was evident a warm Christmas bath under the stars didn't sound half bad.

CHAPTER 28

25 December 1944—Katherine, NT, Australia

As a Christmas present to herself, Ilsa rode Dandy down toward the muddy river, humming her version of an Aboriginal songline. Her father had given everyone the morning off from chores, and the thought of a refreshing swim in one of the streams feeding the Katherine sounded like a logical way to assess her growing frustration.

Her biggest concern was an overwhelming sensation no one in the family, particularly her mother, understood her angst. The war closed some doors, but her father's paranoia about the Graz filming closed the rest. At nearly twenty, she felt like her life was slipping away.

Riding down the steep trail, confident in Dandy's familiarity with the track, Ilsa believed the most important thing to worry about near the water was crocodiles. Reining Dandy loosely, she made for a point where Leight Creek widened into an almond-shaped rock pool. It was grassy for the horse, and she could safely ease her way into the stream.

Removing her boots and rolling up her long pants, she stuck her legs into the rushing water. The sensation was satisfyingly cool, and leaning over, she splashed handfuls onto her bare arms and face.

It was glorious. Momentarily postponing her swim, she climbed up on a giant slab of red sandstone, deciding she would listen to the silence. In the quiet that followed, she felt as if a supreme presence, maybe God, was attempting to connect with her. She was certain it was how Glenno's people felt about places. A human could link oneself to this ledge, flowing water, or infinite sky. In the relative silence, she began recognizing her own breathing. It felt like she could hear the air in her chest.

The sensation was unusual and made Ilsa think about churches and religion. It didn't make much sense. What was its purpose? The family hadn't been to a formal service in years. Was God testing them? Or were they testing God?

An alternative thought was emerging, and it involved the Dreamtime concept Glenn had tried explaining. The one about finding harmony with nature. Hadn't the family stock hand talked about an Earth Mother? Was this peaceful feeling what he meant? Was there an invisible maternalistic spirit?

"It's rather amazing," Ilsa said aloud. "I get the feeling you're trying to tell me something. Like you want me to listen a little more carefully."

For the next few minutes, she let the sun play across her face. Other than the river's burbling, the canyon's magnificent silence enveloped her. Slowly, though, came the twittering of birds. Magpies or kites. Finches or blue and orange kingfishers. Crafty cockatoos pecking at something hard.

There were other noises too, and as her ears became more attuned, she made out a scratching in the dirt. Across the creek. It was as if the entire area was coming alive. It wasn't crackling like the burning bush they wrote about in the Bible. Or crafty like a voice calling in the wilderness. Whatever it was, it didn't matter. For that moment, she had no worries.

She could afford to stretch out on this smooth stretch of ancient lava and close her eyes. The heat coming off the rock would dry her feet and face. A gentle nap would let her dream her way out of the gorge.

Instead, Ilsa found herself in a familiar nightmare. She was back in Graz, handing the films over to Greta. Explaining how the round silver cans were dangerous. She couldn't say what they revealed, but one day she could come back for them. The canisters must stay in the secret hiding place until Ilsa returned.

Greta, you must never look at them. They show Hitler coming to town and him visiting the Zell mansion. But you must never know more. If you try to look, it could kill you. Please, Greta. For both of us.

And then the image of the Reich's fearsome minister appeared. Goebbels was chasing the two girls. He had elongated arms, like an octopus's tentacles, and was reaching for them. His hooded eyes burned bright, as if they were on fire, his pallid face contorted like that of a demon.

Ilsa and Greta were running as fast as they could, but Goebbels was keeping up. Now, Ilsa was falling behind, her lungs seemingly unable to pump enough oxygen and blood to her heart. The terror of Goebbels catching her made her twist and stumble.

She could feel his hand on her shoulder. It was shaking her. He would send her to the concentration camp at Dachau. The one near Munich that Father mentioned that long-ago night in 1938 when she'd been warming her feet by the fire. She would die there. Alone.

Gasping, Ilsa snapped out of her nightmare to see a huge man standing over her, his face obscured in shadow. She was about to scream when the Stulmachers' gentle stock hand bent down, extending his hand.

"It's okay, Missa Ilsa. Don't go yellin'. It's me, Glenn. You havin' a bad dream. Making you upset. Best now if you take Dandy back to the station. 'Member this is Bolung country. Maybe not such a good idea to be down this way. Bad things can happen down here. Many bad things."

CHAPTER 29

25 December 1944—Sermata Islands, Dutch East Indies

Late that afternoon, the two escapees returned to the boat, each carrying a single coconut and a bunch of plantains. Their plan was to play it "light," largely because an enemy patrol had arrived earlier that day before speeding off to the east. No one had come after them.

"We've got more of these for you and nearby," Northgraves said good-naturedly, "but it would go faster if you can give us a hand."

"Not helping. Driving boat. You bring what we agree on. Put in boat."

"What a tosser," Tucker offered when they were out of hearing range. "He can see we're not up to snuff."

"Agree with you, but there's not much we can do. He's enjoying havin' slaves on his plantation. Him givin' orders for a change. I tell you this: when this rotten war is over, these islanders ain't never working for no Dutch, Japanese, English, or anybody ever again."

Tucker didn't care. He'd push coconuts into the clearing with his nose if it meant the islander kept his word and they sailed that night.

"Orright, we're jake. We'll pace ourselves. Let's make sure we don't drop our guard. This work will tire us, but we'll want a bit of reserves when we drop the final lot. Maybe carry less each time but make more trips."

Northgraves agreed on the plan. Slowly, the sweat building on each man with each step, they worked at finishing their task. They stacked the coconuts and bananas, each time sneaking curious glances at the native's craft.

As Tucker had thought, it was nothing special. Primitive with an old white Evinrude motor that might produce ten nautical miles per hour. Maybe more if they caught a following sea. The stern could hold three men with little comfort, but that wasn't its purpose. It was a working boat, designed for interisland trade and transport.

The rough bow, patched frequently with some type of native tar, had endured numerous beachings. Tucker would've wagered the boat didn't displace much water below the gunnels. She'd sit low in the surf and, with breaking waves near the coral reefs, ship water easily. The presence of wooden bailing buckets confirmed his assessment.

The loading finished, the native came over to inspect their work. He rearranged a few piles in the hold, presumably balancing the weight before ordering the two shipwrecked men to push the lightweight prau out into the ocean's shallows.

The sea, coral blue and sparkling clear, felt good. Tucker appreciated the tingling as the saltwater of the South Banda Basin cleansed some of his most recent cuts. It was warmer than the creek, and without hesitating, he dunked his head under.

"Ready to shove off?" asked Northgraves.

"We wait. Wind not right," said the islander as if the American should have been able to read the weather conditions ten miles offshore.

"You're the boss. But hey, what do we call you? I'm Tom Northgraves, US Navy, and this is Brad Tucker, Australian army, I guess."

"Second Australian Imperial Force," corrected Tucker. "AIF for short."

"You call me Lai-lo."

"Lie low, huh? That's a good name for us." As he said it, Tucker glared at the double entendre he was certain Northgraves would soon use. "What's the name of your boat?"

"No name. It's just a boat."

"Okay, got it."

"You need anything else done?"

"We wait. Wind tells us when it's time. Moon too. Moon loves the water."

The words were direct, uttered with generational authority. That suited Tucker. Sitting at the edge of the canal-like confluence of stream and ocean, he scanned the surrounding shoreline. Their exposed visibility didn't stretch more than twenty-five yards, and the soft sound of the onshore break, mixed with the jungle's growing night sounds, produced a cacophony of rumbling moans and evening shrieks.

The gibbous moon soon made its presence known, intent on illuminating and influencing the ocean's tides. Tonight, it was nearly full, and its pale spotlight drifted in and out behind the evening's late-ranging clouds.

It reminded Tucker of nights back on the plateau, looking out toward Long Reef and the moonlight dancing on the parading waves. He thought about Laurel standing somewhere looking at the same sky. Maybe she was wondering where he was. The thought calmed him.

Somehow, some way, I'll see you again.

Northgraves, removed from his daily rituals up in the hills, still hadn't come to grips with moving on. It was one thing to wait for a US Navy PT boat to finally show up and heroically rescue him. It was another risking all the quiet security he savored.

"Hey, Tucker," he whispered, "what do we do when we land on Yamdena? If he puts us ashore at some deserted spot, we're back to scrambling. We'll damn sure be a lot less comfortable."

"Can't say for certain, mate. For two months, all I've known is heading east-northeast. Hunting for a coast watcher. Ain't seen one yet, but by God they're out there."

"Yeah, I did the same thing. Until I stopped running and set up shop. Figured when things quieted down, I'd send word for a ride home. Ended up staying put."

"Can't say I blame you." Tucker was fidgeting with the stringy vine that was gamely trying to hold his torn boots together. "I've got a feeling the time's just about right. Yanks are reclaiming the South Pacific. Can't explain it any other way."

"Yeah, yeah. I get that. But I had it nice up on the hill. Good water, good shade. Decent food supply. You sure you don't want to reconsider?"

"It's not for me, mate. You stay if you fancy a longer holiday. I just have a feeling we'll come good with the next island."

"All right, all right, I'm coming. But we better not see any of those bastards. I'd like to keep my head on."

Their discussion was followed by forty minutes of coastal nightfall watching a thousand gunmetal waves march, with military precision, onto the slightly sloping beach. Offshore, a breeze, the product of early barometric pressure from an equatorial cyclone, started to push volumes of water and, in time, cascading breakers.

"Moon say time now." It was Lai-lo. He was smoking a hand-rolled cigarette, the pungent fumes floating toward the two castaways. "We go now. Go east toward come-up-sun."

"Works for us."

The islander's conviction absolute, Lai-lo untied the bowline from a nearby palm and shoved off. With the agility of a jungle cat, he splashed two quick steps in the shallow water before leaping into the boat's stern.

Realizing the finality of his decision and following the red glow near his face, Tucker and Northgraves followed suit, chasing the boat into the water. Grabbing ahold of the gunnels, weak from fatigue and malnutrition, the two Allied escapees clumsily climbed aboard and made for a pair of uncomfortable slats of wood where they would spend the crossing.

With the sound of waves crashing in their ears, the small craft motored toward the reef, the moon creating a shimmering, luminous road in front of them. Tucker knew the routine, but in all the times he'd slipped between islands on various floating devices, this was the first time he'd done it with an engine, sitting high above the water line, comfortably triangulating the stars.

Almost anything was possible, but this night was a Christmas luxury. It had been a long time since Careening Bay. They'd gone into the water near Pulau Laban before moving down Sumatra's coast, across Java, around Bali, up the Timors, and into Babar. Now, as waves lapped at the hull, Northgraves asleep in the bow, Tucker hoped Lai-lo could coax the small craft across roughly seventy-five miles of open water. There was little chance Tucker could've covered it in a dugout.

An hour later, Tucker tried guessing which way the Banda Sea flowed, but the placement of the bigger islands off New Guinea's western neck clouded his calculations. Combined, the semicircular landmass created a spooling motion. An easterly flow might give them ten sea-miles an hour. They'd reach Yamdena just before sunrise.

Tucker cleared his throat above the oceanic din and got the tillerman's attention. "When do you think we'll make shore? Before daylight?"

"While still dark."

"That's how we like it. Not near anyone else, right?"

"Jap man other side. Near Saumlaki. Near his planes. Where he keeps boat."

"Planes you say, hey? Haven't seen any of those in a while."

Lai-lo didn't respond, and Tucker let the silence settle before tilting his head in respect.

"Oi…thanks, for taking us."

With that, Tucker turned his head away, indicating he'd talk no more. Thirty seconds later, Lai-lo nodded in the slightest of ways, acknowledging the courtesy.

"Maybe you all leave us soon. Christmas gift to everyone."

There was a faint hint of pink, of golden warmth just grabbing the rim of the horizon, when Tucker heard waves breaking on an outer reef. Northgraves, still asleep, rode comfortably, a sailor dreaming at sea. In the stern, Lai-lo searched the unidentifiable shore for a distant landmark he alone would recognize.

"Wake him up."

Tucker gave Northgraves a nudge with his foot. "We're close to shore. Nearly there."

The Black man struggled into a sitting position, stretching and yawning, searching for bearings. A faint pinkish-orange glow to the east was emerging, and the sound of waves crashing on a reef was encouraging. Despite the discomfort of his seat, he looked surprisingly refreshed.

"Where are we?"

"Sydney Harbour, mate. There's the ol' coat-hanger ahead of us."

"No, seriously."

"If I had to guess, west coast of Yamdena. Just like he promised us. Not sure on the time. Five bells or so."

"Good crossing?"

"Yeah. Ran with the wind all night. Smooth. By the way, I talked to the skipper. Sounds like the Japanese have an air base over here."

"You're kidding."

"Not according to him."

"Hmmm. When do we make land?" asked Northgraves.

"Hard to say. Maybe thirty minutes. Better shave and come topside," Tucker joked.

"Haven't seen a razor in years. No sense changing that routine."

Out of the corner of his eye, Tucker saw coral lurking below the surface. But Lai-lo was already steering his craft toward shore as if motoring down a fixed highway. His path was clear, and despite pounding surf to their starboard, he easily brought the boat into a protected inlet with barely a splash reaching his deck.

"Looks like he's done this before," said Northgraves.

"Many times."

"Okay, so what's our plan?"

"We thank him and ask for a heading. We light out from there. If the Rising Sun has a base here, they've got a few sentries down this end of the island."

"Great. That's the last thing we need."

"Keep your head up, mate. Could be a coast watcher nearby with eyes on us, marking down this bloke pulled up with two passengers but went off by himself."

"We come to land soon." It was Lai-lo. "Move fast to trees. No talk. Move."

A fine sandy harbor came up under the boat's timbered frame, and both men vaulted over the side, swimming toward the island's waving palms. The submerged shore sloped upward, and finding his feet among a line of scattered shells, Tucker looked back to the boat and pointed toward a specific section of jungle. It served no purpose. Lai-lo had already turned away.

Moving quickly, the two men carried their belongings and a vine-netting of fruit across the sandy beachfront. The firm footing was cool, and reaching a strand of palm trees, they hustled into the island's fringe vegetation. Tucker knew the morning sun would soon bathe the island in spectacular hues of pink, aquamarine, and gold, making any movement visible from afar. He halted them near a darkened cluster of trees three hundred yards from the sound of the crashing surf.

Walking any longer in the emerging daylight was too risky. Instead, for the next fifteen hours they would hunker down, talking in whispers, letting small, carnivorous creatures discover them. Their inactivity would provide a feast for the curious insects.

"Come dusk, we'll push over to the east and see what Brother Jap has got on."

"I didn't have these worries a week ago, you know," said Northgraves.

"Mate, like I said to myself a while back...when I was pinned inside this gum with a sniper sitting right above me, 'you're in for a penny, in for a pound.'"

"Yeah, I'm in for that penny all right. Nickels and quarters too."

"Hey, no worries. We'll get a feed and see what tomorrow brings."

"That's what I like about you, Tucker. You're pretty upbeat for a skinny little pissant."

"And what I like about you is you cop it sweet and think it's Bush Week."

"What?"

"Too hard to explain. Rest up. We'll check things out tonight."

Once dusk finally arrived, with no beach activity noted, Tucker and Northgraves collected their travel satchels and moved steadily southward along the shore's uneven tree line. They would move counterclockwise around the island, hoping to meet friendly humans. If they didn't, they would stay hidden.

Walking about a mile of uninterrupted beachfront, they found a dirt road snaking its way out of the jungle. In the near distance, a truck's motor was turning over. Growling. Was it the edge of the Japanese base?

Tucker motioned to Northgraves to slide in among the clinging vines and thick loom of the biggest banyans. With extreme caution, the Australian commando pushed forward, crawling up a slight rise until he could see what lay on the other side. He motioned with his arm for Northgraves to crawl up the earthen berm and join him. What he saw was unimaginable. Nothing short of impossible.

CHAPTER 30

"My bleedin' word," said Tucker in disbelief. The short Japanese airfield contained an Australian plane he recognized. "That's not possible. It's a Bristol Beaufort."

"A what?"

"A four-man Aussie torpedo bomber. Used to make 'em outside of Sydney. She's an all-rounder, a strike fighter. Not very fast, but fast enough."

"Yeah, great…how do you know all this stuff? Wait, don't answer that," Northgraves hissed. "Just tell me what it's doing here. And where's the runway?"

"Over there. But it looks far too short."

Northgraves inched his way further up the muddy earthen promontory to look at the landing strip cut diagonally into the island's core.

"Wonder how they built it? Damn tricky beating back the jungle there."

The best solution Tucker could offer involved Allied prisoners hacking it out with machetes. Americans, Australians, New Zealanders, and other POWs must've died constructing the single runway and operations building.

"You think so?" Northgraves asked.

"Dunno. That's just a guess based on what I've heard around the traps. For that bomber to be here, though, it must've come out of Thirty-One Squadron's operation at Coomalie Creek near Darwin. But I thought the Thirty-One flew Beaufighters. Maybe it came out of Goodenough on the Rabaul raids. Sometime in 1943. Wonder what her crew got up to?"

"Probably got shot," spat Northgraves.

"Maybe they got her somewhere else and floated her in here. When they set up this base."

"Do you think she still works?" Northgraves asked about the nearly fifty-foot-long plane and curious runway.

"Hard to say. The Japanese would've smashed her up if they had no use for her. Could be they tried getting over Allied positions in disguise. Or maybe they're studying its design. Did you know there's no copilot seat in a Beaufort?"

At the word "design," the American looked up. As if the idea he'd been forming was too big to tackle.

"I'm wondering...hmm." The American scratched his ragged beard as if he were calculating a difficult math problem. Next, he started itching the back of his head before moving back to an area under his chin. "If we waited until nightfall...nope, that wouldn't work...but if we were able to...no..."

"C'mon, lad...out with it." Tucker knew Northgraves was struggling with an idea.

"See...if we...nope. That dog won't hunt." Northgraves stopped speaking and began absentmindedly picking at a scab on his arm.

"Oi...what're you on about?"

"I know how to fly." The American blurted it, a sheepish, near-guilty grin creeping across his face.

"What?"

"I'm not saying I'm registered or even any good, but when I was at college at Howard, before the war, I wanted to be a pilot. See, at my college, which was just for Blacks, there was this instructor, Chief Anderson, and he started teachin' Negros how to fly. I was learnin' some of the basics, but then the war got goin' in Europe, and he went off to train the Tuskegee Airmen down in

Alabama. I tried gettin' into that squadron but washed out early. Took it pretty hard. Came home, drank a bit. Ended up in the navy."

"Go on..."

"To tell the truth," he stammered, "I wanted to be a fighter pilot so bad. Used to spend my spare nickels on flyin' magazines like *Dare-Devil Aces*. Lots of folks were signing up. There was even this football star from Washington, DC, named Wilmeth Sidat-Singh. Played at Syracuse and then some semipro basketball. He got in. Listen, sorry 'bout my sports stories. That's the thing I think I miss most from back home. Anyways, turned out my eyes weren't good enough. When the navy got hold of me, they just made me a steward like other Black folks. Sent me to the Pacific. My point is...tell me, is that bomber Australian or English?"

"Fair dinkum, it's Aussie built. Good enough for the Brits too. We were making 'em for the Poms to use up in Singapore. You know how that turned out. Complete cock-up. Shambles. But the Beaufort's not for defending. She's more of an all-rounder."

"So the control panels would be labeled in English, then? That's the main thing."

"Too right they would."

"That means if she was fully fueled, I could fly us out of here."

"Yer jokin'."

"I'm not. I know what to do. Sort of."

"Mate, let me see if I have this right. You want to nick the Beaufort, from right under their flamin' noses, and fly her home?"

"I'm not saying it's a piece of cake. But if they gassed her up...then we got the jump on them...we might get airborne. Course, I might crash her if it was dark...'cause I didn't see something...but I'll tell you this much. I'm thinkin' I'm done with jungles. Had it with all this. Maybe it's time to go home. What do you think?"

Tucker was without words.

He'd met a few Americans during the war, and most talked big. Or talked to hear themselves. But this Black American who'd even gone to college was suggesting the unimaginable.

"I think you're a lunatic, cobber. A true-blue lunatic. But if you think you can do it, then we're away." He pounded the American's shoulders to show his support.

"Hey, quiet down, you crazy cracker. We can't get too excited. They might still have patrols operating. The reason I hesitated was because I can't figure out how we get on board."

"Steady on, hey?"

"What I'm saying is we've got forty yards of open space to cover. They'd shoot us like ducks at an arcade. So then I start thinking about the length of the runway. Like how I'd have to taxi down the field before turning her back around."

"What we need is a diversion. Get 'em distracted to buggery."

It was here the Australian recognized a familiar assignment. Neutralize a ground force by drawing the enemy out to a different location. But there were questions to answer. How many men worked this post? Was there fuel in the warbird? Were they even flying this warhorse?

Northgraves watched Tucker working it out. "What are you thinking?"

"That it can be done. Maybe not easily. But there's a way."

"So, who does what?"

"Remember the day we met? Back at that little waterfall?"

Northgraves nodded.

"I said I'd been part of a commando unit. We specialized in demolitions, detonations, raids behind enemy lines…that whole bit. Did some training up in New Guinea."

"Yeah…go on."

"I can get us on that plane."

"What's your scheme? See, back in the States, when we're underdogs, we talk about the plan. We draw up a secret map and stuff. So, how does it work?"

"Ahh, keep forgetting you Yanks like a yarn before you go into action.

First, we get into their ammo dump, grab a jug of petrol. Then we light it off at a different location, create an explosion, maybe some fire in the bush. Their soldiers go investigate."

Tucker guessed the American was uncertain. *He's wondering if he can get her off the ground. The two-seaters he flew in Virginia probably had wingspans under twenty-five feet. This runs closer to sixty.*

"Then, you get on the plane while they're distracted," said Tucker attempting to allay any doubts. "Then come get me down the far end. Lastly, we fly due south to Melville Island or Darwin. Should be pretty simple, right?"

CHAPTER 31

25 December 1944—Katherine, NT, Australia

"Oh, my goodness," Ilsa gasped, catching her breath. "What are you doing here, Glenno?" Above everything else, she wanted to mask the shock of finding the grinning stockman standing over her.

"Out looking for witjuti grubs. Find 'em down here near the river. In the wattle trees."

"The white worms? Ewww. Do you eat them right away or cook them?"

"Either way. Usually roast 'em up back home…which is where you should be headed, Missa Ilsa. Maluka not pleased to find you down here by yourself. Missus Heidi neither."

"What do they taste like?" she persisted, her eyes wandering to where she'd hobbled Dandy, the leather strap keeping the horse from wandering away.

"Dunno. Just taste good to me when Annie cook 'em. Crunchy."

"Glenno, I want to ask you a question about something. Before I head back. In the Dreamtime, are there ever bad people or evil spirits?"

"Plenty. Doolagahs, Waa. Bunyip. Last one, Bunyip, he comes out of water-holes to get you. Fishgirls do too. They hide in rockholes, some not far from here. Eat people all the time."

"In my dream, there was a bad man chasing me. I was so afraid he would catch me. And then, thank heavens, you woke me."

In her mind, Ilsa presumed that early in his life, the stock hand had learned no good came from trying to help Whites interpret dreams. No matter what was offered, the Maluka or his sons were likely to disregard the warning. But the Stulmachers were different from legacy Australians, and the boys were too young. She hoped Glen saw her as trying. As someone who listened because she was willing to learn.

"Our women better at telling dreams than me," he said. "If you want, I'll ask Annie tonight. But she'll tell me this is Bolung's doing. Where we are now, he all around us."

"I don't know about that. There's so much I don't know. But you're right about my getting home. Papa will think I've run off. I can't have that happening. At least not yet."

She smiled at the thought of escaping to a new life but suppressed letting her imagination gallop off toward Mataranka or Alice Springs. Leaving Katherine, especially as a single woman, heading off to a bigger city with lights and shops, seemed like an impossibility.

"You head on up to the station. I'm going to stay. Keep searching for food. Best you get back on that trail and keep things peaceful."

"Remember, now, tomorrow is Boxing Day," she said, "and there's no working. It's a special day. A gift from our mob to yours. That's what you would call us, right?"

"That's right. Not sure why we're getting the day off. Something to do with your Jesus fellow. Celebrating him being true blue."

"That's pretty much it, Glenno. He was a good bloke who tried to help others."

"Got hisself killed for his troubles, Missa Ilsa. But no worries. Me and Annie will stay away tomorrow. Maybe cook up some 'roo and damper."

Ilsa climbed up into her saddle while the muscular man, his brown skin reflecting the sun's warmth, resumed his search for the wood-eating larvae. The thought of eating a fat, wriggling worm was discomforting but once again confirmed how little she knew about surviving the harshness of the NT.

"How will you prepare your kangaroo?"

"Standard way. Start with fire. Singe off the fur. Let coals get going. Then we place 'roo right in the fire. Do some scraping after that with knife."

Glen was not looking up, and Ilsa wondered if he was angry. As if she was keeping him from shopping around. It amazed her how much food the Aboriginal men and women could find in places where she saw nothing but sand and shriveled scrub. She resolved to keep seeking simple lessons from him whenever there was time.

"Living here is hard, isn't it?"

"Why you say that? Our mob been here long time. Creator give us plenty. Living fine until last hundred years."

"Then the English came, right?"

"Yes'm. Whitefellahs. All coming from different tribes. Just like with us when we go walkabout. For secret men's business. Seeing clans down south or out west different from us. Using other words in their country. Sometimes we fight, but we share same Mother. What I mean is, Mother Earth."

"I guess the White people changed things. I mean, the way we live on the land."

"Very different. And ver' hard on us for not thinking exactly same. Important for whitefellahs to *own* the land. Build houses. Jawoyn people, we see things differently. Land owns us. Nobody can own this place. Belong to Creator."

Ilsa wondered how she would approach things when she was older and the important achievement for her new family was buying a station or building a house in town. Would she remember this talk?

"Thank you, Glen. Thank you for trying to help me understand. I'll see you in a few days. That's the plan, okay? Remember to ask Annie about my dream. I want to know what it means."

CHAPTER 32

27 December 1944—Sermata Islands, Dutch East Indies

As Tucker and Northgraves had long known, no war planning ever went to plan. Ever. There were too many variables with inexperienced humans doing unexpected things. All at the last minute.

Waiting through the heat of the next morning and afternoon, pinching off curious ants and centipedes, cleaning or sharpening their knives endlessly, and inspecting their surroundings, the two men noted little Japanese activity around the bomber. It was quiet. Almost too quiet.

One Japanese soldier left the control tower shack every so often to check the two planes and stare with some annoyance at the structure's wispy radio antenna. Each time, he shook his head furiously before fiddling with a device that rotated the metal and wire structure.

Two other Japanese soldiers lounged outside in an area adjacent to the living unit. Besides one wooden and canvas tent, they had a small garrison of supplies. Finally, at one point, one of the men approached the Beaufort, climbed in the hatch, and started the bomber up. It roared to life.

In profile, the Beaufort looked like a mash-up of different aviation designs. The cloudy, Plexiglas nose sat just below the cockpit, while the tail of the plane was inordinately thin, thanks to a bulbous midsection. Taken as a whole, the dirty fuselage looked ungainly, if not susceptible.

No Allied bomber was particularly fast, and this one, like most military planes, would have trouble gaining enough altitude to clear the jungle's tallest trees at this end of the runway.

"I tell you what…we're long odds," said the American. "We can't afford to veer southwest because if we miss the Australian mainland, we'll run out of fuel over the Timor Sea."

"Don't worry about it. If we get out over the ocean, I reckon we'll be happy as Larry."

"I dunno about that."

"Before tomorrow morning, we need to give this ship a proper name. There's nothing painted on the nose that I can see."

"You mean something like *Miss Delores*?"

"Delores is a mean old auntie of mine on my mum's side, so I'd give that one a miss, but *Laurel* could work."

"Laurel, eh? What's the story there?"

"Ahh, a girl I like back home. In my fever dreams, she says when it's safe to get movin.'"

"Dreams, huh? That's as good a name as anything I've got," said Northgraves. "Let's hope *Miss Laurel* takes care of us. I'd like to get out of here before some enemy patrol stumbles on us. But, first, Jessie James, tell me how we pull this bank job off."

Tucker squatted down and cleared away some leaves and sticks before sketching a scale-model of their plan on the jungle floor. He started by scratching out a rough rectangle in the dirt before smoothing in the diagonal Japanese runway.

"This brown rock is our plane, and this nut is their tower," he said moving the small objects like chess pieces. "They don't matter to us yet. This little stick does. This is their barracks. We know they've got at least one recon plane. That's this white stone."

"Then what?"

"Okay, first, down toward the far end of the runway, I create the diversion with a homemade explosion from their petrol that we'll nick tonight."

Northgraves was staring at the dirt map and the specific spot where Tucker indicated he'd distract the Japanese.

"This is the taxi line, start of the runway, right?" Northgraves drew his thick brown thumb through the dirt. "After I get on board and fire her up, I run her to this pivot point."

"Right. And while the sentries are running over to where the commotion is, I maneuver to the same spot...where you pick me up."

"Just like that."

"If you don't, I'm stranded. If you're dead on the ground or killed in the plane, I'm on my own. One other outcome is they kill me. In that case, you fly out solo."

"I don't like any of those options."

"No worries. Just leave that hatch door open coz at some point, I'll break from the brush and dash to the turnaround. You can't help me. You slow down a little before gunning the engines and taking off."

"How will I know you've made it?"

"Mate, they'll hear me hollerin' in Sydney if I'm on board."

"You make it sound simple."

"Yeah, but let's not stir up more snakes than we can kill. Right now, we're a chance. But a lot can go wrong fast."

Just before the next morning came, with one can of petrol safely stolen and the jungle's itchy, uncomfortable darkness beginning to reveal the earliest streaking pinks of a stunning sunrise, it was time for action.

Creeping into position, Tucker went over the specific steps one last time. The Australian would leave first, circumnavigating the runway until he was past the midway point of the hard dirt airfield. Northgraves would wait for the diversion before boarding the bomber.

"You're right about your preflight checklist?"

"Yup. Pretty sure. I check the fuel transfer valves, gear switches, and cowl flaps."

"Right. Let's run through it one last time. There's going to be a lot of knobs and levers."

"Master switch—on. Battery switches and inverters—on. Parking brake—released. Booster pumps and pressure—checked and registering. Carb filters—open. Won't matter on the fuel because we'll have to make do with what's in the tank."

"Last night you mentioned pruning the engines."

"Priming," he corrected. "But that's after I've started the engines. And then only if she's coughing. You know, running thin or rough."

"And you're good with all the dials?"

"I'll have to be. The key ones are the gyros, RPMs, and mixture controls. To make sure they're automatically rich."

"All right, mate. You sound like you know what you're doing. That Anderson bloke must've taught you right. Take your time when you get in the seat. Get it right the first time."

"Hope so," said Northgraves, smirking. "First and last chance I'll get."

"You'll be right. I'm not going to make you more nervous. I'm away. Keep your head on. I'll see you 'round the traps."

"Good luck. Next time I see you, Mister Brad, is on *Miss Laurel*."

Northgraves watched Tucker disappear into the jungle, making for the distinctive palm tree the two men had identified near the beginning of the runway. It stuck out from the cleared underbrush. When the Australian was in place, he'd wave a long branch perpendicular to the tree's leaning trunk.

Seeing the signal, just before the fireworks started, Northgraves would make his move, sliding down the small bank, before sprinting to the plane. On entering he'd pump fuel into the engines, hoping to God the Japanese mechanic had blown out the fuel lines. One of Tucker's last pieces of advice was warning Northgraves about the sentries possibly shooting at the plane. Northgraves should keep low in the elevated cockpit. They might shoot at the windows first.

In the end, the plan relied on Northgraves doing something he'd never done before. Sneaking onto a plane, starting it, and piloting his first solo flight.

CHAPTER 33

Moving off to his left, Tucker soon grasped that his physical weaknesses were slowing him down. It would take much longer to reach the diversion point.

He skirted the edge of the runway, but the stolen petrol can's weight, with its sloshing fuel, plus the rifle, had winded him. At one point, while it was dark, he'd considered coming out onto the airstrip but decided against it because the first pinkish rays of morning sunshine would soon illuminate the field.

The jungle's predawn stillness heightened Tucker's chances of stepping on something that would sound an alarm, drawing the enemy's attention. Precious time was passing, all of it placing Northgraves at a distinct disadvantage.

Well, there's nothing for it. He'll have to make do.

When the Australian reached the massive tree they'd identified, he found a ten-foot branch and trimmed it, leaving just a leafy tip. Then, with consistent up and down thrusts, he began waving it. Thirty seconds later, he saw Northgraves come out of the undergrowth, moving with caution toward the bomber.

Careful now, mate.

Finished with his branch-waving, Tucker began working on creating a sustainable flame in the early-morning humidity. For that he'd brought some dry coconut straw as kindling. He started by digging a small, foot-deep hole to house the petrol can. By walling the tin can into a shallow shaft, the pressure would blow everything skyward. Adding two barky logs on top, both drenched in petrol, would create a bit of fiery display.

Soaking a handful of banana leaves with fuel, he shoved them down along the sides of the can, ensuring a sustained flame. Then he crawled away. The tough part was successfully jumping a spark into his gutter of shavings. The delayed fuse. Past efforts in training camps never failed, but now, with the sun climbing by the minute, the clang of his knife blade on a flat stone echoed loudly.

Noises from the waking jungle, hoots and cries, were common. As he knew, the chaos of the jungle created its own rhythm, and an unexpected metronomic slashing, metal on stone, would stand out. To resolve that challenge, Tucker staggered his pace.

"Jesus wept," he said aloud, before his conscience took over. *Steady on. You can do this.*

His preselected kindling was not the problem. It was his spark tossing. A good strike would send a streaking flash. A weak glancing blow, at the wrong angle, dulled his knife and failed to generate the blue-orange dart he needed.

Tucker was reaching a moment of utter despair when a comet of light leaped from the blade and ignited the dry straw and trace amount of fuel in his capped-off trough. The kindling glowed. For a fraction of a second, Tucker stared in disbelief.

Blow on it, you mad fool. Blow like blazes.

He lunged forward, issuing a long, urgent breath at the ember.

You little beauty.

"Fire going. Check," he said, going through his mental checklist. "Build the primary and backup. Soak them in gas. Scratch out the runner between the firepits. Put a stopper in each. Drizzle both sides of the trench. Screw the cap on. Jam it back in the hole."

Issuing each command, he followed his own orders. It was all going to plan when the flame on the starter pile began flickering. Dimming. Diving across the trampled dirt, he blew carefully, just barely holding on to the nibbling flame.

Bugger. Double bugger.

Tucker transferred the fire to a midsize leaf to jump-start a larger stack of branches. Somehow, the kindling held its glow and started the jittery journey to the petrol can. With every second, the flaming petrol's appetite grew.

Turning to his left, Tucker gathered dry brush and kept building the flame. The Japanese sentry, if he was awake, would soon see a spiral of smoke, hear crackling noises, or pick up on masses of birds taking off.

In training, the commandos used varying types of explosives. Plastique, fused grenades, or limpet mines with magnets. Those were favored choices, but the Z Special Unit men also improvised with pressure-activated bombs meant to destroy train tracks or blow up trucks.

Don't need to destroy anything. Just need an explosion. Enough to bring them running.

Tucker saw his fire growing, the stretching red flames getting greedy. It was time to guide them to his homemade bomb.

Pop the first stopper out of the trough. Careful...pay attention.

Rising from his knees to a crouch, Tucker placed dry strands of husk from the primary fire onto his gas line. He needed about seven seconds to scramble away from the planned explosion.

All right now, pull the gate and get gone.

With a sizzling whoosh, the petrol-rich flame raced across the shallow trough, headed intently toward Tucker's half-buried gas can. There was no value in second-guessing. It either blew, or he'd need to go ba—

PA-WHOOOM.

The thundering explosion was far louder than Tucker had even dared imagine. It was magnificently violent, with auburn flames greedily latching onto numerous nearby trees. The nearby birds let out startled howls while bits of flaming stick and log soared upward. Smoke poured from the black hole in the ground and nearby brush.

Blinking in shock, Tucker stumbled away from the concussion's source to watch the Japanese hut. Hopefully, all of the sleeping soldiers would pour out, racing down the runway toward the disturbance. In the best scenario, Northgraves got on the plane, started it up, and the whole operation took less than five minutes. Leaving the bigger plane unguarded, the outpost would come to Tucker while Northgraves engaged the engines and taxied down the runway.

Hopefully, they don't think to shoot out the tires.

The first curious thing Tucker saw was how the brown-uniformed sentry didn't return to the barracks to sound an alarm but instead raced to the sandbag-lined machine gun pit. Leaping over the edge, the man unlocked the safety mechanism, fed a round of shells into the gun's ammo feeder, and pointed the gun toward the explosion.

The gunner was keenly focused on the source of the billowing flames but instantly began yelling for his comrades. That caused three agitated men to pop out of their canvas hut in various stages of dress.

One man, waving a pistol, raced toward the two planes. He looked at the Beaufort before veering off toward the sleek two-seater stationed further afield. Tucker released a pent-up breath of relief, seeing the aviator dash to the recon plane, pull the wooden chock, and clamber onto the silvery wing.

Jumping into the cockpit, the pilot pulled harnessing straps over his shoulders and initiated his preflight protocol. The craft kicked to life, and after sliding the cowling forward, the Japanese pilot motored away from its stand, heading for the runway.

His orders must call for immediate retreat if they get attacked.

While the pilot revved the engine, a second man, notably smaller than the first, charged out carrying multiple sets of pilot headgear and a small leather pouch stuffed with loose papers. Tucker guessed the man running toward the plane was carrying away their secret codes.

As the second man reached the plane, the clear covering was pushed back and the roaring plane came to a halt. Without waiting, the smaller copilot began climbing up onto the wing. In less than thirty seconds, he had burrowed into the second seat and was jerking the cowling shut as the plane roared down the strip.

Good news for Tom. Two down, two left. The machine gunner and one other.

Tucker couldn't see the American at the far end of the runway, but with the flames from his explosion settling down and the recon plane just lifting off, this was the moment when Northgraves must snatch their ticket for home.

Luck to you, mate. To both of us.

A few seconds later, the American was running, hunched over, scurrying for the big plane's tiny entry. The entire time, Tucker listened for a machine gun's roar and the barking staccato of almost-certain death.

To his adrenalized relief, he heard nothing but the fighter plane's engine. The diversion was working, and after Northgraves finished kicking away the wheel blocks, he slipped through the plane's side hatch, apparently undetected.

The real challenge, the point on which everything now hinged, was whether the Black American, who'd had a few lessons, could start the bomber. Both men had agreed once the Japanese soldiers on the ground saw the big plane coughing to life, someone would come running to investigate.

Don't think about getting shot, mate. Get into your pilot's seat and fire her up.

Tucker shifted his weight, imagining Northgraves moving forward in the plane's tight fuselage. The cockpit's tiny glass instrument dials would glitter in the early-morning light, differing from anything the Virginian had ever seen.

Northgraves had said he'd been taught to go through a complete checklist, but on this morning, he'd face unique challenges. At most, he'd get a few seconds to initiate the proper start-up sequence. But then, like a prayer answered, the big bird's engines began rumbling, with her giant propellers spinning around.

Northgraves had figured it out.

You beauty.

The plan they'd mapped out in the bush was specific. Grab the figure-8 steering wheel and take a breath. Scan the dials. Release the brakes. Open the fuel lines. Pop the engines. Then, without waiting, roll forward and taxi into place. The last preflight instruction Tucker had mentioned was telling the American not to strap into the pilot's seat. If anyone managed to climb on board, Northgraves would need to defend himself.

No sense dwelling on that. Machine gunner is staying at his post. Leaves one other.

Watching the bomber's slender nose wheel with great intentness, Tucker emerged from the jungle knowing Northgraves was seated and using the steering controls to turn the bomber's bow.

Okay, it's now or never, mate. Give 'er the gas. And come get me.

CHAPTER 34

Miss Laurel's lightly used engines had indeed roared to life, coughing out smoke, sputtering with indignity before the torpedo bomber's two eight-foot-long propellers started spinning in synch, propelling the bomber forward. The American was lining himself up for the runway.

The Australian hoped the plane's movement might confuse the Japanese private, the last man, because he would not have seen a pilot enter the craft. What mattered most, though, was praying that same confusion kept the machine gunner from blasting away at the tires or fuel tanks. As Northgraves guided the plane away from the hardstand, the lone remaining Japanese soldier began running alongside the Beaufort, banging on the side, grabbing at handholds.

You may have to deal with that, mate. Before you get to me.

The Australian hoped Northgraves would ignore the pounding and the distinct possibility the sentry might wedge his fingers into the Beaufort's metal framework, getting dragged forward, screaming over the roar of two radial-piston engines.

Tucker had predicted such a possibility and instructed Northgraves any attempt by the Japanese to enter the moving bomber would mean, for the first few seconds, the attacker would be vulnerable, needing two hands to enter the plane.

"The jackknife," Tucker yelled into the wind as he emerged from the jungle onto the runway. "Leave her going forward and go back to deal with him."

All at once, a syncopated rip of machine gun bullets tore into the tail of the plane, the slugs running forward in a rising pattern toward the cockpit's starboard-side window.

Jesus, Joseph, and Janey...keep comin', lad.

That was the moment Tucker felt himself jerking upward and spinning around like a boxer walloped by a left hook. He didn't feel the initial pain or see the slender blossom of red, but by the time he'd collapsed on the ground, he realized a bullet had grazed his leg. Now, with Northgraves maneuvering the plane into position, he must find the strength to reach the wing.

"Keep coming, Tommo. Get here. Fast."

Northgraves was soon pivoting the bomber onto the head of the runway while Tucker scrambled like an agitated crab under the bomber's belly toward the port hatch. Rolling forward past the tail wheel, Tucker had a clear view of the Japanese soldier who had chased after the plane firing successive pistol shots into the plane's interior.

One might've hit the American because Northgraves fell backward. But then, bouncing back up, he shoved the hatch shut again. Distracted by this development, the smallish Asian man never saw Tucker come up behind him.

Using the noise of the twin GM-Holden power plants to mask grunts of pain, Tucker walloped the man in the knees with the long-barreled Arisakas rifle. As he crumbled, Tucker hit him again in the back of the skull. The smaller man was unconscious before he hit the ground.

"Northgraves, reopen the hatch. Open it up, mate, it's me. Open up."

"Crap on a stick, the hell's going on out there?" said the American, sticking his head through the opening. "You need help?"

"Give me a hand up and get out of the way. There's bullets flying."

Reaching down and using a wrist-to-wrist grab, Northgraves roughly yanked Tucker in before racing back to the pilot's seat. The hatch resecured,

Tucker began two-arming his way through the plane's cavernous belly toward the cockpit.

"Give it all you've got," he shouted. "That machine gunner's drawn a bead on us."

"You got that right."

"Go right back past him. Give 'er the goose."

Northgraves didn't need a second verbal shove, and with Tucker positioning himself behind his pilot, the American eased the throttle forward, sending the fourteen-thousand-pound plane hurtling down the runway. They were nearing the trees at the far end, bullets ripping into the plane's rear, prop-wash rushing past them, when the wheels finally lifted. The *Miss Laurel* was climbing out of Yamdena.

For a moment, the plane sputtered. Tucker knew if they stalled or kept dropping, it was over. Northgraves quickly adjusted his flaps, and the bomber, tilting to starboard, roaring at its misuse, cleared the runway's large gums with no more than ten feet to spare.

"Good onya, mate," yelled Tucker.

"Lucky, I'd say," offered Northgraves, looking behind him at the small pool of blood accumulating near Tucker's tattered boot. "Best get that wound addressed. Or tied off. I'd help, but we pitchin' pretty wildly up here. No free hands."

As the plane rose, the last few bullets pinged off the Beaufort's wings, gnats failing to bother the careening hawk as it thundered into the early-morning sky. By that point, both men were hollering from a mixture of joy, relief, pain, and shock.

Two minutes later, the stark reality of what they'd achieved hit them. At a cruising altitude of just under three thousand feet, Northgraves needed to plot a course over the empty Arafura Sea. They must reach Australia or would smash into the ocean, disappearing without a trace. They also needed the Japanese two-seater that took off before them not to come investigate.

"You know, it would've been closer to fly to New Guinea," yelled the

American as Selaru Island appeared out the narrow side window to their west.

"Nothing doing. If we flew north or northeast, we might run into the fighters they keep up that way. But they won't fly south."

"Okay, but let's hope those bullets didn't hit anything. And that we have enough gas. Or I remember how to land a plane."

"You'll be fine," Tucker screamed. "What do your gauges say?"

"Course heading 180, due south with two half tanks of fuel. Pilot must've been siphoning fuel from this one to keep that fighter loaded. If I don't climb any higher than two to three thousand feet, we shouldn't burn too much. Better still, we won't need oxygen."

"Perfect."

"But remember, I've never soloed. This is my virgin flight. We better not hit any weather. We also better hope those peckerheads didn't hit any of our oil lines."

Scanning the horizon, Tucker thought it best to not comment on the ominous cloud bank gathering force about ten miles directly in front of them. After two months of paddling through them, he knew all too well what ocean storms looked like.

Escaping in the bomber with just a gashed leg and Northgraves' grazed skull had been miraculous. Outrunning Mother Nature and the start of the Wet was entirely different. It was this simple: when Mum got angry, someone paid. And gauging by the size of the towering cumulonimbus coming at them, she was already worked up.

CHAPTER 35

Mother Nature was indeed on a tear that afternoon and willing to throw all the wind, rain, and kitchen sink she could find at the Arafura Sea between Yamdena and Australia's remote Arnhem Land. She wound up, much like a baseball pitcher or cricket bowler, and threw it all.

Massive tropical storms regularly hit Australia's northern coast during the Wet and usually savaged the towns and settlements between Arnhem Land, Gulf Country, and Cape York Peninsula. These atmospheric depressions were always fitful in nature, and regardless of where they started, they soon overflowed the Northern Territory's rivers.

As the rain began pounding the bomber's windscreen, Tucker made small talk from the jump seat situated next to the pilot. He began by telling the American about Australians who lived along the desolate northernmost points of Australia. Inhospitable places like Normanton, Burketown, or Borroloola. The men and women up there often joked God was rethinking His promise to Noah about never flooding out mankind again.

It could rain so long and hard in the far north—solid sheets of water, Tucker said—that in certain years, a few old coots simply went mad from the relentless torrents. Up to a certain point, NT folks would accept the misery of puffy skin, invasive mud, and the loss of livestock. Alcohol helped, but not nearly enough.

There was also little hope for planes or ships that went missing in that region because there were no towns, just remote Aboriginal settlements. Tucker knew one story about an American B-24 that went missing in the NT after returning from a mission. *Little Eva* and the crew's navigator got so far off course in December 1942, the pilot ran out of fuel and slammed into the swamps near Moonlight Creek.

In April 1943, far from the crash site, stockmen found one emaciated survivor babbling to himself in a deserted paper-bark hut. During the Wet, this part of Australia was so primeval that it lay virtually unchanged from the prehistoric periods when monster crocodiles, pythons, and Tasmanian tigers ruled the area. Fresh water was scarce, the sun unrelenting, and feasting insects as deadly as the snakes and crocs.

"So, an all-out nasty place to get lost?" said Northgraves.

"Reaching the Aussie coast is no guarantee," said Tucker, doing his best to doctor his leg wound. "But if we go down in the wrong place, it'll be worse than Babar."

"Better than dropping into the drink," said Northgraves, picking at his own dried blood, his wound more a burning graze than a direct hit. "With no life raft, the ocean gets us."

As if listening for that cue, the *Miss Laurel* started shaking and jolting, making their one-in-a-thousand odds worse. To counter the storm, Northgraves brought the juking plane down to about six hundred feet above sea level, working to hold his roll and pitch stability. It was made even harder, given the relentless wave of water pounding the conical Plexiglas nose and thick side windows.

Below them, the riled-up sea was wild, whitecaps smashing into troughs, and more than once, the Beaufort hit air pockets head on, jolting the bomber. In Tucker's weakened condition, it was taking all his strength to stay positive.

"Mate, at this altitude, we're undetectable on any kind of Australian radar.

They'll never see us in this storm."

"Would be a shame to get through all those Japanese islands, reach the mainland…and then get shot down by our own side. Or crash in no-man's-land."

"Chin up. We're too ugly to pull a Kingsford Smith and just disappear."

"Let's hope. I'm having trouble holding a due-south heading because this storm keeps pushing us from the starboard. I know we're getting blown east a bit."

"Give it your best."

"This won't make complete sense, but I'm going to take her up and sacrifice visibility to see if I can get us out of this storm."

Neither man said anything as they entered a vicious-looking cloud and lost sight of the ocean. The plane gurgled a few times, and then the bottom abruptly dropped away after hitting a pocket. If Northgraves was flying blind, they could easily go roaring past the Cobourg Peninsula and crash west of the South Alligator River and the Coomalie Creek airbase.

Tired of wrestling the wheel, Northgraves made the decision to return to a lower altitude. That was the moment Tucker, scanning the horizon from the Beaufort's front bubble, finally spotted land. Jagged, brown uninhabited wilderness.

Prior to that, neither man had known if they were five miles offshore or had flown far into Australia's interior. In front of them, in the near distance, stretched a wide, dark river. One made much fatter by the raging storm.

Wriggling his way upstairs from the navigator's seat, Tucker yelled as he reached the American. "Oi, cobber, we've got a problem."

"What? Not anoth—" Northgraves was interrupted by a seismic dry-heave convulsion and the fuel gauge warning blaring from a small tin speaker.

"We've overshot Darwin, Tommo. That's the Katherine River coming up, mate. We'll run dry over the bloody gorge."

CHAPTER 36

27 December 1944—Katherine, NT, Australia

"What a miserably hot stinking day," Ilsa said to herself. "With no rain in sight."

Having just finished her morning assignments, Ilsa was resting on the verandah, thinking about the noon meal. For five minutes she could wave flies away and glance at a dated copy of *Australian Home Journal* magazine. It was from 1939 and showed prewar fashions that no one within a thousand miles would wear. Certainly not in Katherine, where long-sleeved function made Sydney necklines or Melbourne hems impractical.

But an annoying noise, the droning of a strange-sounding plane, was quietly interrupting her thoughts. It was headed for the gorge, and planes this far south of Darwin were rare. The engine's whine sounded like it was malfunctioning or running out of gas. A thin smile spread across her face. The plane's misfiring might mean something interesting was about to happen.

"Why is this wayward pilot buzzing us?" she said with mock irritability but growing excitement. "It's likely to spook the cattle with all that coughing and sputtering."

Standing up, Ilsa tried locating the plane, searching for the noisy propellers. It was certainly getting closer. She stepped off the verandah to scan more of the sky because whoever it was, Allied or Japanese, they weren't far off.

And then, there it was. At the low edge of the sky. Most importantly, there were no Japanese tail markings. No solid red balls on the wings or fuselage.

"Mama…mach schnell," she screamed. "A big plane is coming down. Near us. It's going to crash. Into the gorge."

Ilsa moved effortlessly toward the dark shed where her father kept the horses, her long stride giving off the impression she was gliding over the scorched earth.

"Ilsa, what on earth are you doing?" her mother asked in German.

"I'm going to ride out and see where the plane is coming down. It's not Japanese. I think it's Australian. Or English. There's no white star like with the Americans. They may need help."

"You will bring water with you and your Abookra hat, yes?"

"Of course, Mama, but it's an Akubra. I've told you that before."

Heidi Stulmacher, old beyond her actual years, did not appear to care. Her words were a strange stew of German and Austrian stock ingredients salted with English and Aboriginal phrases. The result was an unwieldy concoction.

"Look, it's going down. Ach, see where it is headed."

"I know. They're in trouble unless they've come down in the first pool. It's the widest. Lucky for them the river hasn't started coming down yet. If it had, they'd never survive it."

"Where is your father, Ilsa?"

"Papa, Glenno, Hans, and Frederick are working the far paddock. They will hear the engines and come here first. Tell them I've gone to see. Listen. Did you hear that? The whining is wrong. They're crashing."

Racing to the shed, Ilsa ladled cloudy-looking fluid into a watertight oilskin before effortlessly saddling Dandy. Throwing a small feed bag over the curved leather saddle, she raced toward the gate, opened and reset the bar, waved to her mother, setting off along a cantilevered path leading toward the gaping rift. She hoped she wouldn't see a fireball or smoke during her ride.

CHAPTER 37

Tucker's foggy memory of old NT maps and sepia-tinted postcards told him the nasty slab of land in front of them lay somewhere between Darwin and the Kakadu. It made him hesitant to tell Northgraves about Katherine's cavernous gorges because unless they crashed into the walls, it wasn't rocks that would kill them. It was the water. Or saltwater crocs.

The Katherine during the Wet was fearsome, powerfully flowing through sluices that carved out thirteen distinct gorges. Were the two men to have visited in the Dry, they'd have found a peaceful river. During the annual monsoon, though, when billions of gallons fell from the skies and every dry streambed gushed, the big river redressed itself as an inland sea shoving staggering amounts of water across a well-worn gash in the earth.

This was where *Miss Laurel* would crash. And while Northgraves had proven himself every bit the amateur the moment he took the bomber above the storm, managing to lose visual points of reference, he'd impressed Tucker. For his next trick, though, his first solo landing would have to occur at a place lacking a runway.

"Stay over the river, Tommo. There's no more fuel. We've run her dry."

"I'm bringing it down so we're at about fifty feet," Northgraves yelled, wrestling with unseen wind shear, concentrating on the plane's yaw. "If you see a smooth place, some kind of road, I'll try landing there."

"There won't be roads. Not here."

Just then, the plane responded to a murderous air pocket, jolting both men, snapping their heads backward as the bomber bucked, shifted, and slid sideways.

"Hold tight. We gotta get through this."

"What happens next?"

"I lose control and we drop. Might stay up for a minute. Might not."

As they peered through the Plexiglas, the gorge ran away to the south as if a drunken giant had taken a stick or knife to the land and gouged it unevenly. Both rims of the tableland offered so many uneven stone obstacles, it was clear ditching there would kill them on contact. The river would have to do.

"Water landing?" shouted Tucker. "Maybe we can get out before she sinks."

"Sure. Let's give the first-time pilot a water landing. What's to worry about? I'll just put her down in that first section."

Northgraves's sarcastic confidence, shallow as it was, ignored his inexperience. For Tucker, the American's sweaty grit could be summed up easily. In one day, the man had stolen a plane, taken off, fought his way through a tropical storm, and now would attempt the suicidal.

Pushing down on the stick, Northgraves revectored the plane onto a heading consistent with the longest stretch of river in front of them. Once they went down into the abyss, there were no alternatives. If they entered the slot late, the river's short "runway" would send them slamming into a rock wall. If the American flew into the gap at too steep an angle, they would disintegrate the moment they hit the water.

Rushing up at *Miss Laurel's* nose was a half-mile-long strand of muddy greenish blue. As the plane fell below the blurring rim, the canyon's walls closed in around them, scaring Tucker more than a bit. They were far too close.

"All right, all right. You pay for your cards, you take your chances. That's what we'd say in the alley. Instructor always said keep speed strong and take it to the house. Think you better get back to that radio room and strap in. That'll be safest."

Northgraves grinned, the corners of his mouth high in his cheeks as if he were riding a roller coaster. Yet, despite his joker's smile, his eyes stayed fixed on the yoke and bouncing control panel. His management of the spinning altimeter would determine their outcome.

"At some point, I'll throttle back while pulling up on the stick," he yelled, talking himself through his landing procedure. "Gotta go slow as possible at that point. But when the tail hits, we'll slap down like nobody's business."

Tucker was already mentally measuring the distance to the entry hatch and how he'd reach it once they hit. Below him, just as he was leaving the cockpit, he glimpsed crocodile-like shapes on the river's banks. Worse than crocs, though, the rushing red walls of the gorge were just off the tips of the bomber. The river's width seemed barely wider than the plane.

"Mate, you know there are crocs down there, right?"

"Hadn't thought about that."

"I get that a lot from you."

"Get outta here and brace yourself because when she stops bouncing, you have to open that hatch door, or we drown. Get it open and clear out. Don't wait for me because if I'm conscious, I'll be shoving you out of the way. That's a natural fact."

"Right you are, mate. And oi…good luck to you. You've been brilliant. The whole way. As for me, when she hits, I'll be off like a bride's nightie."

"Uh-huh."

"Leave it. Just keep 'er straight and get to shore ahead of the flippin' crocs."

Acting as if it could defy the laws of gravity, the bomber hung in the air for another thirty seconds before Northgraves scored a near-perfect level touch-down. His beginner's luck also defied the laws of probability, coming up roses in a remote setting where months of training might have produced the same result one time in fifty. But the miracle would mean nothing, thought Tucker, if they died in their separate seats.

As the nose of the Beaufort slammed into the Katherine, skipping a few times on the flowing water, the yellow-tipped propellers sheared away amid a small tidal wave washing over the cockpit. At the same time, strips of torn and bent metal, acting as temporary brakes, screeched like wounded animals before the noise-deadening wash of the river silenced them.

Halted by the equivalent of a titan's watery hand, the heavy bomber began settling into the murky river's current. Inside, the two dazed men hung like puppets caught on their strings, heads hanging down, whiplashed. They'd survived a speeding car crash with their various internal organs crashing into ribcages, forcing oxygen out of newly compressed lungs.

Both men likely would have drowned, still strapped to their seats, but the Japanese mechanic on Babar had removed all nonessential items from the plane, including the bombs and machine guns from all the turrets. Thanks to Northgraves, there was no fuel.

This meant instead of driving the fuselage forward and then down into the water, the Beaufort skimmed the river's surface seeking, it seemed, to forestall sinking with a certain dignity. For at least an additional sixty seconds, slowly steered downriver by the current, the seven-ton bomber floated.

In truth, it was shipping gallons of water by the second, creating a fierce rushing sound that slowly revived the groggy Tucker. The Australian was bruised and felt blood trickling from a gash to the back of his head but sensed nothing was broken. The bullet wound that had nicked his outer thigh hadn't resumed bleeding.

Fumbling with the safety straps, he willed himself to start moving.

In the cockpit, Northgraves was hanging limply in his pilot's seat, the imprint of the restraining belts showing deeply on his bare skin. Reaching the cockpit, Tucker shook him.

"Oi, Northy…get up, mate."

For a moment, nothing happened. Then, one of the American's eyes fluttered as if some greater force had flipped a circuit breaker and reset his internal wiring.

"What's going on?"

"We're down…but move it. Back to the hatch." He said the words in a broad Western cowboy accent, like ones he'd heard at the picture shows. "Sailor, you need to get a move on."

"Yes sir."

"And you don't stop until I tell you. Grab hold of me. Let's go."

The next two minutes were largely a blur, but making their way back through the plane's cramped crawlspace, the two men pulled open the hatch and flopped out into the river just rear of the now-submerged port-side wing. For a few seconds, they treaded water as the giant plane settled further into the river.

Water was rushing into the plane from hundreds of bullet holes and crash-related fissures. In mere seconds, she would slip beneath the surface. Remembering his frantic submarine escape, Tucker issued his next command.

"We gotta swim, Tommo. Move. Before it suctions. She'll take us down with her."

Inspired, the two skeletons kicked furiously for the nearby shore. About fifty yards abreast of the plane, Tucker saw the yellowy eyes of three crocodiles watching the two men, but either the giant ripple caused by the crash or the afternoon heat provided enough incentive for the reptiles to stay put.

"Keep swimming, mate. We're almost there."

"That's what you keep telling me," Northgraves said, spitting water over gashed lips. "This war business is getting all day old. I keep ending up in the drink. Should've stayed on the farm, if you ask me."

"Keep swimming, ya big galah. It's my shout tonight."

With that, each man pushed for the shore. Where Tucker's stroke was smooth, the American's frantic efforts alternated between a flustered dog paddle and a panicked overhand crawl. In a battle with the river, the sailor was losing badly. The Katherine was actively sucking Northgraves downstream, deeper into its murk, pulling him like a magnet to his impending death.

CHAPTER 38

At the rim of the first gorge, Ilsa arrived in time to see the tail end of a half-submerged plane sinking. It was sticking up out of the dirty water like a thick gum tree. But there was more.

Two mostly naked men on the river's shallow bank were slapping each other's backs, their animated splashing suggesting they'd somehow escaped drowning. She must hurry down the near side of the chasm and greet them.

Her heart racing, Ilsa was relieved that they did not look at all like Japanese aviators, and this intrusion, thrust into the monotony of farm life, excited her beyond words. She waved furiously at first from atop her horse, but the men were yet to inspect their surroundings.

Ilsa spurred Dandy around the rim of the gorge's precarious maw, heading for the switchback trail leading to the water's edge. She knew she would disappear for a few moments, but there was nowhere for these unexpected visitors to go. The Stulmacher property was the closest station, and if they'd just survived a crash, they certainly wouldn't find any other help. Walking up the path would take ages but, thankfully, it was also the most logical.

As the horse slowly picked its way down into the canyon, careful at points where the lip of the gorge dropped away for hundreds of feet, Ilsa framed her first few questions for the two men. She must ask the right things before her father and brothers arrived.

Her English had developed in uneven spurts, with some coming in Austria and then, for less than two years, at the nearest mission school. Ilsa was conscious of her spotty language skills. More than once, older Australian girls had mocked her accent and word choices.

That wouldn't matter today. She remained the family member best suited to translate discussions between her father and the survivors. But what should she ask? And what if they were badly injured?

"How are you?" or "It is very hot today" couldn't possibly be the best way to greet men from a wreck, although asking about their health felt appropriate. They hadn't looked injured from up on the gorge rim, but she couldn't even attempt a guess on their condition until she arrived at the river.

"I suppose I shall ask them where they came from," she said to the horse. "More than likely, it will have been Darwin…and that won't be interesting in the least. We know about Darwin…or what it used to be…before the Japanese started smashing it to pieces. It's ever so much a pity we haven't been in ages."

In a few moments, the trail broadened out, providing flatter footing for her mare. The spotted horse, his nostrils flared, was not particularly fast or strong but always reliable when handled with authority. Best of all, her brothers knew without question that Dandy was Ilsa's.

"Goodness, this is unusual," Ilsa thought. "Should I greet them like Fizzer would in *Never-Never*? 'Hullo. What ho, boys.'"

That was how Mrs. Gunn made Fizzer, her much-traveled, ever-outgoing bush mailman, speak in the book. It would take considerable cheek and brashness to greet two sopping-wet strangers in that fashion.

"You're both A1, ain't cha?"

That was wrong, too. In English, "ain't" indicated someone was less educated. That would not do, and her Austrian accent was another issue.

What if the two men were Aussie pilots and thought she was a German spy? Papa had talked to the children about the war in Europe and explained why many people around the world disliked Germans and Austrians. They were tired of Germany starting world wars.

"Our accents will make people want to fight you," he'd said one morning. "So the less we say until this war is over, the less we stand out. Am I understood?"

The three children knew to respond in unison, and looking somewhat pleased, Johann Stulmacher returned to his egg-covered steak.

That was all fine, thought Ilsa, but now she must rely on her limited vocabulary. Accent or not. If these men had just crashed into her gorge, they must accept her rescue efforts.

"Steady here, Dandy."

After negotiating the last hairpin turn before the ground leveled out, Ilsa trotted forward toward the water's edge. Just now she could see the two men walking along the edge of the river, talking animatedly. She guessed their discourse was about the three lazy freshwater crocs on the far side of the brown river.

"Hullo," she cried out, standing up in the brass stirrups. It was best to present the largest possible image if the men were blinded in some way.

"Oi...over here, missy."

The voice was Australian and came from the shorter of the two men. He looked younger than the other bushy airman and wore nothing more than ripped green shorts and a torn singlet. The taller one, a Black man, was shirtless and blood splattered. He was waving one arm, hopping about on spindly legs.

This didn't fit Ilsa's image of Australian fighting men. Both looked whip-thin, with protruding ribs and boiled-red insect bites. On closer inspection, the Australian had a bloodstained wrapping on his leg, and the other one was feebly holding his head with one arm.

"Howdy, ma'am. Are we ever glad to see you. You sure are a sight for sore eyes."

This was a different accent. Not posh, like an Englishman's. Could he be an American?

"I am Ilsa Stulmacher," she said without thinking. "Do you need a sister? Are you both all right?"

"Are we ever." It was the non-Australian again. "And if you have a sister, ma'am, that will be swell too. But tell me, where've we come down? Where are we?"

"You are near Katherine. This is the Katherine Gorge. You are from the plane?"

It was a foolish question but the most logical thing she could think to ask.

"Too right we are," said Tucker, tipping his head, picking up on Ilsa's German accent. "And I'm guessing you're not originally from around here. So pardon our manners. G'day miss. I'm Brad Tucker. This is Tom Northgraves. How ya goin'?"

"I am fine," she said awkwardly, struggling with the incongruity of talking with two strangers in an unaccompanied setting. "You are Australian, yes?"

"How do you like that, Northgraves?" Tucker said, turning to his companion. "She's dinky-die. Pegged me straightaway."

The Aussie stopped and performed a strange little two-step jig on the hot sand.

"New dance, Tucker?"

"From when I'd win fights. But like I kept sayin', no fear, mate. We've made it home. Come straight into Oz. Survived it all."

"I told you I could fly," Northgraves interjected.

"That you did, mate. Well and truly. Can't believe it."

For a few moments, while the horse snorted and pawed the dirt, both men forgot the strapping teenage girl sitting above them was trying her best to interpret their words. They had survived the Imperial Japanese navy and gotten back to Allied safety. That took precedence over a female offering to help them.

"Excuse us our behavior, ma'am. We've been on the run from the Japanese for a while and just stole one of our planes back from the dirty mongrels and flew it here from up around Timor way. Bit of a wonder we're even standing here."

"Never flew before," said the dazed American, dropping to his knees and collapsing face-first onto the sandbank.

"Oi, Tommo…you right, mate?"

As Tucker propped up Northgraves's bushy head, a slight sucking noise was sounding behind them. Turning, Tucker watched the tail of the stolen bomber slide slowly under the river's surface. The plane's submission to the dark water created a gentle, spreading ripple racing toward the opposing shorelines.

"Give us a hand, love," said Tucker, turning back toward the blonde girl on the horse. "We'll lift his head up and rest it on your saddlebag. See if we can get him to drink some water."

Instantly, the girl was off her horse, loosening the mare's straps and holding out her oilskin. As she stood over the two men, the sun behind her, Tucker saw the girl's long hair was tied off with a scarlet-colored ribbon.

"Goodness. Is he sick?"

"Reckon it's been a long couple of days for him. He's crook, but he'll be right."

Shaking the leather canteen, Tucker poured water into the American's mouth, causing the Black man to sputter, his eyes blinking open at the unexpected disturbance.

"Hey, what's going on?" he groaned.

"You collapsed, mate. Too much excitement."

"So, what's the plan?"

"This young lady is going to help us get out of the gorge. Take us to her family. To safety."

CHAPTER 39

The journey to the Stulmacher homestead was grueling, with the actual climb out of the gorge gutting the barely revived Northgraves and staggering Tucker with his wounded leg.

"You are both injured," said Ilsa after a short distance. "Shall I ride for help, or will you walk out together?"

"I think we can manage," said Tucker trying to calculate the distance to the rim. "Just go slow for us. We'll lean on each other. Might need to stop a few times along the way."

It took more than an hour, with frequent rest breaks, but when Ilsa brought the two bedraggled men up from the river, she quite expected her father, Johann, and the rest of her family to see two injured and unexpected guests as an enjoyable interruption from their apparent standing as European outcasts.

Life in the Northern Territory had created a lonely, isolated existence, but the prospect of hosting two young soldiers, stranded at their remote station for some amount of time, thrilled her. Instead, for reasons she couldn't fathom, her father, who met them at the top of the trail, came on harshly. Interrupted from his taxing work in the fields, he acted as if they were cattle thieves who hadn't yet stolen his herd. In Ilsa's mind, he was doing his best to hide his emotions, but it wasn't working. His manner was curt, and the creases on his red face were drawn tight, as if he'd contracted a stomach cramp. Where she expected warmth, or at least cheerful curiosity, Johann Stulmacher's countenance was pinched with an almost tic-filled nervousness. Something bordering on fear and distrust.

Over the last six years, Johann had left behind the car-loving, playful film-maker she'd known in childhood. He'd become a stubborn, obstinate man who made their inhospitable pocket of land sustainable by learning the intricate antipodean process of buying and selling livestock, melons, mangos, peanuts, and vegetables.

In Ilsa's simple worldview, her father should at least consider hiring two short-term workers who surely owed the Stulmachers a certain kindness, at least while they visited. Instead, her father was gruff and curiously blunt. Ilsa's mother, Heidi, remained overtly anxious.

She was clearly taking hospitality clues from her husband and diverted her eyes the moment the men from the plane expressed their heartfelt thanks for Ilsa's efforts. It was as if Ilsa had done little more than her daily chores.

"My father and mother don't speak very much English," Ilsa said after going around the circle, introducing the adults and Glenno. The stock hand had nodded with a wry smile but stood mute. "We are not originally from here, and sometimes Glenno has to help us with the right English words."

Almost as an apology, Ilsa explained to her family and Aboriginal station hand that Tucker was in the Australian army and Northgraves had survived a sinking American ship. Both men had been fighting the Japanese. As was family custom, she left out where the Stulmachers had come from and instead offered that they'd been in Katherine for more than five years after leaving the Alps before the war.

"And then this is my brother, Hans, who is speaking some English, and my youngest brother, Frederick, who is turning seven soon but very shy. He usually sticks to Mama or Papa. Like he is now."

"I am ten," said Hans, unprompted. "How are you today?" His stilted English was obvious, but his confidence pleased Tucker, who appreciated anyone giving it a go.

"You right, mate?" he asked while kneeling. "You helping out with your mum and dad on the station?"

The older boy's language proficiency exposed, Ilsa knew he would not answer. She was about to cover for Hans when the American interrupted.

"We're sure pleased to meet y'all," said Northgraves. Having arrived at the Stulmacher homestead, he was showing miraculous signs of recovery from his harrowing swim and clearly showing off. The presence of another Black man was perhaps giving Northgraves new confidence.

"Too right," added Tucker.

"Yes'm, we surely never expected to come crashing down in your neck of the woods," the Virginia native said, tipping a nonexistent hat, his twang a bit broader. "I mean this far inland and all. But that cyclone grabbed us up and spun us around like a big ol' boar coming out of the brush. Spun us all around like one of our hurricanes back home. Pushed us further south than we expected."

"Mate, what are you on about?" Tucker coughed, guessing everyone would still hear him. It seemed like Northgraves was talking just for the sake of being heard, something Australians didn't do. Not even on a first meeting.

"Just acting neighborly," the Black man drawled, sizing up his new audience. "Like coming out after a big storm. I'm just so glad hearing a few more people speaking English."

Understanding very little of what was transpiring, Johann and Heidi nodded their heads but looked to Ilsa to translate.

"They escaped from up north near Dutch New Guinea," she said in German. "They stole a plane...it originally belonged to the Australians...and somehow flew it back here. They are very glad to see us."

The Austrian couple nodded at their daughter's synthesized story, their wooden faces suggesting they were unimpressed with two Allied soldiers standing in their front paddock talking to them or their daughter.

"Ya. Ya. Das ist gut," said Johann, his face stiff, his additional German unapologetic. "The Wehrmacht would not take such men. It explains why this dummkopf war continues."

Ilsa knew her father didn't think anything was even close to good. He was a terrible liar, and she felt bad catching him out in such a situation. In the ensuing silence, Ilsa fretted. What were the soldiers thinking? Where was her family's hospitality? Couldn't everyone see their hideous rib cages and gaunt collarbones? Wasn't the dried blood plastered around their numerous wounds a reason for kindness?

"We must offer them some warm food, Mama, because as you can see, they are not eating often. Almost never. And they have wounds we must help clean."

"Ask them how long they will stay," said Johann in German before his wife could respond. "I do not wish to share with them our story. Do not invite them into the house. Schnell."

Tucker and Northgraves stared at Ilsa, waiting to see how she would explain a stern blast of German phrases and commands mixed with displeasure. Ilsa knew the two visitors were reading her father's tension.

"My father, as you can guess, is new to this country. He is speaking German, the language of our home country, which is Austria. He may sound a little gruff."

"Ahh, no fear, Miss Ilsa," said Tucker, watching the uncomfortable settler. "Reckon if your mob is trying to make a go of it here in the NT, it doesn't matter what language you speak. It's hard getting the hang of things. And Australians, well, we're not always so welcoming to outsiders. Perhaps he's had a rough go here. Mightn't be so keen we just dropped in."

"Oh no, sir, it's nothing like that. He just wants to know your plans now that you've come down safely in Katherine."

She knew it was a bit of white lie, but as only embarrassed teenage daughters would understand, Ilsa was mortified by her father's behavior. She carefully shot him a look to show she was continuing to explain his directions.

"Because we are speaking German, a lot of people here in this End Top suspect us. For five years now, anytime Germany wins a battle—sometimes even the Japanese—people who know us, well, they can be very mean. They think we are for Germany. It is the farthest thing from the truth. We are trying to be Australians."

Tucker eyed the young Austrian girl. Until this point, he had not taken close notice, but the "End Top" phrase was cute, and on closer review, she was as well. Setting that aside, he hoped the Stulmachers weren't a family of tee-totalers because he'd kill for a beer. Murder for a proper pub where he could stand with the lads, hoisting a pint or thick glass pot.

"Reckon you better tell him what you've just said to us. I know my Pa would want to know every word. But do us a favor. Add this in: Tell him we'll head out to the Australian base at Darwin soon as we can sort out some transport. Tell him we didn't intend to crash near his paddock. It happened by accident."

Tucker looked around the corral, still attempting to fully grasp his good fortune. Of getting home after almost four months on the run. Now, in dropping his survive-at-all-costs guard, he looked at Ilsa again, all legs and golden hair tied loosely in a ponytail. She was stunning.

In silence, he listened to Ilsa translate. The family commentary was starting to resemble a German tennis match with a series of pleading serves and forceful return volleys. It was an intense match and one, based on her age and gender, she would lose.

Turning to Northgraves, lips barely moving, teeth clamped shut, Tucker whispered, "Old man's not too keen on us, Tommo. 'Cause of the teenage daughter or 'cause they're Germans. Gonna have to shove off quick if he doesn't warm up."

"That'll suit me," said the American. "Now that I'm safe, I'm thinking about how to spring this on the folks back home. They would've written me off as dead. News I'm alive will give Ma a big ol' heart attack."

"Speaking of mothers," said Ilsa, displaying the capacity to listen and talk in two languages simultaneously, "my mother has insisted you stay for…is it *tea* the Australians call it? In our country, it's the evening meal. But we are working on learning Australian."

"Why, that would be mighty kind," said Northgraves. "And ma'am, if you do figure out what these Aussies are saying, would you fill me in? This skinny one here is always talking about people named Martin, Uncle Bob, and Larry Somebody. Most times, I can't make head or tails what he's saying."

Ilsa laughed, like someone always left on the outside of an adult joke. She turned up her palms with glee.

"You mean starvin' like Marvin."

"Yeah, he's one of 'em."

"And if we get some tucker goin'," she added, "we'll be happy as Larry."

Exhausted but breaking into a broad smile, Tucker added, "Yeah, yeah. And Bob's yer uncle."

"Those are the outlaws I was talkin' about," said Northgraves. "That's the three of 'em."

"Be that as it may, Miss Ilsa," Tucker offered, "make sure your folks really want us around for tea because we can be on our way now if you point us toward town."

"We wouldn't hear of it," Ilsa said, despite her father's glare. He had not appreciated the shared laughter or his daughter's rebelliousness, but in taking command, Ilsa was emerging as the clan's matron. Her father's grimace suggested a concession of sorts.

"You must stay a few nights," said Ilsa, "and recover."

There was a burst of German-sounding words between the icy mother and daughter before Ilsa told the two survivors the evening meal would be prepared within the hour. The men were welcome to rest in the barn and scrub up at the farm's bore. Ilsa would bring them soap and old towels.

"Can't say I've seen a bar of soap in years," said Northgraves. "If it's still December 1944, then I'm all-day dirty. It's almost three full years. Imagine I'm a bit rank. That's how we'd say it back home."

"What my Black friend is saying, Missy, is that he's ugly. And smells," said Tucker. "But then again, I'm not much better."

"Goodness, I can't imagine surviving in the wild that long. It would be ever so hard. But now I am going into the house for the water basin, soap, and scissors. For those bristle beards. Off you go. You are following Papa over to the pump."

Turning toward the Stulmacher cabin, she again spoke to her father in German, spurring him into action. His inelegant wave guided them toward two wooden troughs and a corrugated-tin bathing tank flanking the manual pump.

"Come mit me," Johann said in a resigned voice. "Just so."

If he had once been good at anything else, Tucker thought, here in the NT he was a struggling ploughman. A sunburned man with a good-looking daughter. A bloke who knew that if a soldier in a uniform turned up, she might be off to the races. It explained why the old man probably quarantined her on the family farm, possibly forbidding Ilsa to make unaccompanied trips to Katherine. They needed her to stick with the station.

From the window, Ilsa watched the two men moving slowly, bearded heads down. Their awkward, halting strides revealed their utter fatigue. Both were likely suffering from jungle-related diseases, including worms, malarial dysentery, and sunstroke. Surviving the crash and swimming to shore produced a surge of adrenaline, but in no time at all, both men might fall over. Tucker was no more than skin and poking bones, lucky to reach 140 pounds. The American looked stronger but was almost equally emaciated.

It would take them time to mend, and neither could assist Glenno much on the long list of projects Papa kept putting off. In the morning, or maybe the next, her father would want to send the two strangers off. For a variety of reasons, she decided she must slow down that plan. How could she do that? Perhaps by fussing over them and managing their recovery.

Above her, the sticky linen-colored clouds were aflame as the orange sun moved westward away from the gorge. In the near distance, stunted trees clustered together, creating modest windbreaks.

"Red sky at night, sailor's delight," she said with quiet confidence. "Maybe these men and the New Year are good omens. Wouldn't it be wonderful if something magical came of this?"

CHAPTER 40

Forty minutes later, Hans brought Tucker and Northgraves clean cotton work shirts. They had spent the better part of forty minutes scrubbing off months of grime but could barely stand. Ilsa, in a rough full-length apron, trailed behind her brother carrying warm bread in a red-checkered tea towel. The aroma wafting upward, both placed their noses over the loaf, inhaling.

"My word, that smells good," said Tucker. "Reminds me of home."

"We've got another few minutes until Hans rings the gong, but I asked Mama if I could share this damper early. I am thinking you need it."

"Do we ever," said Tucker, his greedy excitement showing. He'd not eaten bread in months. Just hearing the Australian word "damper" made him hungry. "It's been far too long."

As the three stood sizing each other up, the two men waiting for an approval to approach the house, it became obvious Ilsa's parents had issued an order. The Black American was off limits, verboten. She could speak with the Australian, now returned to his home country. But not the other.

"You will pardon us that our homestead is nothing special," said Ilsa, ignoring Northgraves as if he wasn't there. "It has been hard making a go of things in a new country. Especially during a war."

"It looks wonderful to us," said Tucker just as Hans rang the dinner bell. "We did it tough for a while, so a bit of tucker will work wonders."

Dinner, a fine country affair of chops, vegetables, a pudding, and tea, made the escapees wish they could've licked their plates. When the dishes were cleared and thanks handed around, Johann's curt manner made clear the two men should make for the barn. His gruff responses during Ilsa's translations suggested their heroic escape was not something he wanted his family hearing much about.

Dismissed, Tucker and Northgraves picked their way out of the spartan dining room, through the verandah, and down the wooden steps toward their sleeping quarters for the night. Neither was offended since both were focusing on a good night's sleep and a short-term recovery process designed to nurse them back to something well short of healthy.

Two more uneventful days would pass, and after spending most of them practically bedridden, struggling just to get up for meals, Tucker heard footsteps on the path outside the shed.

"Hullooo," the girl said through cupped hands. "I am coming to see if you need anything."

"Not me, Miss Ilsa," said Northgraves. "I've brung my cattle in for the night. We're finally in Abilene."

"My goodness. I hope this Abilene is a good place," she answered.

"Reckon I'm a bit restless tonight," said Tucker to the warm voice standing below just outside the barn door. "I'm having trouble falling asleep. Not used to civilization anymore. Is there anything more to see on your station? I'd love for us to start helping out if we can."

"I could show you around a little," said Ilsa, coming nearer. "Help you get familiarized with our holding."

"Go for it," whispered the American. "Take in the sights. Walk with her. You know she can't be seen anywhere near me."

"Yeah? I don't get it." Tucker said.

"You saw how she's been acting. I'm Negro. She can't even look my way.

It's like back home, with our segregation and lynchings. In the movies, the old farmer always has a shotgun. I'll get shot for talking to his daughter. You watch."

"You sure? I mean, I'm still holding out hope for Laurel."

"Go have a look at the evening stars. I'm going to climb into that hayloft and not come down until next week. Gonna dream about some moonshine and hamburgers the size of dinner plates. We'll drink some beers in Darwin when we get there."

After the strain of stealing a Japanese plane, getting shot at, and flying through a killer storm, Northgraves had earned his exhaustion. Tucker was certain he'd climb the barn's ladder, arrange the straw to his liking, and conk out. It seemed when evening fell, the American didn't need distractions. He went right to sleep.

Struggling to his feet, Tucker hobbled outside. His stomach felt distended, like he'd swallowed a small coconut. It had him worried about burping or worse, getting the runs. In the purpling darkness, the majestic stars of the Magellan Clouds were appearing overhead.

"You like our lights?" said Ilsa. "I look at them all the time, but they are different here than our patterns in Austria. Australians have the Southern Cross. It is so very different."

"I've never seen the northern stars, except one time in Japan. They sure were different."

Walking side by side, each "accidentally" bumping into the other at every point where the trail narrowed, Ilsa led Tucker down a stone-littered path, pointing out different markers in the approach to the canyon. She started by making apologies for her parents. They were from Graz and didn't trust outsiders. Even airmen who crash-landed nearby.

Growing bolder by the moment, she put her hand in his hand and felt a strange new tingle race up her back. Never having dated or even having gone on a date made holding a soldier's hand the boldest thing she'd ever attempted. Heart fluttering, her head flooding with emotions she didn't quite understand,

Ilsa felt like she was losing her breath.

"This is real pretty," said Tucker. He knew what should happen next. He'd kissed a girl once after a movie. He'd moved her under a towering Norfolk pine near the Collaroy theater and scored his first kiss. That early experience made this moment familiar. It was logical to make the first move.

What Ilsa did next, though, caught Tucker off guard. Thinking about her hand in his, Ilsa was suddenly pulling him toward her. He hadn't planned on any physicality, but here was Ilsa pressing against his chest, pushing her taut body against his. Her cool scent reminded him of freshly sprung flowers in Sydney's Botanical Gardens.

The ensuing kiss jolted Ilsa like she'd touched an electric fence. As the Australian brought his groin next to her pelvis, his first contact with a woman in more than seven months, Ilsa would've sworn she was on fire. She felt him hardening below her waist, and now every part of her was quaking with nervous, tingly explosions. If he kept it up, she'd either go limp in his arms or devour him.

And then, without warning, he stopped.

"I'm sorry, Ilsa. I'm so sorry."

In a childlike way, she leaned into him again. But Tucker's thoughts were of Laurel, and working to control his attraction, he knew he mustn't let this moment ignite. He wanted Ilsa. In the worst way. If it went a moment longer, he'd never turn back. They'd be lying in the dirt with no going back.

The Gordian knot of emotions forced Tucker to place two hands on her shoulders in order to physically stop her.

"I'm not going to say this the right way, Ilsa," said Tucker, "but back in Sydney, I'm keen as mustard on a girl named Laurel, and it wouldn't be right falling for you tonight. I owe it to her to get home. You wouldn't understand me if I said she's been with me the whole time in the jungle. She's helped me stay alive."

"Are you married to her?"

That was the only thing the hurt teenager could think to say in English, but the words didn't fully fit her heartbroken emotions. She had prayed for a visitor, and God had dropped the wrong person out of the sky.

"I'm not, but..."

And at that very moment, they both heard the gunshots. For Ilsa, it was the moment she and her father had feared might come. Hitler had sent his goons after them, and it sounded like they were in the house, and there was horrible screaming.

"Bloody oath, what's going on back there?" said Tucker.

CHAPTER 41

Racing back along a dirt path, Tucker and Ilsa witnessed two men, American soldiers by dress but German by speech, marching Johann and a bawling Hans out of the house toward the impromptu bunkhouse where Tucker and Northgraves were staying. The strangers both held pistols and were barking orders Tucker couldn't understand.

"Shhh…they've come after us," said Ilsa, recovering her composure. "Because of what Papa knows."

"Oi…Ilsa, quick, girl, stay with me in the shadows. They won't know we're here."

Tucker was already circling the couple to his left toward the back of the barn, where a small, dark opening allowed access for the dogs. He went through first before extending his hand to Ilsa to pull her through.

Whoever they were, Johann hadn't been expecting them. It was possible he'd relaxed after dinner, but now the whole family was facing some kind of threat. Weak as Tucker was, he knew he and Northgraves must protect their hosts.

Beside Johann, young Hans was sobbing. The soldier behind him was prodding the boy away from the homestead.

"What are they saying?" he whispered as the foursome approached.

"It takes too long to explain. They are the bad German police. The Gestapo. They want something we filmed six years ago. But it's not here. We don't have it."

"Okay, listen to me. We gotta move fast. Here's what I need you to do. Get up the ladder and wake Tom."

"But…"

"Do it. I need him for this."

Tucker was already pulling his American knife out of the leather sheath he'd hung on the shed's supporting beam. He was calculating how long before the Nazis reached the barn's front door. They had maybe two minutes before the Germans came through the illuminated opening. With any luck, they'd stop for a moment to bash the Stulmachers. It would buy Tucker time.

"Ahh…"

"Listen, there's no time," Tucker hissed. "After you tell Tommo what's on, head back out the way we come in or stay put up in the loft."

Catching on, she climbed the rough-hewn ladder and watched as Northgraves, rubbing his eyes, his fist clenched around his pocketknife, joined Tucker on the ground.

"What's going on?" said Northgraves, rubbing sleep from his eyes.

"Here, mate, grab this hoe. There's trouble. Nazi thugs. Coming for us. So when these two assassins come through the doorway, jump the tall one on the left. I'll take the shorter bloke. Don't ask. Try to kill him."

"What?"

"Kill him."

CHAPTER 42

With Ilsa watching from above, the two Nazis pushed Johann and Hans into the barn, most likely planning to conduct an interrogation. Without warning, Tucker and Northgraves were leaping from the shadows, bringing their attack down on the two Gestapo agents' backs.

But where Tucker was trained in killing and carried a proper weapon, the American's effort revealed a navy steward with a farm tool. Unbriefed, unprepared, and following an order he didn't fully understand, he stunned his German rather than knocking him out.

Tucker's outcome was better. Using a slicing maneuver that severed the carotid artery of the short Nazi's neck, the Australian whirled around as blood sprayed outwardly from the rough incision. Within seconds, the German crumpled to his knees, dropping his gun. For a weak man, Tucker's work had been decisive, fluid. The benefit of surprise had worked. Unfortunately, the American's efforts hadn't.

As Tucker lunged to start his second killing move, he sensed Northgraves hesitating on where to hit his fallen target a second time. It was only a fraction of a second, but by the time Northgraves aimed his wooden hoe at the German's face, the assassin was dodging sideways and firing his gun.

His first shot killed Johann Stulmacher, and then, with great presence of mind, the Nazi turned on Northgraves, clicking off two shots toward the American. Both connected.

Northgraves was dead before he hit the floor.

With the barrel of his Colt .45 still smoking, his gaze jumping wildly, the Nazi realized too late an Australian commando was stabbing him through the left eye socket. The knife met little resistance as it went in, ending the man's life.

There was no thinking left in either fighter. One was clinically dead; the other, sinking to his knees, covered in blood, was screaming.

"Tommo," he howled. "Tommo. No, dear God. No."

Above and behind them, Ilsa, the young woman on the cusp of her first kiss, was bawling. Four bodies lay on the ground surrounded by bits of crimson-colored hair and hay. Three of them were silent. One body, Ilsa's father, was choking, spitting blood, trying to make sense of the slaughter but giving specific orders.

"Ilsa," he gurgled in German. "Herkommen, Fräulein."

Tucker blinked in disbelief at the older man's command. "Mate…"

What he said next in guttural gasps escaped Tucker, but Hans jumped to his feet immediately. The father's words ended with "Mach schnell."

"Ya, Papa," the boy responded over his shoulder. He passed his older sister, who was just then dropping down the last few feet of the ladder from the loft.

"Ilsa, tell him…" Stulmacher continued in German. "Tell the Australian he must do as I say about our film."

The shocked girl began translating, cradling her father's head. He was drooling blood from the corner of his mouth, his rasping breath slowing.

"But my friend…"

"His friend is dead. I know this. Translate, girl. Tell him to listen."

The old man winced, gagging on pooling fluids gathering in his throat. He spat weakly.

"I am dying. He must leave here immediately. Give him my horse. Tell him to take the case from Hans."

He paused to gather his strength for these final orders, his eyes searching to see if Tucker somehow understood any of his German words.

Ilsa saw blood spreading on his chest. Still not comprehending what had happened, she watched Tucker rip off his work shirt and, with his knife, cut one sleeve off at the shoulder. He moved next to Johann, pressing the cloth against the bullet's entry hole to stanch the bleeding. That was when the old man began speaking again. Still in German.

"The film. It can end the war. Tell him where it is hidden in Graz. If someone can see it, they will know what to do. Tell him, Schatzi."

Stroking her father's face, Ilsa guessed her father might not have more than a few words left. Whatever he said, whatever phrases died on his lips, they were not for the Australian.

In his last moments, he saw his beautiful, intelligent nineteen-year-old daughter, a blonde-haired beauty in the classic sense of skater Sonja Henie or the actress Greta Garbo, create a lie with English words he recognized. Ilsa might be shocked and filled with the anger of rejection and the grief of tragedy, but she was capable of words she would come to regret.

"You must leave," she said. "These are Papa's last wishes. That you never return here. Ever. He thinks you were followed."

"But Ilsa, you need help."

"No. Leave. We have our reasons."

Johann's breathing was slowing, his eyes blinking as death enveloped him. "Schnell. Die Filmrolle. Zu Graz."

"What's he saying?" Tucker asked, knowing all too well the look of death.

"He wants you to leave tonight. Right away. Schnell."

Ilsa hoped Tucker couldn't translate the German. But the constant covering up and hiding of truth could not overtake the biggest issue. Her father was dying in her arms.

Without thinking, she kissed him on the forehead, stroking his hair, whispering that she loved him. That she would handle everything.

Wanting to give the girl privacy, Tucker moved away and crawled over to

Northgraves. There was no sign of life and no reason for hope. Either gunshot would have been fatal, and both had turned Northgraves's face into a nightmare skull of blood and bone.

"Ahh, Tommo. What have I done?"

It was quiet for barely a moment, Tucker fighting back his tears, when Hans came trudging back into the barn with a satchel case. The boy's shocked eyes suggested pain he did not understand nor attempt to translate. He indicated, through his tears, that his mother and brother were dead.

"Set that down here, Hans. I will need it for Mutti and Frederick. Go bring me a pail of water. We must wash the bodies."

Then she began explaining to Tucker she would bury his American friend and dispose of the Nazis who had murdered her family. She would make the wretchedness Tucker and his unceasing war represented disappear. She would bury them all. She would bury them and all her tomorrows in shallow, unmarked graves. In the gorge.

But first, she said she would saddle a horse and point Tucker toward Darwin. Help him serve his damned country and return to his stupid girl, Laurel.

"Not on your life, Missy," Tucker responded. "You won't be doing this alone."

"No, I won't. My fiancé will be coming by soon," she said, hoping her words sounded believable. "He will know what to do."

"That's fine. But I'll stay with you and Hans until he arrives. Until we've gotten to the bottom of this."

CHAPTER 43

The horse saddled, Ilsa slapped it on the rump and yelled, "Schnell."
Two days of scorching heat had passed, and as Tucker knew from the moment Ilsa lied about a fiancé supposedly riding to her rescue, there was no one coming. Instead, the trio, working almost exclusively in silence, had done nothing but dig graves for five corpses.

As of this moment, the new level of trauma spreading across Ilsa's tear-streaked face stretched far beyond that of a young woman scorned. It looked more like a vicious, haunting mask. Her command for the horse and rider left little for the unfettered commando to doubt. Her command was simple. Be gone. Don't ever come back.

Tucker tried understanding what had happened, but Ilsa's growing defiance precluded logic. Twenty feet down the track, he pulled back on the reins, halting the gelding's progress, and turned to study the ferocious female he was leaving behind.

This stunning woman had survived the gorge's towering shadows for years. And now, at the very moment she might've dared hope for an escape from a tyrannical father, two unexplained Nazis on a mission he didn't understand had launched a shattering attack. It was the continuing madness of World War II.

There was nothing left for her. Or Hans. They were orphans, stranded like millions of children stretching across Europe and Asia.

In the stillness, all Tucker saw was wisps of smoke coming from the still-smoldering house. All he smelled was the fetid stench of dead bodies dragged into the gorge for burial. None of it made sense. But given the last seventy-two hours, it was hard putting anything into perspective.

Overhead, magpies, kites, and crows swirled, leaving ink stains on the parchment-colored sky. A few hours earlier, the blue-eyed girl's break from her family captivity seemed more than possible. Tucker had fallen from the sky, a figurative rope ladder snaking up out of the fractured abyss. A lifeline that might've taken her away from the unclimbable cliffs.

It was a shimmering mirage, a speck of gold reflecting in the desert sky. Dehydrated dreaming that produced a phantom. One about to ride away.

Tucker stared at her in wonder.

Bold ringlets washed over her shoulders like waterfalls in the Wet. Wild curls tumbling over her ears in a frenzy. No ribbon could hold it back. No velvet restrained the golden locks swarming around her heart-sculptured face. She was tall, and the length of her hair added to her mystifying innocence.

It took him a minute to realize she'd seen Tucker as the rope. Believed he would pull her to safety. Now, she didn't want any of that. She'd told him to put his country and dream girl first.

Tucker watched her turn, moving away from the firelight.

"Ilsa?"

He heard German cursing.

She was already heading back through the spear grass and hedgewood scrub. Head down, shoulders squared. With no apology for the bloodstains on her pants or on the spinifex trail.

Behind her, a slender tongue-like flame burst from the smoking ruins, creating an amber set of diamonds on one of the building's huge beams.

Ilsa looked back at him, wiping rivulets of sweat and strands of long hair away from penetrating, fiery eyes.

Tucker sensed she and Hans would start rebuilding their lives that night. Scratching furiously at the red soil with crooked, rusty shovels and too-heavy picks.

And after that? What dark phoenix possibly rose from those ashes?

Tucker didn't want to guess. His military orders, always on his mind, preempted his guilt. They overrode his infections and many wounds. They mitigated his physical attraction and desire to stay and comfort her.

For now, his blood-soaked, one-sleeved shirt and dirty bandages would have to hold him together. They would have to get him well beyond the voice he hoped would call him back.

Honor the job, mate. Ride north. For Page and Sargent. For the Rimau men.

That was what the grieving voice told him. And this time, the voice didn't belong to Laurel. It was a Z Unit colonel in a large home at 260 Domain Road, South Yarra, Melbourne. He had no choice. Australia's war was his to fight.

Tucker dug his heels into the horse's side and wheeled out of the eerily illuminated yard, not wanting to look back. He guessed Ilsa would never forget his face.

Nor he hers.

CHAPTER 44

2 January 1945—Katherine, NT, Australia

Two days after Tucker left the homestead, riding off to Darwin, Ilsa instructed Hans to search the area, collecting things of value he could salvage. He should move those items into the barn, leaving no trace of any foreign visitors, Americans, Germans, or Australians.

The child was inconsolable most of the time but did as he was commanded, poking around the smoking embers of the house, grabbing small items he imagined Ilsa would want.

While he rested, Ilsa saddled her horse and headed off to meet with Glenno, the family's stockman. He had come to work right after the tragedy, but she had sent him away, explaining there had been a horrific fire and that except for Hans and Tucker, the rest had died. On that mournful day, she committed her second big lie by saying Glenno would be blamed unless he stayed away for a good long while.

The fib was borne of grief and fear. What if it was suggested that German soldiers had been living on the Stulmacher property? That Nazis had sheltered on their land? It would bring more trouble than orphaned Ilsa could manage.

Now, as she approached Logan's humble property and saw the farmhand's smooth face, she could tell he was hurt, crushed. Her words a few days ago had come as protective warning, not blame, but the result had been injurious.

"What happen out there, Missa Ilsa? Must be terrible bad," he said, his shock evident as she dismounted.

Ilsa doubted he believed her then and still might not believe her now.

"It was, Glenno," she said, her eyes watering. "But it's got nothing to do with you. Bad spirits there now. Bolung is mad. You must stay away. For a long time. Otherwise, the whitefellahs in Katherine will think you were involved. They'll use anything as an excuse. Move on. Find another station."

"What about Missus and Redrick? Them gone too?"

"Everybody, Glenno. All gone now. Even one of the new men from the plane. It was very bad. Promise me you won't come out to see the homestead for a very long time."

The Black man looked down at the ground, moving his bare toe around in the vermilion-colored dirt. He said the dream his wife warned him about had come true. Bolung did not like the silver plane it had eaten. Didn't like the disturbance caused by the intruders.

"Must be terrible bad," he repeated. It appeared he didn't know what else to say. He bobbed his head a few times, brown eyes glued to the ground. "I guess you know what's best. Guess you da boss now. You the Maluka."

"I'm sorry, Glenno. Please know that. I will stay on the land and report the fire. I must tell the constable about the deaths. But stay away for a good while. Until I come see you again."

With that, she wheeled Dandy away from the Aboriginal man's lean-to, heading back to comfort Hans. When the heat and humidity from the Wet died down toward evening, she and the small boy would begin dealing with their new reality. They would stay on this land as a way of honoring her parents. They would make it work in Australia. They had to.

And the film, with its damning images of Graz in 1938 and Germany's evil dictator, would remain buried, in two separate tins, in the ruins of a bombed-out city.

CHAPTER 45

February 2005—Narrabeen, NSW, Australia

Ultimately, I did a lot of research on Operation Rimau.

It was in my nature, and while I was obligated to finish the Darwin story for J. B., what I learned from talking to Brad Tucker at the War Vets Village was how, for the rest of his life, his name never once showed up in dispatches or books about the mission to Singapore. In fact, as the fog of history swirled, laying itself across the top of wars in Korea, Vietnam, and Afghanistan, the fate of the young commando from Sydney's Northern Beaches was buried.

The cover-up had started in late 1944. When Ivan Lyon's outfit left Fremantle's Garden Island, Tucker should've been noted as a reserve on the submarine. There should've been records showing Tucker making the journey north. But since Tucker had been on the outer deck when HMS *Porpoise* dropped out from under him, someone, maybe the sub's captain, took Tucker's name off that mission's manifest. For whatever reason—and I later learned the *Porpoise* was sunk by the Japanese in January 1945—Tucker was never shown as rostered.

Then again, maybe the cover-up happened in 1945 after a solitary rider galloped into Darwin and began filling in the blanks on Rimau, revealing how he'd been involved in stealing a dilapidated Beaufort. To my way of thinking, the whole thing would've been problematic for the Australian brass. With little previous intelligence, they were looking at a nonrostered survivor of a hugely failed mission.

Should they make Tucker a hero just as the war in Europe ended, or should they quarantine his improbable story until a later date? There was no doubt Tucker had accepted orders sending him to Fremantle for the Lyon raid on Singapore. But then what?

What I figured out after a few meetings was that Tucker, at least in his head, still saw images of himself on those Indonesian islands. He'd survived the war's terrors, but in his trauma, or delusion, he hadn't forgotten them. Nor mentioned a word to anyone. Like many men of that era, the war never ended. It played like a tape loop, certain cinematic scenes constantly flashing up on an invisible screen in their mind's eye.

Tucker was a lot like Ilsa. Like an entire generation of men and women, they put their war stories to bed and got on with it as best they could. They accepted the hard facts, uncomfortable truths of tragedy, and ran silent like submarines in dark underwater trenches. Many of them simply saw too much death.

What started to emerge from my research was an idea that I would undertake self-producing the story as a documentary. Given I was single (I hadn't found Elle Macpherson yet) and a self-styled adventurer, I thought about retracing Tucker's escape. I doubted whether anyone, even with malaria kits, food supplies, and technology devices (sending messages to satellites) would attempt such an undertaking circa 2005.

Tour groups managed to lead the adventurous over the Kokoda Trail, but to paddle from Singapore to Babar with nothing? And then hire a plane and land near the Katherine Gorge? They'd have to be mad or wealthy with money to burn. My biggest issue was going to be in finding investors.

But something was missing. There were still a few pieces to this jigsaw puzzle missing. Tucker and Ilsa had never reunited. And the naked Hitler film was never shown.

My next port of call, then, was revisiting Tucker at the War Vets. I told the old commando a woman from his past, Ilsa Stulmacher, had sent me to get his side of the story.

Tucker looked pained for a moment but gathered I was telling the truth. That led to the initial story about his escape into the gum tree. When Tucker had finished his long journey, aided by Tom Northgraves, and explained his ride into Darwin, he surprised me by asking if I could "spring" him from the War Vets. Take him up north to see this spectral woman from his past.

"Are you joking?" I asked in disbelief.

The man sitting on a thin mattress was swinging his last legs, and I doubted the risk-averse War Vets administrators would let him out of their sight. Flying to Darwin, mixed with hot weather, jostling in and out of cars, and the new airport security protocol that unfolded following 9-11, would kill him.

"I'm not," Tucker said with a defiant fierceness. His voice had strengthened like a gathering storm. Like in one of those Popeye cartoons where the can of spinach miraculously transforms the hero. "Get Josephine in here and tell her we've got secret men's business to attend to. Tell 'er I'll sign all the papers. Waive all my bleedin' rights."

I stared at him in disbelief.

"But—"

"G'wan. Be quick about it." He was grabbing at the sheets, disturbing the creases in the crisp white sheets. "You know how to book airline tickets, don't you?"

It was time for some quick calculations. I'd have to cover two airfares to Darwin, hotels, a car rental, and a funeral arrangement for one very frail man.

"Shall I tell Ilsa we're coming to visit, or are you hoping the shock alone will kill her?"

"No, Ilsa'll handle it when she sees me. I've always thought she might've hoped I'd turn back up."

"You know you could kick the can in the process, right?"

"No worries. It'll murder me if I don't go. It's been one of my lifelong regrets. Should have done this years ago. I've owed her that much. She patched me and Tom up that day when we come up out of the river. She's paid a pretty steep price for it since."

"But flying all that way?"

"Listen, I saw the first Qantas flying boat go out of Rose Bay in July thirty-eight. I'll be right."

"Well, before I start booking tickets, is there anyone other than these War Vets folks I should be alerting? Any next of kin wanting to float your ashes off some wharf or something if this blows up in our collective faces?"

"No, stuff that." There was a trace of sadness in his voice. "I came home to find Laurel never really loved me. She'd quickly moved on. With my nightmares and issues, I drank, married the wrong girl, and such. Never had kids. Outlived my brothers. There'll be no one to miss me."

I carefully framed the next question as boldly as I could.

"Are you okay if Ilsa doesn't want this?"

"I am. We'll turn around and come right back."

"Okay," I said. "One last mission. If they'll let you out. But I'm sure they'll lay out official paperwork suggesting that with your questionable health, you're in here for life. You've got Buckley's chance. You'd need a stack of politicians or lawyers to get you released."

"Not if I tell them I know about a crashed bomber they've never found. 'Sides, I'm friends with the local member for the Northern Beaches. Comes to see me with his father-in-law, a doc named Harpur when my gout acts up."

The *Miss Laurel*? You'd tell them about her? Where you crashed her?"

"In a flash. There's only two of us left who know where it is."

CHAPTER 46

To my amazement, Tucker pulled the right strings and got himself sprung. Thinking back, I should've sneaked him out of there, but an old girlfriend had been a social worker, and I knew the support staff would have been quick to pick up on an empty bed. It would've become a missing persons case, and as Paul Simon once sang, we'd all have shown up on the cover of *Newsweek*.

Under my quasi-official care, though, he was allowed to visit Katherine by way of Darwin. All because he supposedly knew about a secret World War II crash site. The authorities had to have doubted his story, but they let it go on the stipulation I serve as his guardian, feed the old survivor three square meals a day, and supervise the administration of his meds.

In our subsequent pre-trip meetings, I gathered Tucker never stopped seeing himself as a commando at heart. It made complete sense. A man willing to attack the Japanese in Singapore and, when it all goes to hell, paddle home does not lack for grit.

Ilsa was just as fierce but perhaps more feral. Isolated for much of her teen years, she couldn't have known two men would fly an Australian bomber into the Katherine Gorge or how nearly sixty years later one of them would turn up on her steps, pushed in a wheelchair by an ex-American Air Force officer she'd banished weeks earlier.

Given the trauma she'd endured, I figured Ilsa was the toughest woman I'd ever met. And when I called her from the Darwin airport, her strained tone suggested impatience. She'd made a scene in the hotel pub a few weeks earlier and now was acting fully put out that I'd needed so much time finding Tucker.

Arriving at her door, Ilsa feigned her shock better than I expected. At first, she stepped back, possibly to check her look in the hall mirror. But true to form, she came out swinging, just as gruff as she'd been on the phone. I guessed it was a cover, her protective shield.

"You're late for tea, Brad Tucker. And you, young man" she said to me, "are also tardy. I was beginning to consider you unreliable."

"Uhh, sorry," I replied. "I went as fast as I could."

"Can a man still get a cold beer in the Territory?" Tucker croaked. Dressed in freshly pressed khakis and an R. M. Williams short-sleeve blue-checked plaid shirt, he sounded remarkably young.

"Not on this station he can't," Ilsa said. "But they'll have one down the pub and a bit of what *you Australians* like calling *tucker*."

I picked up on the emphasized words *you Australians* and *tucker*, thinking they were possibly a symbolic reference connecting the two geriatrics back to the day the Beaufort crashed. The night the stars came out and purple Australian sky draped the gorge in velvet. The moment a few nights later when two people not quite ready for each other started walking down a thin dirt path.

"Well then," said Tucker, "let's get to town and pick up where we left off. As I recall, there was one big interruption the last time I came calling."

Thirty minutes later, I had arranged seating for the threesome at a battered wooden table in the same local tavern where this unusual story had started. By habit, I looked around to see if anyone recognized me from a certain night a few weeks previously.

"Your home away from home," Ilsa said to me, lifting a plastic-covered menu off the table. "Nearly walking distance to your fighter pilots and the 75th."

Grinning through yellowing teeth, Tucker gingerly poured Ilsa a glass of water from the metal pitcher. His hand shook a little, but he cut, as they say, to the chase.

"Wouldn't a mattered to her old man if it were ringers, swaggies, cattle barons, or generals come calling," Tucker started without preamble. "Johann wasn't letting anyone near his daughter. And I'll tell you why. She was a beauty. Nineteen, maybe twenty. Brown and built too. Bonza. Couldn't keep my eyes, and, very nearly my hands, off her."

Ilsa blushed. In the pub's muted lighting, Tucker's eyes shone with the memory.

"Do Aussies even say *bonza* anymore?" she asked. "That's very 1940s, isn't it?"

"Well, I use it. Bloody oath. Always have."

"May I remind you, Mr. Tucker, of my role in this story?" Ilsa didn't glare, but it was clear she wanted to return to the past with a different spin. "And to curb that swearing."

"Go on, go on," Tucker said, happy to let Ilsa lead.

"My parents knew we were never going back to Austria," she said evenly. "We had heard the Americans were bombing it regularly. There was even talk of firebombing. Papa was certain Austria would lie in ruins by the end."

"You're right, Ilsa," I said. "The Yanks firebombed Dresden a little more than a month after you two met."

As always, Ilsa was happy ignoring useless historical facts.

"I'll say this…if I was going to fall in love in Australia…and I must've been terribly obvious that night…my father wasn't going to allow it to happen with a Black American. Tom was off-limits. But if I fell for an Aussie, the one right in front of me, well, that might work out differently. At least that's what I envisioned."

"What she didn't know that night," said Tucker, jumping in, "was how I considered myself off-limits. I was pining for a gal named Laurel back in Sydney. Even though this Austrian girl was smart and capable. Way prettier than Laurel too."

"Shush."

"The last Laurel heard from me was from a letter I posted in early September 1944 out in Fremantle. By the time I reached Darwin, three-plus months had gone by. Now, to be honest, it was rare hearing from a soldier at the front. And then I was gone."

"When he entered our lives, he certainly wasn't dead," said Ilsa, "but you had to look hard to see the man he'd been. He was very ill the night we met. I didn't care. A few nights later, I was going to come out with my hair undone, no ribbon, wearing a nice blouse, a top button undone. Make him take a good look. I was naïve. Didn't know anything about love. But I was willing to risk it all to get off our property."

"Well, let me tell you, she fixed up pretty good. Tom knew the game. He was a sharp lad and didn't try to interfere. He could read Ilsa's interest in me. Same as I could. But remember, he barely knew what that girl back home meant to me."

"I certainly didn't know," Ilsa said. "I didn't even know about her. I thought I was a real chance that night."

"In any other situation, I would've been all kisses. No doubt about it. I was a normal bloke. But crook as could be. In my head, I'm thinking, well, Laurel might've moved on. Would be a fair cow, but it happened all the time. Men went off to war, and some bludger who stayed home or came home early got the best girl."

"It sounds pretty honorable to me," I offered sympathetically. "No harm in Ilsa trying. And no crime with you getting tempted."

"Well, that's right," said Tucker, wiping some beer dribble from his shaved chin. "I thought I could play along, and while I wasn't going to get all touchy-feely, I could sure flirt a little. See if I still had some Northern Beaches charm."

In the pub's half-light, it was apparent to me that neither of them had forgotten a single moment from that night. They were ready to finish each other's sentences. Here was a couple reunited after six decades apart, acting like they'd been together forever. Long after an old war, an elderly couple was on a rocket, time-traveling together, jumping over all the failures and shortcomings of their lives. It was a long-overdue closing of that circle that goes unbroken.

Still, a harsh reality lurked in the weeds.

I'd dragged a man out of a nursing home in Sydney. Flown him to Darwin, driven down the Stuart Highway to Katherine, and brought him face-to-face with the woman he had left. I wondered if there was something sacred I wanted them both to say.

Tucker was there the night the Germans came and destroyed any chance of Ilsa living a normal life. And little Hans, the other survivor, probably never recovered. For all I knew, he'd gone off the emotional deep end.

So how was tonight supposed to end? Did Tucker have one last ace up his sleeve?

CHAPTER 47

The three of us looked at our menus and then, perhaps as a means of mending broken fences, Ilsa started detailing for me their combined efforts after the attack.

For Northgraves's final resting place, they'd buried the American's remains overlooking the Katherine River's first pool. The part of the gorge where Tom, in his finest moment, had crash-landed the Beaufort. As a tribute, they'd taken his small jackknife, the one he'd carried with him off USS *Houston*, and wedged it deep into a gum sapling. That tree was his headstone, and a mighty giant had grown up around the rusty blade.

They agreed the setting was honorable. The sailor was near water and close to the one plane he'd heroically flown off Yamdena.

In my notebook, I jotted down a reminder to see if Northgraves was listed as having died on March 1, 1942, near Batavia (now Jakarta), on Java's West Coast. And whether his name lived on in books or KIA plaques honoring the sinking of the warships *Houston* and *Perth*.

The American's parents, while they were still alive, wouldn't have known their son survived the sinking or lived heroically on an obscure island like a modern-day Robinson Crusoe before flying a stolen plane back to Australia. For them, he went down with his ship. That was better than imagining he'd died as a Japanese prisoner of war or that a Nazi killed him during an attack on an innocent Austrian family.

As for Johann, Heidi, and Frederick, Ilsa and Brad buried them in a different location such that Ilsa and Hans could always visit on the times they ventured past the gorge's first pool. Ilsa had decided natural markers would feature prominently over their "plots," and those landmarks were far better than the Dom Mausoleum in Graz.

During the next week, she and Hans gathered the family's remaining items and moved into the barn. They stayed there until the war in the Pacific ended in September. She removed any evidence of an attack. She cleared the burnt buildings and single-handedly refurbished the barn.

"From then on, I was bitter," said Ilsa. "But thorough. I grew up fast. Rebuilt my life. All through it, I was mad at God, at my father, at Hitler, and often enough, at you, Mr. Tucker. I was a right witch to everyone."

"Glad I wasn't here for any of that."

"I knew a few things you didn't."

"I'm sure," Tucker said kindly. "I always had the feeling you were told to send me off. But in our time together, you cast a spell. And it was one where you couldn't have known how you haunted me."

Hans left home the day he turned sixteen. He simply headed south. Never once returning to the NT and rarely offering comfort or correspondence to his sister. He was angry she hadn't done more for him. For them both.

After that, Ilsa came into Katherine a bit more, showing she had proper immigration papers. She told a story that included escaping the Nazis through the mountains. That part of the story was truthful, and the local council never pried for what she'd omitted. The bit about her father and mother dying in a tragic fire in 1944 was always viewed with modest sympathy.

To my way of thinking, the locals back then would've known about a strange Austrian family living up near the gorge. If there were fewer of them because of a fire, maybe that was fine. It was 1945, and Australia had different issues. The war created thousands of heartaches, and an orphaned sister and brother didn't warrant civic intervention.

For the better part of the next fifty years, Ilsa worked various jobs, all while rejecting overtures during the time when her beauty might have brought her romantic suitors and greater standing. She never allowed herself to look attractive and, for the few years he was there, wasn't a happy guardian of Hans.

With his strong German accent, his schooling in the Territory led to healthy doses of bullying and humiliation, all at the hands of postwar Australians offering little tolerance for foreigners. In her words, "he did it tough."

In the modern era, psychologists would have picked up on post-traumatic stress disorder and noted how witnessing a mother and father murdered and then having to bury four corpses (plus burn the remains of two Germans) would easily reach the syndrome's threshold for mental trauma. Ilsa and Hans's emotional scarring would've made them both distrustful of concepts like trust, affection, and love.

Hans dealt with it by leaving. Ilsa, like Garbo before her, chose to be left alone. To live in solitary confinement.

CHAPTER 48

Tucker's story contained trauma as well.

Three days after leaving Ilsa, riding Johann Stulmacher's horse, Tucker reported in at the RAAF base in Darwin. There, he found a bustling hive of Australian and American aircraft since the Americans were now flying B-24 Liberators out of Darwin, targeting oil refineries and shipping harbors in Borneo.

He told them what had happened up in the islands and about crashing into the Katherine Gorge with Northgraves. He left out talking about Ilsa and her family, save to say he'd met a family who loaned him a horse.

He did not get a hero's welcome or even immediate freedom from his servitude to king and country. In fact, Tucker's arrival created nothing but problems for the Australian brass. The reason was simple. It was early January 1945, and the war was still raging.

The commanders in Darwin were obligated to deal with a rail-thin, blood-splattered commando who'd survived a mission that, for all intents and purposes, did not exist.

Two weeks later they officially confirmed how twenty-three men had left Fremantle with Lieutenant-Colonel Ivan Lyon the previous September.

Nothing had been heard from any of them since. It meant all were feared lost.

Tucker dutifully reported the likely deaths of Captain Page, Lieutenant Sargent, and the names of Rimau men he'd seen killed during the firefight on *Mustika*. He explained how he and an American sailor from the USS *Houston* had flown a stolen bomber from Yamdena into Katherine. Northgraves, he said, hadn't survived the crash. There was no body to recover.

What concerned the Australian military exec who took responsibility for Tucker was hearing a Z Special Unit man suggest that none of the men from Rimau survived. Further, after a bit more digging, he determined the assigned British submarine (the HMS *Tantalus*) never went back to the rendezvous island. His conclusion? Every Rimau man had been on his own from the moment Lyon put the crew in the water and left them to sink the *Mustika*.

Tucker repeatedly told the officer that if no one had made it back before him, then he was confident all twenty-three men were dead. Lyon was an incredible leader, but based on what Tucker had just barely survived, the Japanese still controlled the entire area south of Borneo.

He also knew the Aussie brass, cautious to a fault, were assessing liability and career damage. Collectively, they were looking at no known survivors of a secret mission except for an unlisted alternate. Worse, the British purposely (or accidentally) had stranded good Australian men. The prime minister was already infuriated with Churchill. This would make matters worse.

How this translated for Tucker was simple. There'd be no mention in dispatches. In essence, Brad Tucker did not exist. Not yet.

"I wasn't having any of their nonsense," Tucker recalled. "I pitched a fit, demanded my rights. Fought 'em at every turn. Eventually, this colonel named Nabb relented and said I could send a telegram to Laurel. Not to my family, though, because they'd talk or get stinko. But I could write Laurel, and they would hand-deliver it."

"That doesn't sound remotely plausible," I said. "You're an Australian citizen. They couldn't hold you like that or keep you from communicating."

"They sure could, sonny boy. I was in their service, and once I rode onto that base, they owned me. Well and truly. They could treat me like a hero or a deserter. And essentially lock me up if I didn't follow their orders."

"Unbelievable."

"Well, remember, these are war years. There were no legal interventions like today. You copped it good once they got their mitts on you. And they got them on me tight."

CHAPTER 49

Now it was my turn, the American armchair historian, the person called on to fill in the blanks.

"From what I can gather—and mind you, this is all wild speculation—I think Hitler or Goebbels must have sent agents to Sydney to get the film," I said.

"What film?" said Tucker.

"Ahh, that's right. You still don't know why Germans came after the Stulmachers."

"Too right, I don't. Ilsa? You never had a chance to explain the intruders that night."

Straightening her hair, Ilsa paused to consider her words. As we would find out, there was no lie to tell, but there was an omission she needed to come clean about. Something she wanted to condense before the two oldies got sleepy.

"Before you crashed in the gorge," she began, "our family had been living in Katherine for about six years. We'd escaped from Austria because my father accidentally filmed Hitler at a friend's house. Naked. With another man."

"What?"

"Today with Gay Pride and the Sydney Mardi Gras, it's not a big thing.

But in 1938, that would've destroyed Hitler. I hid the film—well, a friend of mine in Graz did—but right after that, our family did a runner through the Alps and all the way down into Australia."

"Oh, my word. That's why they attacked you. They came after the evidence."

"Except it wasn't here. We never brought it with us."

"Actually, I did some research," I interjected, "and found that throughout the midthirties, there was a group in Sydney called the German Workers Front, the DAF, holding organized meetings for German wool buyers. They would meet weekly at Sydney hotels like the Carlton or the Exchange. On top of that, there was a German-language newspaper published called *Die Brucke*. It was supervised by a Nazi firebrand named Walter Karl Ladendorff. He was the most powerful Nazi leader in Australia, reporting directly to Himmler or the Gestapo."

"That doesn't give you agents in Katherine," said Tucker gruffly.

"No, but just as the war broke out in September 1939," I countered, "nearly eighteen months after Ilsa's father films Hitler in Graz, Ladendorff gets called back to Berlin."

"Interesting."

"Exactly. What if the German high command knew the Stulmachers came into Australia? Ladendorff would have had time to check on any German immigrants entering around July thirty-eight. And when he didn't find a family of five turning up in Sydney or Melbourne, he widens the net. Discovers an entry in Darwin."

"Do you think Germany sneaked agents into Australia at some point after that?"

"Not sure. They could've used loyalists who came up from Sydney. But another option is thinking about the US, where the Germans could have had university students studying in America that got sent home in forty-two. It's not impossible Germany sent spies here, dressed as American soldiers during MacArthur's time in Melbourne."

"Bit of a stretch," Tucker said, "but I guess the proof is in the attack. Still, how do they get from Sydney to Katherine?"

"Good question," I offered. "Maybe they took the Ghan train from Adelaide to Alice Springs and hired or commandeered a car. There'd be no records, but two Americans heading north with forged papers wouldn't have attracted much attention. Plus, Australians would've been slapping their backs in the pubs."

"Maybe," Ilsa said. "What I can't work out, though, is that by December 1944, the war in Europe is almost over. The Americans are moving through France and Italy. They're closing in."

"What were the big battles in January forty-five?" asked Tucker.

"The last great German counteroffensive, the Battle of the Bulge, was launched in December around Belgium and France. If two spies came into Oz, it might've been part of a plan to force the Allies into a peace agreement ending the war. If the Stulmacher film surfaces, it kills any sympathy for Germany. Not that there would've been much for the Nazis or the Japanese."

"Still a stretch." It was Tucker arguing for stronger logic.

"Well, out here, two things were working against my father," said Ilsa. "The first was only a handful of German and Austrians immigrated into Australia during the 1937 to '39 time frame. Almost all were Jewish. I checked on this once, and nearly every one of these immigrants came in through Sydney or Melbourne. So, an Austrian family in the Northern Territory, one that came into Darwin, stands out like a rotten mango."

"And the second?"

"Johann Stulmacher doesn't like going into town. He's standoffish. Doesn't drink at the hotel pub. The locals create rumors. They figure *he's* the spy. Now, if two Americans come into the pub with big southern drawls and suggest an Austrian up around the gorge is a Nazi, well, they would've told them which roads to turn down to find us. By 1944, Australians, in general, hate Germans because they're always starting world wars."

"Ilsa? Has it been like that for sixty years?" Tucker's wrinkled face revealed his sadness.

"Seemed that way. It's the whole Teutonic blood thing. Good as engineers, good with cameras. Good at war. But two American agents turn up saying, 'They're up to something out there in Katherine. Can't ever trust 'em, can you, hey?'"

"I would've trusted you. With my life. I dropped out of the sky as a single man and should've been smart enough to marry you. Would've fought 'em all. We would've made a brilliant team."

That was the moment I grasped just how easily life sometimes pivots on the slightest of decisions. We put our money on the roulette number, and Fate spins the wheel. It's rare when the pit boss lets you have a second spin.

CHAPTER 50

"Go back a minute." It was Ilsa lifting her head. "What did you send Laurel from the base in Darwin?"

"They let me construct the shortest telegram ever. Said I had to use something like a spy name so no one else would know it was me…on the possibility she might wave it around. I had to think of a few words, something only she would recognize. So that she'd know it was fair dinkum. Want to see it?"

"Course I do."

"Well, I brought it with me. Figured you would."

Tucker reached into a small folder and produced a see-through plastic sandwich bag. Inside was a dog-eared, yellowed telegram, clearly from the World War II era, the black ink faded but still legible.

```
LAUREL STOP CAN'T WRITE MUCH STOP ALL STILL
SECRET STOP NEED YOU TO KNOW AM STILL
ALIVE STOP HOME SAFELY WHEN THIS WAR ENDS
STOP TELL NO ONE YOU GOT THIS NOT EVEN
FOLKS STOP HOPE YOU CAN WAIT FOR ME STOP
RALEIGH WARRIEWOOD
```

I looked at the signature line. It sounded British, but Tucker explained a Raleigh was the bicycle she'd ridden, followed by the name of the rocky ocean drop where he and Laurel would've visited and jumped around.

"What did she do?" Ilsa finally asked. "Did she try to come find you?"

"The short version is no," Tucker replied.

"Well, how was it when you finally got back to her?" I asked.

"Like I said, she'd moved on. It wasn't easy. I was the opposite of a hero. Up in Darwin, they'd created a new story for me to use. One that took me off the Rimau mission and embedded me in these other settings for the four months I'd been gone plus the eight months they held me."

"The bastards."

"You can say that. They blew hot and cold the whole time. Doctored me up a lot, drugged me. All while saying they were nursing me back to health at the CRS. The Casualty Receiving Station. Mostly, they kept me secluded. Until the Japanese surrendered in September. It was almost exactly one year to the day we'd shipped out of Freo."

"So now what?" I asked. "The Germans and Japanese are beaten, everybody's celebrating, kissing for the cameras. Were you?"

"Yes, tell us," said Ilsa. She'd been quiet most of the evening, but Laurel's entry into the story was revealing. I sensed Ilsa was about to learn about the woman who had commanded Brad's honor and loyalty.

"Well, they discharged me before my condition was fully resolved," Tucker said. "I was still suffering from illusions. Jungle phantoms appearing in my sleep. Certain loud noises, like a door slamming, and I'd get catatonic. I was the equivalent of shell shocked."

"Who wouldn't be?"

"Yes, but here's the rub. This was supposed to be a magical time. The war was won. But for me, there was no "Roll Out the Barrel" or "Rule Britannia" when I came home. No girls selling kisses to me in Sydney's Martin Place. A big reason was because I wasn't fully me. We didn't know about PTSD or any other fancy terms back then."

"Battle fatigue," I offered.

"The world had essentially spun off its moorings for me," said Tucker. "I wasn't nimble anymore. I was wounded."

He drank a mouthful of the amber liquid in front of him. I gathered he still wanted to give Ilsa more details.

"I'll give you an example that gets ahead of things. Either the malaria, beriberi, or drugs shot into me in Darwin made me sterile. Got into my prostate or something. So when I realized Laurel had moved on and I couldn't give anyone kids, I got pretty down on myself."

"Did you find someone else?" Ilsa said the words with something approaching true hope.

"I did, but she was all wrong. We were both victims. I guess when you're down that far, the back alleys and dodgy hotels will do."

"Oh, Brad," Ilsa said. "I'm so sorry."

"It was rough. And me, I'm always thinking it would be nice to plan a trip to Babar. Back then, you'd have to have flown through Dili. It woulda cost a packet, but I'd go to that swimming hole and waterfall where I'd first met Tom. I held onto that dream, but she eventually got sick. Dirty needles. Didn't suffer long. Died in my arms in Kings Cross. After that, I got sober and cleaned up. Got involved with an RSL doing janitorial work."

The old man patted his heart, his eyes watering.

"Many is the day I wished God would have let the emperor's boys get me. I survived the mission only to get clobbered by life. Pretty far from the hero someone deserved."

"Stop that."

It was Austrian Ilsa, stern and fierce. I worried her Mrs. Hyde was about to emerge like the night she'd surprised me in the pub and then sent me looking for Tucker.

"You're right to give me a proper bashing for saying those words," said Tucker. "Have no worries about that. Should've come and found you."

"Too right," said Ilsa. "Because you were, and still are, a good man."

"My last night with Annie—that was her name—she was drifting in and out. Mostly she'd sleep, but I knew our time together was ending. And then she came fully awake one last time and whispered it would be okay. Life was tough. Not everybody got unicorns and rainbows."

Around the trio, the bar traffic was picking up. Someone had just picked the song "Holy Grail" by the Australian band Hunters and Collectors for the jukebox. The big strumming chords underscored something about waking from a strange dream. Halfway through the song, I made out the words *foolish beings dying like flies* and something about *Nobody deserves to die.*

It was followed a stanza later by:

I followed orders
God knows where I'd be
But I woke up alone
All my wounds were clean
I'm still here
I'm still a fool for the Holy Grail

Tucker saw I had turned my head to listen. He interrupted my mental wandering and offered his take on grails and crusades.

"Ilsa sent me away that last night in Katherine. Said she and Hans would be fine. That I wasn't to worry. But I should've. I guess sometimes we settle for surviving instead of fighting for what could be."

Tucker broke down and wept. It was an old man's snort.

"God took Annie's pain away that night. He wasn't so quick with me. Worked me over every bit as good as the Japanese or the Aussies in Darwin. Since then, I've been looking for another Tom Northgraves to get me on that glide path to Katherine. Get me out of the War Vets."

I looked at Ilsa, wondering how she was taking his emotional pain. Her plan and my legwork had somehow reunited them.

Tucker had deftly skipped over his marriage to a woman who sounded like a junkie. A woman fighting her own demons. It would've been hard to give a man, one back from a terrifying mission, transformative love. To fully understand the kind of man who might drink heavily, struggle riding a bike, or find himself incapable of entering salt water. One who might jump about at night while sleeping.

It wasn't hard for me to imagine Annie introducing Tucker to street drugs and steering him away from becoming a productive member of society. Instead, he became residual damage from another war.

A silence settled over the three of us.

I wished I could've met the Brad Tucker, the strapping boxer, who left from Fremantle in a submarine, starting a journey that found him paddling across miles of open water. The man who might've been there for Ilsa as a loving partner playing his part in nursing her emotional wounds.

"So, where do we go from here?" said Ilsa, clearly showing signs of tiring.

"We dump him," said Tucker. "Get him to shout the drinks and mains. That means pay the tab, mate. Then he drives us back to your place. I think we'll both sleep quite well tonight."

"What about himself?" she asked.

"Oh, he'll be right. He'll find a room and start writing this whole thing up. Down the track, he'll find no one believes it. But if he comes back for me in two days' time, I expect we can give him a fairy-tale ending."

Ilsa smiled. Evidently, she had one more concern.

"Before we leave, there's one thing everyone needs to know. I sent Brad away that night without asking him to dig up the Graz rally and Hitler footage on purpose. My father's last words were intended for me to give Brad the film. But that worthless canister had caused enough trouble already. It destroyed a family. I decided it was going to stay in Graz where it couldn't hurt anyone else."

"Ahhh," said Tucker, drumming his digits on the table. "I knew there was something up that night. But I couldn't fully make out what your father was saying, and you didn't let on."

"It was better for you. Maybe worse for me…for both of us…but it had to be done."

I knew how Tucker wanted the rest of the night to play out but wasn't so sure about Ilsa. When she asked to excuse herself, I asked Tucker if he knew what he was doing.

"Course I do," he said. "I can't give her what she wanted all those years ago, but I can give her something she doesn't think exists. She's lived alone for six decades wondering if lying next to me would've worked. It's not about sex now. Neither of us needs that and none of the body parts probably work right anyways. But if I hold her as she falls asleep, as I fall asleep…and she finds me there when she wakes up, well, it might fulfill a small dream for both of us. That little bit of heaven on earth she always deserved. And in my way, I'll finally be there for her. The way Laurel was for me."

"It's an interesting approach to love," I mused, motioning for the check.

"'Tis, but then this isn't the physical kind that everyone gets all hot and bothered about. This is the kind of love where someone says, 'I will hold you.' And for a little while, you relax. Even if your bones ache and you have to get up to pee twice a night."

I smiled and thought about that.

He'd been preaching about kindness in the face of social distortion and civil complexity. Doing it at a time when people were choosing more empty space in a big bed instead of a warm leg brushing up against their own skin. Choosing TV and Internet sites over human touch.

"The next two nights won't solve Ilsa's hang-ups," Tucker said. "Or mine. And both of us could be dead within a year…although judging by her constitution, I reckon she'll be around a while longer. She's a survivor, that one."

"That's for sure."

I could see Ilsa emerging from the bathroom at the far end of the pub where a giant saltwater croc was mounted on the wall. Its use as a decoration made marginal sense this far inland because salties can get into the Katherine River during the Wet. Maybe the crocs in the Katherine dove down to investigate the *Miss Laurel* when they reached the first pool.

"Here she comes," I said. "You want me to come back in two days?"

"Do that for me, will you? I'd like to let Ilsa know she'll get a better journey in the next life. That's certainly something I've learned. Isn't there an old Hebrew proverb that says something like 'Man plans. God laughs?' I'm hoping God's plan for my hereafter leaves me happy as Larry."

"Are we ready, lads?" asked Ilsa as she returned. "It's getting past my bedtime."

"Indeed, we are," said Tucker. "Indeed, we are."

CHAPTER 51

Two days later, when I came to pick Tucker up at Ilsa's place, I couldn't help but notice the big smiles on their geriatric faces. We were running late, and I was obligated to start the process of flying Tucker back to Sydney and Narrabeen's War Vets Village. I told him when I got him home, I intended to record a few more pieces of the story.

Tucker smiled and said, "Better do it quick, lad."

"What do you mean?"

"I'm not long for this particular island. It's time to shove off. Have to get back on the evening currents."

I chuckled at his kayaking reference but knew with near-certain conviction I might not see Tucker very often after our next goodbye. My home in Maryland is a long way from Sydney, and who knew where my next project would take me. Tucker might not be alive the next time I got back to Australia.

As I worked out my traveling calculus, Ilsa was forcing a freezer bag of random items into my hand. From a quick glance, it looked like it held a hairpin, a shell casing, some papers, and a few other items I couldn't quite make out. She said I would be able to connect the dots after I got my nose out of my notebook. But she also had another idea to try out.

"Before you two start getting teary-eyed about the possibility of never seeing each other again, I want to run an idea by you. See if it floats your proverbial boat."

"Lay it on me," I said. We were not in a huge hurry, and a crazy idea from an old Austrian refugee warranted at least some consideration.

"What would you two say if I came to Sydney with Brad? Sold up the station and moved to Narrabeen? Mango and melon developers, the big corporates, have been after my property for years. Turns out my soil is unique. Plus, it's the last great block of land next to the park. I could get a packet for it and afford a unit in or near the War Vets if Brad vouched for me."

"That's brilliant," said Tucker. "Did we discuss it the other night, or did I dream it? It would be the start of a beautiful friendship."

"That's Bogart's line," I said. "You can't use it. And it can't be the *start* because you two codgers met a thousand years ago."

"Call it what you want," said Ilsa, "but we could finish this story in ways no one would ever expect. Two oldies picking up where they left off."

Two days later, during my last few minutes with Ilsa and Brad in Sydney, a taxi waiting outside, Tucker produced a carefully wrapped oilskin package and handed it to me.

Inside the overlapping folds was an old knife in a battered leather sheath. The words *Camillus* and *USMC* were still legible on the polished steel blade. There were a few strands of loose strapping on the knife's handle.

Bringing the blade close to my face, I predicted high-tech scanning devices would find microscopic spots of German blood dried on the raw edge. The gunmetal blade was no longer sharp, but jabbed into a man's chest, the knife would still perform its deadly assignment.

Holding it made me uncomfortable. My own military service had taken place in the sky. Tucker did his up close. Man-to-man. Face-to-face. This pigsticker, as the Aussies called them, came from his story. Not mine.

What struck me as strange was knowing a US Marine Corps knife would survive long after the man who fought with it had expired. Somewhat like sunken ships resting at the bottom of Darwin's harbor. Or a rusted Bristol Beaufort sitting deep in the Katherine River.

The iron and steel lived on. But never the flesh and blood.

I knew then tourists visiting Sydney would enter a different gorge, a man-made one of glitter skyscrapers standing tall over that city's Darling Harbour. There, they would visit the Maritime Museum and, having paid to see all the exhibits, would step outside to the water's edge to investigate an imposing black submarine or the Krait, the little ship Ivan Lyon used during Operation Jaywick on the successful first mission to Singapore.

They wouldn't see Tucker's knife.

That was because I decided, right there on the spot, that my documentary would start with me contacting the Indonesian air force. I would fly into Jakarta to interview some accommodating general, telling him I was doing a story about his islands during World War II. Then I'd tell him about Babar.

"This island is very far from here," he would say with a frown. "More than 2,500 kilometers to Maluku Province. What is out there, friend?"

"Back in 1944, an old Australian friend of mine hid there. The Japanese were chasing him. I want to create a small memorial to him. Something no one will see. Could a short visit be arranged during the next week?"

The general would squint his dark eyes and do some calculating. There would be dark sweat stains on his shirt from the humidity.

"It is almost four hours flying to Ambon, and then you must take a ferry to Tepa. The port in Babar is quite small. These islands hold little economic significance. It is not easy to get there. Does your Australian mean that much to you?"

"He changed my life," I would say.

I wouldn't go into the gory details, because my mission was simple. Brad and Ilsa represented something very romantic to me. They proved it was never too late to love or love again. To rediscover love.

If it took me two days to reach the island, the last portion in a small boat, my time and travel costs were small in comparison to what those two had sacrificed.

CHAPTER 52

April 2007—Annapolis, Maryland

Now, as I look back, a middle-aged man sitting in a distressed brown leather chair, I can write that's almost exactly how things turned out.

Three months after Brad Tucker gave me his knife, I was sitting in the Writers Bar at the Raffles Jakarta admiring artwork styled on that of Hendra Gunawan, the hotel's patron saint. Bored with wandering the streets of Jakarta and the city's notorious Golden Triangle, I was waiting for a call.

Finally, that Indonesian general, a close facsimile of the one I previously imagined, rang the hotel, and a bellman guided me to a beige house phone.

General Giam did not sound enthusiastic but offered me the chance to jump aboard a military transport flight, an old C-141 Starlifter to Ambon the next morning. The ferry to Tepa would get me there by dinnertime.

He had arranged for me to stay with a Christian family, missionaries from Australia, but his superiors, he said, were suspicious of my motives. Would I explain again my intentions? I laughed and repeated the fast version. In my head, though, I wondered whether the general's intelligence group was trying to determine if I was servicing the CIA by inspecting remote places for the US Air Force or Navy.

"My office got you a two-day permit. You know this is the far edge of our country, yes?"

I didn't care. I suspected they would have eyes on me the whole time.

"That's wonderful," I said with appreciation. "I won't need much time. I just want to honor his memory."

In truth, I needed one day to find a giant gum with large soaring branches. Then, taking my time, I'd climb up, far off the ground, and conjure up the frantic, mad world of 1944–'45.

The banyan I'd pick would offer a wide cranny where I could wedge a newly inscribed (and sharpened) blade featuring three names. This slender cenotaph would honor Ilsa, Brad, and Tom. Even if they had been buried or cremated somewhere else.

I imagined God laughing the day I finally reached Babar. I cried. Slow, melancholy tears I couldn't explain.

My backpack contained a change of clothes, a medical kit, and a nice bottle of Australian shiraz, a Penfolds, I'd picked up in the Katherine bottle shop. I drank most of it up in that gum, savoring their individual and collective heroism.

I knew then, as I know now, proper historians reading this book would make clear that Brad Tucker never existed. They'd wave their figurative swords and rant about me getting duped by an old lady in Katherine or an elderly imposter claiming to have survived a 1944 mission so suicidal every heroic man involved was killed in action or beheaded by the Japanese.

For my part, I would have to respectfully ignore their righteous condemnation because I alone had listened to Tucker's story and believed him. Ilsa's tale too. She was the one who stopped me in my tracks that night in Katherine on a warm evening when I ventured out with the brash young pilots of the 75th.

Since that night, I've collected enough material to create a rich story and fit it around the historical details that originated with Operation Rimau. History books detail that mission with certain nuanced facts often disputed.

My effort would simply add to that story, humbly attempting to honor two men and a lonely girl from Graz.

They deserve this small tribute.

CHAPTER 53

March 2005—Narrabeen, NSW, Australia

On our last day together, the day Tucker gave me the Marine Corps knife, the old Aussie warrior was less clear than the first time we met. He rambled, mumbling about ocean conditions. But then, like a dark storm on the horizon, the cloud of fatigue—or maybe it was his early dementia—well, it moved away.

"Turn that foolish recorder off," he instructed me with mild agitation.

"Right. Sorry."

"Laurel got me through the jungles," he said. "Through all the nights on the water. In the gum tree when I was surrounded. In the plane we stole to get off Yamdena. Even up in Katherine when the Nazis came to kill the Stulmachers."

"Back home, she had no idea what you were going through."

"No, she really didn't. Funny, though, that while she was with me in the jungle, she was also with someone else."

Tucker's mind wandered again. The War Vets nurses told me that wasn't unusual. Patients who fought in wars frequently slipped into fits of fear requiring sedation. They felt Tucker should've been at a different facility, but one of the few things sedating him was staring at Narrabeen Lagoon, the place where he once adventured with four teenage friends.

I knew that story and how a teenage Tucker had come face-to-face with Nazis in 1938. Nearly seven years on, he had seen them again. How often had those villains infiltrated his dreams? How often had his time drifting on the open water, ducking the emperor's navy, taken away some foundational part of his soul?

After another two months had passed, I was sitting in yet another hotel, this one in Buenos Aires, when I got an email from the War Vets Village in Narrabeen. They had gotten around to alerting me Tucker had died in his sleep on Boxing Day. That was fitting enough, given Tucker's time in various boxing dens and his amazing journey with Tom Northgraves that same day back in 1944.

It was during those Japanese boxing matches, prior to the 1936 Olympics, when Tucker mastered the handful of Japanese words that saved him from a deadly trap, a "short corner" that would have finished him.

Then, in 1945, when he came home, no one had the proper time or mental health tools to help heal a damaged vet. He would've died alone in Narrabeen if Ilsa hadn't concocted her plan luring us both back to Katherine. That trip completed Tucker's unusual circle and finished something beautiful from a distant December.

I looked at the email and knew my role had made it possible for them to reunite and spend their last month together.

Not long after Brad died, Ilsa by his side, the old girl passed herself. She had returned to Katherine and was found by a couple of New Zealand hikers back in a remote section of Nitmiluk National Park. There wouldn't have been time for her to sell her property.

I was certain I knew where they found the body. It would've been a place overlooking the mysterious gorge where she'd once ridden a horse to rescue two heroes. The place where Bolung, the Rainbow Serpent, protected the Katherine's muddy banks.

According to the bored coroner, her departure came from an overdose of sleeping pills. Wilcox was his name, and he suggested cancer might have influenced the proceedings. He said he hadn't known her more than seeing her in town every now and then. Then he repeated one of those unkind myths about Ilsa. That she'd been a Nazi.

I didn't correct the smug bastard. It wouldn't have done any good. I just asked if there'd been a note or random belongings with the body. He said Ilsa was found holding a torn, bloodied shirtsleeve. It didn't make any sense to him because the stain was quite old, and the cloth didn't go with anything she was wearing. He assumed she might've picked it up during her hike.

I smiled, thinking how that faded piece of fabric had held Ilsa together for nearly sixty years. Kept her slender hopes of happiness alive. I imagined she would have been pleased with my deduction. And satisfied how things ended in the Katherine Gorge.

AUTHOR'S NOTE

The Australian-British World War II mission code-named Operation Rimau, a commando attack on Japanese-held Singapore Harbor during September and October 1944, really did exist, and while I took liberties with a few facts, specifically the inclusion of Brad Tucker on the mission, it's long been established three Australian raiders survived a daring seaborne escape covering more than 3,200 kilometers of open-water navigation along the entire length of modern-day Indonesia's scattered chain of islands. To that end, I'm indebted to Ronald McKie's *The Heroes*, Lynette Ramsay Silver's *Heroes of Rimau*, Macklin and Thompson's *Kill the Tiger* (and *Operation Rimau*), and Ian McPhedran's 2018 book *The Mighty Krait* (HarperCollins Australia).

This spectacular journey was accomplished during two grueling months, just south of the equator, with the trio consistently evading a massive Japanese dragnet designed specifically to find men paddling a battered submersible canoe toward Allied-controlled Dutch New Guinea.

As historians later proved, the Japanese military remained focused on one goal: catching those men before they reached safety. In the end, each of the twenty-three men on the Rimau mission died fighting or was beheaded on 7 July 1945, less than six weeks before Japan surrendered. In Australia, the first official statement about the Rimau raid was not released to the public until 1 August 1946.

This historical fiction attempts to revisit the Rimau mission and the homeward-bound heroism of the three men involved. Please note where Australian dialect has been used (and by today's ears it can sound contrived or colloquial), every effort was made to capture the logical vernacular of Australians circa 1935–45. This era was a different time from the present, and conversations employed different nuances as well as varying insensitivities for matters such as systemic racism, chauvinism, and sexism. This book is set in a different time and deviates from our contemporary attempts to address equality, equity, nondiscrimination, and inclusion.

Also, where possible, and without attempting to confuse the reader, the countries and islands of the Java, Bali, Flores, Banda, and Arafura Seas were identified by their 1944-era designations (for those sections of the book). For example, modern-day Jakarta, Indonesia, was called Batavia (from when it was the capital of the Dutch East Indies), and Portuguese Timor was used instead of East Timor.

On the matter of "found film," I must report that I did see rare family footage of Adolf Hitler's April 4, 1938, Graz rally, and it was provided to me by Chris Weiss, a fellow Syracuse University employee. It is clear to me that Hitler, circa 1938, really did solicit and receive near-hypnotic allegiance from the Austrians visible in that short film. The other filmed event is entirely fictitious.

Lastly, where an Austrian Roman Catholic priest is mentioned in chapters 8 and 9, there was such a person in the Diocese of Innsbruck Feldkirch. His name was Father Carl Lambert, and his rebellious "insurgency" (much like that of the Lutheran pastor Dietrich Bonhoeffer) led to constant surveillance and eventually the torture chambers at Dachau and Sachsenhausen-Oranienburg. Having chosen the Bible over Hitler's Mein Kampf, Lambert was beheaded on 13 November 1944. Bonhoeffer would be hung at Flossenbürg in Bavaria on 9 April 1945, just three weeks before Adolf Hitler would commit suicide in Berlin.

HISTORICAL AFTERWORD

While elements of this story are no longer much discussed in Australia, there was a time in September 1943, well after the Japanese bombed Pearl Harbor and subsequently overran Malaya, Singapore, the Philippines, Dutch Timor, and Rabaul in New Britain, that military men in Melbourne authored a plan to send a disguised fishing boat (named the *Krait*—after a particularly venomous snake) into Singapore Harbor. They hoped Australian commandos could place limpet mines on Japanese supply ships and sink one or two because any disruption to the emperor's war machine was a good one.

While a highly successful outcome would only deliver the slightest of results—during an increasingly brutal war—the real purpose of the mission was much more emotional and so very Australian.

Historically speaking, while the massive conflict throughout the Pacific was continuing to turn in the Allies' favor by early 1943—the Battles of Midway (June 4–7, 1942) and Guadalcanal (August 7, 1942–February 7, 1943) were early indicators of success—the reason for a seemingly desperate Australian commando effort in September 1943 was simple: to hit back at Japan.

The Japanese started bombing Darwin in Australia's far north on 19 February 1942—sinking eight warships there including the US destroyer USS *Peary* during the "Pearl Harbor of Australia"—and decimating Australia's northern coastline until November 1943.

Japan's naval force eventually bombed Broome (Western Australia), Darwin, and other Northern Territory sites more than sixty times during that twenty-month period. Adelaide River, a small township southeast of Darwin and site of the infamous Adelaide River Stakes (the quip used by people joking about their own mass exodus), was the last NT city bombed, taking shells the morning of 12 November 1943.

Meanwhile, due north of Australia (during most of 1942), Japan's navy methodically grabbed key ports, airstrips, and cities throughout the South China, Java, Banda, and Coral Seas, and the northeastern edges of the great Indian Ocean. Until the Americans recovered from the devastation of Pearl Harbor, there was no military force available to stop the Japanese onslaught.

South of Australia's Northern Territory (and this "story" is still routinely recounted by elderly Australians), during the last week of May 1942, Japan dared to attack Sydney using three midget subs that targeted Port Jackson's great harbor. While the Japanese just barely missed out on the chance to sink the cruiser USS *Chicago*, one minisub ended up killing twenty-one when it sank the HMAS *Kuttabul*, an Australian depot ship that was serving as a floating barracks.

By June, Japan's Imperial Navy began working in Australia's shipping lanes, successfully attacking Sydney and Newcastle. In all, more than seventy Aussie sailors died during this month, forcing Australia's government (and frightened population) to concede, albeit briefly, that the threat of a Japanese invasion was not only possible but indeed very real.

Australia's nominal protector, England, had long since pulled most of Australia's fighting-age men into North Africa, the Dutch East Indies, or New Guinea, leaving the "Great Southern Land" vulnerable to the same swift demise witnessed and endured in 1941 and early 1942 by more heavily defended countries to the north. Japan's ruthlessness in striking southward was no less punishing than Germany's blitzkriegs into Poland, Belgium, and France.

Rabaul fell on 23 January 1942 when the Australian garrison of 1,400 men was overwhelmed by more than 5,000 Japanese marines. More than 900 Aussies surrendered that day, with more than 150 of them reportedly slaughtered at the hands of their captors. Notably enough, Japan did not yield Rabaul until the war ended in August 1945 (largely because the Allied command simply bypassed Rabaul, cutting it off as the Allies moved north).

By 15 February 1942, Singapore, the Lion City, long thought by the British to be impregnable, fell (after just seven days of assault), and not long thereafter rumors began circulating that members of Australia's government were considering a concept that, in March 1943, US General Douglas MacArthur ill-advisedly called the Brisbane Line. It was a "plan" whereby Australia's northernmost civilians would retreat southward, burning everything north of the Queensland capital or the twenty-seventh latitudinal line.

A year before, in March 1942, MacArthur himself beat a hasty retreat back to Australia from Corregidor Island (south of the Philippines' Bataan Peninsula), leaving behind a heroic overmatched fortress that fell after months of brutal punishment during 5–6 May 1942. With the American surrender of Corregidor, the Bataan Death March would unfold, with thousands of Allied soldiers and Filipino residents losing their lives.

In short, the middle months of 1942 were frightful and worrisome for nations all around the world but most notably for Australia because the Australian military was fighting overseas. This much was true: a land mass roughly the size of Canada (or the continental forty-eight US states) lay virtually undefended and represented for Japan's military leaders the most attractive marginally populated resource-laden outpost west of the Hawaiian Islands.

This dire abstract is what makes the story of the Krait and the men involved in Operation Jaywick so unusual.

At a time when there was significant doubt if the Axis powers of Germany and Japan could be stopped, a tiny, almost insignificant guerilla mission to Singapore was launched. It was led by the legendary Lieutenant-Colonel Ivan Lyon of the Gordon Highlanders, and when it succeeded, with every man safely returned to Australia's Exmouth Gulf in Western Australia in October

1943, Lyon began planning a second attack on Singapore for 1944. To the exact same spot.

By all reports, Lyon was an amazing soldier. His first legendary escape from Singapore, after setting up various links in a Sumatran escape route (known to many as the Tourist Route), came in March and April 1942. During that tenuous time, as the Japanese moved south out of Singapore, Lyon piloted a small wooden Malayan sailing boat, the *DJohannis*, for thirty-six days across more than 1,650 miles of open water from Padang to a point just off the coast of Ceylon. There, Lyon and his seventeen passengers were picked up in their rotting prahu by the British merchantman *Anglo-Canadian*.

Some contemporary historians now consider Lyon's second guerilla attack on the Japanese at Singapore to have been flawed from the start, and even select members of the assembled team doubted Lyon's logic. But whether bound by the unspoken code of Australian "mateship" or gluttons for hardship and danger, six of the original men indicated they wouldn't let Lyon go back without them…even if Operation Rimau led to their deaths.

Originally, Rimau was to be known as Operation Hornbill, but a shortening of the Malay word for tiger (harimau) was ultimately selected for a mission that clearly must've appeared suicidal from the start.

As those twenty-three men entered the British submarine HMS *Porpoise* (later sunk by the Japanese in January 1945) in Careening Bay near Fremantle's Garden Island on 11 September 1944, each of the commandos knew it was highly unlikely the Japanese would get caught off guard again. In fact, given the concept of a Japanese soldier not "losing face" or betraying (by human failure) the divine nature of the emperor's grand plan, it was likely every Japanese sentry or patrol boat assigned to protect Singapore (known to the Japanese as Shōnantō or "Light of the South") had been reminded of their predecessors' significant failure.

On the night of 23 September 1944, the *Porpoise* dropped anchor off the uninhabited Merapas Island, and two Rimau men scouted what was then designated as Rimau's primary rendezvous point and rear base. The plans called for a British sub to return to Merapas six weeks later on 8 November and evacuate any and all survivors.

Five days later, the *Porpoise* surfaced near a dot in the ocean called Datu (off Borneo), and Lyon's crew commandeered a fishing boat named *Mustika*. They loaded it with twenty-six small submersible low-in-the-water boats (either Australian-built MKIII folboats or British Sleeping Beauties) and returned to Merapas, where Lt. Walter Carey and four men were left behind on the lightly inhabited island to guard provisions.

From there, the remaining eighteen Rimau raiders put back out to sea in the *Mustika* and started a more than one-hundred-nautical-mile journey over the treacherous open waters of the Rhio Archipelago (using the Temiang and Suji Straits) to Singapore.

Unfortunately, this second Australian mission was discovered, most likely in an innocent fashion, by a Malay patrol boat (in the service of the Japanese) late on the afternoon of October 10 near the island of Pulau Laban (some records suggest it was off Kasu Island), and in a moment of unusual panic or extreme provocation, the Rimau men found themselves firing on the police launch. Their cover now blown (because, significantly, one Malayan inspector alertly, or luckily, managed to escape), Lyon turned the *Mustika* south, away from Singapore.

By the time he reached the island of Kapala Jernith (near Batam Island), he'd made the decision to blow up the *Mustika*, his primary transport, thus removing the largest and most obvious evidence of this Allied commando activity. In doing so, he split his men into separate canoe parties. As the largest group went into the water, they knew they were roughly fifty to seventy nautical miles from their rear supply base (depending on the route they selected) and weeks away from a possible submarine rescue off Merapas.

What happened next carries much conjecture, but most historians believe Lyon plus six others—either before the *Mustika* was scuttled or shortly thereafter—were able to attack and sink three Japanese ships in Singapore. Various other Rimau boat parties scattered and raced for the islands at Bintan,

Pompong, Temiang, and Buaja.

According to Australian journalist Ronald McKie (writing in 1960), at least one group of Rimau raiders, in a three-man canoe, headed south by southeast toward Sumatra, Java, Timor (all part of modern-day Indonesia) and undoubtedly would have wanted to move along the island chain until it veered to the northeast (if they made it that far), toward Dutch New Guinea. Having abandoned the risky idea of waiting at Merapas for a sub that might never come back for them—logical reasoning since Merapas was in the middle of a heavily controlled Japanese zone—the three above-mentioned men, one of whom McKie identifies as Lieutenant A. L. "Blondie" Sargent, made first for Mapor Island or Pompong Island. They had little choice but to sail (or row) for home.

At some point, this trio, moving almost exclusively at night, was able to continue evading detection…but the Japanese naval noose around them tightened daily. All of the other Rimau commandos had already been captured or killed. Those kept alive were ultimately headed for Singapore's notorious Outram Road Gaol, where the Japanese secret police, the Kempeitai, were consistently brutal in their management of captured Allied soldiers.

The operative word, though, in that previous sentence is "captured" because the three heroic Aussies who started steering toward Timor were repeatedly outwitting an intensive Japanese manhunt spanning more than three thousand kilometers of open water. Incredibly, after two months at sea, hopping from island to island and surviving on scavenged scraps of food and raw fish, a lone man (likely Blondie Sargent but possibly one of three other Rimau men) is believed to have been "carried into a thicket of fish traps at Cape Sutai," where he was captured on 22 December. Had he reached Romang, a small, undistinguished island northeast of Timor, he would've been less than four hundred miles from Australia.

Still fighting for their lives and largely abandoned by the replacement submarine that haphazardly returned to their rendezvous island, multiple heroic Australians believed they could pull off the impossible and reach Darwin safely by paddling or stealing seaworthy vessels.

Difficult? Undoubtedly, particularly because it was monsoon season, with open-water navigation difficult. But not impossible. And if Page, Sargent, David Gooley, Roland Fletcher, Bruno Reymond, or Colin Craft had reached Romang, they would have been less than 150 nautical miles from Pulau Babar, where much of this fictitious story about Brad Tucker has been centered.

～

The dream of making it back to Australia, idealistic in every sense, was not without precedent. Flight Lieutenant Bryan Rofe, a meteorological officer stationed in Dutch Timor, kept more than thirty men moving through difficult jungle conditions from February to April 1942 to enable a dangerous sea rescue by the American submarine *Searaven* (as detailed in Tom Trumble's superb book *Rescue at 2100 Hours*), depositing the starved and malaria-infected survivors at the Port of Fremantle on 25 April 1942.

Additionally, two Americans, Lt. Damon "Rocky" Gause and Cpt. Bill Osbourne, managed the "home run," escaping from Bataan and Corregidor, eventually sailing the last six hundred nautical (and danger-laden) miles from the island of Sunda through the Java and Timor Seas before finally washing ashore in a bullet-riddled wooden boat in the Western Australian port of Wyndham, southwest of Darwin, in October 1942. Twelve Australians, ever alert for yet another Japanese attack, intercepted Gause and Osbourne in a motor launch and were so stunned by the appearance of two filthy, sunburnt Yanks that they approached with guns drawn before lowering their weapons and welcoming these two amazing survivors.

Similarly, and just as heroically, a Brit named Charles McCormac and R. G. "Don" Donaldson, a Melbournian, escaped from the Japanese when Singapore fell in February 1942 and over the course of five months worked their way back to Broome (the military replacement for Darwin's smashed harbor). During 150 days of uncomfortable jungle conditions, train hopping, and daring fishing boat adventures along the coastal edges of Sumatra and

Java, they lived day-to-day on the most meager of scavenged rations. They were finally flown home by way of a daring Short Sunderland seaplane rescue (despite numerous Japanese checkpoints and patrol boats) and further showed that while the odds were long, recovery of Allied soldiers from within Japan's perimeter of control was clearly possible.

From the Philippines, ten Americans and two Filipinos, led by US pilot William Edwin Dyess, escaped from the Japanese prison at Davao during early 1943 and, with considerable help from Filipino guerillas, made their way to Australia. A very solid account of this event can be found in John Lukacs's 2010 book *Escape from Davao: The Forgotten Story of the Most Daring Prison Break of the Pacific War* (Simon & Schuster).

For the Rimau survivors to pull off an escape of the magnitude I've described above, they needed enormous luck and fortitude. The Japanese navy still controlled parts of the South China, Java, Flores, and Banda Seas as late as December 1944 and had brutalized many of the local islanders into submissive states of fear and loathing. An Allied commando, any White man of European descent, would have known that "washing ashore" on the wrong island would produce almost-certain death.

It is informative to note that a helpful islander who was angry at the Japanese might hide a man. But in doing so, he would know if his act was discovered, he risked the slaughtering of his entire village. Evidence of this was well known in many remote settings the Japanese controlled. On the other hand, a starving Malayan or Sumatran native could avoid risk and earn a substantial reward by informing on a stranded enemy of the empire.

Granted, there were Allied "friends" scattered among the islands of Southeastern Asian theater of the war. Australian Naval Intelligence, under the direction of the portly and mysterious Commander R. B. M. "Cockie" Long, had started setting up Australia's heroic coast watchers as early as 1939. These courageous men (and others like the Lugger Maintenance Section in Darwin) had continually gambled with their lives in and around the Solomon Islands and Coral Sea and had built a network of friendly natives choosing to oppose and harass the Japanese. But the Solomons were much further east and north.

West of New Guinea, shadowy groups like Force 136 (with its irregular warfare school, STS 101, run by F. Spencer Chapman, DSO) and the Malayan Peoples' Anti-Japanese Army in Malaya operated with varying levels of success. In Pierre Boule's novel *The Bridge on the River Kwai*, this unit is presented as Force 316, which military insiders immediately recognized as a simple scrambling of 136's numbers.

In the geographical vicinity of Java, Timor, Borneo, and the Celebes, however, much was unknown. Catholic nuns and missionaries often went missing in these parts or, as of 1942, were forced to retreat into the jungles to escape rape, disembowelment, and decapitation. Even the Australian Army's 2/2nd Independent Company, a forerunner to Australia's famed SAS, had gone into Portuguese Timor in December 1941 but was forced to withdraw by January 1943.

In Babar, a key island in this novel, there remain reports of war atrocities. In October 1944, there is evidence suggesting that at Emplawas village, a significant tobacco hub, 710 natives were slaughtered by the Japanese military.

The cautiousness needed to survive on Japanese-controlled islands during occupation was staggeringly extreme. Chapman, who would write a book called *The Jungle Is Neutral*, lived behind enemy lines for more than three years, most of it while suffering terribly from malaria, coma-inducing fevers, dysentery, beriberi, jungle-rot, and skin ulcers.

Suffice to say, it was a grueling time for anyone hiding on a remote island or laying up in a sweltering jungle. It was a time when failure of caution, simple bad luck, or diminished spiritual and, more so, mental willpower could finish a man off within days.

For the purposes of this novel, my central character was fictitiously named Tucker, and it's clear no such Australian was involved with Rimau...but his fictional heroism here is based largely on the daring homeward-bound journeys of five possible men: Captain Robert Page, AIF; Lieutenant A. L. "Blondie" Sargent, AIF; Warrant Officer Jeffery Willersdorf, AIF; Lance Corporal Hugo Pace, AIF; or Private Douglas Warne, AIF.

In truth, none of the five survived, although, according to authors Peter Thompson and Robert Macklin, Willersdorf, Pace, and Warne came very close, with Willersdorf and Pace reaching Kaju Adi Island near the Celebes in mid-January. Amazingly, Warne stayed uncaptured into March 1945, a feat that truly defies the intensity of the Japanese manhunt that continued long after the mission was discovered in October 1944.

In pure fact, no Rimau participant survived.

Historians are reliably certain thirteen died while fighting, from brutal beatings, sustained torture, starvation, or untreated malaria shortly after their immediate capture. The other ten, taken alive, were beheaded together 7 July 1945, less than one month from the first use of an atomic bomb on Hiroshima on August 6 and less than two months from Japan's formal surrender on September 2, 1945. For the Japanese, execution by sword was not uncommon.

Many readers may, in fact, have seen a particularly gruesome *Life* magazine photograph of a Japanese officer beheading an Australian commando from M Special Unit in New Guinea in 1943. What's most amazing about this horrific image is the apparent quiet dignity of the Australian (later confirmed as twenty-seven-year-old radio operator Sergeant Len Siffleet) who is moments from death. He is surrounded by Japanese soldiers and New Guinean natives, sitting back on his heels in mud, leaning slightly to his right. Moments later he lies dead, a fate he shared with two other men from his Special Ops unit. The three were buried, unceremoniously, on New Guinea's Aitape Beach.

In the case of the two specific Rimau escapees presented in this telling, McKie's version of the Rimau story suggested Blondie Sargent reached Maja off the coast of Borneo but was reportedly captured at Romang (east of Timor). He was reported to have died in captivity, a victim of wounds, malnutrition, and most probably malaria. Amazingly, Bob Page was thought to have traveled even further east during his heroic escape but ultimately was captured and beheaded with nine other Rimau men near Ulu Pandan, a short drive from Singapore's Outram Road prison. Later versions of the Rimau story suggest Blondie Sargent was one of the ten beheaded by the Japanese. As of 2022, seventeen of Operation Rimau's twenty-three commandos remain buried in Singapore's Kranji War Cemetery, including mission commander Lieutenant-Colonel Ivan Lyon.

The ten Australians were executed, according to certain Japanese survivors of World War II, because heroes of their magnitude could not be allowed to exist as prisoners. They would produce too much inspiration. Later, written reports have suggested Page and each of the surviving Rimau raiders, including Major R. N. Ingleton of the Royal Marines, died calmly, with their dignity intact, like Sergeant Siffleet in New Guinea. At the time, this type of noble submission (at the actual point of death) was what the Japanese call "Yu-shi."

Most revealing is that prior to their beheading, the Rimau men had simply shaken hands and wished each other good luck. This act of bravery impressed their Japanese captors deeply. At a time when Japan all but knew the war was over, the Rimau men showed an amazing level of grace (and spirit) in facing their sworn enemy. They'd been heroic in their gritty survival and determination, fighting nobly against fantastic odds.

And then they died, bravely, with honor and courage.

So did many others, with the most horrific case taking place in Borneo starting in January 1945. That month Japanese commanders supervised the organized slaughter of all but six Allied prisoners from a group of 2,400 men. The Bataan Death March in the Philippines is better known, but the Sandakan Death March to Ranau was far deadlier.

As for the Japanese, their efforts officially ended on September 2, 1945, when their foreign minister, Mamoru Shigemitsu, and Japan's chief of the army general staff, General Yoshijiro Umezu, surrendered to US General Douglas MacArthur and leaders from eight other nations (including Australia's General Sir Thomas Blamey) on the American battleship USS *Missouri*. But Japanese soldiers—"stragglers," as they would come to be known—continued hiding out on Filipino and Indonesian islands well into the 1970s.

The last known Japanese soldier to come in from the jungle was Private Teruo Nakamura. He surrendered on the Indonesian island of Morotai in December 1974 and wasn't even the sole Japanese straggler "found" that year. Hiroo Onoda, a second lieutenant, was finally located in March 1974 on Lubang, a small Filipino island about a hundred miles southwest of Manila.

The presence of these soldiers who survived in various jungles for nearly three decades after the war ended was not surprising since many Japanese soldiers believed surrender was worse than death or suicide. In fact, rumors often surfaced during the 1960s and '70s that there were other nonsurrendering Japanese soldiers as far south as the South Banda Basin and small islands like Romang, Yamdena, and Seram.

About reusing captured military equipment, let me offer this mea culpa. One aspect of this story involves Brad Tucker and his fictional American compatriot Tom Northgraves stealing an Australian Bristol Beaufort on Yamdena Island (northeast of modern-day East Timor). Some readers may have found it hard to believe the Japanese army or navy could capture an aircraft or ship and then reconstitute it as their own.

The truth is this: as the war ground into its third and fourth years, Japan's Imperial Navy faced increasing difficulty transporting supplies to the outposts on the outer fringes of their grossly overexpanded empire. As such, captured Allied vehicles were often considered for reuse. This was notably true with the USS *Stewart* (DD-224 and not DE-238), a Clemson-class destroyer "holed" by its American crew in March 1942 in Tjilatjap (now Surabaya), Java. The Japanese soon hauled the ship out of the harbor, completely retrofitted it, and relaunched it as Japanese Patrol Boat No. 102. It served Japan until the emperor's forces surrendered in August 1945.

So, for the Japanese to work with a captured Allied plane and place it back in the air, even from a distant jungle outpost, is not beyond the realm of possibility, and it could have happened when Allied aircraft were not destroyed during interisland missions.

But let me go back to the inspirational heroes of this book.

I first learned about Australians Sargent and Page and their fabled mission on the *Krait* (now on display at Sydney's Australian National Maritime Museum) from my late father, a proud Newfoundlander who sent me hunting through Sydney's once numerous used bookstores to find the work of an Australian war correspondent (McKie) and his great book *The Heroes*. I found it, with notable difficulty, along with two others my father suggested: *Flight to Landfall* by Gerald Glaskin, and Nevil Shute's masterwork *A Town Like Alice*.

After some sweaty digging around, I discovered them all, in various conditions, somewhere on George Street, plus another McKie treasure, *The Survivors*, which told the story of the sinking of the HMAS *Perth* and USS *Houston* off Sumatra's coast on 1 March 1942. Each of the four books served this novel, and there's no hiding from that. Nor should there be.

In honoring those late Australian authors, McKie, Glaskin, and Shute (actually a Brit who moved to Australia), plus Scottish novelist Alastair MacLean, this effort imagines a different historical ending for Rimau because sometimes we need to construct different outcomes for our truths and myths… in order to keep revisiting man's enduring will to survive and return "home."

As is often written by authors and novelists, this story was a labor of love for me and involved the research help of numerous friends, who are mentioned elsewhere.

Notably, I must write that I had the good fortune to hike into the German sailors' camp at Deep Creek in July 2013 and see the real evidence of German "military" in Australia prior to World War II. While this example is historically passive, a small story at best, we know other examples exist of German activities in Australia during or just before the outbreak of Britain's entry into the conflict in 1939. In fact, as late as 1940, Nazi Party supporters were painting slogans, including "Heil Hitler," on broad, whitewashed walls in Sydney's Walsh Bay.

From a war sustainability standpoint, the Germans were most actively interested in Europe and Africa, but their search for raw materials like tungsten (or wolfram) in Portugal and other locales kept the Nazi war machine on constant lookout for easily accessed alloys that facilitated the construction of tanks, armored cars, fighter planes, and guns.

Australia, then, as now, was a treasure trove of industrial metals, and while its landmass was remote, procurement of Australia's natural reserves required notable consideration. Interestingly, until the Americans entered the war at the end of 1941, it was common for Adolf Hitler's generals to factor into their war planning where their needed resources would come from. The reader should know Australia's mining history, especially as it related to gold, lead, copper, tin, silver, and zinc, was frequently noted in Europe. Further, the discovery of wolfram (tungsten) in Tasmania in 1926 did not go unnoticed in Berlin.

Certainly, in writing about Germany's efforts in Australia before and during World War II, I'm obligated (as an armchair historian) to acknowledge the writings of W. A. Scholes and his paper "Nazi Spies Operated in Australia Right Up Until Pearl Harbor." I did not concern myself with the accuracy of Mr. Scholes's writings (nor can I speak to that topic), but I drew on the historical essence of what he revealed in his research, which was that the "clerk attached to the Consulate Officer, Alfred Henschell, was one of the leading men in the [Nazi] party." Henschell, it appears, was the "Manager of the Nazi Party throughout Australia, but this was just a cover for his membership [in] the Gestapo."

So the possibility certainly exists that Gestapo agents (or representatives) operated in Australia prior to 1 September 1939. And it is also possible that my story line of an Austrian family coming to Australia in 1938 is not beyond the pale. Scholes suggests "Australian Military Intelligence had no doubt German agents were at work in Queensland years before the outbreak of the war."

Further, "there were 3600 German citizens, 16,000 German migrants and 100,000 people of German descent in Queensland alone in 1937."

It thus becomes clear (in any reading of various sources) that Nazi Germany created a notable presence in Australia, particularly in Sydney during the 1930s, and did so at places like the German Counsel and the German Workers Front (DAF), or through organized meetings of the German wool buyers, who met weekly at Sydney hotels such as the Carlton and Exchange. Further, the German-language Nazi-influenced newspaper *Die Brucke* was published regularly in Sydney right up until 1939.

One German Australian in particular (referenced in the text), Walter Karl Ladendorff, has been written about as the most powerful Nazi leader in Australia during the thirties and was reportedly recalled to Berlin "just [weeks] before the outbreak of the war." His presence, and reported direct linkage to Heinrich Himmler and the Gestapo, reveals a page of Australian history rarely considered and traditionally not discussed.

Like other political initiatives, Australia's basic freedoms allowed certain partisan communities, like German Australians, to exist and openly congregate. In the case of Nazi sympathizers, though, after 1 September 1939, those views were no longer publicly tolerated and "within a few hours of the declaration of war in September 1939, every known Nazi left in Australia was rounded up and put behind bars."

For some, the presumption is that Australian Nazi members disappeared because they were no longer heard or seen. It is almost certain they did not vanish. And what about the Nazis that Australian Intelligence hadn't discovered? What were they up to?

~

But let me apologize here, to anyone bothered, particularly proper military historians, by creating revisionist history for the purposes of fiction. It's been done (honorably, I can only hope) to feature the indomitable fighting spirit of the Australian men and women who so selflessly served their country during the horrors and privations of World War II.

It is my belief most Australians today, at least those under the age of sixty, have little understanding of how dire things looked for all of Australia in February 1942 or that Australia ultimately built twenty-eight POW camps, including the camp at Cowra in NSW where, on 5 August 1944, a total of 378 Japanese prisoners escaped and 230 were killed or found dead from suicide.

Australia was already a tough land, but World War II brought privations that lasted well beyond the war's end in 1945. To have been attacked (in both Darwin and Sydney) and then to have housed (with the existence of a prisoner-of-war camp) a most-hated enemy was something not easily shrugged off.

In closing, I offer my sincere respect to every Australian family for the courageous ways in which their ancestors may have met their challenges (and fates) from 1933 through 1945. And I apologize in advance to anyone of Japanese ancestry for comments considered racist made by my fictitious characters. This period in Australian history was not immune from racism or language we now consider racist. That does not excuse the errors of our past ways.

World War II was a time, a cauldron, that created countless legends in every theater. So let us not forget any who died for their country.

A FEW PERSONAL ACKNOWLEDGMENTS

No book is ever written without the support of a long list of friends, family, and industry associates contributing in hundreds of different ways. This book is no different, and I'd like to again thank the two patrons for this book, Pat Ryan and Sean Branagan. Their belief in me ensured we summited the mountain.

I'd also like to sincerely thank friends Myles Schrag and Rus Bradburd, who generated profound improvements to this novel through their holistic editing and narrative development. Myles brought me to Rus and then to Amplify, so this book owes him a huge debt. Myles also delivered Dariusz Janczewski, the wonderful map maker whose work helps start this book. I bonded with Dariusz over our shared appreciation of the book *The Long Walk* by Slavomir Rawicz.

Others on the stellar Subplot production team that made this book possible include Naren Aryal, CEO of Amplify Publishing Group, who believed in the wide-ranging vision of the story and encouraged me to push forward; Shannon Sullivan, graphic designer and exemplar of great patience with me; Ray and the Elite Editing team; and Sundar Maruthu, a proofreader who improved the book even at the latest stages.

I'd also like to acknowledge Australian mates Francis Farrelly and Rod Smith. Both kept my historical/factual intentions honest, and for that I am grateful. Special thanks also to former Syracuse University graduate assistant Nick Maranto for unearthing some key material for me on Graz, Austria, and Adolf Hitler's visit to the Weizer Waggonfabrik factory in April 1938, and also Andrew Katz (then with *Time* magazine), who kindly produced great historic readings for me on the Austrian Anschluss of 1938. Both efforts were warranted because Chris Weiss, a noon-ball basketball friend, had casually provided specific cinematic materials and, unwittingly, the shadings of a plot idea I soon developed. For that, Chris deserves full recognition and thanks.

Thanks also to author extraordinaire George Saunders (*Tenth of December; Lincoln in the Bardo*) for his genuine kindness while I was developing this work and readers John Barrows, Daemoni Bishop, and Scott Pitoniak. Their encouragement and constructive suggestions inspired the final product you now see.

I must also particularly honor my legal counsel Jon Stahler and Australian friend Roger Kelly for his tireless efforts in locating maps of Malaysia, Sumatra, New Guinea, and other islands in the South China, Banda, Timor, and Arafura Seas. And for assisting with key plot developments involving German operatives in New South Wales during 1934–39. Australians are frequently surprised to learn German sailors were camping on Sydney's Northern Beaches during that six-year time frame, and Roger showed me firsthand evidence of their Australian visits.

Let me also acknowledge historian Lachlan Grant of the Australian War Memorial's (AWM) Military History Section. Lachlan steered me toward Hank Nelson's *P.O.W.: Prisoners of War: Australians Under Nippon* and Courtney Harrison's *Ambon: Island of Mist* but most importantly was kind enough to meet with me in person at the War Memorial after I'd read his piece "They Called Them Hellships" in AWM's magazine *Wartime*. And to Craig Berelle, assistant curator at the War Memorial, who offered his assistance after a very chance encounter on a train leaving Cronulla.

Another librarian who helped me with maps of Babar and the Arafura Sea was Darle Balfoort of Syracuse University's Bird Library. I'm much indebted to her for her kindness and patience as I measured nautical miles and topographical elevations on Indonesian maps. Thanks also (as always) to the extraordinary Margie Chetney from SU's Falk Sport Management program for daily assistances too numerous to mention.

Full disclosure requires that I mention my reliance on extensive material from *The Royal Australian Air Force in World War II* (Aero Australia Special Edition) with its material on Bristol Beauforts (pp. 88–94) and Bristol Beaufighters (pp. 96–102). From what I can tell, the Thirty-One Squadron at Coomalie Creek in the NT did not have Bristol Beauforts for their Timor Sea missions, but Beauforts were used in raids on Rabaul, and it is not impossible that a wounded or lost Beaufort (from the Six, Eight, or One Hundred Squadron) could have come down on Yamdena in the Tanimbar Islands group (first attacked by the Japanese on 31 July 1942).

I was also much aware of Frank Walker's version of Rimau as told in his book *Commandos* (Hachette Australia, 2015) and acknowledge that his version of Rimau men rowing away from Singapore differs greatly from Ronald McKie's 1960 work. My attempt does not claim (nor probably achieve) perfect accuracy but, rather, attempts to recreate heroic work by courageous AIF participants.

Thanks also to longtime mate and Northern Beaches inspiration David Castle (and his amazing wife, Julianne). David and Julianne have long hosted the Burtons during our frequent visits to Sydney, and certain elements of this book are loosely based on David. I've been blessed to have David treat us like family and show us why Australia is so special.

I must also acknowledge my brother Gary for providing me with Ian Skidmore's 1973 book *Escape from the Rising Sun* (Futura Publications), which so accurately covers the escape of the sailing prahu *Sederhana DJohannis* from Padang to Ceylon. It filled in some missing gaps for me on Rimau's incredible leader, Ivan Lyon. I also borrowed specific facts from James D. Hornfischer's superb *Ship of Ghosts* (Bantam), about the USS *Houston* and her harried survivors, as well as Mitchell Zuckoff's *Lost in Shangri-La* (Harper Perennial) and Leah Garrett's 2021 work *X Troop* (HarperCollins).

I am sincerely grateful to Jonah's publican (Whale Beach) Peter Montgomery for some of my 1936 Australian Olympic team research and to Aussie mate Craig Douglass of Sport Travel Academy in Cary, NC, for research efforts in Queensland.

Further, sincere thanks to Australian agent extraordinaire Selwa Anthony, who read numerous early versions of this work, encouraged its development and continuation, and always gave it "a chance" for succeeding. Her frequent support and engagement of early editor Drew Keys were critical. You wouldn't be reading this story if it weren't for Selwa and Drew. I also owe a word of sincere appreciation and recognition to Australian editor Nicola O'Shea, who helped me greatly with an early version.

Let me also mention I would never have ever met Selwa if it hadn't been for an introduction from longtime Melbourne sports marketing impresario John Tripodi of the Twenty3 Group. Thanks to John for getting this train rolling and to Martin Gasteiger and his staff at the Auracher Löchl in Kufstein, Austria (standing proudly on the banks of the Inn River since about 1409), where I holed up for ten days—fueled largely by pots of black tea and thick, dark bread provided by kindly Ali. For long stretches during that visit, it seemed like I only came out for meals. Their graciousness and hospitality made one of my early writing pushes possible.

Proper notation must also be made of some literary "borrowing" that I made from a single page of unpublished manuscript by Gay Hembach. That cribbing, presented as "The Doctor's Daughter" in Chapter 16, owes much to Gay, a longtime resident of Skaneateles, NY, and daughter of a true WWII hero and doctor.

Finally, thanks and much love to my wonderful wife, Barbara, for abiding my frequent (and passionate) vexation to research and write historical novels. Nothing works for most authors unless they truly have the support of loved ones at home or from afar. I have always been blessed beyond anything I could have ever imagined, and this Australian love letter was important to me for reasons always evident to Barb. Her unrelenting support made it all possible.

I will end here simply by noting any misrepresentations or factual inaccuracies, not to mention possible misuse (or misappropriation) of the Australian "language" (circa 1935–45 and today), are mine and mine alone. The English language is almost always a moving target, and the Aussies (and Yanks) have certainly done their part in corrupting it.

ABOUT THE AUTHOR

Rick Burton is the David B. Falk Endowed Professor of Sport Management at Syracuse University. For four years he lived in Sydney, serving as Commissioner of Australia's National Basketball League. He remains active there as Chief Operating Officer for Australian sports technology firm Playbk Sports.

Burton has spent considerable time overseas as a visiting professor at Kufstein Tirol University in Austria, and he was Chief Marketing Officer for the U.S. Olympic Committee during the 2008 Beijing Summer Olympics. The co-author of numerous sport management books, including *Business the NHL Way* (University of Toronto Press), Burton has written for the *New York Times, Wall Street Journal,* and *Sports Business Journal.*